GW01159404

The Hunter of Fareldin
Book 1

THE HUNTER

K. AAGARD

Copper Fox
Creations Publishing

Copyright © 2024 by Copper Fox Creations LLC

All rights reserved.

No part of this book may be reproduced in any form or by any electronic or mechanical means, including information storage and retrieval systems, without written permission from the author, except for the use of brief quotations in a book review.

No AI was used in the production of this publication.

The store, names, characters, and incidents portrayed in this production are works of fiction. No identification with actual persons (living or dead), places, building, and products is intended or should be inferred.

Cover and internal illustrations drawn by Kylee Aagard.

Page divider and map border designed by Ramona at https://ko-fi.com/alderdoodle or at @Alderdoodle on Twitter.

Interior design by Kylee Aagard

Editors Erin Bledsoe & Pamela Willson

For my family and friends who've encouraged and supported me. For my little co-author, Takari, who 'helped' me write this book, and for Bullet, my sweet boy who inspired Greer. You both will be missed.

Takari　　Bullet

Content Warning

This book contains:
    Harm to animals.
    Overuse of magic leading to sickness and side affects of self loathing/suicidal thoughts.
    Racial discrimination.
    Harm to people and death/murder.
    Past kidnapping/attempted kidnapping.
    Brief and vague mentions of implied SA as a threat to future outcomes.

Contents

1. Stay — 1
2. The Trapped Thief — 6
3. Lost Boots & Little Reward — 15
4. An Offer He Should Refuse — 28
5. Should've Said No — 37
6. A Rocky Start — 48
7. Tiptoeing — 56
8. A Plan Forms — 65
9. Bit Of Everything — 75
10. An Absence Of Rangers — 80
11. Shopping Is Black Magic — 90
12. A Thief In The Night — 100
13. How Not To Steal A Wolf — 106
14. No Trust Between Us — 117
15. Horses Are Hard Work — 123
16. The Trouble With Honor — 134
17. Train, Travel, Repeat — 144
18. The Town Of Borris — 157
19. Stockpile — 168
20. The Ways — 175
21. Keeper Of The Ways — 185
22. Yulie — 194
23. A Deal In The Dark — 203
24. A Promise Between Brothers — 208
25. The Price Of Magic — 214
26. Addy Isn't Any Better At Naming Things — 223
27. The Problem With Rumors — 230
28. Why Didn't She Run? — 239
29. Blasphemy — 244
30. How Not To Avoid An Ambush — 250
31. How Not To Remain Kidnapped — 258
32. Never Leave The Wolf Behind — 268
33. A New "Friend" — 277

34. Question Everything	284
35. First Watch	293
36. The Trouble With Knights	298
37. Swords & Magic	309
38. Burning Bridges	317
39. On The Edge	328
40. Pinned By A Pooch	332
41. Tenuous Cooperation	343
42. Wolves & Lambs	348
43. Regret	355
44. To Track An Addy	363
45. Unsavory Types	367
46. Promises & Apologies	371
47. Pages of Memories	376
48. Tevin Gets A Stick	384
49. Schemes & Stories	392
50. Sabotage	403
51. Burning Bridges, Literally this time	407
52. Wolves In The Mist	415
53. Judgement	421
54. The Touch Of Death	431
55. Usereth Femiera	442
56. Going Through The Front Door	451
57. Cells & Secrets	461
58. The "Dark Ranger"	467
59. Bothersome Brothers	474
60. The Meeting	481
61. The Ranger	493
62. Magic Happy	499
63. Truth Or Lies	507
64. Growing Tension	514
65. The Fluff Always Wins	517
66. Mother & Daughter	530
67. The Dangers Of A Di'horvith	536
68. A Gut Feeling	543
69. Something's Afoot	552
70. Unease	559
71. Books Make Great Tripping blocks	566

72. Obsession	573
73. Sacrifice	578
74. New ties	583
75. Aftermath	592
76. The Debt	600
Thank you for reading	607
Pronunciation Guide	609
Additional Maps	611
About the Author	619

Chapter 1
Stay

2 The Hunter

The sun's dying light cast deep shadows across the darkly clad figure as he limped through the forest. A hand clutched the cut in his side, sliced by his enemy's sword, becoming slick with blood.

Gripping a sheathed sword in his right hand, he wandered deeper into the cover of the trees. His steps faltering, he stumbled into a sturdy trunk. Searing pain ripped through his side like thousands of fiery claws.

Had the tree not been there, he would've collapsed. His breaths came in ragged, shallow gasps as his vision swam. Unsteadily, he turned, his movements slow and careful. His side flared with fresh pain, his vision failing as the dark world turned stark white.

He closed his eyes for a moment, resting his head against the rough bark. The branches overhead shifted, their leaves gently whispering as night creatures sang, unthreatened by the dying man. The world sat in a deceptively peaceful veil of darkness.

His mind ran back over the fight, the flash of swords in the moonlight. The clang and hiss of metal on metal. The coppery scent of blood mixed with the smell of sweat. He'd hardly felt the sting of the blade as it broke through his guard, slicing into his side. His focus was on killing the man who'd killed his loved ones, the man he'd been hunting for decades, even at the cost of his own life.

He'd been the one to walk away from the fight. He'd watched in satisfaction as the light faded from his enemy's eyes, his blood soaking into the dry earth. The man's sword and a necklace of fangs were his physical prize, but revenge had been his goal. Opening his eyes moments later, his gaze drifted back the way he'd come, eyeing the broken branches and crushed grass. The trail he'd left through the undergrowth was obvious to even his cloudy mind.

He'd have scoffed at his clumsiness had he the energy. A bumbling novice could track him right now, even though he knew there was no one left. Still, he needed to move, to distance himself from the body before someone found it. Training and instinct drove him toward the protection of the forest and its singing shadows, where only a Ranger could hope to find him.

The crickets continued to play their lilting song, accompanied by the unsteady beat of his heart in his ears. The world suddenly blurred. He sat at the base of the trunk, blinking in confusion. He hadn't realized he'd slid down the tree, hadn't felt the ground rise to meet him. The sword lay forgotten at his side. He didn't have the strength to reclaim his footing as the shadows grew deeper. Less uncertain in the fading light.

A figure detached itself from the darkness, its form gliding silently and swiftly toward the injured man. It sat before him. A low, worried whine escaped the creature's lips. Using his hand not stained by blood, Strider stroked the beast's head, scratching it softly behind the ears.

"It'll be okay, Greer." The Hunter said in a soft, soothing tone. He went silent for a long moment as his eyes lost focus. Sucking in a sharp breath, his eyes cleared. "Thank you. You saved me... again."

Scooting closer, the creature licked his nose, his deep brown eyes full of concern. The magical ancestor of both wolf and horse, the beast resembled a wolf with a stiffer spine broadening his back, built to carry the weight of a rider. His mother had called them di'horvith. The ummanie and tahrvin called them dire wolves.

Greer gently nudged the man's arm wrapped around his stomach, whining with worry. Strider winced in pain. He could feel his life ebbing away. The man steadied himself, breathing deep, even, and slow. His heart hammered in his head, drumming inside his skull in agonizing waves. Swallowing, he focused, reaching inward with his mind. He felt a well of power within himself.

He imagined an underground pool, deep and seemingly endless as it swirled lazily within, ethereal yet alive. As he sought it, it flooded its banks, reaching for him. His body grew warm as the magic moved through him, trickling from his hand into the wound. He could feel the magic work to close the slash in his side.

The stream of magic he channeled through himself was pitifully small compared to the source he was drawing upon. Like a large container with a tiny opening, it didn't matter how much water it could hold; only a limited amount of it could pour through.

His breathing grew deeper, more labored as his soul felt the strain of using healing magic. He couldn't heal himself completely, but it would be enough to survive. He'd be able to move again. Disappear. After some rest, he could heal his injury completely, and then… then what?

For the first time since he'd entered the forest, he had no reason to go on. He had finally accomplished what he'd set out to do, what he'd dedicated over fifty years of his life to. He'd had his revenge. The assassin that killed his father and familiar was dead.

Vindication had given way to relief, but as time passed, the happiness faded as he was left to face a future of unknowns. The drive that had kept him going died with his enemy. He had nothing left, no purpose to keep him moving forward.

An emptiness sat within his stomach, ringed by twisting vines. There was nothing to fight for, to live for. What was the point of healing himself and pushing on? He'd trained Greer to survive on his own. There was nothing left for him here.

He could simply let the darkness hedging around the corners of his vision claim him. Strider closed his eyes as the shadows stretched across the ground toward him. If he let go, then maybe he would finally find the peace that revenge had denied him? He let the sounds of the forest wash over him. The gentle hiss of the leaves, the warbling tune of the crickets. It wasn't home, but he was content to die here, beneath the forest's canopy, lulled to sleep by its song.

A long, strangled whine pierced the darkness. His eyes snapped open to the forest again. Greer let out another choked, desperate cry. He was pressing his nose firmly against his brother's hand, holding it in place over the wound. Strider hadn't realized it'd fallen onto his lap. Greer whined again, more urgently this time. He pressed harder, pinning the Hunter's hand against his injury. Strider cupped the di'horvith's chin in his free hand, pulling the noble creature's head up so he could peer into his eyes.

Dark brown eyes reflected eyes of gold as the Hunter and di'horvith sat in silence. He lost himself within those brown pools, whose depths seemed to know no bounds. There was wisdom in those eyes, an understanding, and a startling pain. Strider took a deep breath, rested his forehead against Greer's, and whispered. "I do not deserve you."

Greer leaned forward, pressing his own forehead firmly against his brother's. A low sound rumbled in his throat; one the man knew di'horviths made to soothe their own. Greer drew back, head dipping to brush his nose against the blood-stained hand again. His nose hovered there, afraid the Hunter would let it fall again. He watched the man with an intense gaze.

Taking another deep breath, Strider steadied himself. Thoughts of letting himself drift away still pulled at his soul, but he ignored them. His eyes remained fixed on Greer as he channeled magic into his wound once more. The blood stopped flowing as the gash healed to a point that he instinctively knew was survivable.

Releasing the chain of magic, he slumped against the tree. His body and soul drained of all strength. Greer lay down at his side and rested his head on the Hunter's leg, though the position of the di'horvith's ears told Strider he was alert. Grabbing the hilt of his sword, he whispered to Greer. "Wake me when the moon is at its highest."

An ear swiveled to catch his words, but otherwise, Greer gave no sign of confirmation as he kept watch. The man's breathing slowed to an even rhythm as he fell unconscious. Greer kept silent vigil. Both man and beast lay still, wrapped in the comforting blanket of darkness.

Chapter 2
The Trapped Thief

Something woke the Hunter. It wasn't the sound of birdsong, or the lapping of Greer's tongue as he drank from a small stream nearby. Nor was it the sunlight that filtered through the canopy of leaves overhead. None of the natural sounds or sensations of the forest had caused the exhausted man to wake. He'd sensed someone at his side. He heard soft footfalls, the quiet hiss of a scabbard brushing the ground as someone lifted the sword he'd dropped.

Drawing his dagger with one hand, the man grabbed the thief's cloak and yanked them to the ground. The Hunter moved to place himself on top of the intruder, ready to slit their throat. The thief yelped in surprise, kicking out when he hit the ground and striking Strider in his injured side. Sharp pain stole the man's breath, weakening his grip and allowing the thief to break free. They scrambled to their feet and ran; the sword held under their arm.

A deep, feral bark boomed near the stream, and Strider saw the form of Greer bolt past him in pursuit of the would-be thief.

Clutching his side, Strider sheathed his dagger. He stood, cursing as he followed the path Greer left in pursuit of the thief. Though his side burned, and his head felt light, he pushed himself to move faster. Greer was a powerful animal but was as weak to steel as any beast.

It wasn't long before a triumphant bark rang through the trees, accompanied by a shrill scream. He could hear someone yelling, hurling curse words at the di'horvith. The corner of Strider's mouth twitched in amusement. Though the person was clearly distressed, he heard no sounds of concern from Greer, who yipped and whined exuberantly.

His brother wasn't in danger, so the Hunter slowed his pace. Allowing himself time to catch his breath and steady himself against a tree. Though he had healed his wound enough that it wasn't a danger, it hadn't completely sealed. The injury was far too large, too deep. He also hadn't been able to restore the blood he'd lost. His vision swam, and his head grew foggy from the simple exertion.

He should've collapsed again, but he stubbornly stayed upright and pressed on. It took Strider more time than he would've liked to reach the location where Greer had caught the thief. They hadn't made it far before the faster di'horvith had caught up. That wasn't surprising. Di'horviths were endurance runners, and though slower than a horse, they were considerably faster than a person. Greer was small enough to slip through the trees and brush without difficulty, but large enough to throw some serious weight around.

The Hunter stopped at the edge of the trees. His keen eyes took in the situation at a glance. Greer paced eagerly at the crater's edge, whining as he looked out toward the prey trapped within. The crater was large enough to fit a small house. Filled with a shimmering, sandy liquid that rippled as the thief moved and struggled. Still cursing Greer for knocking him into the pool, they stood knee-deep in the strange substance.

Upon sight of the crater, Strider called to Greer sharply. The di'horvith, who had dropped to his elbows as he leaned over the edge of the pool, instantly jerked back. He stood and hurried to stand beside the Hunter, who ruffled the fur atop his head as he stared critically at the person trapped in the pool.

The thief had grown quiet at the sound of his voice. He still held the sword, watching with wide eyes. Now that the Hunter looked at him, he realized they were a girl! Her dull brown hood had fallen back to reveal tangled brown hair. She looked like a trapped bobcat as she gazed up at him with fierce brown eyes. The girl was distinctly ummanie, with her rounded ears that were smaller than those of the tahrvin's and less pointed than the yulie. Given the fact they were within an ummanie kingdom where tahrvin were scarce, and the yulie were hunted, this wasn't surprising.

Despite his injury, Strider walked silently and smoothly toward the edge of the crater. He crouched, arms resting on his knees. His side complained, and his head felt light again, but he gave no outward sign of his discomfort as he regarded her with a cold, emotionless gaze.

The thief couldn't have been older than seventeen. Her tangled brown hair framed an oval, fair skinned face. She might have been pretty, had she not been so thin and dirty. Strider glanced back at Greer, tracing the path he'd followed with his gaze. The churned earth where the wolf's claws had torn up the dirt stood out among the leaf litter as he tried to make a quick halt. The marks stopped dangerously close to the ledge.

Greer must have slammed into the girl, sending her flying into the pool, and out of his reach. She'd been lucky to only end up stuck to her knees. Had she fallen in headfirst, she wouldn't have been able to pull her head out and would've suffocated. Pity, it would've made this easier.

"Aren't you going to say anything?" the girl piped up.

Her tone was considerably less scared, and more heated than he'd been expecting. He raised a brow, pointedly remaining silent as he watched her. That seemed to make her angrier, and she opened her mouth to speak, but he cut her off. "Throw me the sword."

"Like Tarn, I will!" she spat. "If I give you this, you'll just leave me trapped in this magpit."

He cocked his head at the rough term most non-magic users used for the sand entrapping her. The pool was a well of magic, bubbling up to the earth's surface. The concentrated power drew water up from an underground river as it ground the earth, combining the two substances. Over time, it created a deep pool of sand that glistened with a metallic sheen.

Wells like this, as the magic folk called them, were dangerous and impossible to escape without magic or outside help. While quicksand never truly sucked you under and you could swim out, albiet slowly; this sand would hold you fast until you touched something that was connected to the land beyond its borders, slowly sucking you down into its depth, where you would drown and become a part of the magic. Non-magic users only knew about this variety of Well because of their deadly nature. This one was rather tame compared to some the Hunter had encountered.

"Throw me the sword." He repeated, his voice devoid of emotion. "Or drown."

The girl cursed again. "I wouldn't be stuck in this magpit if it weren't for your dumb wolf. He plowed straight into me."

"You wouldn't have gotten trapped, if you had planned properly." the Hunter interjected. "If you're going to steal something, you'd better have a solid plan of escape. You didn't."

The girl's angered expression changed to one of confusion. She narrowed her eyes at him. "Yes, mother," she said. "I'll do better next time. Now get me out!"

"The sword."

"Not until you help me!"

The man stood, his gaze never wavering as he replied in a low, dangerous tone. "Either you give me the sword, or I retrieve it when your body has stopped thrashing. After you've drowned." He had little pity for fools or thieves, and mercy was but a concept he'd abandoned long ago. She'd stolen from him. The item mattered little; it was the act that would cost her life. He turned and began walking back toward the shade of the trees.

The girl looked down at the sand. It was now up to her waist. "I give you the sword, and then you'll help me?" she asked, clutching the sheathed weapon to her chest.

The Hunter turned to face her, his face unreadable as he slowly returned to the edge of the Well. He said nothing; he wouldn't agree to something he didn't intend to do.

The teenager gave one last glance at the sand before raising the sword over her head. With all of her might, she hurled it toward the bank. The action cost her greatly as the force of her efforts caused her to sink past her midriff, but her throw was strong. The Hunter reached out and caught the blade easily enough. He took a moment to belt it on before turning to walk away.

"Wait! You need to get me out of here!"

"You got yourself into this mess," Strider said dismissively. "Get yourself out."

"I gave you the sword!"

"After you stole it. Be glad I didn't put an arrow in you."

The girl cursed at him as he skirted the edge of the crater and headed toward the other side of the clearing. As he walked, the sunlight brushed over a feather attached to the top of his bow. Its colors shifted from blues and greens, to purples and turquoise. The feather was a recognizable symbol within Fareldin.

"Wait! You're a Ranger—?" she yelled as she struggled to pull herself toward the bank. The sand held her fast. "You're supposed to help people!"

Strider didn't stop as he shot back over his shoulder, "I'm not a Ranger."

He disappeared into the trees, Greer vanishing right behind him. He could hear the curses that the girl screamed after him, but he ignored them. Greer caught up to him and whined. He ignored him too. He angled his path toward a town he'd seen a couple days before, but a small tug on his cloak caused him to pause and glance down. Greer whined at him, still clutching the fabric in his mouth. The Hunter stopped as the di'horvith continued to give him a beseeching look.

"No," he ordered.

Greer whined again, looking back toward the Well.

"I said no. I have enough knife marks in my back."

Greer grew silent as he continued to look up at him, the cloak clasped firmly in his mouth. A long moment passed between them. Finally, the Hunter spread his hands in a show of surrender, uttering an exasperated sigh.

"Fine!"

Tears blurred Addy's vision as she suppressed sobs. She tried again to swim toward the bank, willing her legs to move as she reached out with her arms. But her legs remained stuck fast. The sand surrounding them was solid as stone. The earth continued to swallow her. She almost broke down but took a deep, ragged breath and tried again. The sand didn't budge. She had to get out! She couldn't die in a place like this! She gasped, forcng down a large lump in her throat, forcing down the tears and sobs. She had to get home! The magic hummed around her. Addy instinctively knew what it was.

Normally, those not magically inclined couldn't sense magic. But within a Well, it was so strong, even the most magic deaf person could feel it. It swelled around her, pulsing and moving, a heartbeat transmitted through invisible veins. A drum beating to an unknown rhythm. She had been told that magic users once bathed in these magic saturated places. The act was said to be peaceful and reinvigorating.

For her, it was terrible. Everything inside her screamed for her to run. She was going to die, and no one would know. She never should've taken the sword. The thought of having it, alongside her knife, to protect herself with had led to her death. The revelation broke the dam; tears darkened her cheeks as she cried. Overcome by the knowledge that she would never get home.

She'd never get to read in her mother's garden, banter with her brothers while she watched them spar, or ride horses with her father again. A faint whistling sound cut the air, then a rope landed before her with a thick plop! Addy's heart throbbed in her throat as hope surged within her. She looked up at the bank in search of her rescuers. But no one was there.

Reaching out, she grabbed the rope. The moment her hands touched it, the solid stone that held her legs vanished. The magic holding her legs fast was broken when she touched the object connected to the world beyond the Well's borders. Suddenly she was in a pool of soupy, grainy liquid and sank further. Frantically she hauled on the rope, pulling it taut before tying it around her waist to keep herself from going under or losing the rope. Hand over hand, she pulled herself toward the edge of the Well.

Reaching the ledge, she struggled to pull herself out. The sand gave a sucking, popping noise as it refused to release her. It held fast to her feet as she held the rope with one hand and the bank with the other. Her arms shook with the strain of fighting against the force, trying to pull her back in. Her body, weak with hunger, threatened to give out on her. She let out a curse as anger flared within her. She'd escape this pit, this country, and make it home to her family.

She would not die at the edge of this pool!

Her anger gave her the strength she needed. Her feet pulled free of the shoes the sand stubbornly clung to. They snapped back into the liquid, disappearing under the surface. The sudden release sent Addy tumbling away from the edge to safety.

Rolling to her knees, she untied the rope from her waist as she fought back more tears. She'd done it! She knelt there, breathing heavily for several heartbeats to recover some strength. The rope next to her suddenly slipped away with a hiss. She jerked back, startled. The rope slithered away into the trees where it must've been tied off. She watched the sand-covered end as it vanished into the dark cover of the forest.

Addy found herself alone. No one appeared to see if she was alright or take credit for her rescue. She squinted against the sunlight, catching sight of movement in the forest. Her eyes widened. She spotted what she could've sworn had been a furry tail vanishing deeper into the undergrowth. Once she caught her breath, Addy got to her feet and slowly began walking back to town. The soldiers that had come to town would've likely moved on by now. It should be safe to return. Her stomach rumbled, and she hugged herself.

Quietly, she chided herself for thinking she could find any food out here. She didn't know the first thing about gathering food in a forest! She should've stuck to the outer edge of the trees, where she could return to the streets quickly. The forest was no place for her. She became more frustrated when she thought about the man she'd tried to rob. Her ears grew hot with anger at the memory of how he'd spoken to her—like a teacher speaking to a dimwitted child.

What was worse was that he'd been right. She should've had a means of escape before taking the blade. Not that it mattered. Back home, she was never taught these things. She was protected by her father, brothers, guard, and friend Renard. New tears fell. She needed to get back to them.

"Did you really think you could outrun that wolf?" she scolded herself. She glanced about to ensure no one overheard her talking to herself. It was an embarrassing habit she'd picked up after the first moon of being on her own. "You're so stupid. Stick to the town, Addy. Stick to the town and steal from slow-running travelers. If you're lucky, you can get enough coin to get out of this place."

She looked down at her now bare feet and uttered glumly. "And maybe buy some new shoes."

She swore to herself that she'd make no more trips into the forest.

Greer trotted happily beside the Hunter, tongue lolling as he gave a canine grin.

"Oh, shut up," Strider muttered glumly, as he finished winding up the rope in his hands while they walked. The section that had touched the magic, and several feet after, crumbled away while much of it unraveled into a useless tangle of cords. "Had you woken me up when I told you to, we wouldn't have been around for that girl to steal from us."

Greer sucked his tongue back into his mouth with a click of his teeth. Ears twitching. He looked up at the Hunter, still annoyingly happy.

"Don't give me that look." Strider muttered, as he secured the rope back in place on the packs strapped to either side of Greer. "The cost of a new rope is coming out of your share."

Greer simply cocked his head as he continued to smile in the way only canines can.

Chapter 3

Lost Boots & Little Reward

It had taken Addy most of the day to reach the town of Altia. She kept to the sides of the streets, doing her best not to draw attention to herself as she made her way toward the nearest marketplace. Despite only having been in Altia for three moons, Addy had become familiar with its lower district's dirty, crowded streets. The large trading town was only one step away from becoming a full-fledged city within the Denmahr kingdom.

Addy knew she'd missed the morning bustle of the market and mentally kicked herself for going so deep into the forest. Small groups of people flitted back and forth, lazily perusing what remained free of the bustling crowd that bumped and pushed each other out of the way to get the best deal. There was little cover for thieves and cut-purses. She'd arrived early that morning, hoping to get a good haul. Begging in the streets had become less profitable as the cost of food and goods increased.

But the sight of the soldiers bearing the king's crest had caused her to retreat to the forest. The king's men normally didn't bother with lowly thieves, leaving such urchins to the local guard, who'd nearly caught her on more than one occasion. Only her quick feet had saved her. She'd narrowly avoided being recognized while they searched the town.

She had hoped to find food within the forest while waiting for the soldiers to leave. Instead, she found no food and lost her boots for her trouble. Her feet felt cold as they slapped against the dirty street, adding to her misery. Despite the late time, there would still be shops and customers to steal from. If she were lucky, she might be able to grab some leftover food the shops would throw out later.

Tugging her thin cloak around her, Addy pulled her hood over her head before entering the market square. People moved up and down the street. Mostly citizens and workers going about their business in a far less crazed manner than that of the morning crowd who sought the best goods of the day. Addy lingered on the edge of the street, searching for a mark.

This being the market closest to the slums, the crowd it drew was of lower-class. The wares were less fine, catering to the common folk rather than the noblemen. She didn't dare venture into the richer hunting grounds of one of the upper markets, where purses were sure to be full of coin. The Black Teeth wouldn't take kindly to her encroaching deeper into their territory. They chased her out of the richer hunting grounds the first week she arrived in Altia and continued to bully her and others for a tribute to steal in their city.

Someone caught her eye. The man wasn't richly dressed, but she could tell his attire was better than most of the people in the market. Though that wasn't a hard standard to beat. Addy moved into the street as she began following the stranger at a distance. Her target walked toward a stall where more people were gathering.

Addy picked up her pace to shorten the gap between her and her mark. She weaved easily between the small crowd of people as she drew closer to the man, eyes moving to the purse tied to his belt.

Drawing a small knife, Addy waited to strike. A merchant who hollered over the crowd drew her mark's attention. Addy moved in. Darting up to his side, she quickly slit the purse straps. Snatching it in one hand, she wove back through the crowd, putting as much distance between her and the mark she'd stolen from. Her heart pounded in her ears as she left the crowd and broke into a run toward the nearest side street.

"Thief!"

The man's angry shout rang out over the crowd when he realized his purse had been stolen. But when he looked around for any sign of the thief, there was none. No one else had raised their head or offered to help search for this thief. They simply checked their own purses before moving on, glad that it wasn't them who had lost their meager earnings.

Addy didn't stop running until a stitch in her side forced her to stop and catch her breath. She had left the market square behind and took a roundabout way back to her hideout. The lower district stood as an unwanted shadow of Altia's fine cobblestone streets lined with bright lanterns and clean wattle and daub buildings.

With poorly lit dirt roads and ramshackle buildings that leaned against one another for support, this place was where the unwanted were cast aside, left to rot among the putrid rat infested brothels, taverns, and decaying homes.

Addy had made a small hovel from broken crates and barrels in a filthy back-alley, next to a seedy tavern and inn. The inn and tavern owners hadn't driven her out of their alley like they did the other street urchins. They probably hoped she would accept their offer of a job as one of their serving wenches. Addy wasn't naïve enough to not know what they would've expected of her and continued to turn them down. Yet they continued to let her stay, and the large barkeep kept the worst of the rascals away. That was as far as their kindness extended, however. Which was considerably generous in the cutthroat world Addy found herself in.

Her breathing calmed, and her side no longer hurt as she padded down the street outside of the tavern. While walking, she peered into the little purse she'd taken. She frowned at the amount of coin she saw there. Due to rising food prices, it was barely enough to buy scraps from the tavern. She cursed at her misfortune. She could've sworn that the man was more well off than this. Her heart sank. She wasn't any closer to getting enough money to leave this place. She could hardly steal enough to survive.

None of the sellswords would protect her for the amount she'd saved up, at least none of the ones with a reputable reputation. She didn't have enough to hire someone and purchase supplies to reach the fiefdom of Timara either. Were her parents still searching for her? She wished she could get a message to them. To tell them that she wasn't in the kingdom of Myvara, but a little city in Denmahr. But paper was expensive, and the pay would insult a courier.

Dejected, she tucked the few coins into the bag before slipping it into her cloak as she entered her little alleyway. Lost in her misery, she didn't hear the footsteps until it was too late. Two figures emerged from the shadows cast by the tavern. They stepped in front of her, blocking her from going deeper into the alley. She cursed and turned to find two more men cutting off her retreat. Addy looked out into the street, hoping to find someone to help. Those who saw what was going on quickly ducked their heads and hurried away, not wanting to get involved.

She glared at them. Cowards!

"Look a bit happier to see us, Addy." One of the filthy men said. "Or I might be inclined to think you don't like me." He was thinner than her, but a good head taller. He was a foul-smelling skeleton, dressed in rags stained and torn from too much use and too little washing. The others didn't look any better, though they took time to bathe themselves.

"I don't like you, Gen," she retorted, turning her fierce gaze toward him.

"As ill-tempered as ever," Gen said, dismissively. "You should act more grateful. What with me allowing you to steal in our territory and all."

Addy barely bit back another sharp-tongued comment. Gen was in charge of this region for The Black Teeth, who ran the thieves in this town. If you didn't pay tribute to the group, you couldn't steal within the borders of Altia. Failure to pay resulted in punishment that made losing your hand to the local guard sound pleasant.

"What do you want?" Addy asked curtly.

Gen gave her an easy smile as he looked at her. He was missing more than a few teeth. "We've come to collect the rent."

"I already paid you tribute for this moon!"

"The price doubled, princess." Gen held out a hand. "Pay up."

Addy glared and shook her head, taking a step back from the older crook. She knew full well the Black Teeth hadn't driven up their tribute price. It was common practice for Black Teeth members to demand extra tribute from the thieves that refused to join their group. As a result, more and more thieves were joining their ranks to avoid being bullied.

"I'll get you the money next week. I can't pay you right now," Addy told him shortly.

Gen cocked his head, his smile turning dark. "Payment is due today, sweetheart."

"I don't have that kind of money," Addy argued, as she took another step back, her back hitting against the alley wall as the group of thieves closed around her.

Gen regarded her for a moment with a look that made Addy's stomach churn.

"If you can't pay with coin, I'm sure we can work out some other means of payment. The Teeth's brothels are always looking for new girls. We'll even be your first customers."

Addy's fingers clutched at the hilt of her hidden knife as the other thieves chuckled at the implications. She sidestepped, her back sliding along the wall as she shuffled further away from Gen. Angling herself closer to one of the smaller urchins. If she timed her attack right, she might be able to push past him and run out into the street. Seeming to sense her plan, the thieves closed around her, tightening the gaps as the smaller one drew his blade.

A deep growl rumbled from the entrance to the alley. Everyone's gaze turned to see the form of a massive, light-colored wolf as it uttered another threatening snarl. The two men closest to the beast backed away to stand closer to Gen. The wolf stalked closer, forcing the thieves to back up farther as he placed himself between them and Addy.

"What's this?" Gen asked, drawing his dagger as he nervously eyed the snarling beast. "Since when did you get a mutt?"

"She didn't," a cold voice uttered in the darkness behind the men.

Gen and his companions whirled around at the sound of the voice. They could barely make out the form of a darkly clad man. His face lay hidden in the shadows of his hood, though his eyes glinted out from the darkness like two saucers of light. He resembled a demon from The Wilds, eyes glowing gold, silver, and red, the sword he held glinting an icy blue as it caught the dying sunlight. The figure, enshrouded in darkness, took a threatening step forward. The wolf let out another booming snarl, spittle flying from his mouth as he stepped closer, jaws snapping together as he bit at the air. Not ones for bravery, the thieves bolted, fleeing into the street in terror.

Addy's own heart pounded in fear as the figure sheathed his sword and seemed to melt out of the darkness into the sunlight. She blinked in surprise as she found herself faced with the stranger from the woods. She realized the wolf standing in front of her was the one that had knocked her into the magpit earlier that day.

Addy took a moment to study her savior for the first time as he patted the large wolf on the head. His cloak was not quite black, but not quite green either. The shades and colors played tricks with her eyes as she stared at it, causing them to hurt if she stared at the fabric for too long.

His clothes were black, darker than the cloak that blended so perfectly with the shadows. His leather bracers, belts, and satchel were dark brown. On his right hip hung a hand and a half war sword. On his left hung the strange blade she had tried to steal earlier. She didn't know its name. Its form was slightly more curved than the swords she was used to.

A quiver and the same recurve bow she had seen earlier were slung over his back. The feather tied to the top of the bow shifted colors, changing in the light from orange to blue. A black cloth covered the bottom half of the man's face, and two piercing golden eyes stared back at her.

She felt uneasy around the stranger. An instinctual warning told her she was standing before a predator. The man barely regarded her as he walked out of the alley and onto the street toward the tavern. The wolf turned and gave her a friendly look, tongue hanging out of the corner of his mouth. Now that she looked at him too, he looked strange for a wolf. His fur was a light, smoky gray, touched by traces of white and ticks of black.

Such light coloring was extremely rare for a wolf, marking it as a demon in most folklore. Yet she didn't find herself fearing him. The animal gave her a happy yip, tossing his head as if gesturing for her to follow before trotting off after the man. As they rounded the corner, she heard her savior speak to the wolf in a low, annoyed tone. "Are you happy now?"

To which the wolf gave a low bark, his tail wagging.

What happened? Her eyes told her the man she'd stolen from had saved her yet again, but she struggled to believe it. She'd been getting on fine until her encounter with him. Now the small semblance of control she'd fought for was shattered, leaving her breathless and off balance. Still reeling from what had transpired, Addy scrambled after the mysterious man, not wanting to be alone in the alley.

She knew Gen and the others were still close by. She followed the stranger into the tavern, which was as busy as usual at this time of day. The entire tavern fell silent as the man and wolf entered. The customer's eyes traveled from the wolf to the stranger, before settling on the feather tied to the top of his bow that shifted colors in the candlelight.

The man paid them no mind as he walked silently toward a table in the back corner. He selected a seat that put his back to the wall and afforded him a good view of the entryway and doors that led to the kitchen and upper level. The position also offered him a view of most of the tavern and bar. Shrugging off his bow, he rested it against a chair next to him. His wolf flopped down under the table with a huff.

Addy hesitated in the doorway before making up her mind and entering. Slowly, the conversations in the tavern began again, though in more muted tones, as some people cast wary glances toward the stranger and his wolf. Addy heard the word Ranger uttered several times as she skirted the room.

The feather, and title of Ranger, was well known among the kingdoms; many countries employed them to maintain order, act as spies, and strategists. She'd learned that it wasn't common to see one so boldly walk into the slums. Usually, you never knew they were there until it was too late. Most people were wise enough not to mess with them. Their fighting prowess and rank made them deadly opponents.

Addy knew most nobles feared and hated them, for only the king was above a Ranger. Unlike the folks within the tavern, who made a point to not catch their eye, Addy had regular dealings with the Rangers in her home fiefdom. They were kind, free spirited, and rather mischievous. Nothing like the man who sat at the table.

A serving maid approached the table, careful not to approach the side where the wolf had chosen to lay.

"What can I get you, Ranger?" she asked, unable to hide the nervousness in her voice.

Addy paused by the fireplace before slowly getting closer to the table. The man's golden gaze flicked to the serving maid, and Addy half expected him to tell her he wasn't a Ranger like he'd done in the forest. But he said nothing about the matter and instead ordered a plate of mutton and some soup for himself and his wolf.

"And for the girl?" the woman asked, nodding toward Addy, who stood by the table.

Golden eyes focused on her once more, and Addy had a flashback to her childhood when she met the gaze of a great panther in the king's collection at the city of Alvanmir. She'd frozen back then and she froze now. The wolf looked up at her and thumped his tail against the ground in a hearty greeting. The golden eyes shifted to look down at the wolf before he turned and nodded at the server.

"The same order," he said.

The woman nodded before hurrying away.

Addy cautiously took a seat, excitement and mistrust fighting for supremacy within her. "Thank you," she muttered quietly, ...od! in her seat as her excitement won out. She was going to ...hning the

The stranger only cocked his head slightly, his ... room absently. ...dly, unable to

Addy drummed her fingers on the tabl... ...n. She hated the meet his gaze, as the silence stretched b...

silence. All her life, she was used to constant conversations. But she found herself in the rare position of not knowing what to say.

"Why did you help me? And why are you getting me food?" she finally asked. She felt his eyes on her again, but she didn't look up.

"Because I'd never hear the end of it."

She looked up then, surprised. "What?"

The man nodded at the wolf, who gave another thump of his tail when she looked down at him.

"He's the one you should be thanking," the Not-Ranger said, his tone matter-of-fact. "He's nothing but a bleeding heart with fur and refused to let me leave you to drown. He was also the one who helped you with those thugs."

Addy didn't quite understand or believe the man, but she leaned toward the wolf anyway.

"Thank you," she said to the wolf, who lifted his head and kissed her cheek quickly. She giggled and stroked his fur. His tail hammered out a faster beat against the floor. He uttered a sound of pleasure as she scratched his ears. She straightened back in her seat. The man was watching her, regarding her with a look she couldn't read. She shifted in her seat uncomfortably.

"I'm Addy," she offered, unsure how to fill the silence between them.

"Strider," the stranger replied, then gestured at the wolf. "This is Greer."

"Strider," she repeated skeptically. "You mean like a horse?"

His eyes narrowed. "No."

She nodded in acknowledgment. The serving maid brought their food, saving Addy from any further verbal mishaps. She gazed wide-eyed at the steaming plate of mutton, potatoes, and a bowl of vegetables placed before her. The maid placed a loaf of bread on the table between them. The smell of the food caused her stomach to howl and churn.

"Eat slow," the stranger said as he took his plate of food and placed it on the ground for Greer.

The noble beast attacked the plate, downing the food as furiously as she wanted to. But again, those predatory eyes were observing her. It took all her self-control to eat the food slowly.

Her eyes watered with tears as she took the first bite. The mere taste of the food gave her body strength. It was nothing like the fine dishes she was used to, but at the time it tasted better than anything she'd ever eaten. She quickly wiped her tears away, not wanting Strider to see her cry. Satisfied that she wouldn't shovel the food into her mouth as quickly as possible, Strider also began eating.

He pulled the black fabric that covered his neck and lower half of his face down, revealing a short, dark brown beard. His face was rugged, like a sculpture that had endured many hardships. He looked to be in his early thirties, though Addy was terrible at guessing people's ages. Despite the warmth of the tavern, he kept his hood up, casting a dark shadow over his eyes.

Addy wondered if he was some sort of hawk or eagle anumie, which was an ummanie bonded to the spirit of an animal, taking on several of its attributes. That would explain his golden eyes. She would've thought him handsome, had he not been so old. She watched him as he ate slowly, unsure why he let her stick around. Why had he bought her food?

He claimed Greer was the one who wanted to help her, but that sounded ridiculous. Greer was a wolf. She knew he'd had no intention of saving her from the magpit. He would've let her drown and not lost any sleep over it. She had seen it in his eyes. So, the fact that he was now letting her share his table and had bought her food was confusing. She didn't trust it.

Was he planning to take her and sell her as a slave? Maybe he owned or had a deal with one of the local brothels and he intended to make her work off her debt to him? Or was he planning to use her in some other way? Did he know who she was? That last question caused her heart to skip a beat, and her gaze dropped to her plate as she shoveled another spoonful of mutton into her mouth. No, he couldn't know who she was, she told herself. But why was he helping her?

As she thought, she felt someone watching her. Looking down, she met Greer's gaze. He seemed to smile at her. As their eyes locked, she felt less nervous. Was Greer trying to tell her something? To trust the man at the table? She turned her attention back to her food, feeling even more confused. An idea began to form in her head as she ate.

All too soon, the food vanished from the table. Leaving Addy to lean back in her chair, her belly full of food for the first time in moons. Sheepishly, she fished inside her cloak and pulled out the tiny amount of coin she had stolen that day.

Placing them on the table, she said. "I know it won't pay for the food. But—"

"Keep it." Strider cut her off.

She gave him a perplexed look. "But…"

"Keep it," he said, his tone leaving no room for argument as he put the soup bowl on the floor for Greer to finish. He had hardly touched his food, seeming uninterested in it.

Addy retrieved the coins from the table and tucked them back into her cloak. Once again, put off balance by the actions of this stranger. First, he was willing to leave her to die, now he insisted that he pay for her meal.

Strider studied her quietly as she fidgeted in her seat. "You're a terrible thief."

Addy's eyes shot back up to meet his. The same fire blazed in her gaze that he'd seen when she was trapped in the magpit.

"You have no idea whether I am or not!" she shot back. "Just because I messed up stealing from you—"

"You messed up in the market square as well," Strider cut in again, his voice low. "You stole that man's false purse."

Addy's jaw fell open, her mouth working to form words before her anger flared again. "You were watching me?"

Strider's head tilted toward Greer. "He spotted you in the market while I was buying rope."

Addy looked down at Greer, who wagged his tail. "But how did you know the man had a false purse?"

"As he walked, he would subconsciously pat the area near his left shoulder as if checking to make sure something was still there. He was more concerned with whatever he had hidden than that small purse he kept at his side," Strider replied coolly. "If you had taken the time to observe your mark, you would've seen that."

Addy's face grew red. "It's not like I have the luxury of observing every mark. If I don't move fast, I don't eat. How did you know he had a second purse?"

"He pulled it out to purchase fabric from a merchant," Strider said. "Not that you would have been able to get to the purse, given your lack of skill."

Addy threw her hands up in the air in frustration. "Are you a thief or a Ranger?"

Strider fixed her with a flat glare, and she closed her mouth quickly. It didn't stay closed for long.

"Alright," she admitted. "I'm a terrible thief. I haven't been one for very long. I don't even want to be one..."

He said nothing as he watched her. Her temper flared and cooled as rapidly as lightning flashing across the sky.

Addy looked down at her hands as she wrung them together. She took a deep breath before looking at him with a fierce determination.

"I want to hire you."

Chapter 4
An Offer He Should Refuse

Strider raised an eyebrow in response to her words. Addy was certain she was Chaos touched for hiring a man who left her to die. But she was desperate and that deep-seated compulsion to trust him spurred her on.

"Hire me?" he repeated skeptically. Addy nodded, a look of determination flaring like wildfire in her light brown eyes. A warning that he should get out, and fast as she set her resolve.

He would be the one to help her, maybe the gods had finally granted her prayers.

"Yes. I want to hire you to take me home." she confirmed, her voice determined, "I don't have much. But I've saved up enough coins to equal a silver piece. It's yours, if you can get me safely home."

Strider's head tilted to one side, and Addy could see a flash of surprise in his eyes. She'd scraped together everything she had after paying the Black Teeth's tributes, allotting barely anything toward food. She'd nearly spent everything on food several times as the pain in her stomach grew unbearable.

But then she'd remember her home. The soft singing of her mother's voice, the sound of her father's laughter. Was her mom still singing? Could her father laugh knowing his daughter was gone? Or did only tears remain? She refused to give up, and so she grew thinner and thinner.

"Who said I was for hire?" Strider replied, his tone clearly showing that he thought she was being ridiculous.

"You talk and act like a mercenary," Addy began. "You're not a Ranger but have a felaris feather on your bow. You're not a part of the soldiers here, so you must be a sellsword." What else could he be?

"I was willing to let you drown, and you think I'll bring you home safely?" Strider pointed out dryly. Addy fell silent again. The idea really was stupid. She wasn't sure why she felt she could trust him to get her home. But she did. It was a strange certainty, akin to knowing the sun would rise. But far less explainable. Yet she clung to the hope it had planted within her.

Addy knew she'd waste away long before she saved up enough to hire anyone else to get her home. This man was her only hope of escaping this place. Her gaze dropped to her lap for a moment, and she caught Greer looking at her intently, even encouragingly. Which made no sense, but it gave her the resolve she needed to meet Strider's gaze again as she continued to pose her argument.

"You're also the one who came back for me. You helped me outside the tavern and bought me food when you didn't have to."

Strider let out a slow breath. He hated that this girl thought she saw good in him. It was dangerous for her. This wasn't the first time random strangers were inclined to trust him, despite it being glaringly obvious that they shouldn't. He didn't understand it. Frowning, he glanced down at Greer. No, he understood it. He just couldn't explain it. It was as if they suddenly became possessed by this strange idea that he was someone who could solve their problems. He should've let her drown.

Greer was the one who had hassled him into rescuing her. He was the one who always wanted to help. But like with everyone before, Addy hadn't believed him when he'd said so earlier. Clearly thinking he was using Greer as a convenient scapegoat. Knowing how ridiculous it sounded, he wasn't about to argue the point. A man being manipulated by a wolf. But he wasn't about to let Greer's soft heart get him into even more trouble. He knew where this was going; his brother had done it before.

"Will you take the job?" Addy asked hopefully.

"No," Strider replied curtly, then stood. He placed some coins on the table to pay for the meal. Greer, hearing Strider get to his feet, stood also, as he looked up at the man. Strider pointedly did not look back, knowing that he'd be giving him a pleading look.

"Oh, come on!" Addy exclaimed, following Strider out of the tavern. "I promise I can pay you more when I get home!"

"I said no," Strider shot over his shoulder, ignoring the crowd of eyes that watched them leave.

"Please!" Addy begged, as she followed him down the street, past a brothel with women calling out to passersby, heading toward the sagging homes of the lower district.

"There are plenty of swords for hire. Go find someone else."

"I can't hire a decent guard for that price. Plus, I don't trust them. I feel like I can trust Greer."

The wolf paused and looked back at the mention of his name.

"Greer wouldn't be the one having to babysit you all the way back to wherever it is you live," Strider hissed.

"I don't need babysitting!" Addy huffed, as she stomped past Strider before coming to a halt in front of him, arms folded across her chest, chin raised.

Strider stopped and shook his head in frustration, instantly regretting it as his vision blurred, a reminder that he shouldn't push too hard. "I've had to save you twice already. Clearly you do."

Greer whined, and Strider glared at him, not happy for his input.

Addy took advantage of the exchange. "See, Greer wants you to help me," Addy said. "He'll keep you from going back on the job."

A small, grim smile tugged at the corner of Strider's lips, but the shadows of his hood hid his expression from Addy.

"I never said I would take the job." He spoke softly, his voice low and even.

"You haven't said you won't."

"What do you think 'No' meant back in the tavern?"

"You're still standing here listening to me."

Strider tried to move around Addy, but Greer moved quicker, darting in front of him, placing himself between him and Addy. Had Strider not stopped sharply, he would've tripped over the big lug. The movement made Strider very aware of the slash in his side as it sent pain shooting into his abdomen. He shot a murderous glare toward the di'horvith, who returned it with an innocent look of his own.

"I said no," Strider growled through his teeth.

Addy wasn't sure if he was talking to her or Greer. "If you leave me, I'll go find a Ranger," she threatened, her face set in a determined scowl. "I'll tell them about you. About how you wear a felaris feather but are not a Ranger. They'd hunt you down for that."

Strider turned a murderous stare on her, and she had to fight not to shrink back. She was beginning to think that she might have been wrong about him. The moment the thought entered her mind, she felt Greer's eyes on her, which somehow helped her keep her resolve.

"Or I could slit your throat and leave you in the alley I found you in," he stated coldly. "Blackmailing me won't end well for you."

It took every ounce of willpower to stand her ground and meet his gaze defiantly. No one had ever spoken to her like this before. No one would've dared back home. But she wasn't home and needed someone to get her there. "Do that and you miss out on a huge payday."

Strider gave a dismissive laugh, but Addy pressed on, trying to appeal to the man's sense of greed. Hoping that he was the type to be swayed by the promise of a big payout.

"My father is a blacksmith for Lord Fenforde," Addy spoke quickly. "Get me home, and he'll reward you for it. Lord Fenforde is a close family friend. He'd hear about your good deeds and would be inclined to show you favor as well."

"Lord Fenforde is over the fiefdom of Timara in the kingdom of Myvara," Strider said, frustrated, as Greer continued to put himself between him and Addy. Blocking him from carrying out his murderous intent. "Even with a good horse, that is at least two moons of travel. How did you end up in Denmahr?"

He'd seen her once light blue dress, now stained with dirt and grime. Though it wasn't embellished like a noblewoman's, it was made of fine material. Far finer than anything a pauper could afford. That didn't mean she couldn't have stolen the clothes. Her claim was extremely far-fetched.

Only the fact that he had seen her hands, which only had

budding callouses, coupled with how she acted, gave merit to her words. People were usually not aware of their subconscious actions born of lifestyle. None of it was befitting even a high-ranking blacksmith's daughter, but a noblewoman. He didn't care much for those who lied to him, but he didn't call her on it.

Addy bit her lip, her gaze dropping.

"You couldn't have gotten here on your own, so how?"

"I wanted to see the world and convinced my father to fund a trip to the Sea of Donmour." Greer let out a sneeze, but Addy did not notice. A haunted look crossed her face as she remembered that night, her arms folded tighter to hug herself. "Bandits attacked my carriage and killed my escorts while we were traveling through the forest. I escaped. It took me four days to find my way to Altia."

"And you didn't report this to the guards or soldiers?" Strider asked skeptically. Something wasn't right with her story, though her emotions seemed genuine. Likely the last half of her tale was true.

Addy shook her head solemnly. "I hold no titles or rank. My traveling dress, though nice, is rather plain. My clothes were filthy and torn before I even reached Altia. No one believed me." Addy bit out the last few words bitterly. "I looked like a beggar."

"What about the Rangers? They could have and would have easily confirmed your story," he pressed, still blocked by Greer as he tried to move around her.

Addy gave another shake of her head. "I have not seen or heard of any Rangers in Altia in the moons I've been here."

Strider frowned. That couldn't be right. Most of the ummanie kingdoms used Rangers to police their fiefdoms and assist the local populace. It was the Rangers who helped to solve any disputes among the people. A Ranger had skills that far surpassed normal militia. Even most trained soldiers balked at the idea of facing a Ranger in combat.

"Are you sure no Rangers have passed through?" His tone was flat as he observed her.

Addy nodded at his question, not catching on. "I would've heard about it. You know how people whisper. I am sure half of Altia knows you've arrived already."

That was true. Anyone remotely connected to the underside of Altia would know if a Ranger was in town. Word like that spread quickly among thieves and thugs. None of them wanted to attract the attention of a Ranger. Altia should've had at least four Rangers come into town within the last moon alone. They didn't abandon the areas they were assigned to. The lack of Rangers was good for him, but not for the people.

"Tell me, how did you plan to tell a Ranger about me, if none are nearby?" Strider pointed out darkly.

Addy flushed, realizing the vital mistake. She took a step back, trying to gather herself.

Strider's head cocked, eyes hard as flint, as he fingered the hilt of his curved sword.

"I..." She began, her eyes darting from side to side as if searching for an answer. Her face grew redder as she became more flustered and blurted out, "Will you take the job already?" It was a vain attempt to move the conversation away from her blunder as she rambled on, "I can help as we travel. I can cook, and mend clothing, and, and..." Her eyes darted back and forth, searching for an argument that might convince him, now that her threat didn't hold water. Finally, her shoulders slumped, and all she could say was a single word.

"Please."

Her voice was so quiet that anyone else wouldn't have been able to hear her. She looked down quickly, but not before Strider glimpsed tears in her eyes.

Greer let out a small whine as he nudged Addy's hand in concern. She patted him on the head as she fought back tears. She still wouldn't look up at Strider, unwilling to let him see her cry.

"Please, I want to go home."

He could hear the pain in her words but said nothing. Did

nothing as he let her stand there and cry quietly. Strider could feel Greer's eyes on him. He didn't need to look at him to know that he was giving him a beseeching look. Addy was not faking her desperation. She wasn't lying about her desire to get home, though she had lied about plenty of other things. He didn't need Greer to tell him that, like he had done when he sneezed during her story about how she came to Altia. Greer was kind, but he was also scarily good at sensing genuine emotion and the intentions of others.

The meddling di'horvith had become fixated on this girl and was determined to push him toward her. He wouldn't play his brother's game. With Greer distracted by comforting the girl, Strider skirted around Addy and began walking away. He'd gone several paces before realizing that Greer hadn't followed. He turned to see him still sitting with Addy. The admonishing look he gave the Hunter was unmistakable. He was not leaving her. Strider turned and began walking again.

"You know those men will kill me if you leave!" Addy shouted after him.

"That is not my problem," Strider muttered under his breath, as he kept walking. He'd made the mistake of getting involved thus far. He couldn't be roped into helping her further. He had to keep moving. This inexperienced girl would only slow him down.

Greer remained by her side, equally determined to win this battle of wills as he let out a long, howling cry. Greer continued to screech and wail until people stirred in the surrounding houses, jarred from their sleep. Many began cursing at the howling animal. Some threw things out their windows at him, none of them coming close to the shrieking wolf. Greer ignored them as his cries escalated into a hysterical crescendo, sounding scarily similar to the scream of a person. Strider stopped, his jaw working.

He could feel the dumb creature's deep desire to help the girl and knew that he would not abandon her, even if he left them alone. He'd remain by her side and likely die as a result. Strider would never let him die. Greer knew that and used it to his advantage. Strider stopped, the muscles in his shoulders tightening before relaxing in defeat as he sighed.

"Fine, you dumb mutt," he conceded in a low snarl he knew Addy couldn't hear. He turned back to the girl and his annoying di'horvith, saying in a louder, irritated tone.

"Go get your money. I'll take you home."

Chapter 5

Should've Said No

"I know what you're doing," Strider muttered low and harsh toward Greer.

The two waited at the corner of the alley entrance. Addy had returned to the alley to fetch the money she'd hidden among the crates and used barrels she'd built her home out of, leaving him alone with the di'horvith as they kept watch. Greer looked at Strider with a look of pure innocence.

His large brown eyes seemed to say, *'who me?'* as he wagged his tail. Strider's eyes narrowed, giving the di'horvith a look that sent most men running. Greer was unfazed, offering an open-mouthed canine smile, tongue hanging, as he sat. Strider looked to the heavens, letting out a heavy sigh.

"It's not going to work," he rumbled.

Greer merely yawned.

Strider leaned back against the worn brick wall, waiting for Addy, arms folded. Sharp golden eyes watched the street and surrounding shadows. Night had fallen, leaving the world bathed in darkness. He had positioned himself in one of the many shadows covering the dimly lit street, feeling more comfortable within its embrace than in the light. No one noticed him as they walked by.

They didn't notice Greer, either, despite his light gray fur. The dim light cast by the lanterns lining the dirty street impaired their vision. People clung to that light. For them, the shadows meant danger, light meant safety. As if the light could offer them any protection. Be it in light or shadow, death would always find you.

He glanced down the alleyway, easily picking out the form of Addy as she hurried back toward him, a small, ragged piece of cloth tucked under one arm. Her belongings, Strider assumed. She excitedly held out a hand to him, filled with small copper coins.

"Here," she panted, as she wiped dirt from her cheek with the back of her free hand.

"What's this?" Strider asked, as she deposited the collection of coins into his outstretched hand. The dark fabric he'd pulled up to hide his face covered his frown.

"Your payment," she answered, with a nod toward the coins. "Half now. You'll get the rest and anything else my father pays you when we get there."

He nodded silently, tucking the coins away in the shadows of his cloak.

"How long have you been here?" he asked.

"Three moons."

"You should be better at stealing then."

"I didn't start stealing until I had to!" Addy said, defensive. "I survived off of begging for most of it until the drought started and prices began to rise."

"And you didn't try to walk home?"

"A lone girl on the open road, no supplies, and no idea where to go?" Addy said sarcastically. "That sounds like a great plan."

Strider couldn't help the smile that briefly brushed his lips.

"Let's go," he muttered, pushing off the wall and walking out into the street. He set off toward the end of town. Greer trotted to his left. Addy fell into step to his right.

"We're leaving now?" she questioned.

"We are, now that someone foolishly flashed a fistful of money," he replied. "I'm honestly surprised you've survived this long out here."

"No one was around to see," Addy defended. "Plus, everyone thinks you're a Ranger."

"There are plenty of people around who saw. You just didn't see them," Strider corrected her, his voice low. "Some people are more than willing to attack Rangers. Though they usually end up dead for their troubles."

Addy stamped down the spark of anger at being lectured again, her face flushing with fury and embarrassment. She couldn't help glancing around, worried. Strider was right, and she hated it. She'd been so excited by the idea of finally returning home that she'd been reckless. She knew better. But surely no one would be stupid enough to attack him? He had to be making it up. Another idea struck her.

"What about supplies?" she asked, her tone a little too innocent after her blunder.

Strider's head jerked toward Greer. Her gaze drifted to the strange harness that allowed Greer to carry packs on either side. Tied to the top section of the harness, at the rear, was what looked like a blanket and some sort of grey bundle. The packs looked full.

"Never mind, then."

Strider wasn't listening to her anymore, his gaze fixed straight ahead. No, she realized, he wasn't looking forward. She could make out the subtle shift of his head as he used his eyes to look around. Occasionally, his head tilted more to one side when something caught his attention. Had she not been close enough to see a faint outline of his chin in the dim light, she wouldn't have known he had done it. The hood hid most of his actions. Her gaze dropped to Greer again, and she noticed how his ears never sat still as they moved from sound to sound. Both were paying attention to their surroundings, though Greer was more conspicuous than Strider.

She tried to imitate the way Strider surveyed his surroundings. But other than the people who walked out in the light, she saw nothing unusual. Save for the people that actually noticed the felaris feather on Strider's bow or the hulking, light-colored wolf, no one spared them much of a glance. But that didn't mean they weren't being watched. She tried to peer into the shadows, but her eyes couldn't pierce the darkness. She soon grew spooked and jumped at every sound that came from the shadows.

Despite her growing paranoia that someone would spring out and try to mug them, their travel through the slums was quiet. She slowly relaxed, thinking they'd be able to slip out of town unnoticed. Hope began to grow within her, and for the first time in moons, she dared let it. She was going home; her nightmare was about to end. Addy wrapped her arms around herself, imagining her mother's hug. Her father would pick her up in his arms, while her brothers gathered round. They'd all cry in joy and relief.

She'd tell her brother Curthis this wasn't his fault. She was sure Tamous had already tried to reassure him, but he'd listen to her. Her guard, Renard, would likely faint with relief upon seeing her. Her lips curled into a gentle smile as she thought of their smiling faces. Strider led them down a section of town not lit by lanterns. There were no windows to cast light into the street as they approached the edge of town. It wouldn't be long before she was free of Altia forever.

Strider suddenly moved in front of her. Addy stumbled to a halt, barely avoiding running into the man's back. She heard the hiss of metal as Strider drew his blade. She was about to swear at him when Greer let out a low snarl as he positioned himself beside her. Her heart and lungs stopped for a beat as fear tightened her throat. But Greer was not growling at her.

"Now, how did you see us?" A familiar voice said, as Gen and several other thieves slunk out of the dark alleyways.

Addy looked around them frantically. Six men surrounded them. Most held knives, and two had shortswords. A seventh man stood behind Gen; an arrow knocked in an old bow.

"Must be a Ranger thing," Gen dismissed with a shrug, when Strider didn't answer. "Doesn't matter. You're still outnumbered and surrounded." He looked at Addy and smiled. "Where are you going, Addy?"

She shot him a look that could kill as she peered around Strider. "Get out of the way, Gen."

Gen's grin widened. "Sure, sweetheart. Just as soon as you pay the going away tax, and don't tell me you don't have the money." He cut in before she could speak. "Baxter saw the coin you gave the Ranger here."

Addy was glad she was behind Strider so he couldn't shoot her a look that said, *'I told you so.'*

Greer let out another low growl.

"Call that dog off, or we'll put an arrow through him," Gen threatened. The man holding the bow aimed at Greer.

Strider's golden eyes grew hard and his head cocked to one side, as he watched Gen with a look a cat might give a mouse before it tore its throat out.

"He shoots, you die," Strider's words had a murderous edge, as cold and sharp as steel. He didn't appear outwardly troubled by the threat of the arrow.

Greer hardly paid the archer any mind, seeing no threat.

"You're pretty confident, aren't you, Ranger?" Gen said nonchalantly. "Think you can take on all seven of us?"

"Twelve," Strider corrected. "And I only informed you of what would happen to you, specifically, if your friend shot the wolf."

Surprise rippled through the group of thieves at the mention of their numbers. A couple even looked back into the darkness, checking to see if their allies had revealed themselves.

"You Rangers really are something," Gen said, shaking his head.

Strider said nothing.

"I hear they do like their anumi. Freaks, all of you."

"Move, Gen," Addy ordered. "Or do you think The Black Teeth will reward you for starting a war with the Rangers?"

"Oh, we don't have a problem with the Ranger." Gen shrugged. "He can leave. But you need to pay the fee." His confident gaze shifted to Strider.

"What say you, Ranger? Do you feel like fighting off twelve men with those injuries? Is this girl worth it?"

Greer instantly stopped growling. He licked his lips, then snapped his teeth together, head tilted, as he looked up at Strider. Strider gave him a brief glance. He looked back at Addy, considering his answer. She looked up at him pleadingly.

Finally, he shook his head and stepped away from her.

Addy's mouth gaped in shock as Gen grinned.

"Smart man," he said, stepping aside and gesturing for Strider to go through.

Strider strode quietly forward, light as a cat despite the injury. He regarded Gen with a measured gaze, ready for any trouble.

Gen had positioned himself to Strider's left and out of the reach of his sword should he try to strike him. The man with the bow had done the same, an arrow drawn and pointed at him.

Strider knew another archer skulked in the shadows had an arrow trained on him.

"Wait," Addy yelled, as Strider walked toward Gen. "You can't leave me! Your job is to help me!"

Strider didn't look back, ignoring her as he slipped past Gen. Even Greer left her alone, following Strider while he disappeared.

Addy's throat tightened in anger and betrayal as tears welled in her eyes.

"I guess Rangers aren't as brave as people say they are," Gen observed, moving back to fill the hole he made to allow Strider through.

"He's no Ranger," Addy choked out bitterly, hands balling into fists. All hope of returning home vanished and Gen laughed, finding humor in her misery. She wished with everything she had that Renard or Curthis were here. They'd never have abandoned her.

"Whoever he was, he isn't going to help you," Gen smirked. He'd been watching as Strider slipped into the darkness and vanished, ensuring the man left. He had won. Gen turned back to look at Addy, fixing her with a hungry look that made her shiver.

"Now, why don't you give me the rest of that money you so kindly saved up for me?" his voice was slow, unhurried. He was confident she wouldn't escape.

Addy brought a hand up to the small pouch that hung around her neck, hidden under her blouse. She stepped back, shaking her head as she reached for her knife.

"You'll have to take it from me," she hissed, all the anger and hurt turning her words to venom. Just because Strider was too much of a coward to face them didn't mean she wouldn't go down fighting!

"You always make things hard for yourself," Gen sighed, shaking his head. "Be reasonable. Hand over the money and go back to your trash pile like a good little rat."

"Go feed yourself to the pigs," she spat.

Gen gave another shake of his head. "Don't blame me if you get hurt."

He signaled to his men and one holding a shortsword stepped toward her. She turned to face him, knife drawn. The sound of an angry wasp whizzed by her, followed by a resounding thwack! An arrow slammed into the body of the thug, who'd taken a step in her direction.

Now would be the perfect time to leave her, Strider thought, while slipping through the shadows like a phantom. It would be so easy to take the money and leave her to her fate. Yet he wouldn't. A job was a job, money had been exchanged. He'd taken on worse in the past and he'd seen them through till the end. He would do the same here.

As Greer hung back near Gen and the archer, Strider had slipped through the shadows and alleyways as he moved toward the men hiding in the darkness. He could hear Gen speaking, clearly reveling in the victory he thought he'd won. He clearly enjoyed seeing Addy so distraught as he drew out every word, his body language conveying his overconfidence. Everyone was watching Addy. No one was paying attention to the surrounding darkness.

None of the men made a sound when he slipped up behind them and slit their throats before returning to the street behind Gen. The man was making a show of taunting Addy, who, despite her hopeless situation, shot back words laced with fire. Her feisty spirit was amusing and admirable. So long as it wasn't aimed at him.

Strider stood in the darkness, knocking an arrow in his bow. He considered leaving. It would be so easy. But even if he'd agreed to help her because of one stupid wolf, he'd told Addy he'd get her home. As much as Strider hated it, he would get her there. He had very few things left in this world. His word was one of them and he wouldn't lose it now.

Strider watched as Gen decided his gloating was over and signaled to one man. Strider took a deep breath, bracing himself for what he knew would come. He drew back on the string and his side split with pain. He couldn't feel the blood but could smell it as it dampened his shirt. Gritting his teeth, he took aim, all thoughts of the injury forced from his mind as his eyes locked on his target. The man reached for Addy. Strider let out a breath as the string and arrow slipped from his fingers.

The thug was thrown back by the force of the arrow connecting with his chest before skittering across the ground. His body fell silently to the earth, the sword falling into the dirt with a thud. With no plate armor, chain mail, or gambeson to contend with, the arrow passed clean through the man, killing him instantly. Two more bodies fell as Strider's arrows quickly found their marks. Each arrow clattering as they skipped across dirt and stone.

Panicked, the thieves turned in circles, trying to figure out where the shots were coming from and where to run for cover. The archer who'd aimed at Greer earlier slumped silently to the ground, beats before Gen felt a blade kiss his neck, still wet with the archer's blood. He didn't have a chance to beg or scream before the blade sliced his throat.

Strider pushed the limp body away from him, letting it fall to the earth with a thud as he advanced on the two remaining thieves standing out in the moonlight. They stepped back, eyes darting around as they looked for the men who should've appeared when the fight had started. No one came. The shadows were still and silent.

They ran their courage, vanishing now that they no longer had a numerical advantage. With one fluid motion, Strider shrugged his bow into his hand, grabbed an arrow, knocked it, and shot. The arrow sang as it flew, piercing one of the fleeing thieves between the shoulder blades. As quickly as the first flew, Strider had knocked another arrow and aimed. Greer suddenly cried out in pain. Strider whirled, the arrow now aimed to kill whoever dared harm his brother, but no one was there.

Greer stood alone. He cocked his head at Strider, confused. Strider cursed under his breath at the di'horvith, knowing exactly what he'd pulled. The Hunter lowered his bow, placing the arrow back in his quiver. He watched the last thief as he ran like Chaos himself was on his heels. He could've still shot him. The man was well within range. But he only watched a moment longer, eyes like a cat that'd grown bored with its game. With no one left to kill, Strider crouched before Gen's body, using the fabric of his dirty shirt to clean his dagger.

Addy stared at the surrounding devastation. Memories of the night of her escape flashed before her eyes. The cries, the blood, the soldiers dying as the earth slammed into them. A whine startled her out of her memories, and she looked down to see Greer looking up at her in concern. He tenderly licked her hand, his nose bumping into her palm. Addy dropped to her knees and hugged him.

"Let's go," Strider ordered.

She pulled away from the di'horvith, a hand resting on his neck.

Greer gave her a quick kiss before disappearing behind her. She didn't look to see where he went as she eyed Strider. The dead bodies of the thieves lay on either side of him. He watched her with eyes as cold as the moonlight they reflected.

"You came back," she said, finally. Her gaze was glassy. She was in shock, dumbfounded by the sudden explosion of violence around her.

"I never left," he stated. "Come."

Addy shakily got to her feet. She took several deep breaths to steady herself before crossing the street and passing the bodies. She didn't look down at them, feeling numb with disbelief.

Strider silently followed her.

Greer came rushing back, the three arrows Strider had shot in his mouth. He blew past both Addy and Strider before swiftly turning to prance back to them proudly. He tossed his head and lifted his chin to offer the retrieved arrows to Strider, who gave him a scratch behind the ear as a reward.

Addy shuddered at the sight of the vicious arrowheads, the black metal stained scarlet.

Strider inspected the bloody arrows using a piece of Gen's cloak he had cut away to clean the heads as he checked for damage before placing them back in his quiver. Neither of them said anything as they left the town of Altia behind them.

Chapter 6
A Rocky Start

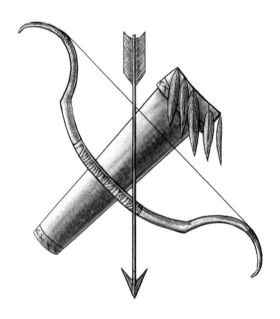

The shock that kept Addy silent wore off when they reached the forest. She whirled on Strider, forcing him to come to a stop, her face red with fury. "You left me again!" she shouted. Her heart and mind couldn't take much more. Twice she believed she would die, forced to stare her mortality in the eye with no hope of rescue. The constant abandonment and rescue left her with emotional whiplash, winding her tight, like a string about to snap. She couldn't handle the pain it inflicted, the trauma of believing she'd be left to die by someone who'd agreed to help her.

Strider looked down at her, meeting the fiery glare Addy leveled upon him with an even stare.

"I'm still here," he stated flatly.

"You left me alone at the magpit, in the street, and with those men! They could've killed me, or worse!"

"They would've done worse and then killed you," Strider said unhelpfully, as he pushed past her.

"And knowing that you abandoned me!" Addy chased after him, which wasn't hard. The man's pace had been slowing gradually as they distanced themselves from Altia. He'd slowed even more when they entered the forest.

"I never gave them a chance," Strider uttered darkly, his voice breathier than before.

"That doesn't change the fact that you walked out on me without a word!"

Strider stopped and gave her a look like he was gauging her intelligence. "You expected me to tell you my plan, surrounded by the people I wanted to use it on?"

"I hired you to get me home safely. I'm not safe if I'm dead!" Addy shouted, nearly hysterical, while tears flowed freely down her face.

"And I will!" Strider barked, his patience growing thin as he began moving again.

Why didn't he understand? She didn't care that he'd wanted to be strategic. But that he'd once again left her. He'd done nothing to communicate a plan to her. Instead, she'd believed he left her high and dry, alone, to face an enemy she couldn't overcome. Addy stormed up to Strider, aiming to hit him as hard as she could when he turned his back on her. Greer hurriedly brushed past her, causing her to stumble. She cursed at the wolf as she sobbed, her body shaking with fury.

"You were supposed to stay with me," she sputtered. No one had ever abandoned her before now. She'd never had to face danger; she'd always had someone to stand between her and the threat. She wanted Curthis and Renard. She wanted her father.

Why was she so surprised by this? Strider had left her to die earlier that morning. She'd given him his sword back, and he'd left her to drown. She was so stupid for thinking he had any good in him! Why had she thought any different?

Strider turned to face her, eyes catching the moonlight and gleaming silver as they shifted to look at her.

"That idiot allowed me to leave with my weapons," Strider explained. "He believed I was going to let them have you and let his guard down. I was never far away. Anyone who tried to get near you died." He nodded toward Greer. "Greer was ready to rush in as well."

"He believed you wouldn't attack him because you were a Ranger."

"I'm not a Ranger."

"But he thought you were!" Addy fumed.

"He was an idiot to trust in that. Not all Rangers are honorable."

Addy ignored him and barreled on, her fury driving her, giving her strength despite her growing exhaustion. "They could've shot me while you were attacking them!"

"They wouldn't have hit you even if they tried," he snorted. "I'm surprised those old bows didn't snap when they were put under tension. They didn't have any spring left. The arrows were in worse condition. Even an expert archer wouldn't have hit you."

That did nothing to calm Addy, as she let out a shriek of frustrated rage. If looks could kill, Strider would've died five times over. He was either too dumb or too stubborn to understand what he did to her, the turmoil and trauma he'd caused. She let out another scream, unable to contain her anger but unable to find the words to accurately express what she was feeling, or how much of an idiot this man was.

She'd been doing fine on her own until he showed up. Gen and the Black Teeth had been an issue, but she'd skirted around them plenty of times. The moment she'd encountered Strider, everything went to Chaos. She considered leaving him, but even in her anger she knew she didn't have the skills to survive or navigate home. She was stuck with this man who attracted trouble.

The Hunter stopped again, his breathing heavy. He grunted in pain as he eased himself to the ground, his back resting against a young tree. Greer looked at him and gave a worried whine. The di'horvith took a step forward but stopped when Strider held up a hand, pointing to the forest. Greer let out a sound of protest but disappeared to scout the area around where they had stopped. Normally, Strider patrolled around the campsite, ensuring that there weren't any surprises. But his injuries forced him to send Greer instead.

Addy hadn't noticed how the Hunter favored his injured side, too caught up in her own emotions. Hurt and anger rolled off her in waves as she paced and continued to berate Strider.

"Even if it seemed like a good plan, you still shouldn't have left me! You have a felaris feather! You must have the skills to hang onto it. The Rangers wouldn't let you walk around with one if you didn't. You could've stood and fought them! Even an injured Ranger could handle twelve measly thieves!"

"I'm. Not. A Ranger." Strider ground out between gritted teeth. The look he shot her as dangerous as what she'd fixed on him.

"Then what are you?" she snapped.

"I'm a Hunter."

Addy threw out her hands in an exasperated gesture. She was about to interrogate him further, but Greer chose that moment to return. Swiftly padding over to Strider, he yipped and whined worriedly as he laid down at a signal from the man.

Strider began rummaging through the packs, ignoring Addy as she continued to pace angrily. He pulled out bandages, a clean cloth, and a small jar. A sharp smell filled the air when he opened the jar, causing Greer to sneeze.

Addy stopped and glared at Strider as he began dipping pieces of clean cloth into the salve. She noticed his shirt was torn and slick with blood. When she'd first met him, she'd thought he was just dirty from travel, his clothes ruffled and worn. She never looked closer or spotted the injury he kept hidden behind his cloak. She hadn't known until Gen pointed it out. He must've seen it when Strider pushed his cloak back to free up his sword. Or maybe one of his men had noticed it while following them. She wouldn't have seen it because he'd stepped before her to shield her from the archer.

His shirt clung to his skin, and he had to pry it away to get at the wound. Addy paled at the sight of the injury that she could tell had been reopened. Had it torn open when he had drawn his bow? A flash of guilt cooled her temper when she realized that even a Ranger would have struggled to fight with such an injury. She now understood why he'd left her. Addy watched Strider place the soaked cloth pieces on the wound, wincing when he stuffed parts of them inside of it to help stem the bleeding.

Slowly, the blood flow stopped as the salve did its job. Greer whined again, placing his head on his paws as he watched Strider, eyes wide with worry.

Strider uttered something to the wolf in a language Addy could not understand. The words were eloquent and soft, unlike the normal sharp tone he took with her. The di'horvith let out a huff. He stopped crying quietly to himself and relaxed a bit, but his eyes never left Strider. Watching every move the man made with great intensity.

Strider put the lid back on the jar, then returned it and the remaining pieces of cloth to the bag he'd pulled them from. Turning his attention to the bandages, he began wrapping it around his midriff awkwardly. A hand gently touched his, and he looked up to see Addy standing over him. Her face was a mixture of unreadable emotions as she nodded to the bandages.

"Let me," she mumbled, her eyes dropping to avoid his gaze. He offered her the bandages with a nod. Addy sat next to him and began binding his wound. He watched her as she worked. Addy never once lifted her eyes to meet his, choosing to focus on her work in silence.

"What happened?" she finally asked, as she bandaged him.

"A sword sliced me," Strider answered.

Addy frowned, looking to the heavens for help.

"How did it happen?"

"The wielder swung their sword."

Addy gritted her teeth in frustration, all guilt vanishing. "I mean, why did someone attack you?"

"I imagine they wanted me dead."

Addy wanted to scream at him again as she hissed through her teeth, "I can guess why."

With a jerk, she tied off the bandages, causing Strider to wince. She turned and began stuffing the remaining bandages back into the bag. Silence resumed as she took her anger out on the packs and bandages, jamming the supplies into the bag with enough force to shake Greer.

Greer widened his stance to steady himself or risk falling over. He shot Strider a look of his own. His eyes shifted to Addy, then back to Strider, clearly wanting him to say something.

Strider frowned at him, not in the mood to humor the nosy beast.

It took Addy a while before she calmed down again. "I'm still mad at you about leaving me," she said, after closing the pack. Her voice had lost all of its earlier heat.

I couldn't tell, Strider thought, wisely not putting it into words, though he made no effort to smooth things over, like Greer wanted. He remained quiet, head resting back against the rough bark. The silence stretched between them. If she expected an apology from him, she wouldn't be getting it anytime soon.

"I was stupid to think I could trust you," she continued. "But you're my only chance at getting home. If you leave me like that again, though, I swear I'll, I'll…"

She wasn't sure what she'd do. What could she do against someone more skilled than her? She bit her lip angrily, and the silence enveloped them again.

Greer placed his head in her lap, his big brown eyes looking up at her as he tried to comfort her. Still, no response came.

Her anger flared anew. "Why won't you—?" she stopped mid-shout when she realized he wasn't listening.

He couldn't. His body was completely limp, his head canted to one side, the great hood of his cloak covering his eyes. He looked even paler in the moonlight than she remembered. For a beat, she thought he was dead until his chest slowly rose. He'd passed out, unable to fend off the exhaustion from blood loss and overuse of magic. He'd looked the same way when she'd found him that morning. Propped against a tree, dead to the world as his body shut down and forced him to rest.

He had to have felt exhausted when he chased her down for his sword, returned and gave her that rope, and stopped to help her in the alley. He'd even bought her food and tolerated her company. Then he told her he would help her when he'd probably wanted nothing more than to spend at least one night sleeping in a bed. But he led her out of town instead when she stupidly flashed money around.

He could've left her when Gen gave him the chance. It would've been easy to take the money she'd given him and never look back. He could've found another inn and used that money to buy himself a soft bed and a warm place to sleep for the night. But he'd stayed and helped her, hurting himself further.

Again, she found herself puzzled by the man who claimed not to be a Ranger. She didn't trust him, and yet she did, which made it all the more confusing. He constantly changed and shifted to the point that her head was left spinning, trying to keep up. Could he really get her home with such an injury? She wondered. Even wounded, he was her best shot.

While Gen and his men were willing to interfere with a Ranger to settle a personal grudge, everyone else would give him a wide berth. She could use that to her advantage. He could get her home. Or he'd attract the attention of real Rangers, who'd help her.

But he could just as easily use her when he found out what really happened the night she escaped, using her as a hostage in place of her kidnappers. The screams of the men and horses that night filled her mind. She bit her cheek, not daring to close her eyes. If she did, she'd see their bodies, half buried in mud and stone, or draped over fallen trees.

Even if he didn't ransom her off, he could abandon her for real the next time she was in danger. Deciding that she wasn't worth the trouble. She stroked Greer's head absentmindedly as she thought.

"What do you say, Greer?" she asked, with a heavy sigh. "What's stopping your master from abandoning me the moment things get rough?"

He looked up at her intently, dark brown eyes searching her face.

As she returned his gaze, she had a strange feeling that Strider needed her as desperately as she needed him.

Chapter 7
Tiptoeing

Birdsong drew Strider from his sleep. He could tell by the shadows that the sun had been in the sky for almost half the morning watch. His body ached, and his mind was hazy, pulsating with pain. He closed his eyes again and lay there in the still of the morning. As he rested, the ice that had settled in his soul became too cold to ignore.

The desire to fall back into sleep's embrace pulled at him. His limbs felt heavy, his soul felt heavier, and he was bone-weary. It'd be so easy to fall back asleep, but he knew that if he gave in, he wouldn't wake up. It was so tempting. He could hear Greer and Addy breathing softly next to him and felt the weight of his brother's head on his leg.

He fought to pry his eyes open, held together by invisible seams stabbed through into each lid with a cruel needle. He finally won the battle, and he saw the light of day once more. How hard it could be to do something so trivial as opening one's eyes. Determined not to relapse, he looked down at the two sleeping figures. Greer was curled around Addy, offering his warmth as she snuggled into him. Both were sleeping soundly.

Strider remained still. He didn't have the strength or desire to bother moving yet, as he fought an internal battle to pull away from the dragging chains of ice that tried to pull him toward death. As he did so, he noticed the pain in his head subsiding. He still felt groggy; a side effect of losing so much blood. But he also felt his magic again.

He latched onto it as he began channeling magic through his body. He was so cold. The warmth of the magic flowed through him, chasing the frigid feeling away. He loosened the bandages and began the painful task of working the cloth out of his wound; wincing as the dried cloth pulled free, taking most of the scabs with it. Blood oozed from the wound once more. Not the best idea, but he didn't have time to soak the cloth to loosen its hold. He placed his hand over the injury, calling to his magic.

His movements woke Greer, who jerked his head up with a snort.

He looked around, dazed. Letting out an enormous yawn, he stretched. He looked at Strider, tail thumping happily on the ground.

Addy stirred with a yawn of her own. She stretched and sat up, before looking around. Her brows knitted together in confusion before remembrance darkened her face. She turned and eyed Strider as if she hadn't expected him to be there when she awoke.

He ignored her while he focused on tapping into his magical well. Having only gained a grasp on his magic eighty years ago, the depths of the magical well within him startled him. It was a gift from his mother's bloodline he could never fully tap into. What magic he did know was built on the foundations she'd laid. It was one of the few things he had left to remember her by, one he'd squandered and tainted.

He was glad she'd never known the crimes he'd committed using what she'd taught him. In the end, it was a blessing that he'd only ever be able to draw on small amounts as he increased his connection with his inner well. It spared her legacy from being corrupted. He couldn't harness all his inner magic, but it would be enough.

The magic to heal was by far one of the most complicated and consuming forms of magical powers. A small amount of healing magic drew far more than some of the most destructive spells. Making powerful healers the most respected and feared in the magical community.

Strider knew he wouldn't be able to heal his wound completely; not because he didn't have the power, but because he couldn't risk completely exhausting himself again, couldn't risk being caught without magic, couldn't risk the cold tempting him away from life. They had a lot of traveling to do. The blood loss would slow him down enough. He didn't need the dark chill that whispered for him to give in, or the exhaustion that made his soul and bones heavy as lead, slowing him down further.

Addy had moved closer, drawn in by the faint light of the healing magic peeking out from between Strider's fingers.

Strider didn't take notice of her until she spoke.

"I didn't know you could use magic," she breathed in amazement. Then her eyes narrowed in suspicion, and she drew away. "Are you sure you're not a Ranger?"

Strider eyed her, intoning slowly, "Yes."

He expected her to yell at him again, or run in fear upon seeing him use magic. But she did neither. Instead, she watched in fascination. There was still a prickliness about her, and she scowled at him every time he caught her eye before glancing away. Her behavior didn't bother him. That would mean he actually cared.

"You can use magic like a Ranger, you shoot a bow like a Ranger, you have a felaris feather like a Ranger, and I am betting you fight like a Ranger," she mused coldly, as she ruffled Greer's fluffy cheeks and ears. "And yet you call yourself a Hunter, why?"

Strider pushed up with his free elbow to shift into a more comfortable position as he considered the question.

"The Rangers call me a Hunter," he replied. Only expounding when Addy shot him a questioning glare. "Someone trained as a Ranger, but is not loyal to them or their code."

"So, it's what they call a Ranger who's betrayed their pact." Her head cocked as she considered this new information. "I bet you're really popular among their group."

Strider gave a ghost of a half-smile but said nothing.

Addy frowned and looked away again. Of course, she'd be the one to hire a dishonored Ranger. Yet she still battled with the idea that she could trust him. But she knew she couldn't. She turned her back to him as she stood and stretched.

Strider watched her like she was a magical item prone to exploding if mishandled. He was becoming well versed in how to handle her the wrong way, though he was too weary to care. No, he told himself, he didn't care. He finally stood, pulling free of the last of the ties, trying to drag him back into the darkness.

"Let's go," he grunted, striding off deeper into the forest with measured steps. He paced himself for the long walk ahead as he set a course Northwest.

Addy frowned. Her stomach growled. Her meal from the previous night had burned away. But before she could say anything in protest, Strider barked over his shoulder, never glancing back.

"There is jerky in Greer's bags. Eat while we walk."

Addy stuck her tongue out at his back.

"Very ladylike," Strider muttered, loud enough for her to hear.

"How did he see that?" she whispered to Greer.

"I'm a Hunter," Strider answered, as if that were enough of an explanation. "Now walk."

Addy made a face, mimicking Strider in silent mockery as she pulled out some pieces of dried meat before following.

Greer smiled at her, amused by the exchange as he padded alongside her. His tail wagged lazily from side to side, hardly ever sitting still.

The pace Strider set was thankfully easy for her to follow as she ate. She was starving and she would've eaten the meat quicker had it not been so tough.

Greer eyed the food in her hand hungrily. She offered him a piece that he swallowed whole with a loud slapping of his jaws. She watched Greer, a plan forming in her mind. They hadn't gotten far before a sharp pain stabbed through Addy's foot, causing her to cry out.

Strider turned, drawing his blade in a single motion, eyes scanning for danger. He frowned at her when he saw no threat.

"What happened?" he asked in annoyance, sheathing his sword.

"I stepped on something sharp," Addy hissed in pain and irritation. She'd dropped to her rear, massaging her bare foot. Strider knelt in front of her, and she jumped in fright. How had he gotten so close so quickly?

"Don't rub it," he ordered, brushing her hands away with a flick of his own.

"Of course, I am going to rub it!"

Strider fixed her with a hard stare. "You'll make it worse."

He let out a frustrated sigh before motioning to Greer to come closer. Opening one of the packs, he pulled out the rest of the clean bandages and began wrapping her hurt foot. The wrap was tight, but not uncomfortable. The cloth covered her foot, secured at her ankle. Strider then wrapped her other foot. He gave a silent nod as he inspected his work.

"There," he breathed, as he stood slowly so as not to cause his own head to spin. He turned and began walking again.

Addy looked down at her bandaged feet. She wiggled her tones, flexing them as she tested the makeshift footwear. As she looked at them, they reminded her of the nice warm shoes she used to have back home, she had several beautiful pairs of shoes; works of art created by skilled cobblers.

She'd spent hours with her mother, picking them out, having them fitted. At the time, such moments together had been fun, the memories trivial. But now they were precious. Now she wondered if she'd be able to make more of those memories. She sniffled as she fought back the urge to cry.

Greer chuffed as he moved in close, his head draping over her shoulder as he inspected what Strider had done to her feet. Satisfied, he licked her on the cheek. She pushed him away, which only encouraged him as he planted another wet kiss on her face.

"Stop it!" she said, trying to be mad at the di'horvith, but not managing it as he scored another kiss.

He let out a mumbling growl as if mimicking her before licking her again.

She giggled as she finally pushed him off.

Greer sneezed before tossing his head playfully.

She laughed again, and he appeared to smile at her.

Greer waited for her to return to her feet, never leaving her side. Addy grinned down at him before looking up to see Strider waiting several paces ahead. He leaned his shoulder against a tree, arms folded as he watched her, his face hidden in shadow. She frowned at him, unable to read his expression. He didn't move until she and Greer had closed the gap. He said nothing as he led the way, following a game trail that took them in the general direction he desired.

The forest hummed around them as they walked. It was a beautiful day, the shade of the trees keeping things at a pleasant temperature. Strider continued leading the way. He followed game trails most of the time. When they started to lead too far West, or East, he'd strike out into the forest. He moved confidently, his cloak blending with the forest, forcing Addy to stay close or risk losing sight of him.

Addy quickly became lost as they traveled deeper into the trees. Strider walked smoothly, his footsteps as quiet as a cat's. As opposed to Addy's own steps that seemed startlingly loud in comparison. She tried to watch how he walked, but his cloak blocked most of his movements from her view.

Seeing him walk so quietly compared to her quickly frustrated her. Taking it as a personal challenge, she tried stepping where he stepped, attempting to be just as quiet. Her steps were quieter, but still obvious.

Brows knitting, she bit her cheek as she tried tiptoeing after Strider. The act threw her off balance. She couldn't match his pace and nearly fell over. She felt eyes on her and froze. Looking up, she saw Strider had stopped to watch her, head cocked to one side. His face was still nothing but a dark void beneath the hood.

She flushed, realizing he'd caught her in the act. Lifting her chin, she shot him a challenging glare, but he said nothing as he turned and resumed walking. His pace was noticeably slower. Her embarrassment didn't take long to wear off, and she began trying to imitate the Hunter again.

"Stop walking on your toes."

Strider's voice startled her, causing her next step to land flat-footed, creating more noise as she snapped a twig. Her eyes shot up to him again, ready to argue, but his back was still to her as he picked his way through the trees. How had he known? As she watched, his cloak shifted while he adjusted his bow and quiver to a more comfortable position. The action pulled his cloak around enough that Addy could see his right foot as he took each step.

She studied how he placed his footing. Each step was planned and careful. His feet found patches of bare earth or green grass. She copied how he stepped on the outer ball of his foot, before rolling it to place his weight on the front of his foot, heel lowering after. He never fully committed to a step until he was certain he wouldn't cause noise. Once she saw him roll his foot as he stepped, only to lift it again to find another place to set it that wouldn't cause needless sound.

As she imitated him, she noticed her steps were softer, but still not right as she shook and wobbled with each attempt. She experimented, finding that if she kept her knees more bent, she could keep her balance and control where she put her feet. It took her a moment to notice how Strider balanced in this manner, and she felt a bit of pride for figuring it out herself. Her steps were considerably quieter, but how she walked was awkward for her and it caused her legs to burn with the strain. Her breath became heavier as she exerted herself.

She worked hard to mirror the Hunter. She was so focused on her task that she didn't notice that their pace had slowed considerably.

He never pointed it out as he listened to her steps gradually get quieter. Though her heavy breathing was easily drowning out any noise her feet might be making. He remained walking at Addy's speed until she called for him to stop, her voice breathless.

"I need to rest," she huffed.

"You need more practice," he responded, stopping. "You're snorting through your nose like a pig."

Addy's skin glistened with sweat, her thin body shaking from the exercise.

"I don't sound like a pig," she said, between heavy breaths.

"You're right," Strider amended. "You sound like a horse."

She glowered at him. "I need to breathe!"

"Not through your nose." Strider stooped over Greer, untied a waterskin, and offered it to her. She lunged for it, but he jerked it out of her reach.

"Drink slowly." His tone was firm.

She shot him another look full of daggers before snatching it from his hand.

He watched her, ensuring she drank slowly to avoid vomiting, before leaving her to sit on a fallen tree nearby. He munched on a piece of jerky, eyeing Greer, who flopped to the ground next to Addy. The corners of his lips twitched downward at the di'horvith. He wasn't used to him favoring another over him. The Hunter wasn't sure how to feel about it, but he brushed the matter aside.

Addy drank over half of the water skin before capping it. She wiped her mouth with the back of her hand, her breath still labored. She would've thought that all the running she'd done through the streets would've made her fit. Boy, had she been wrong! Her legs burned, the muscles twitching in mini spasms after the workout they'd received.

"It'll take years to reach Myvara's border at the pace you're going," Strider noted dryly, after he'd finished eating. He went on before Addy could shoot back a retort. "If you want to practice, do it when we make camp where you can't slow us down."

"I'm too tired to practice now," Addy responded, ill-tempered as usual.

Strider, having gotten to his feet, flashed her a wicked smile. "We're not making camp."

Addy groaned as he started walking. He didn't stop to wait as he disappeared into the trees. She forced herself to her feet and limped after the Hunter, muttering curses under her breath at him. Reaching out, she grabbed the handle that was sewn to the top of Greer's harness, using the wolf to keep herself going as she trudged after Strider. Greer didn't seem bothered by her as he pulled her along, easily following the scent trail left by the Hunter.

Chapter 8

A Plan Forms

Strider had noticed Addy trying to walk quieter. The change in her footfalls and rhythm had alerted him to her actions. He could feel the intensity of her stare as she studied him before focusing on trying to imitate what she saw. She'd been so intent on placing her feet correctly; she didn't notice when he glanced her way. He wasn't sure why she was trying so hard to copy his movements, but he decided to entertain her. It could make his job easier if she could move quietly. Or more difficult if she tried using the skill against him.

He learned Addy could be observant when she wanted to be. When he shifted his cloak so she could watch his movements, she studied his feet and copied him. He occasionally turned in his route to allow her a better view of how he centered himself. He noticed her improvement; she learned quickly when she bothered to pay attention. But like he'd pointed out, her breathing was loud. Her dress was ill-suited for silent movements as it snagged branches and rustled out of rhythm with the forest's natural song.

He'd let Addy have her fun, but indulging her any longer would prove detrimental. They needed to travel as quickly as possible. He avoided the road entirely while leading them through the forest. Though he knew what direction they were traveling on instinct, he still took the time to check the sun's position as he cut a path Northwest through the forest. Their path wound around the more populated areas of Denmahr.

The major trade route would have made travel easier with its well-traveled road. But trade meant people with eyes to report seeing them, and ears to hear the wrong thing being said. He much preferred to face the land and wildlife. The lands of the yulie, ravack, and ummanie were tame compared to The Wilds, where even the ground wanted to kill you. He maintained the same level of vigilance trained into him by the unpredictable wilds, and years of being the hunter and the hunted. Stupidity and complacency killed far more people than many realized.

Strider fell into the steady pace he'd originally set, dictated by what he knew his body could handle in its current condition. He needed to conserve his strength and allow his body to heal. What would be best would be to rest, but he had little hope of that. His side ached, but the worst pain had subsided, numbed by the healing magic he'd used that morning. He'd need to take care not to reopen it again, like he had the night before.

His gaze shifted to glance back toward Addy. He could hear her clumsily plodding behind him. He could tell by her gait that she was reaching the end of her endurance. It surprised the Hunter that she'd lasted for as long as she had. Her stubbornness likely kept her on her feet, but he had to give her a degree of begrudging respect for it.

Greer still walked next to Addy, keeping her company while Strider walked point. He casually maintained alertness about him while his bouncing, happy steps conveyed his relaxed nature. By nature, the sound of his movement through the forest was far quieter than Addy's steps. Several times he pulled her along, lending her his strength as they followed Strider.

Day turned to night earlier within a forest. While the world outside still enjoyed the sun, the light vanished easily within the forest, blocked by the canopy of trees. The temperature dropped as birds sang their final songs, mingling with the sounds of crickets and other night creatures as day transitioned into night. Soon it would become too dark for Addy's eyes to see reliably. Not wishing to drag a blind girl through the trees, Strider selected a small clearing hemmed in by trees to stop for the night.

"We'll camp here," he said. "Wait here while I gather wood."

Addy promptly collapsed with a groan, rubbing her aching legs and feet.

Greer cocked his head, giving her a sympathetic look.

"Finally," Addy breathed, sprawling in dead leaves in a very unladylike fashion. She stared up at Greer, who continued to smile down at her. He didn't appear affected by the long walk.

"How are you not tired?"

The di'horvith tilted his head to the other side before flopping beside her. His wagging tail smacked her in the face as it stirred up dried leaves and pine needles.

"Greer!" she spat, swatting the tail away as she sat up. "That was rude."

Greer rested his head on her legs in response, tail still wagging. She shook her head, then looked around to find that Strider hadn't returned. She shifted while looking behind her.

Greer moved to curl around her more closely, head still resting on her lap. Addy had to situate herself, so the packs secured to him didn't jab into her uncomfortably. She stroked his soft fur thoughtfully.

"You're lucky you're cute."

One of Greer's ears angled to catch her voice, and she gave it an appreciative scratch. His head lifted as he leaned into the welcomed affection.

Addy continued to rub the di'horvith's ears and fluffy cheeks as she sat. Her eyes drifted to the bags and gear secured to the massive wolf's leather harness. She let them linger on the supplies. At least one pack contained rations of jerky, nuts, dried fruits, and other food items. Enough to last her for a decent time if she was careful. Which left three others.

One contained the bandages she had stuffed inside. But she had been so angry with Strider that night, she hadn't taken time to see what else the packs contained. There was a coil of rope tightly woven together, nestled between a rolled-up blanket and what she thought was a one-man tent.

The other packs likely held other things that were useful for survival. All neatly packed away and carried by a wolf who never seemed to tire. A wolf that hadn't left her side all day.

She smiled. It was nice to have someone stay with her. She'd never truly been alone for most of her life. Both Renard and Curthis had grown up beside her, acting as her guards once they were of age.

There were always her parents, siblings, staff, or tutors around her. It'd been terrifying being alone in unknown lands, going from always knowing what the day held to never knowing if you'd survive another moment had left her nerves strained.

But most of all, it had been painfully lonely. As her trust in Greer grew, she found herself relaxing more as her sense of security grew. Greer's head suddenly jerked away from her hand, causing her to start. Her eyes tore away from the packs to focus on whatever had caught his attention.

Strider crouched in the middle of the clearing, a pile of wood next to him. Addy hadn't heard him return.

A light panic fluttered in her stomach. Had he seen her staring at the packs? He didn't look up from his task of building a fire, didn't give any outward signs that he suspected anything. Maybe he didn't notice? She prayed he didn't notice. Greer didn't rise until Addy stood to approach the newly built fire. It crackled and spat, throwing off uneven shadows as it danced. Dusk was quickly becoming night. With it, the temperature dropped. Addy sat beside the fire, hugging her knees as she soaked in the warmth.

"Greer," Strider called softly to the di'horvith, who obediently padded over to him.

Addy ran her fingers through her hair, trying to work out the worst of the tangles. She watched the Hunter undo the harness, relieving Greer of his load.

Greer gave a grateful shake before bounding off with a playful yip. He rushed about the camp, jumping and tossing his head as he released pent-up energy.

Addy laughed at his silly antics. With Greer no longer wearing the packs and harness, Addy could see how different Greer looked compared to other wolves.

"What kind of wolf is he?" she finally asked, as she watched Greer play.

"He is half di'horvith," Strider answered.

Addy gave him a questioning look. "A di-what?"

"A dire wolf," Strider clarified, as he inspected the harness for any wear or damage.

"I thought dire wolves were bigger." Addy watched Greer bound around them, remembering the stories her father had told her of the dread mounts of the ravack. There was no way Greer could carry such a large person.

Seeing nothing that concerned him, Strider moved on to inspecting his own gear and weapons. "He is only half di'horvith," he told her absently, as he studied the grip on his knife.

"I see," she replied, letting the conversation end.

Addy had never seen a di'horvith before. Most ummanie hadn't. The noble beasts lived only in the lands of the ravack tribes. It was said that it took ten men to kill a single di'horvith. Stories of their strength and ferocity abounded in child's tales and history books. They'd decimated yulie forces in the Liberating War. They were a fearsome mount used only by the ravacks, who aided the ummanie in gaining their freedom from yulie oppression.

Addy tried to picture thousands of giant Greers charging into battle with ravacks riding atop their backs. Though she knew little about them, she knew that di'horviths, like normal wolves, did not have light colored fur. The mutation was rare in both wolves and horses.

White or grey-furred wolves were the villains of many dark tales. In some regions, people called them demons. But Greer was nothing like the stories she'd been told. She watched him act like a goofy dog, definitively not a vicious killer. Those stories were obviously false, made up by bards to entertain others.

"How did you get him?" Addy asked.

Strider cocked his head while gazing into the fire. He remained silent for a long while, and Addy thought he'd refuse to tell her. She was preparing to argue with him when he spoke.

"I rescued him," he began, his eyes now following Greer, watching him play. The wolf had stolen a stick from the woodpile

Strider had gathered for the fire and was tossing it around and chasing it with the energy of an excited puppy, though he never shook his head in the violent manner dogs often did when playing. Addy could've sworn she saw Strider smile softly as he gazed at the mutt.

"His pack was killed by a bear consumed with madness. They died defending him. I killed it before it could touch him. But he had no family left. He was alone."

"So you took him in," Addy finished.

Strider nodded. "He's been a good brother."

Addy studied Strider for a long moment. She'd expected him to say he'd bought him off an animal trader. The thought that a man like him would save and then raise an orphaned puppy hadn't occurred to her. He was so cold and distant. But she'd seen the way Strider's eyes softened when he looked at the large mutt and recalled how gently he'd spoken to him the night before. Now he had called him *'brother.'* Not pet or friend, but brother.

Again, Addy wondered if she was missing something. A key part that would help her understand the puzzling man before her. She'd seen him mercilessly kill back at Altia. Had been left by him three times, once to die. But he'd also bought her food for no reason and treated Greer with a kindness she didn't think possible.

She wanted to think there was some good in the Hunter. But she didn't let herself, fighting off that nagging feeling that she should trust him. She'd seen what he was really like when he abandoned her in Altia. When he shot the fleeing thief in the back—he was a killer, and it was only a matter of time before he killed her or left her to die.

Again.

Greer returned to the campfire, having finished playing. Strider didn't reclaim the stick the di'horvith still held in his mouth as he curled up behind Addy. She caught the slight frown Strider gave the wolf when he sat next to her over him. She felt a twinge of satisfaction and patted Greer on the head.

Strider narrowed his eyes at her smug look. He sheathed his

dagger and began fiddling with the packs. Yanking the blanket free, he tossed it to her.

"Here," he barked softly.

Addy barely caught the blanket. She fumbled with it before wrapping it around herself.

Strider was on his feet again, his dark cloak billowing around him.

"Where are you going?" she asked suspiciously.

"To keep watch," he said curtly. "Now go to sleep."

Addy didn't like being ordered around, but she was too tired to argue. The warmth of the fire and the comfort of the blanket wrapped around her had only given her weariness more strength. Her eyes were struggling to focus, begging her to close them. She curled up against Greer as he chewed on his stick.

Strider moved out of sight, vanishing into the darkness. She didn't bother trying to spot him. Her eyes couldn't see beyond the light cast by the fire. But she knew he was out there watching. Snuggled up next to Greer, she felt safe for the first time in a very long time. Her gaze drifted toward the supply packs Strider had left on the ground. They lingered there for a moment longer before she drifted off to sleep.

Strider had taken up a position outside of the ring of firelight. Hidden within the forest's underbrush, he sat, all but invisible in the darkness. His keen golden eyes never stayed in the same place for long, and he took care not to fall into a predictable pattern as he scanned the world around him. The night was filled with the usual sounds of summer. Everything was peaceful as he watched over the camp. Both Addy and Greer had fallen asleep. Greer's snores mingled with the noise of the forest. Again, his brother had chosen Addy over him, which puzzled Strider.

Greer had been glued to him since his fight with the assassin. But now, he clung to Addy. She was their client, he reasoned, so it was perfectly natural for Greer to stick close to her to protect her. The di'horvith always had an uncanny understanding of matters concerning people. He could guard her much more easily than Strider could.

Greer had forced Strider into Addy's life ever since they'd helped her out of the Well. He had worked to get the Hunter to agree to help her. Chasing the girl down after seeing her again in the marketplace. The Chaos-ridden wolf thought they needed to help her. Strider knew why, and it wasn't just because he was a huge softy.

Greer was trying to distract him by giving him a job to do in some misguided attempt to help. It was irritating and inconvenient. After a time, he pushed the thoughts aside. It was pointless working himself up over it. Greer would be Greer, and he couldn't change that.

Strider hated acting as an escort. He was the person who broke through the guards to kill his target. He didn't protect people from being killed unless ordered to do so. Those jobs had never involved protecting a teenager. He rarely associated himself with those younger than him, especially after losing his apprentice decades ago.

Strider's gaze dropped from the canopy of leaves as sorrow shadowed his features. It'd been years since he'd thought about his apprentice, but that didn't stop his chest from tightening, gripped by the claws of grief. He should've insisted on accompanying him on his first mission as a full-fledged assassin, but that wasn't their way. One had to prove themselves.

He couldn't face that kind of loss again, so avoided the young ones when he had to be among people, never wanting to get attached. It had been decades since he'd interacted with anyone, adult or otherwise, in any meaningful way. He didn't remember them being so emotional or irrational. But the teens he'd interacted with had been through rigorous training. Addy hadn't. Her fiery spirit was as admirable as it was exhausting.

As he sat alone with his thoughts, Strider felt the touch of the frozen chains once more. He shuddered despite himself as the growing chill filled him. Closing his eyes, he breathed deeply, fending off the cold within himself. He couldn't answer death's call. As much as he hated it, he had a job to do. And as much as he would've liked to abandon the frustrating teenager, he wouldn't go back on his word.

Chapter 9
Bit Of Everything

Strider woke Greer halfway through the night. The di'horvith carefully extracted himself from Addy. He yawned before shaking out his fur as he stepped toward Strider. The Hunter paid him little mind as he laid down, using the packs as a pillow. Greer bumped his head against the man's arm affectionately. Strider reached up and fondled his ears, smiling softly. Greer made a rumbling noise of pleasure as he leaned into the affection.

With a sigh, the wolf fell on top of Strider, front legs draping over each shoulder as he lay on his chest. Strider bit back a gasp of pain as the wolf's weight landed on top of him, forcing the air from his lungs. The pain in his side did little to help him regain his breath.

"Greer," Strider gasped, trying to keep his voice a whisper, "I said to keep watch, not smother me."

He could hear the thump of the di'horvith's tail as it smacked against the ground. Greer laid his head over his shoulder, his soft cheek resting against Strider's.

"Alright," Strider relented. "If we get taken by surprise and killed because of this, I'll skin your ghost and use your fur as a coat to fend off the cold of Tarn."

He rested a hand over Greer's neck, his thumb stroking behind the mutt's ear. He gazed quietly at the stars, effectively pinned under the large animal. His worries that Greer liked Addy more than him had revealed how much he was unused to sharing Greer with others. His brother was the only family he had, and he'd come to rely heavily on his companionship. He'd done exactly what he never wanted to do again; he'd become too attached to someone.

Though he was sure he never stood a chance the moment he let Greer's charms convince him to let him tag along. It was supposed to be temporary. He'd find someone to leave him with. But Strider always found reasons not to leave behind the puppy that followed him like a fluffy shadow.

Now he couldn't imagine being without him. His earlier anxiety melted alongside the cold that had filled him when he sat alone in the dark. Greer had known, and he'd come to reassure him. Strider could tell by his breathing that Greer wasn't asleep.

"I don't need help," he told Greer. "I'm not going to die or give up. I just need rest, not someone to babysit me."

Greer eyed him out of the corner of his eye as he gave a short grunt, clearly unconvinced. He continued to lay draped over him, staving off the cold inside the man's soul.

The two brothers listened to the song of the forest as they laid together. It had been ten years since Strider had rescued the half di'horvith, yet he found it hard to imagine a time without him. He hardly remembered anything before finding Greer. The time after he'd found his father and animal friend murdered was nothing more than a blur of hatred and blood lust. Greer had grounded him and filled the void left by his father and his last animal companion.

"I'm alright now," Strider muttered, after several moments of silence. "Go keep watch."

The wolf gave a sniff before shifting his great weight off of Strider. He snuffled as his nose sniffed Strider's wound before licking his hand. Strider shooed him away. The wolf snorted again, eyeing Strider one last time before turning away. Wrapping his cloak around himself, Strider shifted into a more comfortable position by the fire before falling asleep.

The next morning saw the trio moving again. After a cold breakfast, Strider took the group in the same direction. Only adjusting his course when the landscape dictated. Addy's malnourished body forced them to stop several times so she could catch her breath. It was frustrating, but Strider knew he couldn't press her to move faster. He didn't want to have to carry her because she fainted. His own body needed to recover, and her inability to handle the rough terrain forced him to take it easier than he might have otherwise.

Seeing how Addy had downed most of the offered water the night before, Strider had kept a close eye on their rations. But Addy seemed to understand they needed to be sparing with the food. She nibbled on the dried meat, fruit, and cheese he'd given her while they sat around the smoldering embers of last night's fire. Prolonging the meal while her stomach growled. She had to be starving, but she kept herself from devouring their entire stock in one sitting.

He was familiar with the soul devouring suffering of starvation. As they continued walking, he gathered edible plants to supplement the midday meal. Addy's endurance had waned. Better, more reliable meals would help restore her energy reserves. Which meant they'd be able to travel longer between breaks.

The Hunter stopped mid watch, selecting a spot near a babbling stream that wound through the trees. Insects buzzed about, dancing in the rays of sunlight breaking through the canopy. Forest birds flitted back and forth overhead, hunting bugs and sounding territorial war songs disguised as pleasant whistles and twitters.

Strider grabbed a small pot secured to Greer's harness and filled it and his water skins at the nearby stream. He set up a firepit and a rig to suspend the pot over the fire. Tossing the herbs and plants he'd gathered into the pot along with some potatoes and dried meat, he let it stew. Addy knelt before the fire.

"What are you making?" she asked, peering into the pot.

"Soup," Strider said.

Addy rolled her eyes. "What kind?"

He glanced up at Addy, a sense of déjà vu causing him to pause as he remembered a similar conversation he'd had with his father when he was younger. He gave the same answer his father had given when he'd asked him what was for dinner while his mother held him on her lap. "BOE Stew."

"Boe?"

"Bit of Everything."

Addy giggled. "That can't be a real soup."

"Probably not, but it's what we're having," Strider said, pushing Greer's nose away as it came too close to the pot.

Guiding Greer alongside him, he retrieved a couple of bowls from the packs on his harness, before filling them and handing one to Addy.

Addy eagerly accepted the bowl from Strider. She blew on the steaming soup to help it cool. She could smell potatoes and strange plants mingled together. It wasn't unpleasant, but it was unlike any soup she'd smelled before. When she tasted it, she knew why. Though mostly potatoes and greens, the soup left a lot to be desired. It tasted mostly like starchy water, seasoned with not enough wild herbs.

"I was right. This isn't real soup," she said into her bowl, her voice full of disappointment.

"It'll give you the strength you need," Strider replied. "If you want flavor, go to an inn."

She hunkered down over her bowl, grumbling as she shoved another spoonful into her mouth. She wasn't sure what to call this atrocity. Slop was too strong a word; it implied the food had a flavor, albeit a bad one. This one was… empty.

She was glad there hadn't been enough soup for Strider to offer her seconds as she forced herself to eat the rest. She was hungry, and the potatoes helped to fill her stomach. But the meal did little to lift her spirits. They didn't linger long after having their meal, and Addy found herself trudging after Strider once more.

Chapter 10

An Absence Of Rangers

The sun was setting when the group reached the edge of the forest. Cresting a rise, they paused, still within the shelter of the trees. Below them lay a small hamlet nestled at the base of the hill. Cultivated fields surrounded the handful of houses that made up the main body of the settlement. Outlying houses sat further away from the single street, running through the middle of the clustered homes. Strider counted ten in all. People could be seen working in the fields, tending to flocks, and taking care of other chores necessary for life.

Strider considered skirting the settlement to avoid as much ummanie contact as possible, but both Addy and Greer started down toward the houses before he could order them away. The girl's speed and mood had picked up considerably at the sight of the hamlet.

Strider gave a small shake of his head but didn't call them back. Pulling the dark fabric up to cover the lower half of his face, he followed the eager girl and wolf. He caught up to the two at the bottom of the hill where Addy had paused to catch her breath. The threesome followed the road as it cut through fields leading toward the heart of the town. Children, who'd been running and playing on the street, stopped to stare at the strangers. When they spotted Strider, one shouted, pointing at the feather atop his bow.

"Ranger!" he cried, in a shrill voice. The others took up the call as they ran back to town. "A Ranger is here!"

They shouted with an energy and enthusiasm only children possessed. The working men and women looked up at the cry of the children. Several offered waves of greetings that Addy happily returned, and Strider ignored. One man left his work in the field to approach them, his hands spreading out in a welcoming gesture.

"Welcome, Ranger!" he greeted them with a smile.

Strider nodded at him quietly.

"I am Helrald," the man went on, unperturbed by Strider's silence. "The leader and founder of Ringo. Who do we have the pleasure of welcoming to our home?"

"Strider," the Hunter responded. "The wolf is Greer, and the girl is Addy."

Addy frowned at being called 'the girl' but smiled at the man. He was well built, with a broad chest and shoulders, and dark brown hair streaked with gray. His skin was tanned to a leather brown from years of being in the sun. He nodded to each person and wolf as they were introduced. His gaze lingered on Greer for a long moment, changing from worried to consideration before he finally seemed to come to a silent conclusion before continuing on.

"We were not expecting to see any Rangers or their company." His face grew hopeful as he looked back at Strider. "Did they decide not to repost Verda and the others?"

The look on the man's face was rather surprising to Addy. She'd heard that most commoners feared and avoided Rangers. Many people in Timara castle gave Rangers a wide berth and never bothered to learn their names, let alone show interest in them.

"I wouldn't know," Strider told him. "We're just passing through."

The founder nodded, his face falling before he smiled again. The setting sun cast a warm golden light over the farmers working in the field. Some paused, leaning on their hoes as they watched the exchange. The forest around them had grown dark, creating a black-green semi-circle around the little hamlet.

"You're welcome to stay and rest here before moving on. It would be our honor," Helrald said.

Strider was shaking his head before Helrald had finished. He had no desire to stay among people. But Addy spoke up hurriedly.

"It is we who would be honored to accept your hospitality." Her tone was proper, and as sweet as honey.

Strider frowned down at her, though neither she nor Helrald could tell. Neither one paid attention to his eyes. The Hunter shook his head and sighed. The damage had been done, and they'd attract more attention if he dragged Addy away now.

Helrald beamed, he gestured toward the cluster of wattle and daub buildings that lined the dirt street, ending at a large well that supplied the town with its water.

"We don't have much, but what's ours is yours. My wife, Illa, will see that you're taken care of. My house is the one nearest the well at the end of the street." He excused himself before hefting a large basket only halfway full of food onto his shoulder. He walked toward the other townsfolk with equally meager spoils from their fields.

Strider shot Addy a hard look. "We don't have time to waste here," he told her. "We can walk for at least a quarter watch more."

Addy gave a dismissive wave. "It won't hurt to stop and rest here. I am exhausted and could use a hot meal." She gave Strider a measured look. Her eyes lingered on his injury before meeting his gaze.

He frowned at the message, narrowing his eyes dangerously.

"You could always tell them you aren't a Ranger," she suggested. "Then we'd have to leave."

He fixed her with a stare she couldn't quite read but said nothing. Addy knew he wouldn't tell. He'd only told her because he thought she was going to die. Word of a dishonored Ranger would travel quickly and attract unwanted attention from any of the Rangers in the area.

The walk to the founder's house took them past several cream-colored houses. Smoke from cook fires curled lazily from stone chimneys, filling the air with the scent of wood smoke and cooking meals. Voices of the farmers in the field, livestock, and the sounds of people in their homes preparing dinner made a peaceful hum against the drawl of crickets.

The walk was short and uneventful; only the children were in the street enjoying the last bit of freedom of the day before they'd be called in for the night. Excited by their arrival, the children peered out from behind the well, giggling and whispering as they watched the trio approach the house.

Addy knocked, feeling that it was better if Illa saw her in the doorway before Strider's imposing figure. Greer had once again stuck close to her, having not left her side all morning. Illa opened the door. She was as short as Addy, her light-colored hair turning gray.

She was a homely woman who offered Addy a friendly smile. Her gaze shifted to Strider, her smile faltering as she peered into the darkness of his hood before shifting to the feather attached to the top of his bow. The shifting colors of the feather caused her smile to grow, her body relaxing at the reassuring sight.

"Why, if it isn't a Ranger! It does my eyes good to see one of you again!" she greeted. "How can I help you?"

Addy stepped forward, greeting her and telling her what her husband had said.

"Why, of course, we're always happy to put up a Ranger and company for the night. Come in!" She gestured for them to enter as she stepped back from the door.

As was common with ummanie wattle and daub dwellings, it was a single-room house with a ladder leading up to a loft that acted as an additional sleeping area. A fire burned in the hearth, and the room smelled of the food Illa had prepared for the evening. Addy's mouth watered, and she gratefully sat at the table when offered. Illa looked to Strider, offering him a place as well. He shook his head, leaning against the stones of the fireplace as he watched Illa serve Addy a warm bowl of stew. Illa didn't seem to find Strider's actions strange, and she simply placed a warm bowl atop the wooden hearth next to him. He accepted it with a quiet nod of thanks.

Addy shot Strider a scornful look. Illa caught it and smiled.

"He's fine, dear," she said good-naturedly. "Rangers will be Rangers. Verda did the same thing when he and his partner Garlen first came to town. He wouldn't sit down and relax until the fourth time they visited."

She smiled fondly at the memory. Strider's lips twitched in a frown at the thought of being compared to a Ranger. Greer lay at Addy's feet, his head warming her bare toes.

"Do Rangers visit here often?" Addy asked, between mouthfuls of stew.

Illa nodded. "Oh yes. It is a part of a Ranger's job to look after the small settlements that don't have enough of a force to employ a sufficient guard. We first met Verda and Garlen about five years after Helrald and some others had founded the town. At the time, a group of men had been stealing our livestock and terrorizing us before retreating into the forest."

"Verda and Garlen are the Rangers responsible for overseeing this section of the kingdom?" Addy surmised.

"There are two more, Taya and Shawn, who also look after this territory." Her face fell. "Or rather, they were."

"What do mean, 'were'?" Strider questioned, eyes narrowing.

Illa looked genuinely surprised. "You mean you haven't heard?"

Both Addy and Strider shook their head, so Illa explained.

"King Elias didn't renew his contract with the Rangers."

Strider raised a brow, his head cocking.

Addy froze, spoon halfway to her mouth as she gaped at Illa. "He did what?"

"He ordered all the Rangers to leave Denmahr," Illa said. "I don't know what we are going to do without them."

"Is king Elias mad?" Addy breathed, looking to Strider as if he had an answer.

He shrugged. "Many kingdoms are unhappy to have to rely upon the Rangers," he informed her.

"But to order them out of your country. That puts you at a serious disadvantage," Addy ranted in a quiet voice. Rangers were known as much for their fighting skills as they were for their information gathering and strategic abilities. "King Elias is going to have to dedicate more of his forces to police his own country, than at the borders where he needs them most."

Illa shook her head solemnly. "Small settlements like Ringo will lose all the support that the Rangers offered. It was a sad day when Verda and the others said goodbye."

No wonder Helrald had looked concerned when Strider said he was just passing through. These places relied upon the safety the Rangers had provided. Now that they were gone, the townspeople had no one to go to for help.

Strider placed his bowl back on the hearth, his gaze thoughtful. Though some nations had never relied on Rangers, of the ones that did, only two other kingdoms had ever tried to sever ties with them. Like Denmahr, the kingdoms of Umanari and Goshon had also refused to renew their contracts.

Of the two, only Umanari still existed, the other fell to neighboring kingdoms when their information network and internal law structure collapsed. The incompetent ruler hadn't realized how much they relied upon the force of the Rangers. While the Rangers hadn't given the enemy kingdoms any information on Goshon, per the contract agreement, their absence in the kingdom had weakened it.

Umanari had survived because they pulled away gradually from the Rangers, allowing their own government the chance to adapt to the change. They'd turned to the Syliceon church and their Ry'arie knights to supplement their forces. Other kingdoms had followed their example. Likely, Denmahr would do the same.

"That explains why I hadn't seen any Rangers in Altia," Addy said.

Had Gen known that the Rangers had been withdrawn, he probably wouldn't have been so willing to let Strider walk to avoid starting a war with the group. She glanced at Strider, who was leaning quietly against the stonework, eyes closed. If Denmahr no longer supported the Rangers, that meant the authority the title offered was null and void. They wouldn't have the king's protection while traveling through his kingdom.

They also wouldn't have the authority to give orders as they did before. Her plan to use Strider's fake rank as a Ranger wouldn't do her any good. However, a single look from him could cause most men to think twice about messing with him. One simply had to look at a panther to know it was dangerous. She wiggled her toes out from under Greer's head. Her mind turned to the other plan that she'd been devising.

Helrald entered the home shortly after the conversation died down. Illa dished him up a bowl of stew as he sat. He thanked her before eagerly digging in. Illa sat next to him and ate.

"The finest cook in the kingdom, my wife," Helrald praised.

Illa smiled, giving him a playful shove with her elbow. "And you're the biggest flatterer of the kingdom," she teased.

"The food was very good," Addy said. "The best I've had in a long time."

"You're too kind," Illa beamed, filling Addy's bowl again and offering it to her.

"It looks like you could do with a few more meals. Thin as a rail, you are!" She looked Addy up and down, spotting her bare feet, she exclaimed. "And where are your shoes?"

Addy eagerly took the bowl, uttering a quick thank you before tucking in. "I lost them in the woods," she said.

"You poor thing!" Illa cooed. "I wish we had a pair to give you. I'll fetch you some thicker cloth to bind them in after dinner."

"We don't get many visitors here in Ringo," Helrald began. "Only the Rangers, really. And they never brought anyone with them. How'd you two end up traveling together?"

Addy chewed her food more slowly, trying to come up with a convincing lie. Her eyes met Strider's, and she was surprised to see him offer a subtle nod.

"Her family asked me to search for her. She'd gotten separated from their caravan while traveling through the forest," Strider said, his tone and face as stoic as usual. "I'm escorting her home."

"You poor thing!" Illa fussed. "The forest is no place for a young lady. You're lucky he found you."

Helrald nodded, studying Addy. "Aye. You're luckier than the girl the guards were searching for a few moons back."

Addy nearly choked on her stew.

"The guards were searching for a girl?" she coughed.

"That they were. Came storming in here a moon after the Rangers left. Ripped apart everyone's homes before stalking off like angry bears." Helrald scowled as he thought about that day. "I don't know why they thought they'd find her here. Had we found a lost girl, we wouldn't have kept it from them."

"Should've given the job to Rangers," Illa tsked. "They're good at finding people, and they don't go tearing apart people's houses for no good reason!"

"Did they say who this girl was?" Strider inquired.

Both Helrald and Illa shook their heads. It was Illa who spoke. "No, but she was important enough for the men to travel all the way out here looking for her. I hope they found her and she's alright."

Addy didn't dare look at Strider. She could feel his eyes on her as she looked at her soup. She focused on taking slow, even breaths to calm herself down.

Greer sat up and rested his head on her lap as if trying to assure her things would be alright. She reached down, running her fingers through his thick neck fur.

The rest of the dinner passed in relative silence. Shortly after, everyone settled down to sleep. Helrald and Illa offered the bed up in the loft to Addy. Which upset Greer, as he couldn't climb up after her. He settled for sleeping at the foot of the ladder as Strider found a corner to rest in that allowed him to watch the door.

It didn't take long for the sound of sleeping people to fill the home. Addy lay awake for a long while, her worries keeping her from slumbering. Strider had to have connected her to the girl the soldiers had been searching for. It was only a matter of time before he questioned her about it. She'd need to put her plan into motion, but she was trapped. She had no hope of slipping out undetected with nothing but a rickety old ladder to get down. Strider would hear her trying to leave and stop her. That'd only confirm any suspicions he had.

Addy wondered if she could somehow get the villagers to send a message to her parents or Renard. She dismissed the idea, the risk of it getting intercepted was too great. Such a letter could put her family and friend in danger. She'd wait until morning, then look for an opportunity to ditch the Hunter. If he didn't torture her for information and then kill her first.

Chapter 11
Shopping Is Black Magic

Strider neither tortured nor killed Addy after leaving the settlement of Ringo behind. He said nothing, hardly regarding her, as he quietly led the group down the road. The occasional road sign pointed them toward the city of Newmen. Addy followed several paces behind him, trying to distance herself from the Hunter. But he slowed to match her pace perfectly, so the distance between them never widened. Addy slowed even further, trying to widen the gap. He slowed again and barked at her over his shoulder.

"If you can't keep up, I'll have Greer drag you."

Greer's ears flicked forward at the mention of his name, his tail wagging as he walked beside Addy. Addy scowled and resumed their usual walking speed. Greer dutifully followed her lead. The end of the strip of cloth Illa had given her to wrap around her feet had begun to come loose on her left foot. The dirtied end flapped with each step, but she didn't call to Strider to stop. As they walked, one of Greer's massive paws stepped on the cloth as it dragged on the ground at the same time she tried to take a step.

Addy jerked forward, tumbling into the dirt. She let out a string of curses as she sat up, her hands and knees covered in scrapes. Her already dirty dress made worse by the fall. She yanked the bandage out from under the wolf's foot, ignoring the apologetic look on Greer's face. She continued to swear as she tried to secure the fabric back into place. Not knowing how Strider had wrapped it, she only loosened it further.

Strider crouched before her again. He took the wrapping from her; she cursed at him but let him have it.

"I can't keep walking like this!" Addy exclaimed. "I need shoes!"

Strider ignored her as he re-wrapped the already worn and dirty bandages around her foot and ankle. He motioned for her other foot tucked underneath her. She kicked it out violently at him. He caught her foot in his hand, blocking it from hitting his injured side. She glowered at him, and he gave her a half-smile as he made sure the other foot-wrapping was secure. Satisfied, he stood and took the lead once more.

Addy stood glaring at him as she dusted off her ruined dress. "I know you heard me," she huffed, falling into step behind him.

"I did. I just didn't listen," Strider answered, never looking back.

"I can't travel to Timara with no shoes," she snapped, her hands spreading out in an exasperated gesture.

"Your ancestors spent their entire life walking without shoes."

"That's because they were slaves! They had to get used to it."

"And so do you."

Addy let out a sound of frustration as she pantomimed strangling Strider behind his back.

"How do you stand him?!" she asked Greer.

The di'horvith cocked his head, flashing her a cheerful smile, pink tongue hanging from his mouth. Seeing that he would be no help, Addy looked to the heavens.

"Please, Great K'yarie, grant me the patience not to strangle this man," she prayed, in a loud, exaggerated voice.

"You'd have better luck praying to Chaos," Strider cut in.

"Of course, a disgraced Ranger would encourage me to pray to Chaos," Addy snorted. "Only Chaos would answer your prayers."

"I don't pray to any gods," Strider growled. "They're more trouble than they're worth. You're welcome to invite their meddling into your life if you desire."

"Why am I not surprised?" Addy shook her head, then looked back at Greer. "I still don't know how you deal with him."

"He's a better person than half the world put together," Strider answered for the di'horvith. "And three times as dangerous."

Addy agreed with the Hunter for once, though not about the dangerous part. Greer was as dangerous as any large animal, but nothing more.

Greer momentarily left Addy to walk next to Strider. He gave him a beseeching look as he rested his cheek against the man's hip.

"The brat hasn't earned them," Strider muttered under his breath.

Greer let out a long, breathy whine as he stared up at Strider. He leaned his head harder against the man's hip.

Strider brushed his head away, but Greer quickly leaned against him again, never hard enough to push the man off balance. He continued to look up at him with puppy dog eyes as he let out small quiet sounds of pleading.

"You're too soft," The Hunter finally relented, as he rubbed Greer's head, pulling it tight against him. "And I am even softer for listening to you."

Greer let out a mix of a bark and a grumbling groan of agreement and pleasure before breaking away. With a snort and a toss of his head, he trotted back to Addy, who gave him a quizzical look. Greer seemed extremely pleased with himself. She had heard Strider mumbling to the wolf, but not what he said to warrant such a self-satisfied expression on Greer's face.

It took half the day to reach Newmen. The large city spread out before them, surrounded by rings of walls. The main body of the Ruea River lazily skirted around the western half of the city. During its construction, the original builders had diverted water to create a large moat around the original outer wall, dividing the city into two parts. Even from a distance, Addy could see the great square building that made up the castle keep rising above its protective battlements.

Houses and businesses dotted the other side of the moat. As more and more people settled in Newmen, it had expanded beyond the walls that'd been built decades before. Addy's eyes traced the new walls that were erected to protect the populace, creating a second outer wall. Outside stood the newer section of town, farmlands, and orchards extending beyond the protection of the castle. The fields were teeming with people, though the crops looked lean and weary.

Addy had expected Strider to move off the main road and skirt around the city. But he didn't. He continued to head straight for the town even as the road grew busier. She'd been expecting to have to convince him to go to Newmen and had planned an argument in her mind to do just that. The wind was taken out of her sails, the butterflies in her stomach turned to pits of disappointment. She'd wasted all that time formulating the perfect responses to his rebuttals.

Strider had slowed to walk next to her, and Addy couldn't help but frown at this. She'd wanted to remain behind him, so losing him in the crowd would be easier. She would have to wait until he dropped his guard in Newmen before slipping away. Again, she felt the overwhelming notion that she could trust Strider. She shouldn't leave him. He would get her home.

But this time, she pushed it away.

Addy continued to look for an opportunity to slip away as they entered the town resting outside the wall. Entering further into the city would require them to seek entry at one of the well-guarded gatehouses. Not something either of them wanted. The Hunter took them to an area closer to the wall where weathered shops lined either side of the street. They would have looked pretty if someone had taken the time to care for them.

The street was clean, speaking of the people's desire to make their area at least somewhat presentable despite their clear lack of money to make other improvements. Despite the lackluster appearance of the shops and the market, there was a lot of traffic. For these people, this was home, for travelers, it was a place to buy goods and services without dealing with the city's guards.

Strider selected a building and started toward it. Cutting through the crowd, he carved a path for the three of them. Addy frowned as she followed, ever aware of Strider's watchful gaze. He held the door open for her, and she had no choice but to go in.

Her frown became an expression of puzzlement. She'd been so focused on watching for an escape that she hadn't paid attention to the shop. The smell of leather, wood, and glue filled the air. Shoes of all sorts of styles and sizes lined the shelves in the little shop. A great wooden work desk made up the front counter where a man sat working on a pair of boots. The elderly man looked up when the three entered the shop, a brow-raising at the sight of the massive wolf and cloaked stranger. The eyebrow fell in a look of displeasure when he noticed the feather on Strider's bow.

"What can I do for you, Ranger?" he asked, still eyeing Greer, whose nose twitched as he took in the enticing scent of leather.

Strider extended a hand toward the wolf, palm out.

Greer sat obediently in the doorway.

Strider stepped further into the shop, nodding toward Addy.

"She needs shoes," He said. "Boots, soft-soled."

Addy, who'd been examining a pair of fine fur boots, jerked her head up in surprise. Had he actually listened to her and decided to get her shoes? The elderly man peered at Addy, taking in her ragged appearance with a frown. He gave Strider a questioning look before shrugging and gesturing for her to take a seat in a chair near his table. She sat, still eyeing Strider in disbelief. The shoemaker measured her feet with a strange wooden tool. He scratched his chin, muttering to himself as he began moving around the room.

"Soft soled, you said?" he questioned over his shoulder while he moved down a hall of shelves stacked with shoes.

Strider nodded. The man turned back to searching and muttering before disappearing into the back of his shop. A moment later, he reappeared with a pair of light tan leather boots.

"They are a little big, but I don't have any in the lady's size. If you give me a couple days, I could rework them to fit..."

"Those will do," Strider said. "We'll take them and a couple pairs of socks."

The old man simply nodded before tallying up the price.

"That'll come to a silver piece."

"A silver piece?" Addy said in shock.

Strider raised a hand, stopping her from arguing as he fished out the amount and handed it to the man. He took the shoes and socks from the shoemaker before herding Addy toward the door.

Addy stomped out. She waited for the door to close behind them before speaking in outrage. "You were just swindled!"

"He was rather reasonable," Strider said, giving her the shoes and socks. "Put both pairs of socks on. It'll be hot, but the shoes will fit better."

"Reasonable? You could have bought three pairs of high-quality boots for that price!"

"Many shop owners in trade towns and larger cities mark their prices higher when dealing with Rangers," Strider explained. "They don't like Rangers scaring customers away."

"Rangers have the power to arrest them, or even demand the goods for free." Addy huffed, pulling on her new socks and boots. "Why aggravate someone who has the power to ruin your business?"

"Because they know the Rangers won't. They'll barter but won't ruin a man's livelihood over a few coins."

Addy shook her head. "I don't get Rangers at all... or you, for that matter,"

Strider offered a rare smile. "Most don't."

"Thank you for the shoes," she muttered.

"Thank your father," Strider said. "He's the one who'll be paying for them."

Addy frowned. Of course, he hadn't done it out of the kindness of his heart.

Strider took her to a tailor shop next. The owner nodded as Strider spoke with her while Addy perused the fine dresses on display. The tailor called her over and took her measurements before disappearing into the back. Both of them could hear her rummaging through her supplies. She returned with a bundle of clothing, which she offered to Addy. Addy looked at the white tunic and a pair of plain brown pants in her arms. Underneath them rested a very warm-looking gray cloak.

"You expect me to wear these?" Addy sniffed, scowling at the clothes.

"Yes," Strider said slowly.

"These are boy's clothes!"

"Women Rangers wear pants."

"They're Rangers!"

"Pretend you're a Ranger. Dresses will catch and tear where we're going."

She gave Strider a beseeching look but found no pity in his eyes. She rolled her eyes and sighed, before disappearing into the dressing room. She fumbled with the clothing. Having never dressed herself, she struggled until the shop owner offered her assistance. With the woman's help, Addy soon emerged dressed in the trousers and tunic. Her gaze never lifted from the floor as she practically hid behind the door of the little room she'd emerged from. She knew her dress was ruined and thinning, but despite that, she still felt more exposed in this outfit.

Strider strode forward, snatched the cloak out of her arms, and wrapped it around her. With a jerk, he secured it before turning to pay the seamstress. Addy wrapped the cloak around her like a security blanket.

"You'll get used to it," Strider growled, as he guided her out of the shop and toward an inn.

Self-conscious, she hunched over, in an attempt to make herself smaller, as she followed him. The pants felt awkward. The only part that fit was the waist. The rest of the pants were baggy, and she had to stuff the ends into her boots to avoid tripping over them. She watched her new boots smack against the dirt road as she let Greer guide her toward the building Strider was aiming for.

It always amazed and irritated Strider how shopping seemed to devour your entire day. Like a magical field that sped up time without you realizing it. The day was drawing to a close, and the streets were filled with the evening bustle of people rushing to the safety of their homes before darkness reigned. Strider cut a path through the crowd toward a single building. He could already hear conversation and laughter coming from within. He opened the door before ushering Addy and Greer inside.

The smell of cooking meat, coffee, and mead drew Addy from her shell as she followed Strider to the bar. An anumi woman stood behind it, serving drinks to customers and making idle conversation. She looked up and smiled a greeting at Strider, her lamb-like ears twitching behind a pair of curled horns.

"Good evening, Ranger," she greeted him, with professional friendliness. "Can I get you anything?"

"I'd like a room for the evening."

Addy's head shot up. "Two rooms!"

The corners of Strider's eyes creased in what Addy recognized as a frown, though the lower half of his face remained hidden. He looked like he was about to say something.

"I'm not sharing a room with you," she insisted heatedly.

For once, the Hunter didn't argue, though he didn't look happy as he asked for two rooms for the night instead of one.

"I'm afraid we don't have two adjacent rooms available. Is that okay?" the woman asked.

"We'll take a single room then."

"No, we won't!" Addy objected, raising her chin in defiance.

Strider gave the roof a long-suffering look. "I need to be close by. I'll sleep on the floor."

"I don't care where you sleep. I'm not sharing a room with you."

"You share a campsite with me."

Addy spread her arms in exasperation. "That's different!"

"I'm sorry," the woman at the counter interrupted. Her voice was still friendly, but her smile was now strained. "Do you want two rooms or one?"

Strider's eyes frowned again. "Two."

"Would you like us to draw up baths for both of you?"

Strider nodded, and Addy grinned. It had been so long since she'd had a bath! Unlike the shoemaker, or tailer, the inn owner did not overcharge for the rooms. Strider paid for the rooms and three meals. The lady thanked him before gesturing for him to take any available table in the tavern.

"We'll bring out your food. One of my girls will let you know when your baths are ready."

Strider selected the table that offered him the best view of the main floor and exits. Positioning his back so it faced a wall. Greer sat next to Addy's seat.

"Greer will sleep with you tonight," Strider said, before Addy could bring up the subject. "Or are you against sharing the room with him?"

"Greer is fine," Addy stated cooly. "He's a gentleman."

Strider gave a shake of his head and focused his attention on the crowds of people while they waited for their food. Addy didn't speak any further. The Hunter was e in a fouler mood than normal. His eyes were sharp as flint and she looked at the table to avoid catching his gaze.

Chapter 12

A Thief In The Night

Addy hardly tasted her dinner. Her stomach was tight as she battled within herself. Her mind was on her plan, but something within her still compelled her to trust the Hunter. It was the same illogical feeling that had led her to make the mistake of hiring him in Altia. She refused to listen to it now. Back then, she had no choice. Now there was another option. A flicker of guilt caused the knot in her stomach to tighten further. She knew Greer would be upset with her betrayal, but it had to be done.

One of the serving girls approached their table, informing them that their baths were ready. Addy jumped to her feet. She didn't see the look Strider gave her as she eagerly followed the woman. The first room she led them to was near the stairs. Before Strider could say anything, Addy rushed forward, like a fox jumping into its den.

Greer bounded after her, squeezing into the room before the door closed behind her. Addy locked the door before turning to the large metal tub sitting in the center of the room. Clean towels sat neatly folded beside it, a scrub brush resting atop them for Addy's convenience. Another smaller tub of water sat propped on three legs, a hairbrush and towel hanging from hooks on the side.

Addy struggled to remove her new clothes before making a beeline for the smaller container. Grabbing the brush, she brushed the worst tangles out of her hair before eyeing the steaming water. She'd never washed her hair on her own before. Normally her lady in waiting would help her. Addy wondered how Tyra was doing. Was she faring well without her? She'd probably laugh at Addy's incompetence.

"It's just a bit of hair, your ladyship!" She could hear her say. "Plop it in the water and scrub, nothing to it!" Bending over the tub, she soaked her hair and began scrubbing.

Greer sniffed the steaming water of the larger bath before growing disinterested and going to lay on the bed.

With dripping wet hair, Addy slipped into the hot water with a sigh. She sat there, letting the warmth soothe her aching muscles.

Then, she slid under the surface, letting the water clean her face. Surfacing, she reached for the brush and began scrubbing herself clean. The water was murky brown and cold by the time Addy slipped out of the tub and into a towel.

Addy dried herself before she wrestled her clothes back on. She'd paid attention to how the seamstress had dressed her, but seeing it only once made repeating the process somewhat difficult. She wasn't used to navigating the pants, and she put her tunic on backward, twice.

She had just pulled her shirt back over her head when a soft knock came at her door.

"May I enter, miss?" The thick door muffled the voice of the serving maid from earlier.

Addy strode over to the door and unlocked it. The young lady smiled at her after offering a quick bow.

"How was your bath, miss?" she asked.

"Wonderful," Addy sighed.

The woman smiled again. "With your permission, we will remove the tubs for you."

Addy nodded and stepped aside. The woman walked in, followed by several other women who worked quickly and professionally to clear the tubs and dirty towels from the room.

"Let us know if there is anything else we can do for you."

The woman offered another bow before shutting the door quietly behind her. Addy locked the door before shoving Greer over so she could sit on the bed. Her body wanted nothing more than to fall asleep. But she kept herself awake as she waited for it to grow late.

A soft knock sounded at Strider's door, followed by the same question the woman had asked Addy.

"Come in," Strider responded to her request.

The woman opened the door and offered a bow.

Strider's own bath was filled with filthy water. He wore his cloak again; the hood pulled up over his head, his face covered once more. His clean shirt and trousers were packed neatly into one of the packs Greer carried. Forcing Strider to wear his dirty clothes or ask Addy to give them to him. He'd fetch them in the morning.

The woman let in a group of maids with Strider's permission.

He watched them from his perch atop the bed, his elbow resting on a raised knee, an open notebook in his hand, its pages pointed downward. Both swords rested within easy reach beside him. He watched the women clear the tubs from the room, offering a nod to the lead maid when she bowed and left. Getting up from the bed, he tossed the notebook atop the sheets before going over to lock the door. He checked the curtains at the window, ensuring they'd remained shut.

Removing his cloak, he draped it on the bedpost. Pulling the cloth down from his face, he settled back onto the bed. Picking up the notebook, he took a moment to study the picture on the first page. His eyes softened as his thumb stroked the edge of the page. He sighed heavily before placing it back into his satchel.

Steadying his breathing, he called upon his magic once more and focused on healing his wound. The magic tugged on his soul. The feeling of heat spread through his body as the healing magic flowed through him. This time he poured more magic into the art, taking care not to drain himself like he'd done the first night. He didn't want to feel the cold or hear the thoughts that whispered to him in the darkness.

The injury sealed itself, becoming nothing more than a raw scar. The warmth within him faded as he released his hold on the magic. He looked for Greer before remembering he was with Addy. He shrugged. It was best she had him with her. The girl was up to something; she had been all day. He didn't trust her, but trusted Greer, so he let it be.

He'd come to expect people to be dishonest in their dealings. Addy was no different. Though he was used to operating without all the information, nobles and criminals liked their secrets. He hadn't expected a person of rank within Denmahr to be in pursuit of her. Perhaps a marriage arrangement gone wrong? She was hot-headed enough to run from such a thing without thinking things through. It wasn't the first time he'd had a noble hunting him, but dragging a teenage girl along would complicate things.

But if she were fleeing from something forced upon her, she wouldn't want to return home. Which meant a reward was not waiting for him. He dismissed the idea. He could tell her desire to return home was genuine. She was brash but wouldn't want to return if her family had sent her away. Which meant someone in Denmahr likely took her.

He wouldn't press her to tell him the truth. She wouldn't tell him, anyway. The Hunter found he learned more from observing and looking for inconsistencies with her stories and actions. He'd wait. She would reveal herself in time. He'd learned in a short time that Addy wasn't the best at lying. He was curious how long she could keep a secret. He laid back on the bed, closing his eyes.

Addy's head fell off the hand she'd been resting her chin on. She jerked awake, cursing when she realized she'd fallen asleep. Moonlight spilled into the room, having risen high in the sky. She jumped out of bed. Her actions woke Greer. His snores ceased as he snorted and looked up, the fur on his right cheek ruffled and messy. She'd only meant to sleep until a quarter of the dusk watch, the third of the four watches that broke the day into six-hour intervals. Peering out the window, she guessed that the night watch had begun.

"Come on, Greer," Addy called softly. She hopped toward the door, struggling to pull on her last boot. The di'horvith leaped out of bed and followed her out into the hall. She shushed him, though he hadn't made a noise as Addy crept down the stairs and out the back of the tavern. The street was deserted, illuminated only by moonlight.

She looked over her shoulder repeatedly, expecting Strider to be there. He never appeared.

Greer followed obediently. He paused every now and again to look back as well before shooting her a meaningful look. A heavy sigh escaped his lips as he followed Addy. He, too, seemed to expect Strider to show up to stop her. Keeping to the shadows, Addy hurried down the alley and out onto the main road leading out of town. It wasn't hard to slip away unnoticed. No one was watching for anyone to leave.

Addy didn't relax her pace until the soft yellow and pink hues of sunrise faded into stronger oranges and reds, driving away the black and purple night sky. The city of Newmen was no longer in view as Addy led Greer down the main road leading North, determined to leave Strider far behind.

Chapter 13

How Not To Steal A Wolf

Strider awoke to the sounds of quiet footsteps creeping up the stairs and down the hall. They were slow and careful; obviously trying to be sneaky, but failing miserably. They paused at the top of the stairs far longer than caution dictated. Addy's room was the only one off the stairs. Strider knew she wasn't in the inn. He knew Greer was gone.

Strider slipped out of bed; his movements far quieter than those moving about. He listened to them sneak down the hall as he pulled on his cloak and buckled on his weapons before slipping on his shoes. He could hear them pause outside his door.

"This is the one, sir," a feminine voice whispered, her tone frightened.

Strider recognized it as the voice belonging to the maid who'd helped them earlier in the evening.

She was hushed by someone, a man. Strider's head cocked back toward the door as he quietly moved toward the window. A voice spoke.

"Remember, he's a Ranger. Don't take him lightly," the man whispered. "On my signal."

Silence filled the inn as the men tensed at the door.

"Now!"

A powerful blow kicked the door in, causing it to slam into the wall with a BANG! Soldiers rushed into the room, swords drawn. They paused, confused, when they encountered the empty room. Only the messy bed showed that someone had occupied it. The men fanned out and searched the little space, turning over the bed and throwing open the small wardrobe. One opened the window and leaned out. Half the empty street lay in the inn's shadow.

"He's not here, captain." The man pointed out the obvious as he withdrew from the window.

"Captain." Another soldier appeared in the doorway. "The girl is not in her room."

"By Chaos!" the captain swore. "They must have known we were coming. Send men to search the roads leading to Myvara immediately! Kill the Ranger and his wolf. Do not harm the girl."

The men murmured words of confirmation before moving to carry out the orders. None of them were aware of the golden, hawk-like eyes that watched them spill out of the inn and hurry down the street. Strider lay on his belly atop the roof, far enough away from the lip so his shadow wouldn't be seen on the street below.

His narrow gaze followed the last soldier as he disappeared around a corner. The man bore the crest of the Denmahr's king, two lions on either side of a shield crossed by swords. They should have born the local noble's crest, identifying them as a part of the lord's own reserve. Why would the king send his own men in search of one girl? Strider pushed up off the roof tiles. The common men at arms were one thing: a noblewoman in a dispute with her father could explain them.

But the king himself was interested in her. This was a far bigger plot than he'd bargained for. He silently cursed Greer for his ever reliable talent for getting them into trouble. What made it worse was he believed he was helping. His brother would be the death of him. As agile as a monkey and as silent as a ghost, he moved across the rooftops after the soldiers.

The men led him directly to their stables. He watched men rush about like a swarm of ants as stable hands scrambled to saddle the soldier's horses. Strider watched the scene below from behind a chimney on a building near the edge of the stable courtyard. He called to his magic as he slowly drew an arrow. Knocking it, he drew back in one fluid motion. The magic flowed from his fingers, through his bow, and into the arrow. He breathed out slowly before letting the string slip from his fingers.

The arrows hissed like an angry hornet before slamming into a pile of hay with a swish. A ripple of magic pulsed outward, unseen by the men, slamming into the horses. They all let out shrill screams of alarm. A second pulse shot out from the hay bale, consuming the arrow as the hay burst into flames, spooking the animals further.

Men were thrown from their saddles as their steeds bolted. Cries of alarm filled the air as the fire spread from the hay to the stable itself. Chaos engulfed the courtyard as alarms sounded and horses ran down the streets. No one noticed the Hunter retreating silently across the rooftops. He struck out Northward toward Greer.

Addy yawned, stretching her hands above her head. She plodded along, blinking the sleep from her eyes. The road she followed traced the bends and curves of the Ruea River. She could see the Tahlrin Mountain piercing the sky like giant dragons' teeth in the distance. Doubt gnawed at the back of her mind. Could she really do this? She'd never traveled this far on her own before. Curthis and Renard were always with her, and she wouldn't have gotten this far without Strider.

Her misgivings shifted to guilt, knowing that she had not only broken her promise of reward, but she'd also stolen the man's best friend. But she couldn't risk traveling with Strider, afraid of what he might do once he figured out who she was. She couldn't risk him betraying her. So, she stamped down the guilt, burying it deep. But the doubt remained.

Greer quietly padded beside her, only veering off the path when he heard people coming. Following his cue, Addy retreated off the road to hide in any cover she could find. The forest near Altia had long given way to plains and dried up farmlands, making finding cover difficult. She had moved at a brisk walk most of the morning; her steps only slowing as tiredness crept in.

Her endurance was getting better, but Strider hadn't pushed her to move at a pace as fast as she'd been going while running from him. The Hunter had to have found her room empty by now and guessed where she'd gone. He'd have to run in order to catch up. The thought of the furious Hunter spurred her to move faster, though the increased pace didn't last long.

Greer faithfully matched her speed. He still glanced back the way they'd come, uttering the occasional whine when he didn't see Strider. He continued to give her pointed looks while they walked, letting out chattering whines as if he were begging her to turn back. But she carried on.

"It's okay, Greer," she cooed. "Strider will be along shortly."

Greer gave her a disbelieving look, his lips twitching before he let out a low whine. He knew she was lying. Somehow Addy knew he knew. He looked at her with eyes full of understanding and concern that startled her.

She found herself unable to meet the wolf's gaze as guilt swept through her. Maybe this was a bad idea. Maybe Strider really was her best shot at getting home. She shook her head. No, she couldn't trust Strider! If he found out the king was searching for her, he'd likely turn her in to gain a reward. He'd already said he was a dishonored Ranger, right?

The promise of payment was the only reason he was taking care of her. Damaged goods didn't fetch as high a price after all. She didn't want or need him. She could ration out the supplies Greer had and sell the stuff she didn't need to get money to buy more. Greer would be enough to deter people from approaching. She no longer looked like herself. Everything would be fine.

She absentmindedly reached down to pat Greer on the head, but he was gone! She stopped abruptly, looking about in a panic. It wasn't hard to spot Greer. The great di'horvith sat in the middle of the road, staring at her with large pleading eyes. He looked over his shoulder, whining through his nose.

"Come on, Greer," she called, patting her knees.

The mutt didn't move. Addy walked back to him and tried pulling him along, using the handle on his harness. He didn't budge. She yanked and heaved before giving up with a frustrated breath. She'd have better luck convincing a mountain to move.

"Fine! I don't need you either!" she shouted.

She stormed off, turning her back on the wolf, ignoring his cries.

Who needed him? She did, she knew. But she couldn't get the di'horvith to go anywhere he didn't want to. Her anger quickly faded, but she didn't turn back. She couldn't. If she waited with Greer, Strider would show up. He'd kill her for trying to run away with his wolf. All that was left was to keep moving. Wrapping her cloak around her, she trudged on, guilt and worry settling in her stomach like two stones.

Addy had been walking alone for an hour when the sound of thundering hooves caused her to pause. Her heart jumped in her throat, and she nearly died right there when she saw the mounted soldiers moving quickly down the road toward her. She looked around frantically for a place to hide. The flat stretch of the road running through an equally flat expanse of grassland offered no cover. One hundred yards away lay a small, wooded area. Addy knew they'd already seen her. Panic filled her as she bolted toward the trees.

The soldiers were still a far enough distance away that she had a chance of reaching the woods and losing them inside. The trees grew tight enough together that they couldn't pursue her on horseback. She had a chance there. The sound of pounding hooves grew so loud it drowned out the pounding of her own heart as she ran. She heard the lead horseman shout for her to stop. Like Tarn, she would!

Fear gave her the energy and speed she needed to run hard and fast. She barely managed to duck into the woods a couple heartbeats before the men reached her. The men and horses came to a skidding halt as Addy pushed her way through the thick underbrush. She could hear the soldiers leaping off their horses, the crash of their boots as they chased her into the woods. Again, they shouted for her to halt. She was too out of breath to shout back some sort of smart remark.

The pursuing footsteps were getting closer as the men closed the distance. Addy's lungs and legs screamed at her to stop, but she fought through the pain, searching for more strength to push her legs harder. Someone tackled her from behind. She screamed and thrashed. Kicking, hitting, and biting as she tried to break free of the soldier's grip. The man wrestled her to the ground, found his feet, then heaved her up over his shoulder.

"Stop fighting, or I'll break your arm!" he threatened, as she spewed a string of very unladylike curse words at him. She had blown her cover the instant she'd opened her mouth, revealing that she was a woman.

She beat against his back and tried to kick and knee him in the chest, but she only hurt herself as she hit the man's breastplate. Her eyes searched wildly for anything she could use to escape. The man's quiver caught her eye. Most of the arrows had spilled out of it when he had tackled her, but a few remained inside. She desperately reached for one.

Her fingers brushed against the first shaft, knocking it away before it rolled back within her reach. Her fingers closed around it. With a strength driven by desperation and fear, Addy drove the arrowhead into the back of the man's neck between the armored guard just above the chain mail. The soldier cried out in pain, dropping her.

Addy hit the ground with a grunt, scrambling to her feet as she ran. She didn't get far before another man grabbed her. Lashing out, she tried to slice at him with the bloody arrow, but he caught her hand and squeezed her wrist. She cried out in pain as the arrow fell from her hand.

"Let me go!" she screamed, as the new assailant dragged her off her feet.

A murderous snarl erupted from the underbrush as Greer slammed into one of the men, knocking him to the ground. He screamed in terror and pain as the di'horvith tore into his throat. The soldier holding Addy turned her to face the chaos in time to watch Greer kill the man with a decisive bite before launching at another soldier, his fangs biting deep into the soldier's sword arm. The man's bracer cracked and bent, crushed under the weight of a di'horvith's jaws.

He let out a strangled cry of agony as the bones in his arm

snapped. The man dropped his sword. Greer yanked his victim's arm to the side, pulling him off balance, before trying to go for the soldier's throat. Only to find another arm coming up to defend it. The metal bracer gave way, and the soldier's arm was crushed between Greer's jaws. Two more soldiers rushed toward the giant wolf as he wrestled with the pinned soldier, swords drawn.

"Greer!" Addy screamed in warning, her voice filled with terror.

Thwack! An arrow slammed into the first man to reach Greer, sending him stumbling backward with a cry before falling silent. Another arrow found its mark as the second man fell dead, wisps of blue smoke seeming to waft from the shafts as they disintegrated.

"The horses!" the soldier holding Addy snarled at the man she'd stabbed in the neck.

The soldier barking orders pulled Addy close, pressing his sword to her neck. She grew very still, doing everything she could to avoid slicing her own throat while being dragged through the trees. The cries of the soldier Greer wrestled with ceased. The woods grew deafeningly silent. The men didn't stop as they forced Addy forward.

She desperately wanted to be rescued but was terrified of the person trying to save her. She could see the horses through the trees, and tears welled in her eyes. They were going to escape with her! She tried digging her heels into the ground; her back pressing against her captor's chest. But he pushed her forward.

Greer's ghostly form appeared in front of them, blocking their path to the horses. White fangs flashed, framed by lips stained with crimson. His fur spiked along his back, making him appear twice as large as he was. A guttural growl of warning rumbled in his chest. The soldiers halted.

The one Addy had stabbed stepped forward to face Greer. His sword flashed as it caught the sunlight that filtered through the trees. Greer didn't run. Man and beast locked eyes as the soldier strode forward. A blade shot out from the trees, pressing against the man's already bloody throat.

"Drop the sword," Strider ordered, his tone as dark as death.

The man obliged, raising his hands before him in surrender. He kicked the blade away at a command from Strider.

"Let the girl go, and drop your sword," Strider ordered the soldier, who still held a blade to Addy's throat.

"You have no authority here, Ranger," the man spoke, his breath hot on Addy's ear.

"You and your dog killed five of us. The king ordered all of you to leave this country four moons ago. He will not take this treachery lightly when he finds out what you've done. The world will know that the Rangers struck out against him."

Strider cocked his head to the side as if pondering the threat. He knew what would happen if he denied the title. He'd already made a mistake telling Addy he wasn't a Ranger. He remembered his father and made his decision. "Then it's a good thing I'm not a Ranger." His eyes narrowed into dangerous slits, his curved blade pressing harder against his hostage's throat. More blood flowed freely down the man's neck from the fresh wound.

"He isn't a Ranger," Addy confirmed. "I watched him shoot a fleeing man in the back. Rangers wouldn't do that. He's-" Her mind whirled, trying to find the right words. "A Dark Ranger."

Strider frowned, his murderous gaze flicking to Addy for a moment as he ground out the words. "Hunter, not Ranger."

"Dark Ranger is more fitting," she shot back, and Strider bared his teeth in a distasteful snarl.

Strider growled as viciously as Greer. "Let her go. So I can kill her."

Greer had moved closer, still uttering low threatening growls, cutting off the man's retreat, should he abandon his fellow soldier and try to escape with Addy. Strider and the soldier locked eyes before the man finally threw his own blade aside. Addy ran several paces away, her hand going to her throat as she took in huge gulps of air. Strider still didn't lower his blade.

"I let her go," the man said. "Release him!"

Strider's eyes were as cold as the steel of his sword. He tilted his head again to look at the man he still held captive. Studying him as if he were a bug he was deciding whether or not to crush.

"Strider," Addy panted, "do as he says."

Strider didn't move. "They're witnesses," he told her coldly.

Addy looked at him in horror. "You made a deal with them!"

"I never told them I'd let them live."

Addy realized he was right. He'd only commanded them to release her.

The soldier who'd held Addy stepped forward, his voice furious. "Do you have no honor?"

Strider huffed at the statement. "Says the man who attacked an unarmed girl."

The man standing with Strider's sword at his neck remained silent, barely willing to breathe as the blade bit into him.

Greer let out a very long-winded whine as he approached Strider. He rested his chin against Strider's leg, angling his head up so he could look up at him with large brown eyes. He made a pleading noise again.

Strider's jaw clenched before he stepped back, withdrawing his blade from the man's throat. He jerked his head back toward town.

"Leave the horses and go. Now!" The words were as rough as grating granite.

The soldiers eyed him with hatred before retreating through the trees toward the road. They took a path away from the horses, giving Strider no reason to shoot them in the back. Not that he normally needed one.

The Hunter stared after them like a beast denied his kill. He fixed his gaze on Addy for a long, hard moment before stalking toward the horses.

Greer walked up to Addy, tail wagging happily. She gave the di'horvith a hug, sobbing into his fur before a bark from Strider forced her to her feet.

"Get on the horse!" he commanded.

She wiped her eyes and moved toward the horses. Greer

remained beside her like he always had. She couldn't meet Strider's gaze as she mounted the horse he'd caught for her.

"Not side saddle," he growled between gritted teeth.

She shifted awkwardly to straddle the animal. She didn't fight him on the matter or tell him she didn't know how to ride this way. Nor did she speak out when he tied the animal's reins to his own horse.

"Hold on," he ordered, before kicking his horse.

Both animals took off at a gallop. Greer ran next to them as they sped toward the road.

Addy clung to the back of her horse as it galloped after its companion. No sense of relief or safety comforted her. Her stomach tied itself into knots as she tried to accept that Strider was her best shot at returning home. That she was stuck with him until they reached the fiefdom of Timara where her father's men patrolled. She had to hold out until then.

Chapter 14
No Trust Between Us

Strider slowed the horses to a trot after their long run down the road. The last thing they needed was to run them to death. The animals fell into the slower rhythm, snorting and huffing from the exertion, foam coating their chests. Greer slowed to match their pace. His own breathing was heavy, but not as labored as the larger animals. He moved ahead, tail bobbing and swaying as he loped twenty feet down the road. Never moving out of sight as he ran point.

Neither Strider nor Addy had spoken since leaving the woods. Addy hadn't tried to take her horse's reins. She couldn't if she'd wanted to. Unused to riding traditionally, it'd been a struggle to stay in the saddle. She never spoke or fussed, cowed by her close call.

She didn't cry for him to slow down when she nearly fell. The most she did was breathe a sigh of relief when their pace slowed. Then the horses started trotting, and she had to focus on staying on again as the rough gait caused her to bob up and down. She still didn't complain. Addy watched when Strider took their coursers off the main road, waiting atop her horse as he left to hide their trail.

She'd expected Strider to lash out at her as soon as he'd found her. But he remained terribly silent. He didn't yell or scream at her. That kind of reaction she could've handled, having grown up with three brothers and a father she had a penchant for setting off.

He didn't strike her, threaten her, or kill her. He didn't leave her behind. His gaze never shifted toward her, never acknowledging her presence. The Hunter hadn't spoken since he'd barked orders for her to hold on to the horse. It was the silence that hit her the hardest. The soundless chasm that stood between them.

Half a watch passed before Addy dared to speak.

"You came back. Why?" her voice was sullen, deflated. Her fire had gone out.

Strider still didn't look at her as he navigated their horses through the trees. She thought he wouldn't answer her, her shoulders slumping further in resignation when he finally spoke, his voice devoid of emotion.

"You stole my wolf."

"He went back to you though... You still came back..."

Again, Strider didn't answer, letting her words hang between them for an uncomfortable amount of time. Her gaze dropped to the saddle horn once more. She still didn't understand this man, and he wasn't helping her to. He should've left her to her fate when Greer had returned to him. Or at least come after her to kill her for trying to take Greer and his supplies. She wasn't naïve enough to believe he hadn't killed her because she was a woman.

"You paid me to do a job." Strider's voice cut into her thoughts, causing her to look at him.

He'd slowed the horses to a walk, so they could more easily navigate the forest terrain, making it easier for her to hold on. Strider gave her a sidelong glare from atop his courser.

"And you're doing a terrible job at letting me do it."

Addy swallowed hard, glancing away guiltily. "You've done nothing to prove that I can trust you."

"You're still alive," he stated flatly. "You have shoes, you're fed, and I came back. Despite you giving me every reason not to."

Addy frowned but didn't lash out without a thought like she normally did. It was her turn to be silent for a long time as she took the time to consider what he said. She hadn't given him any reason to come back. But he'd also left her one time too many. Every action he did seemed perfectly logical to him. He expected her father to pay for her shoes, no doubt her food as well. He didn't think what he did back in Altia was wrong. Stupid Hunter.

The horses stopped, and Addy realized Strider was staring at her. He'd angled his horse, so he was facing her, those golden eyes burrowing into her. He looked like he wanted to say something before giving a slow shake of his head. Tugging on the reins, he turned his horse, sending it down the game trail they'd been following. Addy's own gaze lingered on him, wishing he'd spoken. Had given her an explanation. But he didn't. The quiet engulfed them once more. It was oppressive; she hated it. Finally, the silence proved too much. Her anger found fuel in his silence and she exploded.

"Why won't you say anything!?"

Again, the horses stopped as his mount sidestepped nervously at the sudden noise. It settled down shortly after, and Addy fixed Strider with a furious stare.

"Explain to me why I should trust you! Why shouldn't I expect you to abandon me, or kill me, like you've killed everyone else?" she screamed, taking her fear out on the Hunter. "Why are you not yelling at me? You should be telling me that I was an idiot for running away or trying to kill me for taking Greer!"

She panted heavily, her cheeks flushed and stained with tears. Strider looked at her again, saying nothing. She gritted her teeth in anger as she cried.

A long, slow sigh escaped Strider's lips, and he shook his head.

"Stop doing that!" Addy shrieked.

Strider cocked his head at her, waiting as Addy dissolved into sobs. His gaze shifted toward Greer, as if he expected the di'horvith to have some advice on dealing with a hysterical woman. The wolf gave him a pointed look, his gaze shifting to Addy as if he expected Strider to do something. Strider frowned. He was about to shake his head again, then stopped himself as he felt Addy's eyes on him.

He just wanted to get them moving again, rather than wasting time on words. He'd forgotten how much ummanie liked to talk, how much weight they put on such an easily misleading practice. Beyond necessary interactions, he hadn't been around people for the better part of fifty years. He was used to being alone and had lost a lot of the practiced nuances born from being among society.

Addy's constant company and ever shifting emotions were becoming exhausting. He wasn't so numb to people that he couldn't sense that Addy needed more than action to show his intent. Strider hated dealing with her outbursts, but it'd be unwise for him to continue to let this fester. He let his shoulders sag as he heaved another deep sigh.

"Words are easy to turn into lies, you know that." He cocked his head, shooting her a knowing look. "Do you trust me not to lie to you?"

She shook her head, her jaw clenched. "No."

"Then look at what I've done." He offered.

"You've killed people! And left me!" she shot back. She knew why he left her back at Altia, but she didn't care.

"I've killed people who threatened you. I kept you safe," he corrected her. Pausing, he looked down at Greer, who watched him expectantly. The Hunter scowled at him. "You thought I had abandoned you..." He began, his tone calm and careful. "I apologize for that."

The apology was awkward, like a rusted hinge being forced open. It took Addy by surprise. She hadn't thought him capable of saying sorry or admitting he was wrong. Well, maybe he hadn't admitted that he was wrong, but he acknowledged that what he'd done had hurt her. She caught him shooting Greer a glance. The wolf wagged his tail encouragingly at Strider, who scowled at him before fixing Addy with a level gaze.

"How can I trust *you*?" he mirrored the question back at her.

Addy blinked. Why did she have to prove her trustworthiness to him? She felt ashamed of the thought as soon as it entered her mind. Though she hadn't left him to die, twice, she'd done nothing to earn his trust. There was only one thing she could think of but revealing it could endanger her. He was still so unknown to her, and his misguided attempt to help her against Gen had done little to reassure her.

If he knew who she was, would he turn her in? Then again, him not knowing the danger they were in could prove fatal. She bit her lower lip as she wrestled with the idea of telling him. She sent a quiet prayer to the gods that her earlier belief in him wasn't unfounded. Addy took a deep, steading breath.

"I'm not really the daughter of the blacksmith in Timara, but the daughter of Lord Fenforde."

"I knew that when you hired me," Strider said dismissively, earning him another shocked expression from Addy.

"How did you know I was lying?"

"I have met dying men who could spin more convincing lies. You don't act like the daughter of a blacksmith. Your hands aren't calloused and your mannerisms are that of a noble."

Addy managed to look offended and sheepish at the same time. "If you knew I was lying, then why did you agree to the job?"

Strider shrugged. "I figured it'd be useful to have a powerful lord owe me a favor."

Greer gave what Addy could only describe as a disapproving snort.

Strider shot him a warning look.

"You still haven't answered my question," he pointed out.

Addy looked confused. "I told you the truth."

"Words hold little merit," he said roughly. "You left me and stole my wolf. You put his life in danger. How can I trust you?"

Addy wanted to defend herself. To tell him she'd only done it because she'd thought he would hurt her. But she fought the impulse as she tried to think of why he should trust her. Finally, her shoulders slumped in defeat.

"You can't," she muttered solemnly.

Strider nodded, his point proven. Satisfied, he tossed her the reins to her horse. He gave her one last look before sending his courser walking down the trail.

Addy watched him as he rode further into the trees. Looking over her shoulder, she was tempted to ride back to the road, but thought better of it. Clucking at the horse, she sent it following Strider's mount. Greer trotted past her. She hadn't realized that he hadn't accompanied Strider. Her gaze followed him as he took the lead before looking up to catch the subtle nod of Strider's head.

Chapter 15

Horses Are Hard Work

Strider didn't stop for camp after nightfall, forcing Addy to let her horse follow its companion because she couldn't see where they were going. The Hunter didn't seem bothered by the darkness as he navigated his horse with pressure from his knees, leaving Addy to wonder what he might be. Maybe he was some sort of cat anumie, though his pupils were not slits like those of a cat. Owls could see in the dark. Maybe he was an owl?

The coursers hadn't slowed. They apparently saw better in the dark, too. Addy's mount needed no prodding from her to follow its friend, as Strider's horse picked its way down an embankment. Her horse rocked, and she swayed in the saddle, growing accustomed to riding traditionally.

Greer still led the way, disappearing into the underbrush as he scouted ahead before doubling back to the party. He'd linger a moment before running off again. Even he tired from moving back and forth after a hard run.

Addy hadn't spoken to Strider since their last exchange. While he was completely comfortable with the lack of conversation, she wasn't. Even in the city of Altia, she'd spoken to herself or found people to talk to. At home, she had her brother, Curthis, Tyra, or her retainer, Renard, as constant companions. She wasn't used to the silence that hung between them.

Her rear ached after riding in such rough terrain for so long and she needed something to distract her. But Strider had gone back to ignoring her as he focused on picking the best route for their mounts to follow. She couldn't see. He was her only guide through the darkness. She didn't dare distract him from his task, leaving her alone with her thoughts. A place she didn't want to be.

The night was dark, the forest was alive around her. The cries and shifting of creatures hiding behind a black curtain, wreathed in the earthy scent of the forest, caused her mind to wander to old stories about monsters and demons that her brothers loved telling. Creatures that hid in a blanket of inky blackness, waiting to strike.

She pulled her cloak tighter around her and tried to think about other things, but those tales lurked in the back of her mind. The loud cry of a night creature made her jump. Her horse's ears swiveled back to her, and she noticed a change in his step for a moment before he dismissed her alarm and continue walking.

Addy tried to tell herself that monsters only existed in The Wilds. It didn't work. She tried thinking of other things to distract herself. She only thought about Strider's words. He told her to look back at what he'd done, but she was more fixated on the fact that he'd said he had no reason to trust her. It was true, but she wasn't sure why it bothered her.

"We'll stop here."

Addy started at the sound of Strider's voice. She'd been so wrapped up in her thoughts she hadn't realized that he'd slid off his mount and was gripping her horse's reins. She could hardly see him as he held the courser steady while she awkwardly dismounted. Addy gasped, grabbing onto the saddle as her sore legs nearly buckled underneath her. The horse stood firm, allowing her to hang there while she gingerly regained use of her feet. She rubbed her backside, groaning.

"I think I liked walking better," she moaned, as she hobbled around trying to ease stiff muscles.

She didn't see the small smile Strider gave her.

"You'll get used to it," he told her, handing the horse's reins to her. "You can stretch your muscles while walking your friend around."

Addy's brows knit together as she looked up at the humanoid shadow in puzzlement.

"Why would I walk the horse around?"

She could feel the disapproving look he gave her as he walked his own mount around the area he'd selected to camp.

"He carried you. Now you need to take care of him. You need to walk him, allowing him to cool down. You can't just ride the horse and then leave it to servants to tend to."

Addy moaned, then nearly jumped out of her skin as Strider appeared next to her. He led her around the clearing he'd picked out. Her horse followed behind as he walked her through the proper way to prepare a horse before removing its saddle to prevent it from getting bruised. She couldn't see a thing, forcing Strider to help her do most of the work before securing both horses near a small stream. Addy dropped the heavy saddle to the ground, throwing the riding blanket atop it in a jumbled heap.

"You need to rub him down," Strider said, before she could sit down.

Addy released an exasperated breath as she returned to her now grazing horse. She used the discarded saddle as a stool as Strider used a spare shirt he found in a saddlebag to show Addy how to massage the animal. She felt more than saw what he did as he directed her hands before stepping back to allow her to do it.

He picked up the riding blanket and ensured no brambles or other irritants had tangled in it before re-saddling the horse. He didn't tighten the girth completely, so the animal would remain comfortable but ready to ride if needed.

"Horses are so much work," Addy groaned, as she slumped to the ground.

"They probably think the same thing about hauling loud ummanie around." Strider's voice drifted up from where he lay.

Greer had walked off to sit among the deeper shadows of the forest as he stood on watch. There was no fire, and the moonlight couldn't find its way through the canopy of leaves. Addy couldn't tell whether her eyes were open or closed. It was unnerving to be in total darkness.

Laying on the ground, wrapped in Strider's blanket, she realized that this was the first time she'd heard Strider sound amused and looked over to him. She saw only black and gave up trying to see him.

"If I promise to get my dad to pay you extra, would you take care of my horse for me?" she asked innocently.

". "You need to build trust between the

'It isn't my horse."

home."

shaggy brown horse. It was a common

common soldier. Nothing like the fine animals

I am not the one riding it home," Strider told her in a low growl. "You're the one it needs to trust."

Addy heaved another sigh. "I never had to do this with my horse at home."

"Your horse at home has a stronger bond with its trainer and caretakers, then."

Addy scowled. She'd never really thought about it. Or cared. The animal was something to ride whenever the urge overtook her. It didn't really make sense to her that what she'd done tonight would improve her standing with the animal.

"How does walking a horse around and then rubbing it make it trust me?"

Strider yawned as he rolled over. "Your actions prove to him you will care for him as a herd-mate. It is creating a bond."

"So, the horse will think I am a part of its family." That was a weird thought.

Strider gave a grunt of agreement in response. She thought about that for a moment.

"Kind of like how Greer thinks you are a part of his pack."

"I am a part of his pack." Strider yawned again. "We're brothers."

"Of course, Greer thinks that though. You raised him," Addy pointed out.

"You can raise something, be it a person or animal, and still not have it trust you," Strider stated, though he didn't sound nearly as harsh or annoyed as normal.

Addy grew quiet again, her fingers drumming thoughtfully

against her stomach. Her thoughts didn't go very far as came her.

Strider watched her for a moment longer. She'd been t. ponderous as she'd asked each question. He considered this moment. He'd first thought she'd be too stubborn to listen to him, she was now showing signs of trying to learn. Her bristles were stil. quick to come up, and she had no shortage of snark. But she did pick up on things quickly when she was willing. Maybe he'd be able to teach her something?

Strider knew he shouldn't. He'd risk becoming attached to the girl. But he knew he had to train her. He couldn't let himself grow fond of her. He wouldn't put her or himself through that. Strider listened to the surrounding forest, allowing the sounds of the shifting leaves and nocturnal animals to drown out his thoughts before he, too, fell asleep.

Another morning brought another day of travel. They slept only half a night, but Strider insisted they get moving while the sky was barely blushing behind the mountains. Addy nearly fell asleep several times while riding in the saddle that morning. Strider had stopped them and forced her to run ahead of the horses when she nearly toppled from the saddle. She wasn't tired after that and had thrown a few choice words at Strider while running, which prompted him to pick up the pace.

"If you have enough breath to swear, you have enough breath to run faster," he told her, spurring his horse to increase its speed, forcing her to move quicker or be trampled.

Strider was no longer taking them on a Northwestern route but had instead headed Northeast to avoid the main roads and towns that were likely being searched. He still thought they should've killed the two soldiers, who no doubt had informed their captain of their direction of travel, and of Addy's disguise. They ate in the saddle, having found additional food in the horse's saddlebags. Strider didn't let them stop until they made camp again.

He made Addy take care of her horse on her own, doing his best to brush out the hair on his varnish roan's back where the saddle and blanket rested. But without a proper brush, he could do little to work out the dust and sweat. The courser was a rather scraggly looking horse; sturdy, but annoyingly jumpy. Securing the saddle back on his horse, his gaze traveled to the bay Addy was tending to. His brow raised when he saw her standing back several paces, staring at the horse with a critical eye.

"What is it?" he asked, leaving the grazing horse to sit beside the saddlebags on the ground. Pulling out the arrows that Greer had returned to him in Altia, he inspected them for any damage, painfully aware of the two arrows he destroyed when saving Addy. The magic he'd channeled through them had destroyed them like it always did when one enchanted an item too quickly.

The magic held within them, becoming unstable as the item fell apart, unable to handle the strain of further magic being forced into it and woven into an enchantment. Because of this, arrows and other projectiles had to be created with a preset enchantment. He'd witnessed how Rangers bemoaned having to take up space in their quivers for arrows they had to use sparingly.

But Strider's father had taught him how to create arrows that held any spell he attached to them instantly, remaining together long enough to reach their target. It was an art his mother had taught him, and he honored her memory by passing the skill down to their son. They both had given him a gift, and he guarded their secret fiercely. But such arrows were difficult to craft, requiring time and patience to ensure he didn't disintegrate the shafts instantly.

This quiver was his reserve of arrows, having used his first batch long before meeting Addy. He didn't have the time needed to make more to replace the arrows he'd sacrificed. He would need to take care not to lose anymore.

"I don't know what to name him," Addy said, after a moment.

She cocked her head to one side as if viewing the horse from a different angle would help her know its name.

"Call it Su'lris," Strider suggested, as he held up an arrow to peer down it. It was as straight as a rail. He placed it back in the quiver and picked up another one.

Addy touched a finger to her chin as she considered the name. She turned to him, smiling.

"I like it. What language is it, and what does it mean?"

Strider's lips curled in a catlike smile. "It is the yulie word for brown."

Addy gave him a look. "Seriously? You couldn't be a little more creative?"

Strider gave a dismissive shrug. "You don't need to use it."

"I'll use it. I'm just taken aback by your naming skills."

"I have many talents," Strider responded, never looking up from his work. Having finished inspecting the first few arrows, he went through the rest of his quiver, searching for any wear or damage.

"What does Greer's name mean, wolf?"

"It means nothing."

Addy gave him an incredulous look. "You named your wolf, Nothing?"

Strider raised a brow as he looked down the shaft of an arrow at her. "No, I made the name up."

"And Greer was the best thing you could come up with?"

Strider gave another dismissive shrug as he moved from his arrows to caring for his swords.

"He doesn't seem to mind."

"He's a wolf," Addy pointed out flatly.

"Try explaining that to him."

The soldiers finally reached Newmen. Their bodies were haggard and weary as they stumbled down the streets. They'd pushed themselves to the point of exhaustion in their efforts to return to town as quickly as possible. Their ragged forms collapsed before the barracks, raising shouts of concern from the other soldiers. The noise drew the captain from his quarters. He stomped toward the crowd gathering in the courtyard.

"Step aside!" he boomed. The crowd of men parted. Seeing his injured men, the captain began barking orders.

"Fetch some water and a healer!" He pointed to two of his soldiers, who saluted before rushing off toward the well.

"Help me get these men out of their armor and to a bed."

The soldiers carried the two men into the barracks, while those not helping lift the bodies hastily prepared beds before helping strip the injured soldiers of their heavy plate armor. The other soldiers returned as they laid their comrades on their beds. One man carried the bucket that belonged to the well outside, having stolen it from off its hook in a rush to bring his comrades water.

A healer followed the other man, his hair ruffled, his clothes skewed from having been pulled out of bed and made to dress quickly. The captain and his men stepped aside to let the healer look at the unconscious men. He focused on the one that had blood caked on his neck and shoulder while the captain approached the uninjured man, who stirred. His eyes flew open, wild with alarm as he flailed about in confusion. The captain placed a firm hand on his shoulder to keep him from hurting himself.

"Easy now," he said, his tone soft but authoritative.

The man calmed when he saw his commanding officer standing over him.

"Captain," he croaked, then coughed.

"Drink first," the knight ordered. His soldier greedily accepted the ladle of water offered to him. He gasped and coughed, before downing another ladle full. Finally, he'd regained enough breath to speak. His voice was scratchy from the dust of the road.

"What happened, Arden?" his leader asked.

"We found the girl," he began, wheezing. "She was alone. She ran. We gave chase. She ran into a thicket... of trees."

The captain nodded as the words tumbled out of the man.

"We caught her. She put up a fight, even managed to stab Joshen with one of his arrows."

A murmur of amusement rippled through the soldiers crowded around the beds. They'd not be letting Joshen live that moment down anytime soon. The captain shot them a warning glance, and they quieted. Arden didn't seem to notice his companions as he continued.

"We were about to bring her back... when the wolf attacked. Bigger than any wolf I've ever seen. It killed Micheal and Grimly..."

He trailed off for a moment. "Then the arrows came, killing Connor and Will. The arrows, they pierced their armor... I don't know how. Joshen and I took the girl and tried to get to the horses."

The entire room had grown silent. Arden kept speaking in a rambling manner, born from shock. "The man appeared out of nowhere and held Joshen at blade point."

"The Ranger," the captain clarified, but Arden shook his head.

"No, sir. He said he wasn't a Ranger, called himself a Hunter. The girl said he was... A Dark Ranger. That he killed without honor." His face grew dark. "He planned to kill Joshen and me even after we'd let the girl go. Didn't want to leave any witnesses."

"How did you escape?" the captain prodded.

Arden had grown silent, staring at the blanket that covered his legs. He blinked, his eyes clearing for a moment as he looked at his captain.

"The girl begged him to, and he let us go. I was expecting to be shot in the back as we left."

The captain nodded. "Rest now," he ordered, placing a hand on Arden's shoulder. "We'll see that justice is done."

He left his men to the healer, barking orders for a horse to be prepared as he summoned one of his lighter built soldiers to his quarters. After being briefed on all that had happened, and armed with a full report, the soldier spurred his horse out of Newmen and raced toward the capital.

Chapter 16
The Trouble With Honor

"How did the soldiers find you?" Strider asked, as he ran a whetstone along the edge of his war sword. Greer snored, asleep at his feet.

Addy, who'd been practicing moving silently, paused mid-step. Straightening, she recounted her story from the point where she'd left Greer in the road.

Strider stopped sharpening his blade to fix her with a level stare. "It didn't occur to you to pull up your hood and get out of the way?" he asked, as if the idea should've been obvious.

"They were after me."

"They were after a girl in a dress, traveling with a Ranger and a wolf. Not some random boy walking down the road. They wouldn't have given you a second glance. When you ran, you admitted guilt, so they chased you."

That hadn't occurred to her. Something clicked inside her head. He hadn't let the seamstress fit her clothes, keeping them loose and bulky on purpose, because he wanted the outfit to disguise her feminine features to help pass her off as a peasant boy. She'd just assumed he didn't want to spend more money on her than he had to. He'd put a lot more thought into his actions than she'd given him credit for. Now those soldiers whom he'd let go would report that she was disguised as a boy.

Strider nodded when her face showed understanding. "You should've let me kill them," he said in disappointment. "Witnesses cause trouble." Although they couldn't do much about it now.

"They let me go. Honor demands you do the same," Addy said, her anger bubbling to the surface. Who had she hired? How many people had he killed? What kind of person could kill so easily?

Strider sighed and shook his head, muttering something in the same rough language she'd heard him speak in before. It differed from the yulie tongue; it sounded familiar, but she couldn't quite place it. Addy frowned at him; pretty sure he'd just sworn, given his tone.

"I am paying you to do a job, Strider," Addy said, her voice taking on an air of a noble speaking to a servant. This caused the man's brow to raise. "While under my employment, you will not kill unless you have to."

Strider ran the whetstone across his blade with more force. The metal made a savage hiss. He looked as if he were contemplating using the sword on her as he spoke in a low, slow tone.

"You are paying me to get you home safe, not to follow your idea of honor. I will get you home, and I will do it in any way I see fit."

He stood abruptly, thrusting the hilt of the war sword into her stomach. She gasped as she fumbled with the blade.

"What was that for?" she shouted after him as he walked toward the horses.

Strider turned to face her. "It's for practice," he growled. "You have a talent for getting yourself into trouble. You're going to learn how to get yourself out of it."

She held the sword awkwardly; it was much lighter than expected. It sat in her hand, perfectly balanced, despite being too long for her height. Her arms were stiff and graceless, unused to holding a blade.

"You want me to learn to fight?"

Strider nodded and gestured for her to stand before him. The area where he stood was flat and clear of their gear.

"But ladies don't fight," Addy argued weakly, parroting her mother's words. Words she'd been told all her life.

Strider's eyebrow shot up. "Ladies don't steal, curse, or cause trouble, either. You were perfectly willing to fight when your life was in danger." A look of dark approval shadowed his face, his lips curling into an amused smile. "Or did that soldier accidentally stab himself in the neck?"

Addy's face flushed. "That was different."

"Survival is survival. The difference is that you lack the skills to increase your chances," Strider said firmly. "You should've gone for his eyes, or at least sliced open his artery."

Addy would've thrown out her arms in exasperation had she not been trying to hold the sword steady. "I wasn't trying to kill him!" she exclaimed.

"Then what were you trying to do?"

"I wanted him to let me go. I'm not a killer!" *I'm not like you.* She wanted to say.

He seemed to get the unspoken message. "You don't want to put me in a situation where I'll kill without discretion? Then make my job easier and learn how to get out of or avoid putting yourself in such a position."

Addy considered his words for a moment. She'd been told all her life that swordplay and violence were for the men of the family. Her mother had been strict about it, and many other values and practices that were deemed unacceptable for a lady.

"Women are to be revered," her mother would say. "They have men to fight for them and they shouldn't sully their own hands with such violent and bloody actions."

But was it wrong that she learn to defend herself? She knew other women of the court learned, and even knew her father employed a few women within his military. She made up her mind, before nodding.

"Fine, teach me."

Strider ran over the basics. Stance, hand positioning, edge alignment, and so on. Allowing her to feel how it should be with a real sword before putting a stick in her hand and making her practice with that.

"Tell me about your kidnapping."

Addy stopped swinging her stick to look at Strider. But she didn't see him, instead she saw the bloodied body of a soldier bearing Denmahr's crest. Her breath hitched in her throat. She blinked rapidly. The dead man vanished. Strider returned. He gave her an inquiring look, to which she offered a wan smile.

When she didn't speak, he gestured for her to continue practicing while he unharnessed Greer. She turned her back on him and began working on a general thrust and block he'd shown her, trying to work the memory away.

"I don't remember how I was taken from the castle," she began. "I remember going to bed the night before, then waking up in a dark carriage bumping along the road. I only saw my kidnappers when they opened the door to give me food or let me relieve myself. They were dressed in armor bearing the crest of Denmahr."

She stopped moving again as she remembered the events. The stuffy carriage, the pain in her throat and head after crying and screaming for someone to help her. No one heard, no one came to her call. All she got for her troubles was a sharp pounding on the wood, and threats breathed at her.

"Who was guarding you that night?" Strider prodded.

"Curthis, my brother."

"Your brother?" It was unusual for a sibling to act as a guard.

"He's the third son, born a year before me. Father arranged for him to be my guard rather than sending him away. He grew up fulfilling that role."

"How generous," Strider muttered. Being a third son, Curthis wouldn't stand to inherit anything of his father's. "How does he handle his fate of forever serving his younger sister?"

"He didn't help my kidnappers!" Addy snapped. "He'd die before-" Her words caught in her throat as she realized her brother might be dead. She shook her head. He couldn't be. If word of her kidnapping had reached Altia, then her brother's death would've reached her on the lips of gossips. She had to believe he was alive.

"How did you escape?" Strider prompted, steering the conversation back to her kidnapping.

Addy took in a breath, pulled out of her thoughts. "There was a storm. The dry earth couldn't handle the water. A mudslide took the road out from underneath the carriage. The door broke open, and I ran. I reached Altia several days later and hid there until I met you."

Strider placed the harness on the ground, nodding his understanding. He asked no more questions as he resumed instructing her in the art of swordplay.

Training with the sword became a part of her daily routine. Every time they stopped for camp, she would practice moving quietly after caring for Su'lris and then work on drills with a dummy sword Strider fashioned out of a sturdy stick. After she'd grasped the foundational practices and control, Strider made a sword of his own and began running through the drills with her.

He never shied away from whacking her when she failed to execute a move he'd shown her. Or when her actions left her open. It was never hard enough to do serious damage, but she ended up with a lot of bumps and bruises.

She collapsed by the fire after a particularly difficult practice session, her sides heaving from the exertion.

"There is no way I'll be able to beat a solider!" she exclaimed in frustration, as she rubbed a nasty bruise on her back. Strider sat in front of the fire, tending to his curved blade after their practice bout.

"Most soldiers have minimal training and skill. With clever tactics and training, you can beat them."

"But I can't match their strength, height, or reach!" Addy protested. "If I end up fighting a man as skilled as me, someone I can't outsmart, I'll lose if the fight goes on for too long."

Strider nodded slowly, his eyes glinting silver in the firelight. "You're clever, and don't hesitate when making a snap decision, like stabbing a man with his own arrow. We only need to close the gap in strength."

Addy raised her hands in an exasperated gesture. "I can't!"

Strider's head tilted to one side as he studied her. "Magic is a great equalizer."

Addy gave him a long, hard look. Many people feared magic. Most ummanie didn't practice magic because of its close ties to the yulie. As such, it was looked upon with suspicion and hostility. Most ummanie had abandoned the practice a few hundred years after the fall of the Devain Empire.

The Syliceon church had dedicated itself to preserving their views of the old magic, believing that one day the ummanie would need it again to defend against the great yulie threat. But they frowned upon any practices of the arts that didn't fall under their strict views. Such as the magic of the Rangers and other races. That was dark magic. Addy chewed her lip as she considered the possibility.

"I can't use magic," Addy finally stated, though the look in her eye told Strider the offer tempted her.

"Everyone is born with magic," Strider told her. "Some have a natural connection to it, while others must work to create one."

Addy dropped her gaze as she mulled over the idea. Her parents would be furious if they knew she allowed Strider to teach her magic, and that she possessed such a dark and unknown power. Very few people in the ummanie kingdom could use magic outside of the Syliceon and Rangers.

She'd grown up being taught that magic not approved by the Syliceon was evil. The church closely monitored the use of it, either scooping up children said to be blessed by K'yarie or trying them for witchcraft and sentencing them to death. They hardly tolerated the anumi, as they bonded with the spirits of animals, the goddess Layura's creations.

Even the Rangers called upon dark magic, magic that went unspoken, an art used by the yulie. She knew very little of it beyond what she'd learned in history. If the Syliceon found out, she'd be tried as a witch and killed. But she'd seen how Strider had used the power to heal himself. Was it so bad if it could help her protect herself and maybe heal others?

"How does it work?" she asked.

"You use magic to increase your natural abilities, such as strength, speed, and endurance," Strider told her. "It is a technique taught to the Rangers by the ravack women."

"So, all Rangers can do it?"

"Yes, though women are often more adept at it. The ravack

taught the Rangers this magic when they taught them the secret to crafting their recurve bows." Strider grew serious, reiterating what she already knew. "Use of this magic is considered evil by the ummanie. You must never let them know you can use it."

Addy looked away, unable to meet his intense stare.

Taking a breath, she steeled herself and met his gaze. "You have my word. I won't tell a soul."

Strider didn't look convinced, but he sheathed his sword and moved closer to crouch before her.

"Internal magic is difficult to detect, and while it can be weakened, it cannot be blocked like external magic," he explained. "You will first need to form your own connection with the magic before you can practice using it."

He extended his hand, palm up. A leaf rested in the center of his palm. His hand didn't glow as it had when he'd healed himself. The air shifted around them as it was pulled toward him. It swirled in his palm, tearing the leaf into thousands of tiny pieces before hurling them around in a tornado of wind. If it weren't for the tumbling debris she wouldn't have been able to tell the air was moving. She was completely deaf to the magic itself.

"You've felt magic before," Strider said. "The pulse that beat through the Well Greer knocked you into when you stole my sword."

Addy thought back to when she'd been trapped in the shimmering sand. She had felt the pulse of magic. It had terrified her, and every fiber of her being told her to run.

"Listen for that heartbeat in the wind," Strider challenged, grabbing her hand and bringing it closer to his own that channeled the magic. The wind swirled around her hand as she placed it inside of the small tornado. The pieces of leaf pelted her skin as they swirled about.

She closed her eyes, trying to sense the same throbbing pulse that she had when she was stuck within the magical Well. She felt nothing. Her eyebrows furrowed as she concentrated harder. Finally, she leaned back, letting out a breath. "I can't feel anything."

Strider let the wind dissipate and sat back. His face was as unreadable as usual. "You'll try again tomorrow while we ride," he said, returning to his place by the fire.

She frowned, unused to him not pointing out where she needed to improve. He returned to quietly polishing his blade, its blue surface glinting red in the firelight. Addy curled up in the blanket, head cradled in her arm as she watched him. Unlike the war sword, his curved blade was longer with a single edge. Its blade curved upward halfway down, unlike the straight blades of the arming swords and shortswords her father's men used.

Intricate runes and designs laced the guard, handle, and pommel. On the flat of the blade, inches before the guard, was a small symbol that she couldn't make out in the firelight. The metal held a blue tint to it. It was bluer than the normal color of spring steel and appeared to glow in the darkness like soft moonlight. This sword held an unnatural beauty no mortal hand could craft.

"What kind of sword is that?" she finally asked.

"It is a yulie blade," Strider answered, as he worked. "A saber."

"How did you get it?" Addy asked, propping herself up on an elbow.

Yulie blades were incredibly rare. Many people had claimed yulie weapons as prizes after the Liberating Wars when the ummanie, tahrvin, and ravack pushed them back into the lands they now inhabited. Most had been lost over time; forgotten relics of a time long passed. The few remaining were treasured heirlooms of noble or royal families. Her own father had a long sword made of the magical steel passed down from generation to generation, but it never glowed the way Strider's did.

"Did you steal it?"

Strider gave her a withering look. "I won it."

She rolled over on her stomach, chin resting in her hands as she looked at him expectantly.

He frowned at her. "Go to sleep."

"I won't be able to sleep after hearing that!" she protested. "Did you win it off a noble, or was it a prize in some grand contest?"

"It was the blade of an assassin I killed," Strider stated flatly, clearly not willing to share anymore.

"Did the Rangers send them after you?"

That drew a small laugh from the man. "Rangers working with assassins. You'd sooner see Chaos change his nature."

"So, why were you fighting him?"

Strider looked like he wanted to whack her with the stick he used in their training matches. "He killed people who were dear to me."

"Oh." Her voice grew subdued, her gaze dropping to study the ground.

She didn't press him for any more answers as he got up and left the firelight to relieve Greer from his post, clearly trying to distance himself from her and her questions.

Chapter 17
Train, Travel, Repeat

Addy helped Strider forage for food while they traveled. She'd never realized how many plants were edible until now. He took the time to name each plant and their various uses, and how to tell the edible from the poisonous doppelgänger many plants had. Not all the greenery tasted very good, but they gave her body the strength it needed. She wrote down each plant in a small leather-bound book she found in a saddlebag, doing her best to sketch each plant next to their information.

Greer hunted for himself, occasionally bringing back a rabbit that Strider would prepare for them, keeping the pelt—supplementing their supply of dried meat.

As they drew further from the towns and roads the soldiers might search, Strider began to set traps to snare small animals. Addy followed him, asking questions on how and why he placed his snares in certain areas. He showed her tracks and other signs that animals had passed that way, and how certain animals favored different routes over others. Eventually, she began setting traps under his guidance. They would leave them overnight, checking them in the morning before they left.

"Why don't you shoot a rabbit?" Addy asked, on a day when the traps were empty. "You have a bow and arrows."

He fixed her with a level look as he undid the empty snare from the wetland they found themselves in. "An arrow designed to tear through armor would decimate a rabbit," he told her. "There'd be nothing left to eat."

"How about a deer, then?"

"I don't have the supplies or time to treat the meat. Most of it would spoil."

Addy wrote down the information in her book in the section she'd made about trapping and hunting. She tucked the book away and walked ahead, doing her best to step on the firmer ground, avoiding the mud and marsh. They stopped near an area where the banks of the Tahl River sloped, and the water spilled out into marshland.

Greer had spent most of his time attempting to hunt the wild birds that flocked here. He'd snagged a duck for himself the night before. He now waited back at camp with the horses while they checked their traps. The drought that plagued Denmahr could be seen within the wetlands. Water levels were not as high and many reeds and plant life that thrived on the banks and in the shallows had died, denied of the water they desperately needed.

Addy pulled ahead of Strider, eager to leave the area quickly. The place buzzed with annoying insects.

"Addy," Strider called to her, his voice hushed and urgent. "Stop."

She turned back to look at him, confused, when a loud splash caught her attention. Whirling to face the noise, she found herself staring at a giant animal, standing in the water twenty feet from her. Covered in dark brown fur, it looked like a bulky elk, with a more rounded nose and strange antlers that had fused together to create solid, spiked structures resembling spiked bowls on either side of its head. It was huge! It snorted as it locked eyes with her. Rolling its great head, the deformed elk aggressively flashed its large antlers. The beast's ears pinned back as it licked its lips.

"Back up. Slowly," Strider told her.

Addy backed away, her eyes locked on the hulking beast. It snorted again, more violently, before charging. Addy turned and tried to run. Not watching where she stepped, her shoe slipped off solid ground, into the thick mud. Her shoe stuck in the sucking mud, tripping her. She fell, landing with a grunt. She pulled free of the mud, but long reeds had tangled around her legs.

The massive beast bore down on her; its pounding hooves caused the ground to shake beneath her. Addy kicked free of the reeds, scrambling to get to her feet. She looked back, her heart freezing as she saw nothing but a mass of antlers and fur. There was no time to run or dodge. She was going to die!

A wave of invisible energy slammed into the horned animal's side, sending it flying off to the right. Addy could feel the sour breath forced from the animal's lungs on her face before it disappeared. Water erupted into the air, where the animal landed in the middle of the bog, over sixty feet away. The creature's head burst through the surface as it kicked and thrashed, fighting free of the muck and weeds to reach the opposite shore.

Addy sat on the ground, panting. She stared, dumbstruck, at the retreating animal. "What was that?" she gasped.

Strider appeared beside her. "That was a moose," he said, offering her a hand up.

Addy accepted his help, too stunned to insist on doing it herself. Strider pulled her to her feet before retreating to drier ground.

"That was a moose?!" she breathed, as she followed Strider back the way they'd come. She'd heard about moose before but had never seen one. No one had ever told her they were so hostile. "Why'd it attack me?"

"The ill-tempered chwytes will attack just about anything," Strider answered, grabbing the last of their traps before heading back toward camp.

Addy continued glancing back toward the bog while they walked, half expecting the moose to race after them. "What kind of magic was that? Can I learn to blow things away too?"

"You can if you connect with the magic," he informed her.

She'd never seen such a display of magic until encountering Strider. The thought of being able to blast a charging moose away excited her. Bolting ahead of Strider, she rushed back toward camp, calling over her shoulder as she ran.

"I'll practice while we ride."

The Hunter shook his head as he trailed behind the enthusiastic girl.

The land began to raise in elevation while they traveled. Slowly the marsh and forest gave way to craggy grassland. The open land offered little shelter from the wind. Strider had taken care to avoid any well-traveled roads, steering clear of any sign of population. Black rock and scrub grass replaced trees and bushes. The party paused at the edge of a sheer cliff running alongside their path.

Below them stretched a green-gray grassland. Scraggly trees and bushes dotted the windswept moorland, interspaced with jagged black rocks. The land looked forlorn and barren. The Tahl River cut a lazy 'S' far to the west on its path to meet the Ruea River down south.

Far in the distance, they could see the Tahlvin Mountains marking the border between Denmahr and Myvara. Their towering peaks appeared massive even from a distance. Great gray clouds filled the sky, casting the world in a dreary light, the first sign of rain the kingdom had seen in months. Addy shivered at the unwelcoming sight of the moors.

The mountains were so far off. Beyond the moors lay Bayvar Pass, the only safe way through the Tahlrin Mountains. Both Myvara and Denmahr had built imposing fortresses at the mouth of the pass to guard against invasion. Over time, great towns grew around the key trading points. In the center of the canyon lay a third fortress, constructed by the tahrvin who owned the land within the pass.

Bayvar Pass was the only path the tahrvin allowed the ummanie of this area to take through their mountain kingdom. A kingdom sandwiched between several other kingdoms, the tahrvin would've fallen long ago had it not been for the Tahlrin Mountains. The imposing peaks proved to be nearly impenetrable. A sufficient army could never hope to traverse the rugged terrain of the Tahlrin to go to battle with the tahrvin towns that rested aboveground, and no one could reach the cities below.

The tahrvin were entrenched in those mountains so deeply the ummanie had no hope of ever driving them out. Addy had learned from her tutor how they benefited from charging tolls to pass through their mountains, while the ummanie kingdoms traded for goods they couldn't normally acquire with the mountain folk. The fortress within the pass, like the fortresses of Denmahr and Myvara, had grown into a bustling trade town where both races mingled and haggled. She'd fallen asleep shortly afterward, earning a good scolding.

Addy knew the pass was being watched. It was the only accessible point they had to reach Timara fiefdom.

"They've likely sealed off the pass," Strider said, noting her gaze as it lingered on the mountains.

"How will we get through?" Addy asked, hoping he had some sort of plan.

His eyes traced a path over the mountains. "We go around."

"You want to go over the mountains?"

"Something like that." He nodded before steering his horse down the trail toward the moors.

They descended into the moor. No longer having the advantage of height, Addy lost sight of the river and surrounding landscape, though the towering mountains still loomed. The rolling hills and flatland offered few places for the small group to hide. Strider took care not to let them skyline themselves on the tall hills that sat near the base of the small mountain they'd left behind. Sheep dotted the land here and there. The occasional farmhouse popped up, along with other signs of those trying to eke out a living on the lonely moor.

Addy could count on one hand the number of people they saw. Their path through the moors angled in a wide arch away from the pass.

Strider was quiet again and Addy was beginning to understand the differences in the silence that came from the Hunter. While it drove her nuts when he didn't talk, she understood that he felt comfortable in the quiet. It made her feel awkward and fidgety.

Addy jumped when a distant howl cut through the air. Several more followed the haunting call. Greer, who had been walking ahead, stopped, lifted his head, and let out his own reply. His howl made Addy shiver. Something about it struck her more deeply than the cries of the wolves. The howls ceased for several heartbeats, as if stunned by the response. Then their howls began anew, with far more enthusiasm.

"Don't encourage them," Strider told Greer.

Greer sniffed dismissively. He tossed his head before trotting ahead.

The howling grew silent. Addy didn't hear from the wolves again as they rode. Stuck on Su'lris, she had nothing to do to keep herself occupied. Talking was all she had, especially given the boring blandness of the moor. She toyed with the buttons on her sleeves, shifted about on the saddle, and fiddled with her packs while riding. Strider had shown her she didn't have to have her hands constantly on the reigns.

Su'lris was trained to follow the simple pressure of her knees. A trick she'd never known existed. A proper lady sat side-saddle and did not need to learn such things. Su'lris was an excellent horse. His manners were gentle and obedient, and he didn't startle easily, which allowed Addy to fidget while in the saddle without worrying that he would take advantage of having his head free. He was content plodding along behind his friend.

Her fidgeting soon caught Strider's attention.

"Here." He summoned another ball of wind and sent it her way.

Again, she only saw the wind because he had dirt spinning within it. Addy relaxed in her saddle, grateful for something to do. The ball of air hovered before her. The air was cold as it slid over her skin when she rested her hands at the rim of the swirling element. She closed her eyes and began trying to feel the rhythm of the magic. She had done this every day since Strider had started teaching her magic. It gave her something to do while they rode, and she wondered if he taught her to keep her quiet.

Addy blocked out everything around her. She focused only on the ball of magic between her hands, trying to feel its presence, its heartbeat. The wind hissed as it spun. It lapped at her hands, the tiny particles of dirt pattering against her fingers and palms. She concentrated harder. Still nothing. Addy didn't know how long she sat there trying to connect with the magic before she grew frustrated and gave up.

Letting out an exasperated breath, she said. "I'm never going to get this!"

Greer looked up at her curiously.

Strider continued to scan the moor. Unperturbed by her newest outburst. While he was hard on her every time she practiced sneaking about or fighting, he was distinctly more patient when teaching magic. He didn't lecture her, only prodded and prompted her with occasional guidance. None of it had helped.

"Isn't there some sort of trick you can teach me?" she asked for the hundredth time.

"You know the tricks," Strider told her again. "You're just especially magic deaf."

"Not helping," Addy said between gritted teeth. "I've felt magic before, back in the magpit."

Strider's head cocked. "The Well," he corrected. "Is a powerful concentration of magic. Even the dead could feel its magic."

"So why can't I feel it now?" She thought she saw the slight tilt of the man's head as he looked up at the sky.

"Because," he explained carefully. "The magic I am using doesn't give off nearly as strong a heartbeat."

"Can't you use a more powerful spell?"

"I could."

"Then why don't you?"

"Waste magic in hostile territory?" Addy could picture him raising a brow. "That sounds like a smart idea."

Addy frowned. "How am I supposed to get any better?"

"You can't," Strider stated.

"Then what am I supposed to do?"

"Hope we stumble across another Well I can throw you into."

Addy glared daggers at the back of Strider's head, wishing she had some sort of magic she could use to slap him from this distance.

The overcast sky wept shortly after the sun disappeared behind the Tahlrin Mountains, as if the sky was mourning the disappearance of the sun's light. Strider put up the small tent Greer carried on his back when they stopped for camp. An icy drizzle tapped out a loud beat against its walls.

Addy was grateful for the protection the little tent offered. She lay curled up in the warmth of her cloak and blanket. Greer had tried to stuff himself in the tent with her, but she'd forced him out, not wanting to cook inside of the small space.

The large wolf huffed before padding over to sit next to Strider.

The man's cloak was wrapped around him, protecting him from the chill in the air. Rain slid off the treated material like water off duck feathers. Again, Strider had taken up a spot outside of the camp in the shadow of a large outcropping of rocks.

Greer bumped his head against his shoulder.

"Go mind the horses," Strider said, softly rubbing the di'horvith's head.

Greer obeyed with a low woof.

The horses stood huddled closely together. Their heads held low as the rain beat against their backs. Thunder rumbled through the sky and Strider's horse jumped. The animal pulled at its tether, spooked by the noise. Su'lris remained impassive.

Greer approached the startled varnish roan, uttering that same low rumbling sound he'd used to try to comfort Strider.

The horse calmed in Greer's presence. Ears perking forward, he lowered his head to blow a puff of air into the mutt's face. Greer did the same, his nose bumping against the horse's. Velvet lips nuzzled the wolf's head before lipping at Greer's ear affectionately. Greer snorted, tossing his head.

The horse bobbed his own head, nickering. Su'lris had moved so he, too, could stand closer to Greer. Both animals appeared calmer in the di'horvith's presence. Another clap of thunder boomed, but this time, neither horse spooked.

Candlelight reflected in the well-polished wood of the study desk; a flickering flame suspended in dark water. The dancing light cast king Elias's shadow against a wall, its form seeming to move with a life of its own. Bishop Markane stood on the other side of the desk as they both looked at maps strewn on the table. They were in the middle of discussing the deployment of Syliceon's Ry'arie knights for the past week.

Bishop Markane was a middle-aged man, though his black hair was already showing signs of gray. The candlelight tinted his aging skin a sickly yellow. He eyed the maps where small wooden circles with the Ranger's symbol still dotted the map. The Rangers were systematically leaving the country of Denmahr so as not to cause alarm and unbalance in the kingdom.

As they left a region, Syliceon's knights and mages moved in to bolster the kingdom's security. The church had always held a serious presence in Denmahr. Their influence would now grow even further as their disciplined men replaced the free-spirited Rangers.

The Syliceon boasted a very impressive number of magic users and skilled knights within their ranks. The Ry'arie, Syliceon's elite soldiers, were one of the few warriors capable of contending with the Rangers. They also held a healthy distrust for the Rangers and the way they practiced dark magic. He and the king were trading the Ranger tokens on a section of the map for tokens bearing the crest of the Ry'arie, a dragon encircling a star within a shield, when a knock at the door caused them to pause.

"What is it?" King Elias asked, as the servant entered with an apologetic bow.

"I am sorry to disturb you, your highness, but a soldier has come bearing an urgent message from Captain Kenthis."

"Send him in," the king said, taking a seat in his large leather chair.

The servant gave another bow before ducking back out into the hall. It took a moment for the man to fetch the soldier who'd been forced to wait in one of the side rooms near the throne room. They ushered the soldier into the study, the door closing tightly behind him.

The man looked travel-worn and dirty. Despite this, he dropped to his knee before his king. The smell of horse and man sweat filled the room, causing the bishop's nose to wrinkle. But the king showed no outward sign of disgust as he bade the soldier rise and present his message. Obediently, the soldier stood and repeated the message Captain Kenthis had sent him to deliver.

Bishop Markane's face changed from disgust to shock.

"You're saying a Ranger is with the girl?" King Elias questioned.

"No, sire, he claims not to be associated with the Rangers. The surviving soldier called him a Hunter and a Dark Ranger. Captain Kenthis has written a full report on the matter and has taken his men to intercept this Dark Ranger at Bayvar Pass."

With a gesture from his king, the messenger placed the message satchel on the table.

"Thank you, soldier," King Elias said, before calling for the servant. When he entered, the king addressed him. "Escort this man to the kitchen and have the cook prepare him a good meal, then see to it he is given a proper bed and a hot bath."

Both servant and soldier bowed.

"Thank you, my lord," the soldier said gratefully, before following the servant out.

King Elias read over the report before passing it to Bishop Markane for his perusal.

"So, she was hiding in Altia where she met this man," the bishop mused.

"Even if I risked arousing Myvara's suspicion by sending more forces to enforce the pass," King Elias said. "They would never reach it in time to help. If this man returns Lord Fenforde's daughter, we'll be at war within the month. King Renmous will not stand for it. We need to get her back before then. We shouldn't have changed the plan. *You* shouldn't have agreed to change the plan. You're too soft, Markane."

"My man asked for the girl as his reward. He's spent years integrating himself into the family and flawlessly performed his end of the task," Markane countered. "Your men allowed her to escape and failed to recapture her."

"They should never have been put in this situation in the first place!"

"Perhaps we could use this to our advantage," Bishop Markane suggested.

The King gave him a sideways glance; he said nothing, so the bishop continued.

"Lord Fenforde still does not know who stole his daughter. We have yet to send any demands, either. Spread the word to Myvara, to the towns and cities between Newman and Timara. Tell them this Dark Ranger was the one responsible for kidnapping Lady Fenforde and issue a reward for his death and her safe return. Every peasant, sell-sword, and soldier will be on the lookout for them. The people of Myvara will also aid us. Though it is not a favorable outcome, the Rangers will hear word of this man who dishonors them by claiming their name. They would kill him on sight for the offense."

"And what will stop the dear lady from revealing who actually kidnapped her?" the king questioned.

"The only proof they have is that men wearing the emblem of your men held her. My people have been careful to ensure any evidence found doesn't lead back to you. Send word asking after the delegate visiting King Renmous on your behalf. He is long past due to return. People will assume that this man had stolen and used the carriage to pass through Bayvar Pass to enter Denmhar." The bishop shrugged dismissively, as he exchanged another Ranger tile with that of the Ry'arie. "If she still claims he is innocent, well, it is not uncommon for a captive to sympathize with her captor. She will be a young lady in great distress. Deceived by her kidnapper into believing that he was protecting her. If our men take her, we can quietly bring her back here and proceed as planned, using the Dark Ranger's name instead. If not, we have other plans in motion that will allow us to adapt."

King Elias thought about it for a moment before nodding. Pulling out a paper from his desk, he began writing the official decree. He would have his scribes make copies. The falcons would deliver the pamphlet to the surrounding area, where heralds would spread the word to every town. They'd dispatch messengers to Myvara asking for aid in the search for Lady Fenforde and her kidnapper.

Chapter 18

The Town Of Borris

"Strider," Addy whispered, her voice shaking as she stared wide-eyed at the figures that circled their camp. "There are wolves."

Strider sat before the fire, drinking a cup of steaming coffee while she hid within the tent. He looked around exaggeratedly, taking in the large animals before going back to sipping his coffee.

"So there are" he mused, watching the animals with disinterest.

The forms of dark-furred wolves circled the camp, their eyes glinting in the dim morning light. Among them danced the lighter-colored Greer. Barks and cries of delight escaped his lips as he played with the wolf pack.

"We're surrounded by wolves, and you're not worried?" Addy said in disbelief.

"They won't harm us."

"How do you know that?"

"They're here because of Greer," he explained. "They're here to pay him respect."

"Respect, like in the stories?" She'd grown up with bedtime stories told by her parents of a time before the Chaos portals dragged the ummanie into the world. Back when the ravack had their loyal di'horvith, and the yulie had their powerful moose, the tahrvin found themselves without a mount of their own.

She could hear her dad making his voice deep and dramatic as he pretended to be the tahrvin king, beseeching the goddess Layura for an animal as loyal as the di'horvith, but easier to handle and bond with than a moose. Taking pity on her brother's creations, Layura agreed. Addy smiled, remembering how she'd laugh at her father's impression of Layura's voice.

The story ended with the goddess taking the di'horvith and splitting it in two. Creating both the wolf and the horse. She gave the first horse to the tahrvin leader, who named it Strider. The story had been one of her favorites as a little girl, mostly because her father would play horse afterwards, and she'd be the tahrvin king riding his great mount into battle.

Strider nodded as he took another drink. "Ignore them. They'll leave when they feel like it."

Addy continued to eye the large canines as she went about helping take down the camp, unconvinced that they wouldn't try anything.

The wolves left before the rain returned, having come only to greet Greer before bounding off into the morning mist. Rain blanketed the moors in a silver curtain, obscuring the world around the soaked travelers as they rode. Addy was grateful for her cloak that kept the water and cold at bay. The days were growing colder as the season of harvest approached, though it would prove to be a lean one for the kingdom of Denmahr. The land had suffered from a lack of rain.

With the wolves gone, there appeared to be no life visible on the moors. Even the sheep had vanished. It felt as if they were the only living souls out in the storm. The Tahlrin Mountains had disappeared, hidden behind a wall of rain. Yet Strider knew which direction he needed to travel. The weather was miserable but helped to conceal their passage through open land. The few people who lived here were likely holed up in their homes, safe and warm. Addy shivered, wishing she had a warm place to curl up in.

"When we get to Myvara, I want to stay in an inn," she called over the din of the rain. The idea of a hot bath sounded wonderful, the steam clearing out her lungs, the hot water on her skin easing her sore muscles.

Strider didn't respond. He sat hunched in the saddle against the rain. Like all archers, he had covered his quiver. Yet his bow remained strung on his back. Addy thought the bow looked oddly dry despite the rain, though it was hard to tell. The Hunter looked as miserable in the rain as her, and a flash of guilt swept over her. He had spent the night out in the cold and damp, while she slept in a warm, dry tent. She hadn't asked him to pitch the little tent. She'd actually forgotten about it.

He'd set up the tent while she practiced trying to sneak up on Greer as he slept. Strider didn't speak. He hadn't said anything while he'd bandaged her feet after stepping on a sharp rock, or when he stepped in front of her as they'd been surrounded in Altia. He simply did it. She smiled despite the rain, touched by his thoughtfulness. He was prickly, and his appearance and willingness to kill would make him right at home in a dark alley, but he had a soft side.

Her mind flashed back to him telling her to watch his actions and saying he also did not trust her. Her smile faded. He was doing something; she wasn't. But what could she do? She couldn't set up a camp; she could barely gather food and firewood.

She considered what she could do. The wet, sucking sound of hooves plodding through mud and the drum of rain on her hood offered her no help in figuring out what to do. She'd lied to him. Her head shot up. That was it!

"Strider," she began, not sure how she wanted to phrase this. "If I promise to be honest with you, will you begin to trust me?"

"I don't care if you lie to me," Strider stated flatly. "Just do a better job of it and accept the consequences that will follow when I find out."

She was taken aback by his response. "Then how am I supposed to prove my trustworthiness?"

He turned enough so she could see one eye fixing her with a hard look.

"You already have been." He turned back to face the path ahead without offering further explanation.

Addy wasn't sure what she'd been doing to prove to him that he could trust her. She'd been following him and working hard to improve upon the skills he was teaching her, nothing more. No grand gestures or displays of loyalty. Nothing in what she'd been doing should be enough. Not understanding what he meant, Addy shrugged the thoughts away before she drove herself mad.

The town of Borris was a dull and forlorn sight. Like a half-starved vagrant squatting at the base of the mountains, it stood almost entirely forgotten by the world. The Talhrin Mountains jutted from the ground like petrified fangs, their tips sunk into gray storm clouds as if it were its prey. Strider stopped them while the town was still nothing but a gloomy outline. He fixed Addy with an unwavering stare.

"Stay close. Don't speak. Keep your hood up and your head down," he told Addy, as he pulled his face mask up around his nose.

"Because keeping my head down will hide the fact that a Ranger and his wolf are accompanying me," Addy said, rolling her eyes. "They'll be looking for you, too."

Strider shrugged off his bow. He held it near the top with one hand, the main shaft hanging down past his leg. Keeping a firm grip on the bow, he reached for the felaris feather. He gently brushed the feather down, causing it to hug against the curved bow.

Addy watched in amazement as the feather melded with the wood. The shimmering, colorful feather turned a dull silver as Strider's hand passed over it. When he removed his hand, the feather had completely fused with the bow, appearing to be nothing more than a decorative design inlaid into the wood.

"Can all Rangers do that?" Addy asked.

Strider nodded. "A Ranger will never remove their felaris feather. To do so is to cease being a Ranger. But sometimes a Ranger needs to hide the fact that they are one."

Aside from the feather, Rangers resembled normal mercenaries or sell-swords. Remove the feather, and no one would ever guess who they were.

Addy cocked her head. She wanted to ask him why he insisted on keeping the feather when he insisted he wasn't a Ranger. But she instead asked, "How are you going to hide, Greer?"

The di'horvith perked up at the sound of his name.

"Do you plan to leave him outside of town?"

The idea didn't sit well with Addy. The flat land of the moors offered little cover for the enormous wolf. If the locals saw him, they'd likely start a hunting party to kill the demon haunting their town.

Strider pulled out a pendant he had hidden under his shirt. It was the shape of a long, thin rectangle made of what appeared to be ivory.

The item gave no sign that it was doing anything, but Addy watched it closely, expecting to see magic. Movement flashed in the corner of her eye where Greer stood. She gasped when she looked at him. The di'horvith was dissolving into a silver mist. His great form growing translucent before vanishing altogether.

"What did you do?" she exclaimed.

"I hid Greer," Strider stated, tucking the pendant back under his shirt. Dismounting, Strider quickly fetched the pelts he'd gathered from the squirrels, rabbits, and the occasional raccoon they'd captured for food.

"How?!" Addy asked, as Strider secured the pelts to his saddle, so they draped over his horse's crop.

"Magic."

Addy scowled, letting out an exasperated huff. She gave the furs a puzzled look but didn't ask him about it. She expected Strider not to explain, as he mounted his horse and sent it trotting toward the town of Borris. The animal snorted as it plodded through the mud and rain. Both horses seemed as miserable as their riders.

The town looked far worse up close. Its streets were dirty, the squat buildings sagged under the weight of time and neglect. The place was as unwelcoming as the surrounding moors. Even the gray church sitting in the center of town looked uninviting. The eyes of the people were cold and suspicious. They scowled and glared at the strangers as they themselves scurried toward what little safety their dilapidated homes offered. A man approached them, toting a pike as straight and stiff as his posture.

"State your business here!" he sniffed, speaking in the tone of someone who thought his small bit of authority meant something to anyone other than himself.

Strider's posture had grown sloppier, and his shoulders slumped as if weighed down by life's hardships. He nodded his head in deference to the man, his gaze never meeting the other man's, though he took in every inch of him. Clearly, a member of the town acting in the role of a guard or postman. His stance was too stiff, his feet too close together. His poster told Strider that he had no idea how to wield his weapon. "We're just passing through on our way to sell furs in Talma," Strider responded, his voice softer than before.

Addy had to hide her surprise when she heard Strider's response. Not only was his voice softer, it held the accent of someone from eastern Denmahr rather than his usual, rougher accent pegging him as someone from Roxbi.

The man sniffed as he took in the meager supply of furs. "Not much in the way of stock. Who is this?" He gestured toward Addy, who'd copied the weary body posture Strider had adopted. She kept her head bowed, hiding most of her face, allowing the baggy clothes to hide her figure.

"My son, he helps me hunt, for all the good it did us," Strider replied, his voice tired, haggard by the trial they all faced. "We sold some wares at Black Rock. Though the drought has been hard on us all."

"Carry on then. Don't cause trouble. Curfew is at half dusk watch." The postman dismissed them, hardly taking in Addy as he moved along. Strider tilted his head in another nod before clucking to his horse to move along.

Addy pulled her cloak tighter around herself before urging Su'lris to follow Strider's horse more closely. She kept her hood up and her eyes down as instructed. She found her gaze searching the ground for Greer. His absence unnerved her. Addy wondered if he knew what was going on right now.

Her gaze drifted toward Strider. She'd never seen him behave this way. His posture never changed, remaining as tired and world-weary as those around him. From behind, he looked and sounded like someone completely different. Only the clothes and gear were distinctly his. She wondered if his Roxbi accent was real or if he had also faked it. She didn't dare ask for fear of being overheard.

The rain clouds above had stopped weeping, but they remained overhead. Only one tavern existed in town, and it had done little to appear welcoming. It didn't have to. Those traveling through these parts didn't have the money to be picky. Addy found herself casting longing looks toward the warm light that spilled from the tavern's grimy windows.

Used to sleeping in a bed that likely cost more than the building itself, and being fed meals curated by a chef who was only second to the king's own cook, she'd have never willingly gone into such a filthy looking place. But her time on the streets and long, hard travel had severely decreased her standards for establishments.

The tavern didn't have an attached inn, but the owner might allow them to purchase a bit of floor for the night. A roof and four walls made the place far better than sleeping out on the cold, damp moors.

Strider brought the horses to a stop before the tavern. Even he was growing tired of the wet. The storm had stopped, but he knew it wasn't over. He cast a look toward Addy before dismounting.

"Head down, keep quiet," he reminded her.

"I know, I know," Addy grumbled, as she swung down from the saddle.

Strider took Su'lris' reins and looped them around the saddle horn. He held onto each horse's bridle as he took the time to whisper into their ears. The animals became alert. Both bobbed their heads when he stepped away. Strider offered them a nod before turning to the tavern.

Addy gave Strider and the horses a puzzled look, before following the Hunter inside. The inside of the tavern was as sad as the exterior, despite being crowded with people. The damp chill of the day had driven many people into the warmth of the decrepit building. Addy noticed the usual lull in the conversations ripple through the room as they entered, though it didn't hold the same air of suspicion and fear as it normally did.

It was incredible how one little feather could affect the mood of a room. Unlike out on the streets, the stares didn't last. People returned to their dinner and conversation. Only a few eyes remained, watching them take their seats at a table near the fire.

Addy eagerly slid into the chair closest to the fire's warmth, letting out a sigh of contentment when the heat spread through her. She loved curling up by the fire back home, where she would read or practice needlepoint with her mother. She'd gained her love for books from her mother, who often joined her by the fire with a book or project of her own.

Addy had to stifle a laugh as the thought of Strider sitting across from her doing needlepoint flashed across her mind, earning a warning look from him. Addy's back straightened as she placed her hands on her lap. She pursed her lips, fighting off the urge to laugh as she sat. To keep from giggling, she watched the logs burn in the fire.

Strider ordered a bowl of pottage for Addy, but nothing for himself. He propped his feet up on an empty chair, relaxing as his cloak dried. He hadn't come for the food, but for warmth and information. The Hunter listened to the surrounding conversations, allowing his attention to roam from table to table, listening to each conversation for a moment before moving on to the next.

Taverns were wells of information, especially when the patrons believed they couldn't be overheard. Most of the talk was inconsequential. A rise in food cost caused by the scarce crops for this year remained an ever-present topic for the inhabitants of Denmahr. He also heard rumblings of worry about flooding if the rain didn't let up. The parched earth did not absorb water well, and the rain was heavy.

A word caught his attention, and he subtly tilted his head toward the table. Not enough to indicate that he was listening to anyone, should anyone be watching. The men at the table behind him spoke again.

"Ya think it's them?" one of them whispered.

"They ain't got no wolf," another said, his tone as low as his companion's.

"Coulda left it outside," a third man suggested.

"He ain't got no Ranger feather neither," the second man piped up, his tone scrutinizing.

"Could be hid'n it."

"The postmen will stop 'em when they leave town. Leave it to them to ask."

The conversation continued as the men quietly bickered amongst themselves, unaware of Strider's eavesdropping. Strider's gaze drifted toward another table that had become rather boisterous, allowing him to observe the table behind him out of the corner of his eye. The men sat with their heads close together. Their weapons sat within easy reach. It would seem whoever kidnapped Addy had taken to hiring sellswords to aid in their search. Mercenaries didn't concern him; he'd dealt with their kind before.

He didn't care for the postmen and what they entailed. Addy's kidnappers were thorough enough to have a town as far from the pass as Borris under curfew. Like the man they'd encountered upon entering the town, the night postmen would question anyone trying to leave during night and dusk watch. It'd be safer to stay the night and leave in the morning, but there was something they had to do tonight. He leaned back in his chair, seeming to grow bored with the raucous being caused by the other table.

"We're going," Strider said, after Addy had shoveled the last spoonful of food into her mouth.

She looked at him, surprised. "We're not staying the night?"

"We have some business to take care of first."

He tossed a few coins on the table before leading the way out of the tavern.

Addy wearily got to her feet. She could feel eyes watching them, but she didn't look up as she followed Strider. The Hunter held the door open for her, falling behind her and blocking the stares before the door swung shut.

The street outside was dark, and it took Addy's eyes a moment to adjust. Her dinner sat heavily in her stomach, weighed down with worry. Strider didn't do things for no reason. Had he heard something that concerned him? Keeping her head down, she broke off from Strider, making her way to Su'lris. She patted his neck and was about to pull herself back into the saddle when someone grabbed her from behind.

Chapter 19
Stockpile

A firm hand clamped over Addy's mouth before she could scream. Her assailant yanked her backward while she thrashed and kicked, her hands grabbing for her knife.

"Hold still," Strider hissed in her ear, as he dragged her into the shadows of an alleyway.

Addy froze, her chest heaving.

Strider let her go, gesturing for her to remain quiet.

She looked up at him, her eyes alight with anger. But he wasn't looking at her, his eyes fixed on the dark street. The clouds still hadn't cleared, making the night darker than usual. Addy strained her eyes, trying to see what Strider was looking at.

"Look out of the corner of your eye," his voice was barely audible next to her ear. "Don't focus directly on the spot you're looking at."

She shifted from staring directly at the darkness to watching the area out of the corner of her eye. Movement in the shadows caught her attention. Figures moved down the streets as people rushed back to their homes. But they weren't what concerned Strider. It was the armed men that'd given him pause.

"Postmen. Paid to question any visitors to the town at night," Strider explained, his breath hot in her ear. "There's a curfew for the townsfolk."

He fell silent when three men came out of the tavern.

"I'm just say'n it's suspicious that they left all'a sudden," one man said. "I say we at least alert the postmen."

Strider recognized the voice as belonging to the first man in the tavern that caught his attention.

"They left, 'cause they were done eat'n," the one who'd cast doubt inside spat grumpily. "The postmen will stop'n question them when they leave, anyway. I don't see why we need to go bother'n them."

The third man had stopped to look at the horses. "These here horses don't belong to anyone in this here town," he muttered. "Do you think they belong to those two strangers?"

"Now, why would they leave two perfectly good horses?" the first man mused. "They probably belong to someone inside."

"Not anymore. Idiots didn't even tie them up. What's stop'n 'em from walk'n off?"

He reached out to grab Su'lris reins. The horse threw his head back with a shrill cry. He bucked, striking out with his front hooves. The man reeled back, barely avoiding being struck. Off balance, he fell into the squelching mud. Su'lris let out another loud scream and bolted, the varnish roan following close behind as they ran full tilt for the end of town. Kicking and lashing out at anyone who attempted to stop them. The man's companions laughed. He cursed as he got to his feet, caked in soupy mud, and the group moved on.

Addy gaped at the display, having never seen her horse react so violently. A tap on her elbow drew her attention in time to see Strider disappearing further into the shadows. Addy looked at him, then back to where Su'lris had run. A hand grabbed her arm and tugged her deeper into the alley.

"Su'lris," she whispered urgently, resisting Strider's pull.

"You can't help if you're caught," he whispered.

Addy couldn't argue the point. She followed Strider through the dirty maze of alleyways that made up the back end of the town of Borris. He had her stop and wait for him while he slipped into the main street. Addy tried following him with her eyes, using the method he'd just taught her, but she quickly lost track of the man. Moments later, he returned for her.

They passed the church building, using its structure as cover. The main road cut straight from the church to the end of town. But the Hunter didn't follow it. He ushered her into another side street. A door burst open, spilling light into the alleyway. Strider pushed her down behind a pile of barrels a heartbeat before a group of men walked out.

Addy didn't dare breathe. She held perfectly still. Her cloak wrapped around her like a blanket of ink. The illuminated doorway cast the shadows of the men against the adjacent wall. She could hear them talking and the soft giggle of women as they bid them farewell. The light from the door vanished. The men made their way down the street, their footfalls coming closer. Addy kept her head bowed as she waited for the men to pass by. The door opened again as a woman called out. The men stopped, turning back. Addy's heart stopped. She could see their feet right next to her.

Everything inside of her screamed to run. These men would see her, they'd sound the alarm. She needed to get away! *Stay still!* Strider's words echoed in her head. He'd drilled them into her during training. *Stay still, stay still.* She told herself, forcing her muscles to relax.

One man walked back to the light of the doorway while the others waited for him. Addy fought down the growing desire to bolt. The door closed again and the light vanished. She watched the men's shoes turn and walk away, still quietly chattering among themselves. She stayed still, listening to their voices fade into the distance as her heart hammered against her ribcage.

Strider appeared next to her again. His touch was gentle as he helped her to her feet and guided her through the darkness. Though the town of Borris was small, it felt as if an entire watch passed before they reached the building Strider was looking for. It was a rundown, unassuming building.

Squat and sagging, it sat wedged between two taller buildings. No lights filtered through the cracks in the door facing the small alley. Strider gestured for Addy to remain hidden further back as he approached the door. She watched him inspect the door, surrounding frame, and steps as if looking for something.

Seeming not to find anything amiss, he picked the lock of the door before slowly opening it and disappearing inside. He returned moments later, signaling for her to come in. The room was small and full of dust, clearly not having been touched in a long time. Addy didn't see Strider at all until his head poked up out of a dark hole in the floor.

"Here," he said, tossing her a bundle of something.

She caught it and approached the hole. As she drew closer, she could tell that the hole was a hidden cellar of some sort, once covered by a trapdoor. She couldn't see inside. Strider didn't use a light as he rummaged down below. Occasionally, he'd toss another bundle of something up into the main room as he ransacked the hidden cellar.

He appeared again, handing something long and slender to her. She took it, realizing that it was a sword.

"Put that on," he ordered, before vanishing into the darkness again.

"What is this place?" she whispered, as she buckled on the sword. Unlike Strider's sword, which was the proper length for his height and arm length, this one was closer to what she needed.

"It's a hidden cache," Strider stated the obvious from within the darkness once more.

"One of yours?"

"No."

"Then how do you know about it?"

"I know a lot of things."

"Just not how to answer questions," she said, rolling her eyes.

"I answered, just not in the way you wanted."

He climbed out of the hole a moment later and handed her another bundle before pulling out what looked to be a charcoal pencil. He marked the button of the trapdoor with half of a strange symbol before closing it. The seam of the door flashed a brief silver after it closed. He moved to the door, drawing half the symbol on the door, the other half on the frame as he marked around it, muttering softly under his breath.

He worked quickly, before signaling to Addy that they were leaving. Addy followed him out, and Strider locked the door behind them. Addy thought she saw another dim glow of silver around the door.

"What was that?" she asked, her tone barely audible.

"Nothing important," he answered.

"That's why you took the time to do it," she said flippantly. "Because it wasn't important."

He didn't answer.

Addy let out a huff as she followed him toward the town's limit.

"I thought you said we were going back?" she asked, in a hushed whisper.

"That was before we had men taking an interest in us and trying to steal our horses."

"I was really looking forward to sleeping in a bed," Addy lamented.

"I bet your kidnappers have a bed they can let you sleep in."

"That's not funny."

"It wasn't meant to be," he stated, less than empathetic to her plight. "Hide."

Addy could make out the lantern light of a patrol walking along the border of the town less than a hundred yards away. Looking in the other direction, she saw another patrol. Both were converging on their location. She crouched behind a woodpile. Strider slid up next to her. Even sitting next to him, his shape was hard to make out in the darkness, his strange cloak blending in perfectly with the night.

His head turned to her, slow and measured. All she saw was darkness within. He reminded her of the pictures depicting the god of Chaos dressed in black and purple robes, the hooded face enshrouded in shadow. Her life had been nothing but chaos lately. That chaos had only increased as she spent more time with Strider. The Hunter reached over, pulling her hood further down to better hide her face, breaking her train of thought. Her attention returned to their current situation.

Addy could hear her heartbeat in her ears as she waited beside Strider, her eyes fixed on one of the approaching patrols. A hand came up between her gaze and the approaching men, blocking her view, preventing her night vision from being ruined by the light. She shot Strider a sideways glance, but he didn't acknowledge her.

The two groups of postmen greeted one another as they passed, though they didn't stop to visit as they continued on their designated patrols. Strider didn't move when the men began walking away. He remained still until they had covered a third of their route, just before the point where they'd double back again, before he moved, leading Addy out of town and into the darkness of the moors.

Chapter 20
The Ways

They moved low and slow, never rising to full height as they crept away from town. They made their way to a small hill, using it to block the line of sight from the town. Addy stretched, glad to be able to walk upright again. A heavy snort sent a gust of air into Addy's face. She yelped in surprise, stumbling backward.

"Shh!" Strider hissed, shoving something into her hands.

It took her a moment to realize she was holding Su'Iris' reins. The steady horse had been the one that snorted in her face in greeting. Addy reached up to stroke Su'Iris' cheek, her eyes watering with tears of relief. She hadn't realized how worried she'd been about the big animal. Su'Iris bumped her hand with his velvet nose, causing her to smile.

"Get on," Strider said in a firm whisper, after securing some of their stolen supplies to Su'Iris' saddle.

She slowly navigated around Su'Iris, groping in the dark for the stirrups. She heard an exasperated breath to her right. Strider appeared beside her, helping her into the saddle.

"Well, I'm sorry—" She began, her tone heated.

He cut her off with another furious hiss. Was he a snake now?

She felt Su'Iris begin moving forward as he resumed his normal routine of following Strider's horse. Strider continued to silence Addy for the next few miles. She'd grown frustrated with his paranoia but bit back a remark. He had more experience in sneaking out of places than her. Maybe he was right to be concerned? The sound might travel over the moor. That didn't mean he had to be a jerk about it.

"You can talk now," Strider said, although his tone indicated he wished she wouldn't.

"Oh, thank you for granting me such an honor," she said, feigning gratitude.

"I changed my mind. Stay quiet."

"Too late," Addy retorted in a singsong voice.

Strider grumbled a word in a language she couldn't understand but had long figured out was some kind of curse. She stroked Su'lris' mane, smiling with pleasure. "How did you know where to find them?"

"I told them where to wait."

"You told them to run and hide when you whispered in their ear?"

There was no answer, and Addy assumed Strider had merely nodded.

"I can't see in the dark, remember?" Addy heard a very audible sigh.

"Yes, that is what I told them," he answered gruffly.

"Is that another Ranger trick?"

"Not exclusively."

"Will you teach me?"

"That would require you learn to use magic first."

"Fine," Addy relented, verbally backing away from the conversation. "One day then?"

"Maybe one day."

They rode through the night, not stopping even when the rain began to fall again. Travel was slow and miserable. Strider did not push the horses hard, not wanting them to slip in the mud that sucked at their hooves. The rain relented as morning light seeped through the clouds, casting the world in a dull gray light.

The daylight did little to improve the somber air of the mud-filled moors. Without the warmth of the sun to drive it away, a fog hung in the air, blanketing the land in further gray. The scent of heather, rain, and wet loam filled the damp air with a fresh earthy scent mixing with the smell of wet horse and leather.

The great Talhrin Mountains stood before them; cold, dark, and imposing. Broken boulders and pieces of giant stone lay strewn about them, cast down from the mountain long ago. Addy tilted her head back, but she couldn't see the tops of the mountain range, its peaks vanishing into the cloud cover. The world around them was silent.

Strider brought them to a halt. Then, rummaging through the sacks, he pulled out a bundle of clothing. He handed them to Addy, saying, "Put these on. We have a cold trek ahead."

Addy dismounted before accepting the clothes. With a warning look, she vanished behind one of the giant rocks to change. When she emerged, she noticed that Strider hadn't changed to thicker clothing. Though his clothes looked like a clean pair, he wore the same shirt and pants. He kept the hood of his cloak over his head, though now the weather called for it, unlike before. Despite how hot it became, she'd never seen him take it off. It was yet another one of his strange behaviors she had shrugged off.

At least he took his mask off whenever they were out of town. It made it easier for her to read his facial expressions when half of his face wasn't covered. Not interested in starting a conversation about Strider's fashion choices, Addy busied herself by running her fingers through her tangled mess of hair, grunting in frustration as she fought a stubborn patch.

Strider watched her for a moment, before pulling something out of his satchel. He plucked something off the item while circling around his horse toward her. Addy couldn't quite make out what he held as he approached.

"Here." He handed her the object.

Addy looked to see a simple brush being held out to her. Letting out a gasp of wonderment, she snatched up the offered bush.

"When did you get this?" she asked, holding the brush as if it were a precious gem.

"It's Greer's."

Her excitement faded a moment as the thought sank in, but it quickly rekindled. It could've been the horse's brush and she wouldn't have cared. Letting out a noise of joy, she wrapped her arms around Strider, giving him a swift hug before pulling away to brush her hair.

The Hunter stood there momentarily, surprised at the sudden show of affection. He blinked uncertainly at the girl as she trotted away before shaking his head and walking back to his horse. He touched the pendant under his shirt, releasing Greer, who appeared like an apparition before him. The di'horvith gave a brisk shake before bounding around the two of them in excitement.

Addy happily perched atop Su'lris, her hair freshly combed, while Strider walked his own horse up to a section of sheer cliff.

Greer ran circles around him, chattering excitedly. Strider placed a hand on the cold stone, his eyes searching for something before he walked several paces to the right. Stopping, he cocked his head as if listening to something, then uttered a word under his breath. The cliff looked as cold and uninviting as ever, yet he signaled for Addy to come closer.

She dismounted and led Su'lris over. Standing next to Strider, she looked at the cliff, puzzled.

"It's a really nice wall," she commented. "I thought you said we were going to go over the mountain?"

"I never said we were going over the mountain," Strider told her, stretching out his hand again. His palm touched the surface, and to her amazement, the stone rippled like water. His lips twitched in an amused smile at her expression. "We're going through it."

"You know how to enter the tahrvin tunnels?" Addy asked in amazement.

The tahrvin had created intricate tunnels running throughout the entire Tahlrin Mountain range, connecting their great cities, towns, and capital in a warren-like network. These tunnels allowed them to move their armies into position to defend against potential attacks from the outside, though no one had been stupid enough to try.

The mountains had protected the tahrvin from being destroyed long before the ummanie had entered this world. During their wars with the yulie, they'd fled underground to avoid being wiped out by the other race. Only the ravacks had fended off the yulie's attempts to claim their territory.

The war had come to a stalemate before the ummanie appeared. They ended everything when the ummanie united with the tahrvin and ravack to drive back the yulie. Ending the war and winning the freedom for the ummanie race.

Even now, the tahrvin didn't share the secrets of their tunnels, guarding their Ways fiercely. Addy looked at Strider with renewed suspicion. How had he learned about them?

"Keep Su'lris close to Greer. He isn't going to like the tunnels," Strider told her, as he pulled his mask back over his face.

He turned to his horse, grabbing something out of his packs. He bent down and began covering his horse's hooves in sackcloth; the animal snorted and stomped a hoof. Both Greer and Strider had to calm the skittish horse to keep him from trying to throw the makeshift shoes off. He then placed the sackcloth on Su'lris' hooves, who wasn't as agitated by the strange things on his feet, and Strider wished he had chosen the steadier bay for his horse rather than the jumpy roan. He'd never had the best luck with horses.

Strider returned to his horse. Using the last of the sackcloth, he covered the animal's eyes to keep him calm. He kept a firm hold on his horse's reins as he led him toward the cliff face. Deeper ripples warped the stone as Strider and his horse disappeared through it.

Addy gawked as she watched the stone swallow Strider and his horse. She'd never seen anything like it. No wonder no one could ever find the entrances to the tunnels. Even when opened, they looked like solid stone.

Greer waited beside Addy, looking up at her expectantly. She took a deep breath before following Strider. She felt nothing as she passed through the stone. No lapping of cold against her skin, no feeling of moving through gritty sand, like with the Well. It was as if the cliff face never existed as she left the outside world and entered the tunnels. Sunlight illuminated the tunnel entrance she'd stepped into with dull gray light.

Puzzled, Addy looked back to the doorway to find that she could see outside. There was no sign of a door or wall. The moment Su'lris cleared the entrance, however, the world outside shifted. With a ripple, the view of the outside changed from the dull colors of the moor to a black and white rendition. As if an artist had sketched the landscape in charcoal, the details sharp and real. The sunlight filtering through the magical screen now stained the gray stone white.

The stone passage inside was wide enough to allow three large carts to move abreast. Dim sunlight revealed the roof of the tunnel before shadows swallowed it deeper within. The roof arched high above their heads, as seamless as the stone walls around them. The stone held no signs of tool work.

Polished to a smooth shine, it reflected the dark forms of the trespassers. Addy ran a hand along the smooth, icy surface in amazement. Her fingers found no hidden seams or blemishes. Columns extended from the stone at evenly spaced intervals, providing a visual break to the cylindrical tunnel. Faintly glowing crystals mounted on these columns cast the tunnels in soft blue light.

"Keep the horses close to Greer," Strider reminded her in a hushed tones, as he handed his horse's reins to her.

Strider's courser shifted uncomfortably, rocking its weight from side to side as he bobbed his head slightly. His eyes remained covered, though it was doing little to keep him calm. Even steady, Su'lris seemed unsettled by the tunnels. Greer took up a position between the two horses, who relaxed in his presence. Addy herself felt unnerved. The tunnels were otherworldly; it was as if she'd been swallowed by a Chaos portal and thrown into another dimension.

Strider remained as composed as ever, as still as a lake of ice. He strode forward with a silent, careful gait.

"Keep the horses in the center of the path," Strider ordered. "I don't want you bringing the tunnel down on our heads."

Addy shivered at the thought and followed more slowly. The two horses kept pace with her, or maybe they were matching pace with Greer, who walked beside her? She didn't know, but she appreciated the di'horvith's company. Addy watched Strider as he moved with purpose, searching for any traps along their path. How he'd see anything among the smooth stone was beyond her, but she led the horses as directed. He constantly cocked his head as if listening to something.

The dark world of the tahrvin tunnels was eerily quiet. There were no sounds of dripping water or scurrying animal life. The world beneath the mountain was disconcertingly void of sound. She didn't even feel a noticeable breeze, yet the cold, earthy air never smelled stale. She was grateful for the thick wool clothes. The world of stone possessed a chill that she wasn't used to this time of year.

"It's kind of crazy," she whispered, her hushed voice echoing off the stone walls. "These tunnels don't collapse despite supporting the weight of a mountain. I wonder how the tahrvin built them, how they kept them from caving in. Do they ever worry they'll give way?"

"Enough," Strider said sharply.

Addy paused, shocked by how tense and threatening he sounded as he walked. "You don't like the tunnels?"

"Do you like the thought of a mountain hovering over your head, ready to cave in on you at any moment?"

Addy thought about it for a moment and couldn't help but shiver. "No, I guess not."

"Then don't bring it up again," he growled.

Addy's head tilted in thought. Though his body appeared as calm and stoic as usual, his voice had held a bite to it. Not one out of anger, but something else. Was he scared? The idea seemed impossible. She doubted there was anything that could scare the irritable Hunter. Addy watched him more closely, noticing a subtle shake in his hands that he tried to hide by slowly curling and uncurling his fingers.

She wasn't cruel or stupid enough to try to play upon this potential fear. It was possible she was misinterpreting his tone. For all she knew, he could be trying to concentrate on locating traps, and the act of splitting his focus to listen and talk to her had been a frustrating strain. The idea that he might be afraid of something, like how she feared snakes, made him appear a little more normal, more ummanie. Maybe he wasn't as hardened as he wanted her to believe?

Shadows filled the tunnel, the soft glow of the crystals barely providing any light for her to see by. She could make out the form of Strider easily enough, but it wouldn't be hard for him to vanish if he tried. They passed several off-shooting tunnels, creating large four-way intersections, or deep holes in the wall, where only a single passage spouted off of the major thoroughfare.

They were approaching one of these single passageways when Strider signaled for her to stop. He turned, holding two fingers to his lips in a signal for her to be quiet. He motioned for her to stay with Greer, before pointing at himself then further down the hall, signaling that he was going ahead. Then he disappeared.

After a time, Addy heard footsteps coming down the hall. She knew they couldn't be Strider's. She'd never have heard them if they were. The steps were heavy and loud, made with sturdy boots. Addy stood there, frozen. She held the reins of both horses. Greer stood next to her, ears angled forward as he listened to the approaching feet. He didn't seem bothered by the noise. Addy's own heart pounded anxiously.

Had Strider seriously left her alone in the middle of the hall? Even if she were to ditch the horses and try to hide, there was no cover. She didn't know where the traps were, and she might trigger one if she ran. She couldn't move without risking death. The feet were almost to the end of the hall. She could see a dim shadow being cast onto the floor by the blue crystals. She watched the shadow touch the far wall and crawling up it. Then the man appeared. His eyes instantly focused on Addy.

"Wha—" he began, before being cut off by a knife pressed to his throat.

Strider had come from the opposite side of the tunnel they were in. The tahrvin hadn't noticed him as he'd instead focused on the obvious sight of Addy and the animals standing in the middle of the road. The tahrvin grew still as he uttered a curse under his breath. Addy noticed it was the same curse Strider favored.

"Good evening, Toris." Strider's voice drifted out from the shadow of his hood.

Chapter 21
Keeper Of The Ways

Lord Fenforde clutched the parchment in his fist like it was the throat of a hated enemy. King Elias's courier had delivered the letter that morning. He'd read it several times, growing angrier with each pass. The door to his study opened, drawing his gaze from the hated letter to the two resident Rangers of his castle. Kyre Bree and Elyphain Winnow slipped quietly into the room. He'd worked with Kyre for almost a decade, having known the Ranger through most of his apprenticeship, and he'd come to trust his judgment.

His partner, Elyphain, had replaced Kyre's old mentor after he returned to The Sanctuary, the headquarters and capitol of the Rangers within The Wilds. The anumi woman had quickly proven herself a valuable asset as a Ranger.

Placing both hands on his desk, Lord Fenforde hunched over it like a bear waiting to charge.

"I take it that letter isn't good news," Kyre said, as informal as ever as he approached the desk.

Being a Ranger, he outranked the nobleman despite having the decorum of a peasant. Like most Rangers, he didn't bother with the pompous niceties of the nobility. Lord Fenforde said nothing as he thrust the paper toward Kyre, who read it.

"The Dark Ranger?" he exclaimed incredulously, handing the paper to Elyphain. "What in Tarn is a Dark Ranger?"

"Someone with a death wish," Elyphain muttered. "Claiming that name will bring the entire Sanctuary down on top of them."

"How did old Elias figure out this man was the one who kidnapped Adelin?" Kyre mused, while Elyphain returned the letter to Lord Fenforde. "She was in a section of his kingdom the Rangers have cleared out from."

"Syliceon established their own network even before we began to withdraw," Elyphain pointed out.

"That isn't suspicious at all." Kyre smiled, sounding far too cheerful for this meeting.

Lord Fenforde had been listening, his shoulders tense. "I need someone to go into Denmahr and find out what is happening," he said, through gritted teeth. "The letter claims this Dark Ranger was last seen traveling toward Timara. I need to know if my daughter is safe and if this information is credible. I don't trust King Elias."

"I think we can do that," Kyre beamed, looking at his partner. "Do you want the honor, or shall I?"

"I'll go," Elyphain said. "I can cross the border much faster."

"Please leave as soon as possible," Lord Fenforde said, the urgency in his voice spurred by his overwhelming desire to see his daughter's return. He looked haggard and tired. Bags had formed under his eyes and his face had grown gaunt.

Worn out by the constant worry for his child, the overpowering fear that she'd never come home, that he would never see her again, had robbed the nobleman of his sleep. It had strained the entire castle, as months passed with no news. Now, something had come, and no one dared to hope that it was true.

Elyphain nodded curtly. "I will leave tonight."

"Leave now," Lord Fenforde ordered, before realizing his place. "Please."

Elyphain regarded him with a cool look, before nodding her understanding. Moving toward the large double doors behind the nobleman's desk, she threw them open.

"Mind the fiefdom until I return," she told Kyre. "And don't do anything stupid while I'm gone."

"Never," Kyre grinned.

She gave him a disbelieving look before running out onto the balcony and jumping off. Her body dissolved as she ran, dispersing into dust when she leaped off the railing before reforming into the form of a great bird of prey. The magic had taken less than a beat to transform the woman. With powerful thrusts of her wings, Elyphain flew off into the sky, letting out one last cry before vanishing around the other side of the keep.

"I wish I could do that," Kyre breathed. "It always looks so impressive."

Lord Fenforde gave the jovial Ranger a long-suffering look.

"I'll start my own patrols, then."

Lord Fenforde spoke before he could leave. "Take Curthis with you. Maybe he can redeem himself."

Kyre turned back to the nobleman. "Don't be too hard on the boy. He already carries a heavy weight of guilt on his shoulders."

"I allowed him to stay, trained him, tutored him, and in exchange, he was to dedicate his life to protecting his sister." Lord Fenforde's voice was taut and cold. "I held up my end of the deal, and he did not."

"He was drugged, just the same as any other guard would've been," Kyre reasoned. "Renard wasn't even there and was bedridden for days with guilt. Imagine the burden Curthis bears."

"And if he were any other guard, he'd no longer be in my service. I am at least giving him a chance to make things right."

Though his words were harsh, Kyre knew much of it was redirected anger and pain. He doubted the nobleman would throw his own son out for what had happened. Over the years of working with the man, Kyre had gathered that the deal with his son acted more as a show for the other nobility than a reflection of the man's affection for his child. As the third son, Curthis had nothing to his name. Acting as Addy's guard, he could remain under the protection of his family without appearing to be given favor from his father to the other nobles.

"We'll get her back," Kyre replied firmly.

Lord Fenforde nodded as he stared down at his desk, overcome with emotion. When he looked up again, Kyre was gone.

The tahrvin relaxed, a frustrated scowl darkening his face.

"I shoulda known it was you," he snarled.

Strider stepped away, withdrawing the saber he held to the tahrvin's throat. Toris rubbed his neck where the blade had been moments before.

"I stick my neck out for you every time you decide to come gallivanting down our bloody Ways, and this is the thanks I get?"

"You help because you want to save your own neck," Strider remarked darkly, earning a glower from the tahrvin.

He wasn't a tall man. Though even at their tallest, tahrvin people stood only around five feet. Toris stood shorter than Addy, meaning he was well under their tallest on record. He wore rough wool clothes and fur dyed in bright blues and greens, contrasting with the dull tones of the corridor. On his belt were several tools, hammers, picks, and other things Addy couldn't identify. Other belts and straps held more equipment.

A large pack nearly bursting at the seams was slung over his back, adorned with other odd gadgets and utensils. A sword hung from his hip, shorter than Addy's own blade. He wore thick leather boots and sported a nice woolen hat with flaps that covered his large, round tahrvin ears. His skin was pale, marking him as someone who rarely left the mountain.

"Curse that Chaos loving Minkus for teaching an outsider The Ways," Toris spat. "I shoulda turned him in long before he began bringing you and that other brat with him."

"If you'd done that, you'd be swinging from a rope," Strider reminded him, eyes narrowing.

"At least there wouldn't be a yulie mutt tainting our Ways with his filth."

That earned a growl from Strider, who advanced on the man, saber drawn. "Maybe I should add your blood to the filth, then."

Toris backpedaled, eyes wide with fear. His back hit the stone wall as he tried to distance himself from Strider, who quickly closed the gap.

"Stop!" Addy shouted in horror.

To her surprise, Strider stopped his sword a hair's breadth from

Toris's throat. He fixed a golden eye on her as she looked at him. She looked like a ghost, standing in the pale blue light of the crystals. Her brown eyes were wide as she stared at him.

"Yulie?" she said in disbelief. "I thought you were an anumie!"

Toris chuckled, the sound like gravel in his throat. "The kid here's a bloody half-breed." The cold blade pressed against his throat. He raised his hands in surrender as he protested. "It ain't my fault you didn't tell her."

"It isn't your place, either." Strider's voice held a dangerous edge.

"Is he telling the truth?" Addy asked, eyes narrowing.

Strider kept the blade to Toris' throat, his gaze fixed on the shorter man. He nodded slowly.

"But that doesn't make sense, yulie don't have golden eyes."

"It depends on the bloodline from what I hear," Toris commented, before biting back a curse as the sword drew blood.

"Shut up." Strider's tone was eerily calm, as devoid of emotion as the tunnels were devoid of sound.

Addy had fallen silent, her eyes moving back and forth as she processed the new information. All this time, she'd assumed Strider to be anumie. Never once had she thought he'd be part yulie. Her tutor had taught her about the enemy of ummanie. All ummanie were taught to despise and fear yulie ever since they were dumped in this world by a Chaos portal. All the legends and stories her parents, tutor, and brothers told depicted them as heartless demons who tricked, killed, and tormented the ummanie for sport.

They were her people's cruel slavers, who they had fought desperately against to earn their freedom. She'd cheered on the heroes who fought against them and jeered when the yulie appeared in the old tales. Though she'd never faced the fear and persecution of her ancestors, fear and revulsion, bred by such stories and bias, rose up within her now.

She felt dirty for being near him and wanted to slap him for daring to even be in her presence after all his kind had done. Addy sensed someone watching her intently. She glanced up to meet Strider's steady gaze. Those golden eyes glinted in the dim light, glowing in the darkness like the eyes belonging to the demons of those stories. He said nothing as he watched her. She'd never thought about the yulie as individual people. They were a collective group that'd committed great crimes against her ancestors. She'd never knowingly met a yulie, until now.

Greer brushed against her, drawing her gaze. He looked up at her, head cocked in his usual goofy fashion. His soft brown eyes bored into her. They seemed to hold an understanding and hurt as they pleaded with her. But that was impossible. He was only a wolf.

Seeing Greer, the kind and gentle creature who remained close to her throughout this adventure, made her pause. The sweet creature Strider had rescued and raised. How had a man so cold and distant, one with the blood of monsters, not have corrupted the half-di'horvith? She'd seen dogs made vicious by the cruel treatment of their masters. She'd seen how they would flinch when they approached.

Yet Greer showed nothing but complete trust and love toward Strider. He was light, raised by a creature of the dark. Wasn't Greer considered a monster as well? Her bedtime stories also held tales of evil, light-furred wolves who devoured whole towns. Beasts of wicked cunning that were slain by only the bravest and strongest heroes. Yet she'd never feared him.

Look what I have done. She reflected on Strider's words, on what he'd done. Not just the times he'd left her or killed people. But the times he'd stayed with her, had bound her feet, had slowed to let her practice imitating him. The night he'd gone through the trouble to pitch a tent he would never sleep in and instead spent a miserable night in the rain.

Her fingers found the brush he'd given her secured to her belt. Strider was rough and uncivilized, but he'd been helping her this entire time, not simply by bringing her home. He didn't need to buy her shoes, clothes, or teach her how to survive to do that. He didn't even need to come back for her when she'd run away from him and tried to take Greer with her.

But he had come back. Knowing that her father would never agree to owe someone like him a favor, knowing that he'd likely be cast out without a reward or killed. He was still watching her, and Addy got the impression that he was waiting to see how she reacted. The tahrvin had fallen silent as well, obviously unwilling to see how much further Strider would slice into his neck. He was watching her as well.

Finally, Addy shrugged.

"It really makes no difference if you're anumie or part yulie. I know you'll get me home either way." She believed her own words, feeling that familiar surety that had prompted her to hire him. He would get her home. Though him being part yulie would make things more difficult when she tried to smooth things over with her father.

Strider's head tilted to the side before he finally stepped away from Toris.

The tahrvin let out a long breath, wincing as his fingers brushed the cut the blade had left. "You really shouldn't treat me so badly."

"You really should've kept your mouth shut," Strider replied.

Toris rolled his eyes. "So ye don't want me to tell ya the change in patrols or whether they've had me install any new traps?"

Strider frowned at him, that murderous glint returning to his eye.

Toris held up his hands again in a placating gesture. "Alright, alright. Calm down!"

Addy looked from Strider to Toris.

"How would you know what patrols are coming through?" she asked.

"I'm the Keeper of this here section of The Ways," Toris said, with pride. "Nothing comes through without my approval, nor are any changes made to the traps or structure without me oversee'n it."

"That's a fancy way of saying that he's in charge of one of the least traveled tunnels in this part of the mountain," Strider said, his tone flat. "They're almost completely abandoned, save for the standard patrols."

Toris gave him a baleful look.

"A Way is a Way, no matter how deserted. It is an honor to be a Keeper of The Ways. Though I'm cursed to have to let people like you walk them." His last words were venomous, though Strider didn't seem bothered.

"The patrols and traps," the Hunter reminded him.

"Don't get your whiskers in a twist!" snapped Toris. "There ain't another patrol due down here for another week. Their route won't intersect yours at all, and I've added no new traps. Though I shoulda." He muttered the last bit under his breath, earning a sharp look from the Hunter.

"Thank you," Strider said curtly, though he sounded more like he was trying to cut the man with words than showing any gratitude.

"If you do end up being stupid enough to get caught."

"I'll be sure to tell them all about you and your little secret," Strider finished, as he left the tahrvin and began picking his way down the tunnel Toris had come from.

Addy shuffled after him, offering a bob of her head and shoulders toward Toris as she passed.

"Thank you!" Her tone was far brighter and more genuine than Strider's.

Toris gave her a startled look, not expecting the pretty girl to thank him or flash him such a bright smile. He touched two fingers to the rim of his woolen hat and tipped his head toward her.

"Be careful around that one, miss," Toris warned, jabbing a thumb in Strider's direction. "He's nastier than a dragon with a toothache and as wicked as a viper." He muttered what sounded like a stream of curses under his breath, toward this Minkus character for bringing such ilk into his Ways, as he walked off.

Chapter 22
Yulie

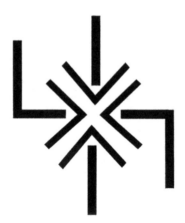

Addy could distinguish Strider's different levels of quiet. There was an edge to him now. He was angry. Her eyes dropped to the floor. She had thought he was going to kill Toris, but he stopped when she screamed. That had surprised her as much as learning what he was. Her eyes flicked back to Strider's hood before dropping to the floor again.

"Can I see?" she finally asked, her voice barely a whisper.

Addy braced for his anger to focus on her. She had no right to ask, but she had to see for herself to face it. She'd said that she trusted him to get her home. She knew he would. But it was hard to forget beliefs ingrained in her since birth. It was something she had to face before she spoke with her parents. Her mother she would be able to reason with, but her father was a very passionate man and she worried he'd let himself be carried away by his emotions.

She hoped the joy of having her home and his gratitude toward her rescuer would be enough to outweigh the anger Strider's heritage would evoke. Her mother would be the tipping point though; angry or not, her father would pay heed to his wife's words. If she thought Strider should be rewarded instead of punished, he would consider it. Addy snuck another timid glance up at his hood. Her heart skipped a beat when she found her eyes meeting one of Strider's instead. She quickly glanced away, focusing on her boots.

"Please?" she added, lifting her gaze just enough to peek out from underneath her hood.

Strider looked away when their eyes met. Letting out a heavy breath, he reached up and pulled down his hood. Even in the dim light, Addy could make out dark, medium-length brown hair; messy from being under the hood. But that wasn't what caught her eye.

The pointed ears that made yulie so different from the ummanie, whose ears were rounded at the top. The sight of those ears cemented what Toris had said, and Addy's heart pounded like a rabbit who suddenly found itself face to face with a fox. She always knew he was a deadly, cunning predator.

She swallowed hard. He wasn't just a predator, but a monster she'd been taught to loath and fear. But she didn't.

Strider let out another breath and began pulling the hood back over his head.

"No!" she held out a hand, her voice urgent.

Strider shot her a sideways glance, eyes narrowed.

In a more subdued voice, Addy continued. "Please. Don't."

Strider said nothing, but left the hood down as he resumed searching for traps. He didn't trust Toris. He didn't trust anyone, save for a certain furry monster. The Hunter kept an eye out for new additions to the tunnel's nasty surprises, and an ear out for the sound of approaching patrols. Nothing had changed from when he'd last traversed The Ways.

The magic he felt in the stone walls hummed its steady, familiar tune. The heartbeat of the Tahlrin Mountains. It became background noise for the Hunter as he listened for viable threats. There was nothing. Only the sound of muffled hoofbeats of the horses and the clicking of Greer's claws reached his ears.

Even shod in cloth, the horse's hooves were loud drumbeats in the stillness of The Ways. No matter how hard you tried, you could never make a horse completely silent. It was one reason he usually avoided using the animals. That, and he had a hard time keeping them alive. At least Addy was becoming better at walking around without making noise. Greer wasn't even trying, which was the most annoying of all.

They encountered no other soul. No life existed in The Ways. It struck Addy as strange that there wasn't any dust in a tunnel that wasn't frequented. Yet Strider didn't seem to notice, or he did and knew something she didn't. Her eyes fell on his ears again, and she looked away. The knee jerk reaction angered her.

"Toris said someone named Minkus taught you how to use The Ways," she began. "Did he also teach you to speak tahrvin?"

"He taught me many things," Strider answered curtly.

"Did he also teach you how to fight like a Ranger?"

"My father taught me that. Not that *tahrvin*." He uttered the word as if it were a vile insult.

Addy took a moment to steel herself before asking what she truly wanted to know. "Was your father a-"

"My mother," Strider cut her off.

Addy was taken aback. She had expected his father to be the yulie, not his mother. Stories of the yulie men ravaging women and burning farms near the borders had been whispered around firelight for years. She had assumed... Her ears grew warm, and she felt the anger flare inside her. Not at Strider, but herself.

The history of the yulie deceiving, then enslaving her people, after they were stolen from their world by the god of Chaos. And the Liberating War that followed was known by all. They kept the wounds open and festering for countless generations, passing from parent to child, feeding the flames of animosity.

She had also carried those wounds, cultivated by bedtime stories her father told, the history lessons of her tutor, and the games she played with her brothers where she was the ummanie princess being rescued from yulie warriors. She doubted she could trust a yulie until they proved they were different. Addy felt resentment and guilt toward herself for feeling that way, and toward the tales. But she was unable to resent the people who told them to her. Well, she already resented her tutor, but not her parents and brothers.

"How did they meet?" Addy asked, after steadying herself. "Your parents."

"My father was a Ranger set to guard my mother while she lived in the kingdom of Ullefen."

"Your mother lived among the ummanie?" She had heard stories of some of the border kingdoms letting yulie live among them, but had never believed them.

"My mother was a part of the yulie who are of the mind that ummanie and yulie could learn to live and work together. She was young and naïve."

"But your father loved her," Addy defended, feeling offended for Strider's mother. How could her own son insult her like that?

"And when he was gone, no one tried to help a sick, widowed yulie woman and her eight-year-old child. They let them starve!" His voice was as sharp as a knife dipped in poison.

Addy looked away, feeling guilty, even though she hadn't been the one to not help a widow and her child. Would she have helped? She liked to think she would have. She hoped she would. The hatred for the yulie ran as deep as a trench on the ocean floor. So deep that it clearly still tainted the hearts of the ummanie enough to let them watch a mother and child starve.

She knew her mother wouldn't hesitate. Addy didn't know a lot about the kingdom of Rachia, where her mother was from, but she knew that she could never see a child suffer without helping. She and her husband worked hard to ensure Timara's children always had somewhere safe to go.

It was common knowledge that Rangers often took in orphans, and many kingdoms were more than happy to offload the burden of caring for these children onto them. Several fiefdoms in Myvara did this. Her parents had instead built homes specifically to house these children, providing them with the opportunity to stay in Timara and learn trades when they were older, or go with the Rangers. Rumors spoke of them even using young Rangers to secretly check in on these homes to ensure they were treating the children properly.

They paid for healers from the Syliceon church or the Rangers to visit towns and help the sick. Knowing they often couldn't afford to leave their farms or pay the high prices Syliceon charged for their services. Yet people still suffered; she'd seen her parents listen to subjects asking for aid on the days they opened their doors to the people.

"Did your mother starve to death?"

"She was murdered," Strider ground out, his eyes growing dark as the memories seemed to play before his mind's eye. He looked like a wolf; snarling, ready to kill.

Addy didn't speak for a long time as she waited for that look to fade.

"How did your father train you, if he left you at the age of eight?"

Strider looked at her, and she thought she saw the corner of his eyes wrinkle. Had he smiled?

"He left to try to find a cure for my mother's illness. He never returned. We thought he was dead. It broke my mother's heart."

"He wasn't?"

"No. A lord in Umanarie threw him into a dungeon when he refused to bow to him. How that lord kept the Rangers from finding out, I'll never know. He never told me before I killed him a year after I found my father."

"How did you find your dad?" Addy questioned, eyes narrowing as she looked at him. "If you thought he was dead."

Strider shrugged. "I happened upon him while doing a job."

"A job. In a dungeon?" she said skeptically.

Strider didn't seem interested in elaborating. He offered a curt nod, giving her a look that told her not to ask any more questions.

Addy backed off. Having already learned far more about Strider than she expected. The man was usually so tight-lipped. His answers were short and didn't paint the whole picture, but he had answered. It was enough to shed a little light on the life of the man.

"So, you're half yulie," she mused, putting her hands behind her back as she led the horses. "I guess that's why you can see in the dark and wear that stuffy hood all the time."

"I don't wear the hood to hide what I am," Strider clarified. "I do it to make it harder for people to identify me should there be trouble."

"The pointed ears do stand out."

Strider gave her a look, and she couldn't help but smile.

"You pretend to be a Ranger, so people give you a wide birth," Addy pondered.

"I wear the felaris feather because it was a gift," he told her. "If they want it back, they can try to take it."

"You don't tell people you *aren't* a Ranger, though. At least not since I've been around," Addy pointed out.

"It causes less trouble that way; raises fewer questions."

Addy felt like he wasn't telling her everything, but she didn't press the matter. If she pressed too hard, he'd stop answering. She wondered if there was some sort of magic she could use that would help her better understand the Hunter. Not that she could use magic and her inability to do so vexed her. She wanted to learn the Ranger magic Strider told her about.

She wanted to be as strong as a Ranger. But she couldn't. Perhaps that was for the best. Her father would already have a heart attack when he saw what she'd become. He'd be scandalized. If anyone found out she had also learned dark magic, he'd be ruined. His name dragged through the mud. The Syliceon would kill her. No one could ever find out.

Addy smirked at the thought of her parents' expressions when they learned she could fight with the sword. "It isn't lady-like at all!" She could hear her mother saying.

"It's good that she knows," her father would reply. He'd always wanted her to learn but respected his wife's insistence on raising their daughter in the Rachian manner.

All other noblewomen in Myvara knew how to use a sword. But in Rachia they didn't. Addy didn't listen well enough to her tutor to know why; she'd never listened to her mother either when they fought. Her mother would probably faint when she saw her daughter dressed like a boy wielding a sword. Served her right. If they had taught her to fight, then maybe she wouldn't be here?

At least Strider took the time to show her some useful skills. The only thing that had proven useful from her tutor's training was needlepoint. Addy continued to watch Strider closely, finding that if she copied him, she could learn even more. She could never match his level of grace and athleticism, but she could become better than most ummanie.

Strider had fallen quiet again, the silent rage that coursed through him dissipating. He could feel the mountain above him as they traveled, a constant reminder of how deep underground they were. It hung over his shoulder like a ghost, never letting him feel at ease within The Ways.

As they walked, Addy noticed something strange. It was the same feeling that had touched her soul and sent shivers down her spine. One she had felt only once before, like a drumbeat that thumped low, vibrating the earth, shaking her core. It started slow and quiet. She wasn't aware of it until it grew louder.

She had felt this throbbing beat before in the Well back in Altia. The sensation of the rhythmic heartbeat grew louder, causing her own heart to pound in time to it. Her eyes widened as they stepped out of the tunnel into a vast cavern. Here, the world practically shook with the booming beat of magic.

The cavern was massive! Not even Strider could see the top swallowed by inky black shadows. Ancient etchings and symbols lined the walls, all glowing a soft blue. These carvings covered the walls at the equivalent height of at least four stories. Also carved into the floor, the writing was set in a swirling circular pattern that matched the shape of the room.

A soft blue glow, cast by the symbols, hung in the air like a light mist. Addy could feel the magic beating within her, vibrating in her chest, shaking her bones. Greer stood beside her, face-up, eyes closed. He held a look of pure bliss, as if he were basking in warm sunlight.

"I can feel it," Addy squeaked, her throat tight. "I can feel the magic!"

Strider didn't look back, but his voice drifted toward her. "Then connect with it."

Addy concentrated on what Strider had taught her. She had no trouble finding the magic as it pulsed in the center of her being. She stopped walking as she focused. Eyes closed, she mentally reached out toward the well of magic. It reached back as if all it needed was for her to invite it.

She felt a tug on her soul as her and the magic connected. It was not a huge channel that she'd opened, but it would grow with practice. The small amount of magic that filled her was wonderful! Her body flooded with warmth and exhilaration. She felt alive as the power surged through her, finding a home within her.

"I did it!" she exclaimed, her eyes snapping open to look at Strider in excitement.

But he wasn't looking at her. His hood was up as he stood in front of her, bow drawn and pointed beyond her line of sight.

"Yes, you did." A soft, singsong voice carried through the cavern.

Addy's heart jumped, and she looked around Strider to see who the beautiful voice belonged to. On the other side of the cavern stood a small company of tahrvin soldiers, their own bows drawn, with arrows aimed at the Hunter and his wolf.

Chapter 23
A Deal In The Dark

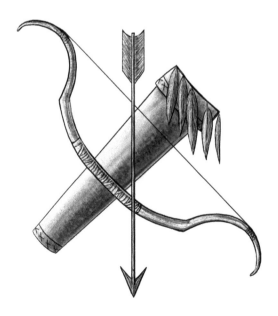

There were at least six soldiers. All of them had their arrows aimed at Strider and Greer. Strider's cold eyes focused on his target, the woman who'd spoken. She sat on a cushioned chair, secured to a wheeled platform, pulled by two small horses. Her shimmering white dress flowed around her and pooled at her feet.

Like many tahrvin who lived underground, her skin was ivory. Her light hair held a silken sheen to it, and Addy couldn't tell if it was gold or silver. She had been the one to speak, her voice a light purr as she looked at them. Or toward them. Her eyes were milky white and unseeing.

"How did you get in here?" one guard, dressed in full plate armor, barked. "Who taught you The Ways and gave you a keystone?"

"He's long dead," Strider responded gruffly. His voice took on a harsher tone as he ordered, "tell your men to get out of the shadows, or the woman dies."

The tahrvin man looked surprised, before he frowned and snarled an order in his native tongue. Six more soldiers slunk out of the shadows, their attempts to flank the intruders thwarted.

"How dare you threaten Lady Tourmaline, High Priestess of Zircion!"

"It wasn't a threat," Strider growled.

Lady Tourmaline raised a hand, waving it up and down gently as she spoke, her quiet voice carrying with unnatural ease. "Lower your weapons, Captain Marvern. No blood need be spilled tonight."

"My lady!" the knight protested.

Her white eyes shifted to stare at Marvern, her face expressionless, and his argument died in his throat. Her gaze returned to Strider, who found it hard to meet her eyes. Not because he'd never seen a blind person before. But because he had a sense beyond words that she could see far more than she should. He lowered his bow when the soldiers did the same, keeping the arrow knocked.

Once the priestess was certain people were no longer aiming pointed sticks at each other, she smiled and offered a soft thank you. She held an unearthly beauty, and an air of quiet authority hung about her like a veil.

"Now tell me, man touched by many worlds," she began, addressing Strider. "Why did you risk losing your passage through the mountain for the girl you are protecting?"

Strider felt Addy start at the mention of her. She'd fallen silent, transfixed by the beautiful tahrvin woman. Strider narrowed his eyes as he looked at the high priestess. The sense that something wasn't quite right with the woman only grew. She cocked her head as if waiting for his answer. He said nothing.

"A soul, drowned in blood," she spoke again. "Guarding a soul who bears purity despite her hardships." Her gaze shifted in Greer's direction. "Tell me, Marvern. What color is the dire wolf's pelt?"

No one had told her of Greer's presence. Unlike Addy, he made no sound to tell the blind woman he was there. Strider watched her more closely, wary of the connection she had with the surrounding magic.

"Light gray, my lady," Marven answered curtly, his gaze still locked on Strider.

The priestess smiled as if someone had told her a funny joke. "A rare creature indeed. Even rarer considering the soul of light, raised by a soul so tainted." she mused, more to herself than anyone else, though Strider still heard it.

"As entertaining as this is," he cut in. "We need you to move or die. I'm not picky."

The soldiers moved before their high priestess, but the raised platform exposed her completely. She would be the first to die should they make any move toward him.

"No blood need be shed," Lady Tourmaline reinforced.

"So, you plan to move. Good." Strider met her gaze and looked away. Hating that he found it impossible to meet those eyes.

"Leave now and lose The Ways," Tourmaline countered, her

voice echoing off of the stone. "We cannot change the keystone ingrained into the magic of these tunnels. But we can seal them, blocking the passage that your key opens."

Strider was about to speak, but she cut him off.

"Kill us, and our bodies will be found. The Ways will be sealed, and the ummanie kingdoms blamed. The tahrvin will declare war on the kingdoms that border it, and needless blood will be spilled."

Addy looked up sharply at Strider, a small gasp escaping her lips. Her father's lands were on the border of the tahrvin empire. His men manned the fortress at Bayvar Pass. If the tahrvin attacked, her father and brothers would be pulled into the war and possibly killed. She balled her fists and pressed them against her lips in horror. She knew Strider hated to leave witnesses. He would kill them and put her father and brothers in danger.

"Or," the priestess proposed, "I can let you pass with my blessing. You'd be permitted to travel these Ways as you please."

"And the catch?" Strider questioned flatly.

The woman smiled. "You would owe me one favor. A debt I can call on at any time."

Strider scoffed, his golden eyes becoming murderous. "I do not owe people favors."

"I wouldn't ask anything beyond your capabilities or moral limits."

It was Addy's turn to scoff. "That could be anything from having tea to murdering a king!" she thought for a moment, then amended her statement, "No, he wouldn't sit down to have tea; more like coffee."

The priestess nodded. "A favor, to prevent a war. Fulfill it and I will also open more Ways to you. You would always have a secure way to enter any kingdom bordering our realm."

Strider still eyed her harshly.

Addy fixed him with a pleading look. She didn't want her people drawn into a war she caused. She didn't want her brothers and father being called to fight, while she waited at home to hear word of their death.

Strider cocked his head to one side. There was more to this deal than met the eye. There was something behind Tourmaline's desire to negotiate. It went beyond simply avoiding bloodshed, but he didn't know what she stood to gain. As it stood, he'd be receiving the better end of the deal. He didn't trust it.

Greer let out a low woof, wagging his tail as he looked up at Strider as happy as ever. The tahrvin hadn't threatened him, nor was he bothered by the priestess's intentions. Strider glanced at him and thought for a moment. Finally, he gave a small nod, his rough voice spilling out of the darkness of his hood.

"You have a deal."

The knight turned to face his priestess, outrage darkening his features. "My lady!"

She raised her hand, cutting him off.

"Trust me, Marvern." She fixed him with an unseeing stare that stopped any further protest.

The man lowered his gaze respectfully, though his face remained red. He gave a harsh, jerking gesture, signaling to his men. The company moved away from the entrance to the tunnel behind them.

"Continue to protect her well, Hunter," Tourmaline purred in parting.

Strider didn't move until the woman and her escort vanished deep into The Ways.

As they crossed the cavern into the tunnel, Addy uttered in a low voice. "Thank you."

Strider glanced at her briefly before turning back to the tunnel ahead. Silence fell between them as they resumed their travel through The Ways.

Chapter 24
A Promise Between Brothers

Addy lost track of how many days they'd been traveling through The Ways. She didn't know how Strider knew where to go. The walls were all the same. She saw no distinguishing marks or anything that indicated where they were going. But he moved down each passage with confidence. After leaving the priestess behind, they had stopped at what Strider called a waypoint. A large room cut into the mountain filled with water, hay, and food. All apparently stocked and maintained by Toris.

There were waypoints set throughout The Ways for tahrvin traveling within the tunnels to ensure no one died of starvation or lack of water while traveling. They took advantage of the stores to bolster their own supplies of food. They'd rested in four other waypoints since entering The Ways, breaking up the monotonous routine of travel.

The lack of variance and the ability to tell time grated on Addy. At least while traveling outside, she had things to look at. Here it was all the same. The same walls, the same tunnels, the same silent darkness. Nothing changed. Even the waypoints looked the same to her, as everything blurred together in a never-ending stream of stone and darkness. She needed to get out!

"How much further?" she asked for the thousandth time.

"A ways," Strider remarked curtly.

Greer gave an amused snort, the only one to catch what Strider said.

Addy sighed as she followed, always careful to stay in the center of the path, as Strider had instructed.

"Are we close?"

She heard him swear under his breath.

"Only ten snatches closer than the last time you asked," he rumbled. "If you keep asking me, I'll leave you at the next waypoint and let you find your own way out."

"Well, excuse me for asking!" she snapped back. "I'm not able to tell time in here like you can!"

"Asking is fine but doing it repeatedly over a short time is extremely irritating."

"It's not like I have anything else to do! You're as talkative as these Chaos ridden tunnels!" she'd sped up as she spoke, pulling the horses behind her. "Greer has been a better conversationalist, and he's a wolf!"

"Then do me a favor and ask him the time from now on!"

They turned to enter another boring waypoint when something dark rippled through the tunnels, like a foul wind. They stopped. The magic shifted; its melody overpowered by the malicious intent surging through it with a song of bloodlust. Su'lris nervously danced in place, and Addy turned to face him. As she did, Strider's horse spooked. He reared, letting out a scream of terror.

"Addy!" Strider shouted a warning, as he lunged for the horse's reins.

The animal's hooves slammed into the ground, his shoulder ramming into Addy, knocking her off the safe path. She couldn't correct herself as she fell. She heard Strider shout her name as he reached for her. But it was too late. He couldn't reach her in time.

Strider reached for his magic, but a gray flash appeared behind Addy, throwing its weight against her. She fell forward, back onto the safe path as Greer's body landed at the tunnel's side. Strider couldn't stop what happened. He felt the magic ripple through The Ways as a click reverberated through the stone, and a fraction of a beat later, several spikes shot out of the floor, impaling the di'horvith. Greer's scream of pain echoed sharply off the cold stone.

"Greer!" Strider moved faster than Addy had ever seen as he rushed toward his friend.

With a groan, the spikes retracted, and Greer's body dropped to the floor. Strider grabbed him, dragging him free of the danger. The di'horvith whined pitifully as blood stained the stone floor.

"No, no, no," Strider pleaded under his breath, as he placed both hands on the wolf's reddening fur.

"Greer," Addy choked out, tears spilling down her cheeks as she held onto both horses, watching helplessly.

Strider's hands glowed with magic as he poured everything he had into his brother. He could feel the extent of the damage. The internal bleeding, punctured organs. His life was draining from him.

"No," Strider rasped through gritted death. "You are not leaving me, Greer. You promised me!"

He sent his magic coursing through his friend, aiming at every wound, attacking the injuries with everything he had. The bleeding didn't stop, and Strider forced more magic to come. He fought within himself, tearing and grasping at the channel as he used every ounce of magic within himself to heal Greer.

The tightness in his chest grew as he strained his magical channel. He bled himself dry and still kept grasping for that well of magic within himself. He felt his soul tearing under the stress. It bled into the magic, feeding into Greer to heal him.

Greer's whine changed to growls of warning, but Strider ignored them as he continued to search for more magic. The tightness in his chest became a dull ache, then a burning pain. His fracturing soul felt like he was ripping pieces of his heart out to give to Greer. But he pressed on, desperate to save his brother.

Greer let out a loud snarl that boomed off the walls, but Strider didn't stop. Greer whipped his head around, his jaw clamping down on Strider's left arm. Fangs sank deep into his flesh as Greer pulled Strider's hand off him. Strider barely flinched, numb to the pain as he glared at Greer. He didn't remove his other hand as he channeled his magic and soul into healing the di'horvith.

"You promised me!" he repeated, as they glared at each other.

Strider could hardly see. White blotches blocked his fading vision. His head and chest were pounding with bolts of pain as his soul and body screamed for him to stop. He didn't. He could feel Greer's wounds sealing, the damage being repaired. But it wasn't enough. He dug deeper, as he did so, he felt another power channel through him

It was not his magic, or his soul, but his mind was too hazy to figure out its source. Like a drowning man, he latched onto that power, adding it to his own before feeding it into Greer. Organs healed, the internal damage repaired, as the magic began knitting the rest of the wounds together.

Greer continued to snarl and whine, trying to get Strider to stop. But he kept pushing. Greer, finding strength in his own desperation, gave a hard kick with his back legs. His paws struck Strider square in the chest, knocking him away. The Hunter fell back into the waypoint they'd been aiming for, ending the flow of magic that he'd been forcing through his body. But it was too late. The damage had been done.

"Greer! Strider!" Addy shouted in shock, as she brought both horses inside. She fumbled with the reins, clumsily tying the knots around iron rings secured to the wall in her rush to return to them. "Stop it!"

Strider barely propped himself up on his elbow as Greer snarled and yowled at him as if he were lecturing him.

"I don't care what you have to say about it!" Strider shot back. "You promised I would die first! Not you, me!"

"ARR WAAAAHOOOO ROOOO!" Greer howled back.

"I AM SUPPOSED TO DIE FIRST!" Strider bellowed, spending every ounce of strength he had left.

Addy froze. She'd never heard Strider shout before. It terrified her.

Strider panted, the pain worsening. He clutched at his chest as he continued to gasp heavily.

"I'm supposed to die first," he said in a harsh whisper. "You promised me; I go first."

Greer's own tone softened as he continued to whine and yowl at Strider. He crawled toward the Hunter. When he reached him,

Strider wrapped his arms around Greer, drawing him close. His body shook from shock and fear.

"I die first," the Hunter said again, his voice cracking as his arms tightened around the wolf, terrified of losing him. He repeated the words over and over as he buried his face in his brother's fur, his shoulders shaking in quiet sobs. He couldn't lose him; he couldn't handle that, not again.

Icy stabs of pain replaced the burning in his chest, tearing through him like vicious knives. They ripped at his soul like starved beasts, and Strider found himself unable to breathe as he clung to Greer. His strength failed him. He sank to the floor, his fingers weakly grasping at Greer's thick fur, his vision darkening. Strider realized he was dying, but he was so cold and numb, he hardly cared. Greer was safe. He was alive. That was all that mattered.

Greer lay atop him, making low, rumbling, and chuffing noises as he tried to comfort his brother, who'd soaked his fur with his tears. His tone grew more urgent as he felt Strider slipping away. An arm came back up to wrap around his neck and he heard Strider mutter softly in his ear.

"I told you," Strider said. His weak voice was tainted with cheeky pride, as if he'd outsmarted the di'horvith. "I die first."

Chapter 25
The Price Of Magic

Addy stood to the side as she watched Strider and Greer in horror. She'd cried out when Greer had bitten Strider, but neither heard her. They ignored her as they both yelled at each other. She couldn't do anything to help as she watched Strider desperately pour everything he had into healing Greer.

Never had she seen the Hunter's face filled with an expression of such fear and anguish. She'd never heard him shout before, never heard such pain as his voice broke. All she could do was stand there, useless. The spell that held her broke the moment Strider slumped to the floor with Greer on top of him.

"Strider!" she said, tears streaming down her face as she knelt beside them.

She shook his shoulder, trying to get him to respond as she called his name again. But he didn't stir. Greer let out a long, pained whine as he pressed himself harder into Strider. Addy watched Greer, still as helpless and useless as before. She didn't know what to do. Strider wasn't breathing.

"Strider!" she yelled again, shaking him. "Strider-" Her voice shrank as she choked out. "Come back."

Greer let out a low groan, his head lowering to rest in the crook of Strider's neck. Addy looked at him pitifully, her vision blurred with tears. She couldn't find her voice to tell him that Strider was gone.

Greer continued to lay there, whining and chuffing. She watched him, trying to find the strength to tell him. As she did so, she thought she saw the underpart of his coat shimmer blue as the rest of his pelt seemed to shift color the same way the felaris feather did. She blinked, but it didn't help to clear her vision.

Greer continued to whimper softly, and Addy buried her face in her hands. Her heart broke even more for Greer. How was she supposed to tell him? Sobbing harder, she reached down and hugged both him and Strider, her tears dampening the Hunter's shirt as her heart ached with loss. A weak breath brushed across her ear. She choked back a gasp as she pulled away.

"Strider?" She placed her ear to his chest, her head poking into Greer's side. Greer had grown silent as he lay on top of Strider. She listened, and her own heart leaped when she heard the weak beat of Strider's heart. She sat up and looked at Greer.

"He's alive!" she shouted.

Greer grunted and gave a single, tired thump of his tail as he lay limp atop his brother.

He was drowning in frigid darkness. No matter how hard he kicked and thrashed, he found himself unable to reach the surface. His chest burned in pain, and a writhing monster inside his skull was trying to split it open. Chains grabbed at his limbs, trying to pull him under. Their touch froze his skin. Still, he fought to reach the surface, fought to get back. With each passing beat, the pain grew worse as the cold sapped the strength from his bones.

He clawed weakly, losing his will to fight against the dark cold and the dragging chains. He was so cold, colder than anything he could remember experiencing in life. It hurt, like thousands of tiny blades stabbing through him, as his blood began to freeze, sending great waves of agony through him, clutching at his heart with every struggle. Slowly, he found his vision fading as he lost sight of the surface- of Greer. His will faded, until he finally stopped fighting and let the chains drag him down further.

A single thread shot through the oppressive void. It wrapped firmly around Strider's wrist, jerking him to a stop as it pulled against the force of the frozen chains. Its touch sent a shock of warmth racing through his body as it strained against the force dragging him down.

"Strider!" A voice echoed in the darkness. He didn't recognize it but knew it was crying for him.

Another voice drifted down to him as it whined and chuffed in a rumbling manner. He faintly remembered that this was Greer, crying for him. Strider slowly opened his eyes as he looked at the single thread that kept him bound to the world of the living. It vibrated with the strain, fighting to keep him from being dragged deeper into the cold abyss.

He considered cutting the string and letting himself sink. Living was painful. Letting the cold claim him and be done with it would be easier. Greer and the other voice continued to cry, begging him to return. But did he really want to? As the warmth of the string spread through him, he remembered. He had made a promise. To whom he couldn't remember. But he'd promised them something important. To get them home, he thought. Was this the voice crying for him?

It was. His foggy mind remembered. This was the person whom he'd made a promise to, and he'd yet to fulfill it. Greer let out another low rumble. It vibrated through the thread and into his soul. Strider could feel the di'horvith's pain and fear. He didn't want to lose him. He couldn't lose him, not yet. Greer's pain was more than he could bear. Strider looked up toward the surface, and with the strength he had left, he took hold of the thread.

"He's alive!" that same voice cried. They sounded distant and garbled, like they were talking underwater. He was vaguely aware of weight on him as the thing let out a warped grunt. He heard the voice saying other things but couldn't make them out as he faded into unconsciousness.

The sound of a crackling fire slowly drew Strider into the waking world. He opened his eyes, his head pounding. It was hard to breathe, and he took a deep gasp of breath as a weight pressed down on his chest. The weight stirred, and Strider realized Greer was on top of him.

He let out the breath he'd taken with a heavy sigh. He couldn't move, not because of the di'horvith on top of him, but because he had no strength. A face appeared in his field of vision, and he found Addy smiling down at him, her puffy red eyes glistening with barely suppressed tears.

"You're awake," she choked out, placing a damp cloth on his forehead and picking up the old one that had fallen off when he had stirred. "You stopped breathing. I thought you had- I was so worried."

"How long-?" he asked, too tired to complete his question. Which was probably good, as he slurred his words together like a drunken sailor.

Addy shook her head. "I can't tell time in here, remember?" She bit her cheek and looked at the fire. "A long time, though; I went through half the woodpile. Neither you or Greer have woken up since he got hurt."

Strider grunted, his eyes closing as he let out another breath. He could hear Greer breathing steadily in his ear. He could feel his heart beating next to him, providing comfort.

The woodpiles in most waypoints could last a week. If she'd used up half the pile, that meant he'd been out almost four days. Addy disappeared and returned with a waterskin. She helped to prop him up on her lap. Greer didn't stir as Strider struggled to help Addy. His body could hardly find the strength. Breathing was a challenge, made harder by the heavy animal lying on him. But he didn't ask Addy to shove him off. He didn't want to be that far from Greer.

Addy uncorked the water skin and helped him drink. It was fresh from the spring that bubbled into a small dais. It helped to ease the scratch in his dry throat.

"Do you think you can eat?" she asked him. "I can make you some soup."

Strider knew he needed to eat; his body needed the strength. But the thought made him ill. He thought he told her that before falling unconscious again, but he didn't know.

Addy left Strider to sleep. Her hands shook as she refilled the waterskin at the basin. She didn't know what to do, stuck in these tunnels with no hope of navigating them. Her eyes lingered on the horses. Even if she could, she didn't have the strength to lift Strider up into the saddle. Addy hugged the waterskin close to her chest, curling in on herself as she sucked in short, strangled breaths, trying to suppress her sobs.

Wiping her eyes, she took a deep breath, steadying herself. She couldn't cry, couldn't let fear freeze her. Strider and Greer were relying on her. Her body still shaking, she returned to Strider's side, sitting in silence as she changed out the wet cloth on his head for another one.

When Strider woke up again, another day had passed, according to the woodpile.

Addy came over with a bowl of something. "I know you're tired," she said. "But you need to eat something."

He gave the bowl a dubious look. "You...cook?" It took a lot to speak, and his words bled together.

Addy frowned. "You're one to talk. Can you eat or not?"

He bolstered enough strength to eat a bit of the soup Addy prepared for him, noting that it had a little more flavor than what he usually made.

Greer also woke up and devoured the bowl offered to him with far more energy than Strider had in his entire body. Greer had slid off Strider to eat, but he still stayed next to him underneath the warmth of the blanket. He lapped steadily at the soup, his tongue making loud slapping noises that seemed louder in the silence of The Ways.

"What happened?" Addy asked, as she stroked Greer's head. "I thought I'd lost you." The idea brought a tightness to Addy's throat. She hadn't realized how attached she'd gotten to him until now. When she'd first met Strider, she'd wanted nothing more than to get away from him. Now the thought of losing him had her choking back tears.

Strider closed his eyes again, gathering his thoughts and energy. It was a long time before he opened them to reply. "I used more magic... than my soul was... capable... channeling..." He breathed out, stopping to catch his breath every few words as they slurred together. Even with Greer no longer laying on him, breathing was hard. The energy required to speak drained him quickly, and he found himself on the edge of unconsciousness once more. He closed his eyes and his head lolled to one side.

"Channel too much... Your soul tears itself... apart... to feed... power..." The darkness claimed him again.

Addy resorted to only building a fire when she needed to cook food for Strider in order to stretch out the rest of their supply. She considered going to find another waypoint but decided against it; she didn't want to risk getting lost or triggering another trap. She continued to retrieve cold water from the small spring that fed into a raised bowl before falling into a trough for the horses. Using a bowl she found in the stash of supplies left in the waypoint, she filled it with water and dipped pieces of cloth into it before placing them on Strider's forehead.

He'd been burning up the entire time, and his body was drenched in sweat. He rested fitfully, muttering words she couldn't make out before waking up, sometimes in a panic that he didn't have the strength for, that only subsided once he confirmed Greer was still with him, before falling back asleep. Greer stayed beside him, faring far better than Strider, though he also mostly slept.

She busied herself as best she could tending to the horses and any gear she could repair with a needle and thread she found. There had been no sign of the dark presence that had spooked the horses since. But Addy kept a wary eye on the entrance to the waypoint, still terrified that something might appear there. But nothing ever did.

When Strider woke, she would make sure he got water and as much food as he could handle before he fell back unconscious, leaving her alone. Eventually, Greer woke up, but he did little more than watch her go about her busy work as Strider used him for a pillow.

The Hunter rested easier knowing Greer was close by, waking up in a panic whenever the wolf left him. Eventually, Strider found the strength to sit up as Addy helped him eat a bowl of stew. Two days later, he could stand again, though unsteadily, as his body slowly bounced back from the shock it had endured.

Greer shadowed his every step as the Hunter walked around the room, using the walls as support. They no longer had wood for a fire and the hay was running out. They would need to go. Strider barely pulled himself up into Sul'ris' saddle, his muscles shaking with the strain. Addy had insisted he ride Sul'ris rather than his jumpier mount.

Greer and Addy eyed him worriedly, but he said nothing as he waited for her to pack the few things she still had before sending Sul'ris out into the tunnels at a slow walk. Despite wavering in the saddle like a drunk, Strider led them through The Ways.

"What about traps?" Addy asked. He'd insisted on walking the entire way to avoid missing any.

"If we hit them, hope we die quickly," Strider grunted. "Just stay in the center of the path."

"Strider... I'm sorry."

"For what?"

Addy bit her lip, holding back tears. "If it weren't for me, Greer wouldn't have gotten hurt, and you wouldn't have had to heal him."

"Did you spook the horses?"

"No, but-"

"Then it wasn't your fault."

Addy didn't agree, but she didn't argue further. She knew Strider didn't have the strength for it.

They eventually stopped at another waypoint, where Strider slid out of the saddle and slumped to the ground with an annoyed grunt. Addy had to help him to a pile of hay she arranged as a bed before caring for the horses. Greer flopped down next to him, and the Hunter soon fell asleep, unable to stay conscious any longer. By the time they bled this waypoint of its supplies, Strider's strength had returned, and he could walk under his own power as he led them back into The Ways.

Chapter 26

Addy Isn't Any Better At Naming Things

The sun was approaching its zenith when Addy and Strider emerged from The Ways. Addy stretched her arms over her head, letting out a deep breath. She savored the sun's warmth against her skin, grateful to be out of the dark tunnels.

"Finally free!" she exclaimed. "How long has it been?"

With no way to tell the passage of time, Addy had lost track of how long they'd been underground.

Strider tilted his head to one side, considering the question as he took his horse's reins.

"Almost three weeks," he answered.

Addy's jaw dropped. "Three weeks?"

He nodded as he swung into the saddle. "Let's go."

Addy mounted Su'lris and sent him clopping after Strider's horse. They'd emerged onto a small grassy plain surrounded by trees. She didn't know where she was within Myvara. But she knew she was back in her own kingdom. She was closer to home than she ever thought she'd be. The thought caused her eyes to water, but she didn't cry. She'd save the tears for when she was actually home.

"I want to stay in an inn in the next town," Addy piped up.

Strider shook his head.

"I want a bath, and after sleeping on the stone for weeks, I want to sleep in a bed," she argued. "It's not like anyone is after us anymore. No one knows we are here. No one will be looking for me."

He shook his head again. Addy puffed out her cheeks, letting out an angry breath.

"A good night's sleep would do both of us some good."

Strider stopped shaking his head, but he still didn't reply.

Addy looked to the sky again, beseeching the gods to grant her strength when dealing with the infuriating man. She wondered what part of Myvara they were in and if they were near a town she knew. The tunnels had not been a direct shot, and she had long since lost her sense of direction.

Like in The Ways, Strider seemed to know where he was going.

Addy Isn't Any Better At Naming Things

They rode a short distance before he brought his horse to a stop near a tightly packed cluster of trees and bushes.

"Change in there," he told her, nodding toward the trees as he dismounted.

No longer in the tunnels, the warm clothing was stifling, even in the forest's shade. The land was beginning to cool, as summer moved toward autumn, causing the days to remain hot as the nights became pleasant. Addy slid off Sul'ris, rummaging through her saddlebags as she pulled out her clothes and ran toward the trees.

Strider slipped into a fresher set of clothes. As he changed, his eyes fell to his side. The cut was nothing more than an angry scar, another reminder of what he'd lost.

His soul shivered, causing his body to react in kind. He couldn't shake the weariness that clung to his bones. While his body had recovered from overusing his magic, his soul hadn't. Only time could heal that wound. Until then, he'd never escape the chill that settled inside him or the tiredness that hounded him. He'd push through it, like he always did. Slipping on his shirt, he reached for his cloak, which hung on the saddle next to his weapons. He'd just swung his cloak around his shoulders when Addy emerged.

She approached the horse while he fastened the cloak, straightening it on his shoulders before putting on his quiver. She reached up and lifted his recurve bow from where it hung on the saddle horn. He eyed her but didn't move to stop her.

Her head cocked as she looked at the weapon. It didn't look unique or interesting. Clearly made of fine craft. Its ash gray color was the only distinguishable note about the bow. Its elegance was in its design rather than in adornments. Only the felaris feather, which Strider had returned to normal, set it apart. It was not nearly as tall as a longbow, though it was still too big for her. Attached near the bowstring's top and bottom were strange puffballs of fur.

She didn't know the purpose of the funny looking balls. They couldn't be decorations. Strider wasn't the type. Maybe it was another Ranger thing? She'd done archery with low-powered bows and understood the fundamentals. She gripped the bow in her left hand and tried to draw back on the string. It didn't budge. Determined, she pulled with all her strength. The string still didn't move.

Strider watched as she struggled with the bow before finally giving up with a heavy breath.

"How do you pull this back so quickly? It weighs a ton."

"Practice," he answered.

"I can't imagine how strong you'd need to be to pull back a warbow. My brothers say they are the hardest to draw."

"Maybe compared to a normal recurve bow," Strider agreed, as he buckled on his longsword. "That bow has the highest poundage found in a warbow, despite its size. The arrows are special as well. They travel with little resistance, keeping the force they hit with, while maintaining the speed this type of bow allows."

Addy looked at the bow with new admiration. "Is that why it also doesn't get wet in the rain?"

Strider nodded, as he straightened his longsword and then grabbed his yulie saber. He worked on fastening its buckle.

"The Ravack taught the Rangers their art of crafting with wood and magic. The bow has significant power, can be used in the rain, and doesn't need to be unstrung to preserve it. Among other things."

He folded his winter clothes up tightly before stuffing them in a saddlebag. Addy had thrown her own clothes onto the saddle, where they draped limply.

"Were you given the bow too?" Addy asked, handing the bow back when Strider motioned for it. He pointed at the mess of clothes on the saddle. Addy frowned, snatching at the items.

"I made it," he grunted, swinging into the saddle with the grace of a cat.

She paused in the middle of stuffing her clothes into the pack to pose another question. "Do all Rangers know how to make these bows?"

"No. But they know how to make longbows if they somehow break their recurve bow."

Addy Isn't Any Better At Naming Things

Addy finished stuffing the clothes haphazardly into the pack before climbing into the saddle. The bag bulged, and a pant leg hung out of the top, but she didn't care. Strider let out a heavy sigh, but didn't tell her to redo her packs, having long given up on that battle.

"So, your father taught you how to make your bow. Like he taught you how to be a Ranger?"

She got a nod from Strider as her answer. With a kick, he sent his horse into a walk, taking the lead.

"And Minkus taught you tahrvin, The Ways, and gave you some sort of key to enter them. What else did he teach you?"

"How to silence nosey girls who ask too many questions," Strider rumbled, his tone marking the end of his willingness to answer questions.

She made a face at him. "Kill me, and you don't get paid."

"I expect to be awarded land from the king for having to put up with you."

"I haven't been that bad."

He shot her a look.

She frowned. "I could be a lot worse!"

"So could I," Strider countered, and the two lapsed into silence once more.

While Addy was growing used to the quiet, she still couldn't resist talking to fill the silence. Which clearly annoyed Strider, so she kept doing it. This time, her focus changed to the horse Strider rode. The animal had always been skittish, but even more so in the tunnels. Now that they were outside, it had calmed down. It seemed both rider and horse loathed being underneath the mountain.

"Have you named him yet?" she began. "The horse."

Strider once again did not look at her as he rode, speaking to her over his shoulder. "No."

"Why not?"

"Because I am not keeping it."

"Why? He's a good horse."

"I have bad luck with horses," he stated, but didn't elaborate.

"What do you plan to do with him, then?"

"Sell him."

Addy's eyes widened in shock. She hadn't considered selling Su'lris. She'd grown attached to the scruffy horse and couldn't bear the thought of getting rid of him. Hunching her shoulders, she narrowed her eyes at Strider. "Well, you're the one riding him right now. Bad luck or not, he deserves a name."

"He doesn't need a name to trust me or get me to where I want to go."

"If you won't name him, I will."

"You name it, you keep it," Strider responded, as toneless as ever.

"I will. Su'lris would probably miss his friend if I let you take him. And I'd treat him better, anyway."

Strider scoffed but said nothing.

Addy began watching the horse intently, trying to figure out a name for the animal. "What is the yulie name for horse?" she asked cheekily.

"The yulie don't have a word for horse. They stole the name from the tahrvin," Strider answered. "They were the only ones given horses, so only they had a word for them."

"What is the tahrvin name for the horse, then?"

Strider's lips twitched into a smile. "Horse."

Well, that was less than helpful. Addy went back to trying to come up with a name on her own. This occupied her for half a watch as she muttered names to herself, testing each on her tongue.

"How about Tiller?"

"He is a horse, not a ship," Strider stated blandly.

"Then Dusty."

"No."

"If you're not keeping the horse, then you don't get a say in what I name him!" Addy snapped, and Strider shrugged.

She went back to thinking. Finally, she snapped her fingers.

"Copper!" she exclaimed happily. "I'll call him Copper."

"That is about as bad as Tiller."

"Doesn't matter. Copper is his name," Addy asserted.

Strider shook his head once more. What did it matter to him? He wasn't keeping the animal.

"I'd have named him Strider, but that was already taken," Addy added in her own flat tone. "Who gave you that nickname? Or did your parents decide to name you after a favorite horse?"

Strider was a popular name for horses. She'd never heard of a person with such a name.

Strider's eyes flicked toward the sky as if he were searching for something. "It is short for Longstride," he explained with a heavy breath.

"Is that your last name?" Addy inquired, her head cocking. "I've never heard of that last name before."

"Yes." The tone held an edge to it, tight and sharp. A warning that Addy ignored.

"What is your first name?"

"That is none of your concern." Strider's tone grew sharper. "Don't utter my last name, or tell anyone about The Ways, or the Rangers. You'll attract the attention of people who'll make you wish I was the one that killed you."

"That is the nicest way anyone has ever asked me to keep a secret," Addy said sarcastically.

He finally turned and eyed her for a long moment. She met his gaze steadily. He kept staring at her until she grew uncomfortable and looked away. He continued staring, and she fidgeted in her saddle.

"I won't tell, alright!?"

He eyed her a moment longer before turning back around to face forward. She rolled her eyes, letting silence reclaim the space between them.

Chapter 27

The Problem With Rumors

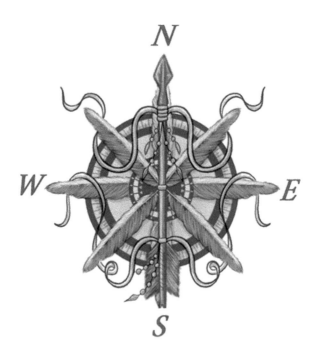

A ddy wasn't sure how he'd done it, but Strider led them directly to a road. The landscape placed them within the borders of Timara fiefdom, but that did little to help her know where she was in Timara. None of the surrounding fields or forests gave her a clue. Having spent most of her time traveling through the fiefdom inside a carriage, Addy couldn't recall any distinguishing landmarks outside.

She'd never noticed the world creeping by outside her window. Now she regretted it and envied the way Strider always knew where he was. Had she been on her own, she never would've been able to find her way. Strider hadn't paused, hadn't stopped to consider, or second guess himself. He continued in silent confidence.

Now on the road, Greer took to running several meters ahead before doubling back. When he got too far for Strider's liking, the Hunter would softly call to him, drawing the di'horvith back. Greer continued zooming back and forth between the trail ahead and the horses for several miles before settling to a steady pace beside Copper.

Now that they were no longer on the narrow paths of the forest, Addy brought Su'Iris to walk beside Copper. Strider glanced her way but said nothing. Addy let the quiet hang between them. After a moment of thought, she spoke.

"What was that feeling back in the tunnel? The one that scared the horses."

"That was the intent of something," Strider explained. "You felt its malevolence through the magic."

"Magic can transmit intent?"

"When you use magic, it always transmits the wielder's intent through it. Magic will also transmit the intent of those who do not wield it, though they are unaware of how they are affecting the surrounding magic. In both cases, it is usually so subtle people can't detect it. When they do, it is often what you'd call a gut feeling. That was an overwhelming amount of bloodlust and magical power for it to transmit through The Ways so clearly."

Addy shuddered. "I'm glad we're out of there."

Strider grunted in agreement.

Addy studied him for a moment. He seemed more at ease now that they were out of the mountain, though he continued to watch Greer closely. He'd reverted back to his same quiet self. Addy didn't want to dwell on the memory of what happened for long. It had scared her to see Strider lose his composure. It terrified her to think he could have died in those dark tunnels.

Addy opened her mouth to ask Strider another question, then closed it. He answered many of her questions but clammed up if she pried too deeply into his personal life. She realized he never asked her about her own life, save for the story of her kidnapping. He never pried into her life or attempted to make small talk by asking her about herself. Addy bit the inside of her cheek and let out a deep breath, irritated.

She didn't speak, letting the Hunter have his silence. She fidgeted with the reins out of boredom. Reaching into a saddlebag, she pulled out a lock and a set of picks Strider had given her and began trying to pick the lock like he'd shown her. Working the tumblers free while riding on a horse was even more difficult, but she kept at it.

Strider kept the same pace he'd set since acquiring the horses, alternating the speed with which they traveled to allow the animals a chance to rest. The horses could keep up the rhythm for miles. Greer never seemed to tire, and Strider had the impression that the horses would drop dead long before the di'horvith became worn out. Addy was blessedly quiet. Her constant need to talk exhausted him. Worse, he found himself answering more and more of her questions.

He kept them following the road toward the nearest town. His body was weary from travel, the exhaustion in his soul only amplifying it, and the thought of a good bed appealed to him. But he would never let Addy know it, or risk entering a town for such a stupid reason.

He wanted to hear what was being said in the taverns. They'd been underground for so long, he didn't know what the current state the fiefdom was in, or how far rumors of the hunt for him and Addy had spread. A tavern was the perfect place to hear local gossip, but it was still a risk. If word had spread, he'd be in danger. But he could use it to his advantage if he played his cards right.

It didn't take them long to reach the town after taking the road. Minkus had called the town Fair Fork, deriving its name from the road that forked in its center, dividing the town into thirds. His old mentor had stopped in the town many times after leaving The Ways, dragging both of his apprentices with him. He hadn't been back in over sixty years. The place had grown, yet that was as far as it appeared to have changed.

Any ummanie he'd once known would be old, or dead. But that was the case with most places he found himself in. He had nothing left but ghosts and shadows. There would be fewer people capable of identifying him. There'd be fewer trying to kill him. He noticed Addy had leaned forward in her saddle when the town came into view. She looked at him like she wanted to say something but didn't. He could see the excitement growing within her as they drew closer to the town. She beamed when it became apparent they were actually going to enter it. Her innocent joy amused him.

He caught Greer looking up at him with a pleased expression. Strider frowned. He pulled the black fabric over his face as he'd done with every town they entered, and shifted the hood so it cast his face in deeper shadows. Given the dust kicked up from travel, it wasn't uncommon to see people with face coverings.

The sound of the horses' hoofbeats changed from the muffled thump to a loud clopping as dirt gave way to rough cobblestone. That was new. The Fair Fork he'd known had dirt roads. Growth had brought wealth with it. The buildings lining the street were the same. Well maintained and painted in white accented with more expensive colors such as blue, red, and yellow. It was a pretty town, befitting its name. But Strider knew that behind the pretty exterior, darkness lay in the town's underbelly. All towns and cities had them. Fair Fork just hid theirs better.

Strider picked an inn and tavern he knew, the sign above it bearing the name The Blue Ivy Inn. The name had changed; it had been The Laying Dog Inn years ago, but the building was the same. It would have the same back entrance that led to a small alley, the same escape routes via the upper levels he could use to jump to the rooftops on three sides of the building if he couldn't escape via the ground floor. The entryways on the main level made it easy to watch the comings and goings of the customers and workers while they ate.

Strider led them to a stable built at the side of the inn. A stable boy rushed out to offer them aid. He waved the boy away, and Addy frowned. But she said nothing as she tended to Su'lris, whispering to him as she cooled him down. Once the two horses were bedded down, Strider flicked the stable boy a quarter-silver coin. "Take care of them and keep an eye on them."

"Yes, sir!" the kid beamed, still staring at the coin with wide eyes. It was likely more money than he'd ever seen in his life.

Addy stretched, rolling her shoulders as she tried to ease her stiff muscles. When they entered the town, she didn't bother to put her hood up. Strider had given her a disapproving look, but she didn't care. They were in no danger here. No one knew who they were. The hood was hot and stuffy, and she didn't know how Strider could stand keeping his on all day. She followed him into the tavern. Unlike in Denmahr, the conversations didn't fall silent at the sight of a Ranger. They lulled as the patrons looked to see who entered, but quickly started up again.

Myvara had a greater Ranger presence than a lot of other countries. As a result, their information network was one of the strongest and their borders the most secure. While Rangers wouldn't fight against their own, they had no qualms about fighting anyone that tried to invade the country they were posted in. It was part of their contract, and Myvara employed their tactical services more than most. Soldiers and commanders of armies tended to not like outsiders giving input or advice. They also didn't like the fact that the Rangers played both sides and refused to attack their own in battle.

Though they would listen, the relationship was not one of comradery, but necessity. It was a madness Addy never quite understood, and she didn't know how the Rangers had positioned themselves in such a way that nearly every ummanie country relied on them.

Over the centuries, they'd placed themselves in a key position. If they really wanted to, they could overthrow almost every ummanie kingdom. A fact that all the nobility and leaders were very aware of and hated. But they needed them. They'd become crucial parts of their order system. Though more than a few were turning to the Syliceon and the Ry'arie for support rather than relying on the Rangers.

Addy slid into her seat at the table. Strider let her order the food as he leaned back in his seat, feet crossed. Greer lay underneath his legs and Addy thought he looked bigger than before. Or maybe these chairs were shorter. Strider's chin rested against his chest; if Addy didn't know better, she'd think he was sleeping. She drummed her hands against the table and bounced her legs.

"Stop fidgeting," Strider ordered, his voice low so it wouldn't carry to the other tables. "Don't draw attention to yourself and listen."

Addy rolled her eyes. "I'm not drawing any more attention than you are."

"Movement catches the eye," he told her. "Spend your energy listening and observing, and you might learn something."

Addy looked at him, her tone cheeky. "I thought you didn't trust the words of people."

Strider eyed her from under his hood. "I don't, but even gossip can be useful. Alcohol and trusted company have a way of loosening people's lips."

Addy sat back in her chair with a sigh. She tried listening to the surrounding conversations. She only heard the conversation the people to her right were having—something about the price of wool going up.

She tried listening to another table. Their conversation was more interesting. They were talking about Denmahr ending their contract with the Rangers and how the Ry'arie had moved in to fill the gap. Her attention shifted from the conversation to food when the server brought their meals to the table. Addy greedily tucked in; thoughts of eavesdropping forgotten.

Strider shook his head and ate his own meal in silence. His discipline had not lapsed at the presence of food. He listened as he ate, keen ears picking up conversations from the far end of the tavern. He drifted his attention from table to table to give himself a better chance at catching anything of interest. It was a table near the center of the room that caught it.

"Aye, they say she was kidnapped right out of her home." The man spoke in conspiratorial tones. "Stolen from the great Timara castle without so much as a sign of a struggle. No one knows how he did it, only that he did."

A murmur ran around the table.

"King Elias is the one who discovered that he brought her to Denmahr. He's posted a reward for the girl's safe return. Even King Renmous is offering a reward for her return. He and Lord Fenforde are rather close."

One man scoffed. "If'n he can snatch her right out from under her own guard's noses. How does the king expect anyone to catch this Dark Ranger?"

Strider wanted to put his face in his hand and shake his head in exasperation. Of course, that name would spread! He shot a glare in Addy's direction. She looked at him, puzzled.

"What?" she asked in a low voice.

"It seems your story about the Dark Ranger has spread," he growled under his breath.

Addy gave him a sheepish look. "How do you know?"

"Because I listen and observe," he stated flatly. "They're talking about how a Dark Ranger kidnapped Lord Fenforde's daughter."

Addy's look changed to shock. "But you didn't kidnap me."

"No, but it is a clever move by those who did. I would've done the same. Deflect the blame of their crimes onto me and get the populace of both Denmahr and Myvara in on the manhunt. They've even offered a reward for your safe return, and my death."

The horror of realization crossed her face. "If you take me back... My father's men will try to kill you."

Strider nodded slowly, folding his arms across his chest, then leaning back further in his chair.

"I'll tell them what really happened," Addy offered hastily, her eyes darting back and forth as she thought. "They won't kill you if I order them not to. I could talk to my father. He'll believe me."

Strider's brow raised skeptically. "Would he? Would he listen to what you have to say before killing the man he thought stole his daughter?"

Addy looked down at her food, no longer hungry. She knew the answer but didn't want to say it.

Strider gave another nod.

"But if we don't do anything, everyone will continue to blame you for the crime," Addy muttered softly.

Strider shrugged dismissively. "I've been blamed for worse."

Addy paused, giving him a questioning look. What had he been blamed for in the past? When he didn't elaborate, her brows knit in an annoyed scowl. "So, you're not going to try to clear your name?"

"I never said that, but we aren't safe here."

He let out a long, heavy breath as he considered his options. Movement caught his eye. He watched out of the corner of his vision as a group of men looked toward him and Addy, then ducked their heads together again, occasionally casting glances their way. Finally, one got up and, doing his best not to attract attention, slipped out the front door. Strider cursed under his breath. Why in Chaos did he agree to bring this girl home? She was more trouble than she was worth!

"Finish your food," he growled. "We're leaving."

Chapter 28

Why Didn't She Run?

Strider gestured toward the back entrance he knew let out into the alley behind the building. He disappeared after Addy down the hallway when two men dressed in gambeson and chain mail entered the front entrance. Strider took the lead as they hurried out the door. He turned toward the stables, intending to retrieve their horses. Three men in light armor walked around the corner into the alley. Addy recognized her father's coat of arms on the men's uniform. Strider cursed. Turning back the way he'd come, he saw two more men coming down the alley on the opposite end. They'd surrounded the building. He swore again.

"Stop there!" one man shouted as they drew their swords.

Drawing his own blade, Strider moved away from the tavern. He kept his back to the wall, motioning for Addy toward some barrels stacked next to the back door. She crouched behind them, dragging Greer with her to keep him out of the fight. She had barely pulled Greer out of the way when two soldiers came bursting from the tavern door. It took them a moment to size up the situation before they also drew their swords and advanced on the Hunter.

Addy poked her head up from behind the barrel. "Don't kill them!" she ordered Strider, as the first man lunged at him.

Strider countered the blade, parrying before answering with his own counterstrike. He struck the man with the blade out of edge alignment, inhibiting its ability to cut effectively, but still focused enough to transfer most of its force on a single point. The blow caused the man to stagger. He hit the dirt, clutching his side, a rib broken. Strider kicked him in the head to ensure he didn't get back up to join the fight.

"They're trying to kill me, remember?" Strider snarled, as he blocked an overhead strike by another soldier. He grappled the man's wrist and used his own momentum to set him off balance, breaking his grip on his sword as Strider slid to the side of him. Using his attacker's own sword, the Hunter pommeled him in the back of the head. Another fighter hit the ground.

"I don't care, just don't kill them!" Addy shouted from her spot behind the barrels.

He countered another attack with his yulie blade.

"Why don't you tie my ankles to a boulder and throw me in the lake while you're at it?" he snarled, as he brought the stolen sword down on the man's hand, using the flat of the blade to crush the bone. The soldier shrieked in pain as he stumbled back, his sword falling from his broken hand.

Two men rushed him this time, all thoughts of an honorable fight forgotten. Strider stepped back. The first soldier's attack missed as he overextended, but Strider didn't take the opening as the man exposed his head and left side. The second soldier's attack came. He knocked the other blade aside before driving in past the man's guard.

Shifting his yulie blade so he gripped it in reverse, he drove the pommel up into the man's jaw before switching back into the normal grip with a flick of his wrist in time to parry another blow. Strider sensed another man coming up behind him for an attack.

A resounding crack filled the air before he could move. The soldier facing him faltered, his concentration lapsing for half a beat. It was a moment too long. Strider knocked his blade aside, leaving him wide open. Another strike from his blade's pommel planted the man in the dirt.

Turning around, Strider found Addy standing over the last soldier, a board clasped in her hands. She looked down at the man, stunned that she'd actually snuck up behind him and hit him.

Greer stood beside her, head canted to one side, as he also looked down at the still man. A groan came up from the soldier she hit, and Addy let out a squeal before smacking him again.

Strider shook his head and sheathed his sword. He eyed Addy in confusion before shaking his head again and moving swiftly down the road. He could hear the shouts of more men as they approached the tavern. They'd swarm the place in a few moments. Swiftly moving toward a dividing wall, he jerked his head for Addy to follow. He crouched, cupping his hands.

"Put your foot in my hands, and I'll boost you up," he told her. "Don't go completely over the wall until you've seen what is on the other side."

Addy did as instructed. With a single thrust, he sent her flying upward. Her heart leaped into her throat in the instant she felt weightless, then gravity took hold, bringing her down atop the wall. Dividing walls between the buildings were capped with tiny roofs, imitating the surrounding buildings. Addy scrambled onto the tiles. The clay cracked beneath her feet.

The alley beyond the wall was empty. She didn't see any danger, and so she let herself down. A few beats later, Greer came vaulting up to the top of the wall. He perched awkwardly for a moment, snout in the air as he sniffed. Addy gave him a perplexed look. How had he jumped that high? A beat later, Strider joined him atop the wall, and the two jumped down together. Strider gave Addy a look like he wanted to say something, but didn't, as he stalked down the alley. Addy realized he was about to lead them out of the city and stopped.

"What about Su'lris and Copper?"

"What about them?"

"We can't leave them!"

"We can, and we are," Strider told her.

Addy stopped, folding her arms across her chest. "You can. I'm not abandoning Su'lris."

Greer sat beside her, a look of defiance also on his face. Strider gave Greer a disbelieving look before the expression turned to exasperation. "You want me to risk getting caught and killed for a horse?"

"Just don't get caught," Addy said, with a cheeky smile.

He didn't have time to argue; he had to get her to safety. The window was closing fast, they needed to leave. He shook his head and took another route that didn't lead out of town. Addy and Greer followed. He realized it would've been better for her if he'd left and let the soldiers escort her home. He could've followed at a distance. Instead, he'd instinctively brought her with him. His frown deepened as he thought about Addy standing over that soldier with her plank of wood. She'd helped him fight off her father's men. But why?

Chapter 29
Blasphemy

Why? He asked himself again, as he led Addy and Greer through the maze of streets and back alleys, dodging soldiers as they rushed about the city in search of them. Why had she not run away the moment the soldiers cornered him? Why didn't she let them attack him while she ran and found more of her father's men to take her home? Why had she helped him? It'd be in her best interest to let them capture or kill him. He'd gotten her to Timara. Here she could rely on her station and connections to get her home. She didn't need him. She could've cut him out.

The entire kingdom thought he was the villain that'd kidnapped her. They'd do everything in their power to see him dead. And while the act of trying to cut him out would be a foolish and fatal one, it made the most sense. He'd grown up around people who would've betrayed him without a second thought. He'd seen many nobles do the same. But she didn't stab him in the back, which left him confused. Why hadn't she?

This led him to his next question. Why hadn't he left her with her father's men?? Even if she didn't plan to betray him, he, as her protector, should've let the soldiers take her. Yet he hadn't. His first instinct had been to take her with him when he'd normally consider leaving her behind. He was getting too attached. Was she doing the same?

The night was closing in, lending aid to their escape by creating uncertain lighting and shadows to hide in. Using the darkness as cover, Strider picked the lock to a back door before ushering Addy and Greer inside. He swiftly locked the door behind them as the day gave way to night, plunging everything into total darkness. The building was completely black inside, and he could hear Addy fumbling through the darkness behind him.

He felt a tug on his cloak as she grabbed it, using it to help guide her as he nimbly navigated the dark storeroom. He quietly opened the door to the little storage room and peered out. Rows of wooden benches sat empty, abandoned for the day. Greer pushed his way out into the chapel, his claws clicking against the wooden floor.

He sniffed and snuffled as he searched about before settling on a bench, certain there was no one here. Strider moved more cautiously into the chapel, never caring to be inside of Syliceon's churches as he walked down the pews. Addy clung to him until he stopped and moved her to sit down next to Greer. Her hands fumbled about, feeling the seat, her face growing perplexed.

"Are we in a church?" she asked, as she felt about.

"Yes," Strider said, moving to check the main door.

It was locked via an exterior lock. No one thought to make it accessible from the inside. A heavy wooden beam lay off to the side. Strider hefted the beam into the iron fixtures designed to hold it, barring the door from the inside.

Addy's head cocked as she listened to Strider shove the beam into place. "Won't they think to look inside of the church?"

"You'd be surprised," Strider muttered. "Most people avoid the building, thinking its sacredness somehow means people won't use it to hide. Most wouldn't, fearing the wrath of the gods."

"And you don't?" Addy asked.

Strider shrugged, forgetting that Addy couldn't see him. "They've never complained when I've done it before."

"So, you've used their churches to hide out in before." Addy's tone was incredulous.

"Why not? It's a dry place to sleep."

Addy let out a long-suffering sigh, unsurprised by the casual way Strider treated such a blasphemous act. She pulled her cloak tighter around her and bowed her head to utter a quiet prayer to the gods, asking for their forgiveness for trespassing on holy ground.

Strider left Addy to pray. He returned to the storage room. He locked the door before sliding some heavy boxes in front of it. The Hunter continued moving boxes in front of one another in a line until they touched the wall opposite the door. Taking care to perch a bucket of various items on the edge of a box in such a way that it would fall the moment anyone tried to force their way in, he surveyed his work.

The arrangement of boxes would mean those attempting to break in would fight against the wall's strength, their antics knocking the bucket off the box, alerting anyone inside to their presence. Satisfied that he had reinforced the doors, Strider returned to the chapel and claimed a bench.

The only window in the building was a solid stained-glass piece placed high above the altars. One would create quite the ruckus breaking through it. A fall from that height in pitch darkness was a recipe for a broken leg or neck. The circular stained-glass window sat above a wall mural depicting the gods. Strider took a moment to study the image. The goddess K'yarie was the largest, most central image. She was the creator of the worlds. The goddess of matter and magic. The artist depicted her as a woman of great beauty whose dark hair and dress held the stars.

Around her were the other gods within the Syliceon's pantheon. The twins, the god and goddess of life, were the second largest of the top portion of the picture. The goddess Layura, creator of animals and monsters, and her brother Takari, creator of the people that populated the planets, stood in silent judgement of the world's inhabitants.

Smaller gods dedicated to the elements, harvest, and much more framed the three deities. Beneath them was the form of a terrible dragon-looking creature with darkness surrounding him. He lay beneath K'yarie, staring up at the gods with a malevolent glare. The god of Chaos, as depicted by the Syliceon church.

He was the only god not given an altar of worship. Though also a giver of magic and father to the twin gods of life, most people feared the enormous beast. Though in the stories all the gods and goddesses, even K'yarie, possessed a truly terrifying form, but they were rarely depicted.

Strider cared little for the myths and legends surrounding these divine beings. To him, all of them caused more trouble than they were worth as they meddled in the affairs of mortals. Strider lay on his back, gazing up at the rafters. As he stretched out, the nagging question came back to him.

"Why?" Strider finally asked.

Addy's confused voice filled the darkness. "I don't understand."

"You could've left me to take the fall back at the tavern. Why didn't you?"

"You're innocent of the crime they think you've committed," Addy stated, as if that were all the answer he needed.

"But they don't know that. You could've played your part and they would've rescued you, leaving you free of me and any debt you owed. So why did you help me and then run away with me?"

Addy gave an exasperated gesture. "I didn't consider it."

"Why not?" Anyone else would. He would. Yet he didn't.

"Because it would be wrong!" she snapped. "I won't stab someone in the back just because it's convenient for me!"

"Everyone else I've known would have."

"Well, I'm not like them!"

Strider didn't respond. He still thought she was naïve.

"Why didn't you leave me?" Addy shot back. "You could've gotten rid of me today."

It would've been better for you if I had, he thought, but Greer appeared before he could voice it.

Greer, who had slipped off the bench during their conversation, leaped up, landing on top of him. The Hunter let out a loud *humph* as the air was driven out of him. Greer panted in a pleased manner as he snuggled on top of the Hunter, who was found it very hard to breathe with the massive dir'horvith on his chest, ending any conversation he might have intended to have with Addy. Greer rested his head on Strider's shoulder, quickly falling asleep. In the quiet of the church, Strider heard Addy's breathing grow slow and even as she drifted off.

He stared up at the rafters as he listened to the breathing of his two sleeping companions. He knew why he hadn't left her behind, and a plan was forming in his mind to return her to the soldiers. She wouldn't like it. But he had something different in mind than abandoning her. He still didn't understand why she'd chosen to stay with him. Why she hadn't helped frame him. But her actions were not lost on him.

Chapter 30
How Not To Avoid An Ambush

Addy jerked awake when someone gently shook her shoulder. Her eyes flashed open to see an unfamiliar man hovering over her. Shrieking, she lashed out, slapping the person hard across the face as panic filled her. The stranger reeled back in shock as she reached for her sword. The sound of laughter exploded around her, causing her to freeze. Looking around, she saw several armed men standing in the surrounding aisles.

"I'm sorry for startling you, my lady!" the first man said, a hand covering the cheek she'd slapped while he held up the other in a placating gesture.

Addy's brows knit in confusion, her hand on the hilt of her sword. She took in the surrounding men. None of them showed any sign of aggression. The slapped knight looked apologetic while the others struggled to hold back more laughter. He was the only one dressed in plated armor. The rest bore the typical light gambeson and chain mail of men at arms. The knight's armor bore king Renmous' crest while the foot soldiers wore her family's emblem. These were her father's men!

Addy sat up in alarm, eyes searching the church as her heartbeat quickened. She looked at the man kneeling before her, her tone holding the authority of a noblewoman. "Where is the man that was with me?"

The soldier she'd struck glanced at the floor when she made eye contact with him.

"He wasn't here when we entered. The scoundrel must've fled before we arrived," he informed her. "You're safe now, my lady."

"Fled?" Addy repeated in disbelief. Her eyes searched the dimly lit corners of the room, expecting to see a dark figure standing there. But both Strider and Greer were gone. Her jaw tightened as she drew a deep breath, fueling the anger that burned within her. After all they'd been through, he'd abandoned her!

"How did you know I was here?" she turned back to the guard, heat flushing her cheeks.

"An anonymous tip said you entered the church last night," the soldier answered, still down on one knee.

Addy scowled. Had something happened to Strider? She couldn't believe it. No one was in the streets to see them; she trusted that Strider would've spotted them if they were, and the interior lights of the houses would've made anyone inside blind to the outside world. She had a sneaking suspicion that Strider had coerced this person into tipping off these men.

Her chest tightened with growing anger and hurt. It made sense that he would run. It was safer to let her father's men take her the rest of the way rather than risk being caught or killed. Though it made sense, it still hurt. It hurt far more than it should have, and she realized she'd begun to believe that Greer and Strider would always be there for her.

Something scratched against her neck and she irritably reached into the folds of her cloak, pulling out a folded piece of paper. She looked at it, confused. Opening it she found a note written in the formal language.

Neat letters scrawled across the paper. "We're not gone."

She had no idea that Strider could write. There was another paper folded within the first. Addy unfolded it to find a drawing of a large stone carved with markings she did not recognize. Next to it stood a dark figure with his hood up. Written below it in Strider's handwriting, the note said, "Look for us here."

Her hurt turned to confusion when she realized Strider had not abandoned her but planned to follow her. Her anger flared again, however, as she noticed the last message he'd written.

"Behave yourself."

Crumpling up the papers, she threw them with a huff. The ball cleared three benches before smacking against the back of the fourth with a crumpling sound.

"My lady, we need to go." The knight stood, beckoning her.

He held out a hand to her, which she took as he helped her to her feet. They ushered her out of the church in a flurry of motion, hefting her up into the saddle in front of the man she'd assaulted. With a flick of the reins, he sent his horse into a brisk trot.

"Wait!" she cried in alarm. "My horse, he is back at The Blue Ivy Inn!"

"I'm sorry, my lady, but we have strict orders to not delay in getting you home."

"Getting a horse won't delay us by much," Addy protested, but she could feel the knight shaking his head.

"Direct orders from your father, my lady. We cannot deny them."

The idea of diving off the horse flashed through Addy's mind, but the knight placed a muscular arm around her waist as if he was afraid she'd fall off. Or was he afraid she'd fight him? She had slapped him earlier.

"Could you at least send a man to fetch him?" she proposed. "He is a bay horse, black mane, with a white blaze on his face. Ask the stable boy about the animals someone paid him a quarter-silver to watch. He can point them out. Grab the roan while you're at it."

She doubted Strider would risk going back for the horses while the city was swarming with guards.

The knight gave the order to one of the men, who broke away to retrieve the two horses while the main company headed out of town toward castle Timara. The man also sent a rider ahead to inform her father of her rescue.

Addy's heart ached at the thought of going home. Strider was the one that was supposed to bring her home, not these men. It angered her that he'd left her without discussing things with her. But he had at least attempted to tell her of his plans to hang around. The thought comforted her despite her anger. She'd still smack the Hunter when she saw him again for putting her through this.

Addy and her new entourage traveled for several days. The men did their best to make her comfortable, treating her like the noblewoman she was. The treatment felt strange after spending so long with Strider. No one made her cook, set up camp, or care for the horses. The soldiers waited on her to the best of their ability, often fumbling in their efforts. They'd procured a tent for her, and she hoped they'd paid the merchant they'd taken it from. The tent was large enough to fit at least five people, but they apologized for the meager offering.

She ignored them and sequestered herself inside the large tent, wishing it was the one Strider had pitched for her whenever the weather turned bad. That tent was small, but it was warm and cozy. This felt empty. There was no Greer trying to squeeze his way inside to join her. No sound of Strider tending to his weapons or sketching in his book as she fell asleep.

She was still angry at him for leaving her. But as each day passed, she found herself missing him. Once she even thought she saw Greer standing in the trees. But when she looked back, the form had vanished. Leaving her to wonder if it was ever there. She should've been more excited about going home, but the moment was soured by the fact that Strider and Greer weren't here.

Greer was a lovable ball of fluff; she couldn't help but get attached. But she hadn't realized how much she cared about Strider and enjoyed traveling with him. She rode on the horse belonging to the same knight who had awoken her in the temple, wishing it was Sul'ris instead.

He had introduced himself as Tevin Ulwick, one of the king's knights. After the first day of riding, he'd opted to walk when she assured him she could ride alone. The mortified look he gave her when she straddled the horse was priceless. The other men stopped as well, confused by the sight. She looked at Tevin and the other men in annoyance.

"Have you never seen a woman ride like this before?" she asked sharply.

"Not a noblewoman, my lady," Tevin answered.

"Well, now you have."

With a flick of the reins, she sent the horse into a trot, forcing the men to scramble to their own mounts or be left behind. They set a leisurely pace, as if concerned she'd fall off her horse. She scoffed at the idea. Strider had taken her and Su'lris over far rougher terrain at a much more agonizing pace. This was a leisurely ride compared to what she'd grown accustomed to. She rode with confidence, easily adjusting to the new gait of this horse.

Tevin had to shorten the stirrups on his saddle for her. Like most men, he was taller than her. This caused Addy to wonder about Su'lris' stirrups. They'd been the perfect length for her ever since she'd first gotten into his saddle. She couldn't help but think of Strider. He had to have adjusted them so she could ride. She scanned the landscape, looking for the large stone monolith in Strider's drawing.

Tevin took notice of what she was doing.

"Don't worry, my lady," he assured her. "We'll keep you safe from the Dark Ranger."

Addy's anger flared again. This time at hearing yet again how these big powerful men would protect her from the big bad Dark Ranger. It irked her to hear them speak so badly of the Hunter. He was cold and merciless, but he'd done nothing to her to warrant this kind of treatment—at least not anything recently.

"I doubt he will be interested in getting me back," she replied curtly. "He's likely celebrating being rid of me."

The thought of Strider kicking up his feet and having a toast to her being gone made her face flush with anger.

Tevin nodded, but he didn't look like he understood. To them, the Dark Ranger was the enemy who took their dear lord's daughter. A villain for the brave soldiers to slay.

Addy watched these men. They had watched her vigilantly and did their best to make her feel comfortable, but she doubted they had any idea what kind of threat Strider could be. Addy wasn't sure she understood, either. She continued looking for the stone that stood as tall as a tree. She spotted it toward the evening. It stood four-hundred feet off the trail, embedded into the side of a small rise.

As Addy watched, she saw a dark figure detach itself from the stone's shadow. Her heart skipped as she recognized the hooded figure. He did not linger out in the open for long, vanishing back behind the obelisk before any soldiers spotted him. Had she not been looking for him, she never would've seen him.

Day seven came and went peacefully. On day eight, a messenger arrived on a horse covered in a lather from a hard run. The messenger bore the uniform of the Fenforde house.

Tevin raised a hand in greeting. "State your business," he said, his tone friendly but cautious. His hand rested on the hilt of his sword as he took up position in front of Addy's horse.

The messenger was puffing as hard as his horse. "Message from the house of Fenforde," he gasped. "Lord Fenforde is not at castle Timara to receive his daughter. He is in Tucket on business; it has been requested that she meet him there."

Tevin looked up at Addy for her input. She was the lady after all.

Addy heart's throbbed with longing at the idea of seeing her father. Tucket was not very far away, far closer than her home. She could rendezvous with her father and explain to him what really happened as they traveled home. While her heart jumped at the idea, something felt off. Something in the pit of her stomach warned her against it.

Something wasn't right. She couldn't explain the feeling. It was strikingly similar to the one that had compelled her to trust Strider back in Altia. The thought of her father being so close made her want to cry. She could see him again, to feel his arms wrap around her, as he hugged her and told her everything would be okay. But the feeling of ill ease wouldn't go away. She ignored it, nodding her consent to Tevin. "We'll go to Tucket."

Tevin nodded, before gesturing for the messenger to lead the way. The man bowed and whirled his horse around. The animal snorted and puffed as it fell into the slower pace the rest of the horses had been following.

Addy couldn't help but think of Su'Iris as she watched the tired bay. The soldier sent to fetch him had reported that both horses weren't there when he arrived at the stable and the man they posted to watch the horses, to make sure the Dark Ranger didn't use them to escape, had been knocked unconscious. She wanted her horse. Addy rode in the center of the group of soldiers as they all moved off the main road toward Tucket.

The smaller road forced the men to form up into two lines as it sloped down into the forest. They continued traveling, and excitement bubbled in Addy's stomach at the thought of seeing her father. She hardly noticed the surrounding forest or the earthen banks rising around them on either side as they entered an old gully. A scream tore through the air, snapping her out of her happy thoughts. Another man cried out. Horses screamed as arrows rained down on the soldiers. Tevin gripped the reins of Addy's horse.

"Ride my lady!" he shouted, slapping the flank of her horse.

The animal lunged forward with a cry of its own. Several horses ran alongside her, their saddles empty. A couple dragged the bodies of their fallen riders as they fled. Her horse leapt over a log placed across the road. Its front hooves landed in a tangle of branches, causing it to stumble and pitch forward. Addy went flying as her horse fell out from under her.

She hit the ground, doing her best to roll with the impact. Her head slammed into the ground. Light and shadow danced in her vision, drowning out the world around her. Her head spun and ears rang. Rough hands grabbed her, wrestling her up into a rider's arms. She heard the sounds of battle and the shout of Tevin before everything went dark.

Chapter 31

How Not To Remain Kidnapped

S trider was nothing more than a shadow among the trees. A hidden figure the riders were oblivious to. He remained crouched within the protection of the forest, watching as the messenger approached Addy and her new escorts.

Like his note said, he continued to watch over her from afar, shadowing the group every day. Content to follow to ensure Addy got home. It was laughable how close he could come to their camp without them noticing his presence. Had he intended to reclaim Addy, he'd have done so with little trouble. But he was happy to let them take the glory. Then the messenger appeared.

A quiet rumbling ground in the back of Greer's throat. His eyes fixed on the messenger as he snarled again, his hair standing on end.

Strider placed a hand on his head, fondling the di'horvith's ears, quieting him. "I know," Strider growled, fingering his bow with his other hand. He considered shooting the man, saving Addy the trouble. But he stopped, deciding to wait and see what Addy would do.

Greer continued to watch the stranger with a deadly focus.

Addy appeared to be hesitating, and for a moment, it looked like she was going to trust her instincts and refuse the man. But she let her impatient nature take over, opting to trust the stranger. Strider sighed, shaking his head for the hundredth time.

"What are we going to do with her?" he quietly asked Greer.

Greer snorted, giving his own head a vigorous shake that traveled down the length of his body.

Strider pulled Greer's head against his chest, rubbing the di'horvith's cheek before patting his side. "You're the one who stuck us with her. You get to figure it out," he replied, earning a kiss on the nose from the gray di'horvith before he bounded off after the company.

An ambusher walked among the dead bodies, sword in hand.

"Why'd I have to be the one to go through the bodies?" he grumbled angrily to himself, as he stabbed at the corpses, slitting the throat of those who cried out. He stood over the form of an unconscious knight who was clearly still breathing. The outlaw's blood-soaked blade shifted in his hand as he looked down at the injured man.

He spat on the ground before the knight, hefted his blade to deal a deathblow, then froze. A strangled gasp left his throat as he looked down at the arrow that sprouted from his chest with a dumbfounded expression. He was dead before he hit the ground, the shocked look forever plastered on his face.

Strider melted from the shadows, surveying the carnage with little regard. He crouched before the mass of bodies, bow resting across his knees, as he envisioned the ambush in his mind. There was no sign of Addy. They'd at least gone to the trouble of taking her alive.

Greer trotted among the corpses, looking for survivors. Several horses followed him, having latched onto the half di'horvith as their new herd leader when they'd encountered him after the battle.

Strider figured he'd be able to make a nice profit selling the animals and hadn't bothered to chase them away. He moved from body to body, quickly searching for valuables. Though the weapons could be sold for a decent profit, he didn't take them. He didn't have the time to gather them and secure them to the horses.

There wasn't much to find on the dead men; neither the soldiers nor attackers had much to their names. But they wouldn't miss the few coins he found. A low woof drew his attention from the soldier he was searching. Greer was standing over the knight, clutching Strider's arrow in his jaws. He nudged the knight's arm before letting out another woof.

Strider stood and walked over. Using the toe of his boot, he rolled the survivor over, his head cocking as he looked at him. He was young for a king's knight. An arrow protruded from his collarbone. It hadn't had enough force to kill, but it had pierced deep enough to wedge into the bone. Blood stained his side where a blade had slipped past armor and mail.

Greer let out a small whine, and Strider sighed. "I'll take care of him if he survives," he told the wolf. "After we get Addy."

Greer gave a disapproving sniff, but he didn't protest.

Strider removed the knight's armor and relieved him of any weapons. He looked at the sword; considered leaving it behind. It'd be best not to give his enemy a pointy stick to attack with. He toyed with the string of his pendant for a moment before deciding. The blade faded like mist in sunlight. Finished, the Hunter unceremoniously hefted the man into the saddle of one of his extra horses, tying him to the saddle so he wouldn't fall off.

Nimbly climbing into Copper's saddle, Strider set off. The trail the attackers left behind was extremely easy to follow, despite their sloppy attempts to cover their tracks. Su'lris followed behind Copper, his reins tied to his own saddle. Strider secured the horse, now toting the injured man, to Su'lris. The four other horses fell in line behind them, creating a train behind Greer. He didn't bother to tie off the others; they were content to follow Greer. He would eventually have to secure the six horses deep in the forest, as the animals weren't exactly quiet.

After a while, he left Greer to guard the horses and the unconscious man, to continue tracking Addy on foot. He tracked Addy's kidnappers to an old, abandoned keep. The building stood alone and forgotten, its rotting structure dark and forlorn. Crumbling patches of a low wall surrounded the keep as a skeletal reminder of what it had been. A few lights flickered in the windows like foxfire, indicating that the building was occupied. A light rain fell, and a fog rolled in as the day cooled. Keeping to the edge of the forest, he stalked around the building, plotting, as he waited for night to fall.

Addy awoke to a deep throbbing in her skull. Clutching her head, she let out a soft moan as she rolled over. The ground beneath her was hard. Her hand brushed a thin, scratchy canvas that someone had laid beneath her. Opening her eyes, Addy found herself in a small room, lit by light coming from a small window. Ancient stone walls surrounded her as she lay on the decaying wooden floor.

Her mind was foggy and pulsed with pain. How had she gotten here? Where was Strider? She continued to look around the room, not really taking any of it in as her mind worked. The memories trickled through the haze, like morning light dissolving the mist. Her heart pounded, increasing the pain in her head as she relived the violence. She pushed herself to her feet, wobbling unsteadily.

She moved slowly, finding that as she spent more time upright, the pain lessened to a dull throb. She didn't know where she was, but the men who took her must be beyond the door. Patting herself down, she took stock of what she had. They'd taken her sword, but she still had her knife hidden in the folds of her clothes, and the lock pick set Strider had given her to practice picking his locks.

It would seem the men hadn't bothered to search her for hidden weapons. She was just a noble's daughter, after all. Addy cringed as each step brought a creak from the floor. What was it Strider had said about floors? The words eluded her.

Addy first moved to the small window in the room carved out of the stone, but it was too small for her to fit through. Peering out, she searched for a recognizable landmark or a passerby she could shout to for help. She could see an overgrown field and a forest beyond, but nothing more. The light was fading as well as a light rain turned to fog. But it was still light enough in the room for her to see. Addy turned away from the window and noticed that the floor didn't protest as she moved. The act brought what Strider had said to mind.

"Keep to the edges."

She skirted the room, making considerably less noise as she stalked to the old door. It held fast when she pushed on it. Peeking through the keyhole, she caught sight of a man as he walked by the door, then disappeared from sight before reappearing a moment later, walking the other way on his patrol. He took a significantly longer time to return on the second pass. Addy assumed this was the direction she needed to go to get out. She pulled back from the door and studied the lock. It was old, like a lock Strider had taken from the cache he'd raided in Borris—one she'd picked before.

She pressed her face to the door again, watching the man outside walk back and forth as she tried to get down the timing. She counted how long it took for the guard to pass by her door. That would be all the time she had to get out and get down the hall before he spotted her. The creaking floor outside told her when he was approaching. She set to work, counting in her head to keep time with the guard outside as his footsteps appeared and faded.

Pulling out her lock picks, she began teasing the tumblers inside, trying to find the right combination. The mechanisms were old and stiff, but whoever had previously used the lock had worked them loose. Still, it was an effort to get the pieces to move, made even more agonizing because she had to freeze each time the footsteps came too close. She couldn't have the man hear her work.

She was teasing one tumbler into place when her set slipped. She tried to tease the tumbler back into place as she uttered Strider's favorite curse when it wouldn't budge. Addy froze as the footsteps came again. She dared not breathe as the steps paused in front of her door. Had he heard her? She resisted the urge to look through the keyhole, fearing she would make a noise that would give her away.

She waited, her heart hammering inside her chest. Tense beats stretched into agonizing heartbeats before the man turned away. His footsteps faded as he resumed his patrol. Addy let out her breath in a quiet gasp. Her body relaxed against the door in relief. Gathering herself, she waited for the guard to pass by a couple more times before attacking the lock again. The lock released with an old, tired click.

Excitement brightened her face. Had she not needed to remain silent, she'd have let out a delighted squeal at her accomplishment. Returning the lock picks to their hiding place, she listened at the door to the footsteps. The man showed no sign of noticing that the door was unlocked. Waiting for his steps to grow distant, she eased the door open enough to slip out.

Not wanting to alert the man that she'd left, she closed the door. It let out a low creak as it shut. Her heart stopped; the footsteps began stomping her way. Keeping to the wall, Addy moved down the hall, away from the approaching guard.

She reached the stone steps and hurried down, hugging the edge. She reached the bottom and scurried down the hall, ducking into a dark doorway when she heard someone coming toward her. Pulling up her hood, she froze, letting the darkness envelop her. The man didn't even glance her way as he walked by and mounted the stairs. Addy slipped back into the hallway, pausing at an open doorway as voices of several men drifted to her. Carefully, she peered in.

The men had their backs to her. Focused on a group gathered at a table as they played some sort of dice game. She wanted to dart across the doorway, but Strider had warned her that sudden movement would catch the eye. She'd also look suspicious if someone saw her. Still dressed in the clothes Strider had bought her, she looked like a short man if glanced at casually. Pulling her hood down a little further to ensure it was hiding her hair, she prayed quietly to the gods. Straightening, she walked with purpose past the door.

No one called out to her. They remained focused on the dice as one man tossed them onto the table, eliciting cheers and groans from the observers, when they'd stopped rolling. If anyone glanced up, they would've seen what they had expected to see: one of their men moving down the hall.

Addy couldn't believe her heart hadn't stopped with how quickly it was pounding. She'd made it out! The fog was growing thicker as the night cooled and the rain had stopped. Addy sidestepped toward the horses tied up near the door. She'd untied a horse when a shout of alarm sounded.

"She's escaped!"

Cursing again, Addy pulled herself up into the saddle. She hadn't been able to shorten the straps on the horse's saddle; she didn't know how to. Forced to cling to the beast with her knees, she sent it into a gallop with a whip of its reins. There was more shouting behind her as men poured from the building.

She looked back to see men mounting their own horses as they chased after her, but she had a good lead. She followed the overgrown road that once led to the old keep, hoping to provide steady ground for her stolen animal. Thwack! The horse let out a terrible cry as an arrow slammed into its hindquarters. The animal's leg buckled, and it stumbled.

Addy slipped off the horse as it struggled to keep its footing, hitting the ground for the second time that day. She rolled with the impact, avoiding hitting her head. Though it throbbed painfully, jarred by the impact. The injured horse found its footing. It continued running, blood streaming from the wound as the arrow bit deeper.

Addy scrambled to her feet, swearing as she ran into the forest, hoping to lose the men in the trees and fog. She kept low to present a harder target for the archer. But no arrows came. The men on horseback plunged their horses into the forest after her.

Like her, the mercenary's vision was impeded by the darkness and growing fog. They'd closed the distance at an alarming rate, and Addy tried to move toward thicker terrain to force them off their horses. Some slowed, unwilling to risk their horses, but one man pushed his animal through despite the tangle of brambles and uneven ground.

Bringing his horse up alongside her, he leaped from the saddle, his weight slamming into her and knocking her to the ground. Again, she rolled, trying to use the momentum to bring herself back to her feet, but the man grabbed her and tried to pin her. She reached inside her cloak for her dagger. With a fierce shriek, she struck out blindly.

The man fell away with a cry of his own as the blade stabbed him in the stomach. Addy grabbed for the man's sword, drawing it from its scabbard before taking off into the forest again. The others were catching up, having abandoned their horses.

None of them had thought to bring torches. Without them, they didn't have a light source to weaken their night vision further. The glowing light would've also bounced off the fog, making it harder for them to see, aiding Addy in her escape. Instead, they were on an even playing field. And they had longer legs than her.

She needed to hide! But for that, she needed to break their line of sight. If she could avoid them long enough, the fog would become thick enough to make it hard for them to see. She could get away. And that was when she hit a wall.

Unable to see far herself, Addy hadn't seen the looming wall of earth and stone until she was in front of it. The cliff was too steep to climb. She whirled, intending to run down the length of it and back into the forest when the men appeared. There were seven of them. She could've sworn there had been more.

Sheathing her dagger, she raised the stolen sword. Her body fell into the defensive stance Strider had taught her. The sword was weighted terribly and felt wrong in her hands. It was nothing like her own sword or the finely crafted blades Strider wielded. She could feel how it would strain her arms and wrists as she used it. The men paused and laughed.

"Come on, princess," the apparent leader said confidently, clearly believing he'd won. "We don't want to hurt you. Put that down and come with us."

Addy glowered at the man as she shot back, "Or you can leave, and this princess will forget that you've wronged her and let you live."

The men laughed again, clearly not threatened. He drew his own sword, the fog closing in around them until Addy could only see the advancing men and nothing else. The leader sauntered toward her. He didn't take up a serious fighting stance, clearly not threatened, or not trained enough to know what a proper sword stance was. Addy wasn't seasoned enough to tell the difference. What she could tell, was what he was about to do. He didn't try to hide his first attack.

The swing was obvious but held significant force behind it. The strike was only aimed at her sword, not her. He expected to knock the weapon out of her hand with a powerful blow. But her sword wasn't there to hit, and he overextended and stumbled, his footing not aiding his balance.

Training kicked in and Addy answered with her own attack, aiming to slice deep into her opponent's side. The idea startled her, and she suddenly pulled back in her swing. Her sword still sliced through her attacker, but the wound was not fatal like it would've been. The action saved his life but threw her off balance.

The burning pain that tore through the man caused him to react reflexively. He struck out at her again with his blade, aiming at her head. Addy barely brought her sword up to block as she ducked, using her blade to deflect the attack. She didn't answer with her own attack, not wanting to kill him. Instead, she parried his attacks, stepping back each time. Her arms and wrists grew tired quickly from wielding the unruly sword against her opponent's powerful blows.

Her stamina was running out, and there were still other men to fight. Again, the man overextended, leaving his other side wide open for a thrust. But Addy couldn't take advantage of it. She couldn't kill him. He went for her sword again, this time the blow connecting. The weapons clanged together. The sword flew out of Addy's hands. She stepped back again and found her back against the cliff wall.

Caught up in the moment, he lost sight of his true goal as battle rage overtook him. The man gave a triumphant cry as he brought his weapon around to deal the final blow. His companions yelled out. But he was deaf to their cries as he swung the blade down in an attack aimed to split her from shoulder to ribcage. Blue silver flashed out from the darkness, knocking the enemy's sword aside with tremendous force and filling the air with a resounding CLANG!

Chapter 32
Never Leave The Wolf Behind

Using the cover of the darkness and fog, Strider drew closer to the keep. Hidden behind a surviving section of the low, crumbling perimeter wall, he had the perfect vantage point to watch without being observed. He'd held off sneaking into the keep, curious to see if Addy would utilize the skills he'd taught her. His wait proved fruitful. He watched Addy exit the keep, a small smile of approval tugging at the corners of his lips.

She'd just finished untying a horse when an alarm sounded. She swung into the saddle and fled. Strider watched as men swarmed out of the keep and rode off after her. His eye caught movement above where he knew a man kept watch. The man fired an arrow, striking Addy's horse, sending her tumbling to the ground. Strider's own arrow slammed into the archer before he could reach for another. The man tumbled backward, out of sight.

Strider vaulted over the wall and rushed to the horse left for the archer. He kicked the animal into a hard run. He wasn't far behind Addy and her kidnappers. To the girl's credit, she'd led them into the forest, using the rough, bramble-filled terrain to force her pursuers to dismount. Strider didn't wait for his animal to come to a stop as he leaped off, darting into the forest at a different location, so as not to come up directly behind his prey.

He moved through the fog like a phantom. Arriving in time to see Addy stab one man and steal his sword. Strider spotted another man sneaking around her in the shadows as she fought. When she fled, the mercenary crouched, poised to jump her. But a hand wrapped around his mouth, jerking his head back as a blade slit his throat. Strider quietly pulled the limp body further into the dark fog.

Addy ran past, unaware of the dead body hidden in the underbrush. At least twelve men remained. Strider slipped back into the night, quietly moving in on them. He caught up to the last pursuer in the group. Slipping out from the trees, he seemed to materialize before the man who had no chance to react as Strider's blade found its mark.

He stepped back into the fog, vanishing like a ghost. Like a wolf, he hunted his enemy, picking the stragglers off one by one, killing them with silent efficiency. Their comrades were none the wiser as they focused on their pursuit.

The next man fell as Strider dropped from a small embankment, rising in time to kill a third with an arrow to the back. Another man stopped, turning in time to be transfixed by another arrow. Strider was on the move again, quickly blending into the forest. He silenced another enemy before the group came to a halt. Strider skirted them as he searched for Addy. He spotted her wreathed in fog and darkness as she stood facing the remaining men.

Strider stayed still, a shadow among the fog, as he watched Addy predict her attacker's movement and counter. Her opponent should've dropped at the first strike, having severely underestimated the girl. But she drew back, throwing herself off balance in a desperate attempt to keep from killing the man. Strider would've shaken his head in disappointment had he not thought the movement would give him away. All the training he'd given her would prove useless if she refused to take a life to save her own.

The fog was growing thicker, allowing him to move closer. He watched Addy let the lesser swordsman dictate the battle. Time and time again, she didn't take advantage of the openings he offered her. The fight had ended the moment she refused to deal the killing blow. The Hunter began moving forward before the man knocked Addy's blade from her hand. He drew his blade when the two weapons clanged together, masking the sound of his sword being drawn.

The attacker raised his weapon as his companions, having seen the dark figure appear, tried to warn him. But he could not hear them. The fog of battle had deafened him from anything other than his kill. The blue yulie saber met ummanie steel, causing both swords to sing. The man hadn't expected Strider's powerful counter. It knocked his blade away, completely exposing him to a counterstrike.

The blue sword flashed again as Strider reversed the direction of his own attack to slash down, nearly severing the mercenary in two.

He pushed the body away, stepping between Addy and her kidnappers. The fog swallowed the fallen fighter. Even the thud he created when hitting the ground was dampened. Crimson stained the curved sword's tip, which glowed with an unnatural light in the darkness.

"Addy," he said, his voice low but firm. "Raise your sword."

His gaze never left the men as he waited for her to join him.

But she didn't. Instead, her quiet, shaking voice drifted to him in the darkness. "No… I can't."

The shock and brokenness in her voice stabbed his heart. He understood it far too well. He'd trained her to defend herself, but no amount of training could prepare one of such tender heart for the act of taking another person's life. She would need to come to terms with it; would need to find the resolve within herself. She would have to if she wanted to survive, but he wouldn't force her tonight.

The fog swirled around Strider's dark figure as he moved toward the six remaining mercenaries. They drew their blades, but Strider could see their fear. He attacked. The first man fell as he raised his sword to block a downward slice, but found the blade thrust into his side instead. The second came in with a charging swing, which Strider knocked aside, using the momentum of the attack to move around and behind the man, using the motion to bring his blade around to cut his enemy across the back, severing his spine. He advanced on the remaining men, leaving the fog to devour the bodies.

Three men rushed him at the same time, as it occurred to them to use superior numbers on the terrifying monster that'd killed three of them with contemptuous ease. Strider shifted to the right, moving forward with a surprising swiftness as he met the closest opponent who aimed a thrust at his side. Strider stepped aside, the saber now in his left hand as he brought it up to throw off the attacker's thrust, sending it away from his body. The force behind the block created enough of an opening to answer with his own counter thrust.

He'd just pierced up under the man's ribcage when the other two reached them. Strider leaped out of reach of the first blade, ducking under the other man's attack aimed at his head. The last remaining fighter hung back, unwilling to fight the hooded figure.

Strider parried, or completely dodged, each attack thrown at him by the men. Had they been skilled fighters, they would've likely worked in tandem against him. But both were as clumsy and untrained as the others Strider had dealt with. Nothing more than hired thugs, good for shock attacks against unsuspecting victims, but terrible in an actual fight and completely uncoordinated in their assault. Still, it was annoying to fight two at once. Their lack of training made them reckless and potentially more dangerous than even a skilled swordsman.

One fighter stepped forward, slashing at him. He met the attack and blocked it. The two swords locked, and Strider grabbed the other blade at the cross guard. He thrust his own blade, now free of having to block his opponent's sword, into the mercenary's stomach, pulling his enemy off balance and into the path of his companion's blade. The other mercenary's sword sliced a deep cut down his cohort's back.

Strider held onto the blade he'd stolen from the now-dead man. The other thug stepped back, shocked that he'd killed his companion. He wasn't prepared to block the sword that Strider threw directly at him like a javelin. It slammed into him, knocking him to the ground. He didn't rise, his eyes staring at nothing before being covered by the gray fog.

It swirled around the Hunter like eager spirits excited by the bloodshed. Blood dripped from his blade as he set his sights on the final thug, his face nothing but a pit of shadow. He was a demon of the night, out for blood. Strider advanced on the man, who fled in fear.

The mercenary's breaths came in panicked gasps as he stumbled through the dark and foggy forest. He was disoriented by fog and fear and didn't know where the horses were. Something moved to his left, and he lashed out with his blade. The sword hissed hollowly as it sliced through nothing but air. A shadow slid up behind him. The blue blade flashed one last time in the darkness.

Strider returned to find Addy hadn't moved from her spot. She stood back against the cliff, staring blankly into the darkness. The fog blanketed the floor of the forest, covering the bodies the Hunter had left behind in its tender mercy. Strider cleaned and sheathed his blade before he cautiously approached her.

Addy watched in shock as Strider appeared out of nowhere and killed her attacker. She continued to stare as he vanished into the fog and darkness. She could see the first two men, their dark forms in the fog, and she watched, as the shadow of Strider slew both of them. The fog hid the other men from view, but she heard their screams and cries as one after the other fell to the Hunter's blade. Then silence enveloped the world. The only sound she heard was her heart pounding in her ears as she leaned against the cliff for support.

Adrenaline pumped through her body, sapping her strength as her mind processed what had transpired. Her eyes stared into the dark fog without seeing, her emotions and thoughts whirling. Her body shook as the initial flurry of chaos, heart-stopping panic, and the drive to survive wore off. The memories of what had happened played back in her mind. She remembered the man she'd stabbed. Had she really stabbed someone? Did she kill him?

"Let's go," Strider said softly.

She felt his hand on her shoulder, gentle, but firm. She slowly looked up at him and in that moment, everything collided within her. Tears filled her eyes, and she moved without thinking. Reaching out for the only familiar thing there, she wrapped her arms around him.

Strider froze. He stood awkwardly as Addy continued crying, her tears already soaking into his shirt. She shook violently, her legs giving out on her as she leaned into him. He was forced to hold onto her to keep her upright. His body stiffened at the unexpected and unwelcome contact. He didn't know what to do. Greer wasn't here, the one she always hugged before. The one who always seemed to know what people needed. He had stupidly left him back with the horses and injured knight. He was now the only one around to offer comfort. But how did he do that?

He stood there a moment longer. For the first time since he sat bleeding in the forest, he was unsure of what to do. He finally settled on awkwardly patting her on the head like he would do with Greer when he was upset. The action felt inadequate. He was out of his depth as he stood with an arm around Addy to hold her up while he stroked her head.

Memories of his mother holding him while he cried flashed briefly in his mind, memories of them holding each other, as they both wept the day they had to accept that his father was never coming back. The image of himself crying alone as he held her limp hand, the world filled with the scent of her blood. Sorrow and guilt filled his chest, coating his ribs in frost and darkness, pressing in on his heart like an iron maiden. He blinked away the memories, but the pain remained.

His actions seemed to work, and he felt Addy slowly relax, her sobs quieting. She still buried her face in his shirt and refused to move, even as she calmed down. They needed to leave. But if he stepped away and let her go, she would fall. She seemed unable to stand on her own. He didn't snap at her like he'd done when he had saved her the last time, didn't press her to move. Instead, after a moment of thought, he swept her up into his arms. She didn't fight him as he picked her up. She simply curled against him, eyes closed. He said nothing as he walked, leaving the bodies buried in the fog.

Addy was vaguely aware of being picked up and carried. It reminded her of her father, who'd carried her this way a year ago when she collapsed from a fever. He'd cradled her just as gently in his arms.

"It'll be okay Addy," he had said, as her mother rushed about ordering servants to fetch water and towels and summoning the healer. They'd both tucked her in and one of them always slept in her reading chair beside the bed at night until she recovered.

At some point, she was lifted into a saddle. She sat sidesaddle, resting against the warmth of Strider as he rode in the saddle behind her. She didn't open her eyes as she muttered softly, her voice haunted, "I killed someone."

He didn't respond for a long time. All she heard was the clomping of hooves and the steady beat of Strider's heart.

"No, you didn't," she heard his voice rumble in his chest.

"I did. I stabbed a man."

"He was still alive when I found him. I slit his throat to keep him quiet."

"You killed him?" Addy whispered, her eyes still closed. *Like you kill everyone.* The thought drifted through her mind. *No, not everyone,* she reminded herself. He hadn't killed Toris, or her father's men. He hadn't killed her.

"How do you do it?" she asked. "How do you kill?"

"I used to kill because I had to. Now I do it because I am good at it."

"Don't you feel guilty? Doesn't it bother you?"

"Does a wolf apologize while eating a fawn in front of its bleating mother?"

The words were like a growl vibrating from his chest. Addy said nothing for a long time, wondering how a man became like Strider. How many lives had he taken to grow so calloused? What horrors had driven him to this life? Or did he walk into it happy and willing? She didn't have the strength to ask. She didn't want to know.

"Thank you," she mumbled, wrapping her arms around him again. She felt him stiffen for a moment before relaxing again. Strider didn't respond, and after a time, she drifted into sleep.

Strider felt Addy relax as she fell asleep. He glanced down at her still form, unsure why he had lied about killing the man she'd stabbed. He had found him alive. That was true. But he'd left him knowing the man was going to die. There was too much blood. It was dark blood. The kind that came from deep inside a man—the kind that signaled death.

Addy had killed him. But he'd taken the blame to shield her.

What was one more death on his hands? Hers were clean. Was it so bad that he tried to keep them that way?

"You're welcome," he said quietly, though she never heard him.

His eyes found Greer as he padded faithfully beside Copper. He was looking up at them with a knowing look. He knew the Hunter lied, and he knew why. Strider let out a defeated sigh before growling at the wolf, "You win."

Greer smiled as his tail wagged.

Strider eyed him, reminded for the hundredth time how dangerous Greer could be if he put his mind to it.

Chapter 33
A New "Friend"

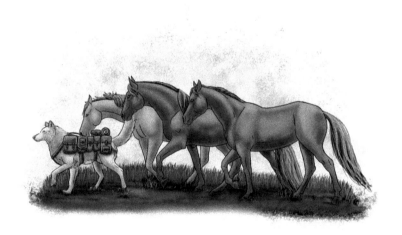

The sound of jingling gear and the snort of a horse drew Addy from her sleep. She slowly opened her eyes, before closing them again quickly, as the memories of the night before hit her. Her father's soldiers were dead. She hadn't let herself think about it while trying to escape, but now she had nothing to keep her from dwelling on the fact that she'd led them into an ambush.

Addy subconsciously snuggled closer to the warmth beside her before remembering who it was. She jerked away from Strider, whom she'd cuddled into, her face turning red. She looked up at him with a sheepish look. He hardly glanced down at her as he continued to watch the surrounding land, always looking for danger.

She put her hands in her lap, aware that she'd had them wrapped around him for most of the ride. He said nothing. Somehow, that made things worse. Pulling her cloak tighter around her, she straightened and cleared her throat, trying to find something to say. All she could think of were the chastising words her mother and lady-in-waiting would have for her.

Her father was furiously ranting in her head about proper decorum. She shut all of them out as she began stroking her own hair, her thoughts turning back to how Strider had awkwardly patted her on the head, in an attempt to comfort her the night before. She'd felt how stiff he'd been as she cried into his shirt. Like he was made of stone. But she hadn't cared. She'd needed someone, and he had at least tried to help.

Her eyes began wandering, looking anywhere but at Strider, as she tried to act normal. They were still in the forest. Weak sunlight streamed through the fog that still hung thick in the air, casting silhouettes of trees through the white screen. She heard the clopping of hooves; many hooves, in fact. She peaked around Strider, spotted Su'lris, and beamed. Her smile faded into a look of puzzlement when she saw a body draped over his saddle, arms bound behind their back.

"Who is that?" she asked, grateful for something to distract her.

"One of your kidnappers."

Addy raised a brow. "So, you didn't kill all of them?"

"I still plan to kill him. How quickly depends on how well he answers my questions."

"What questions?"

"Who the traitor is inside your father's house, for one."

Addy's back stiffened, and the knot that had settled in her stomach ever since the messenger first appeared tightened. "So there really is a traitor," she whispered. "You don't think the messenger we sent to the castle was intercepted?"

"Who would know to intercept him?" Strider asked. "It'd be far easier to wait for word of your location and send men to stop you than recruit enough manpower to watch every single road. That many hired swords would draw attention as quickly as they would drain the coffers."

She let out a heavy sigh. It made sense, but she still didn't want to believe it. "Or they could have an information network throughout the cities, and one of them sent the message," Addy suggested.

Strider gave a small nod before speaking. "That is possible." His gaze slid over to the man. "We'll see if he has any input."

Addy's own gaze traveled back to the man on her horse. Then something else caught her eye. Other horses! They followed behind Su'lris, and Addy had to lean out further to see them. She cried out when she spotted a new figure slumped over a saddle. "Tevin!"

Strider pulled Copper to a halt as Addy scrambled out of the saddle. She barely landed on her feet as she rushed toward the knight. His horse shied away. Addy grabbed its reins as she worked to steady it.

"Is he alive?" she asked, moving to the side of the animal.

"He was last time I checked," Strider replied flatly. "Though it's been a while. At least he's stopped mumbling your name every time he became semi-conscious."

She glared at Strider as she fumbled with the rope he'd used to tie the man to the saddle.

"Why didn't you use magic to heal him?"

"I was kind of busy trying to save you," Strider pointed out dryly. "His wounds are bandaged."

He climbed off Copper as Addy reached for her dagger. He grabbed her hand, stopping her from cutting the knots when they wouldn't give. Gently nudging her aside, he began untying the ropes.

"Well, help him now!" Addy ordered.

"This is a waste of time," Strider muttered under his breath.

"Gently!" Addy scolded Strider, as he roughly pulled the man down from the saddle.

Strider grunted a less than flattering tahrvin word as he carried the dead weight off the trail they'd been following and into the trees. There wasn't much in the way of clear ground in the area, and Strider settled for depositing Tevin on top of a bush.

"That wasn't gentle. You just dropped him in a bush!"

"I'll drop him on the open ground if you wish," Strider responded, drawing his dagger. "After you help me clear a camp." He started cutting away the brush with his blade.

Addy helped cut and hack at the branches. Strider moved much quicker than her—his speed born from practice. He soon overtook her but didn't clear the area she had started. Leaving her to finish, he built a small fire pit. They threw most of the green wood away as burning it would create too much smoke. Strider bundled several stacks to take with them later, securing them to the saddles of a couple of horses.

Finished clearing her part of the camp, Addy knelt beside Tevin, where he now lay on a blanket. Strider returned to the horses, bringing them closer and off the game trail. The thug moaned. Strider hit him over the head with his dagger hilt before taking the man and tying him to a sturdy tree, arms and hands still bound behind his back. Greer sat near the man, keeping watch over their prisoner. Addy bounced and fidgeted as she sat there, watching Strider with accusing eyes as he did everything but heal Tevin.

"Are you done now?" she snapped, after Strider finished checking his knots. "And why did you tie up Tevin?"

The knight's hands were tied behind his back.

"Because he thinks I kidnapped you," Strider said matter-of-factly, as he came to crouch before the injured man. "I'd rather he not try to strangle me while I am saving him."

"We're untying him after I explain everything."

"Do what you like."

Addy folded her arms across her chest, fixing him with a stern stare. She eyed him as he undid the bandages he'd wrapped around the man's chest and abdomen. He had pulled the arrow out with little trouble. The arrow hadn't pierced far enough to become stuck. There had been a lot of blood, but Strider realized the injury was fairly superficial once he cleaned it.

As he removed the bandages, Addy could smell the pungent scent of the strange mixture he'd used on his own wound to help stop the bleeding. Her hands went to her mouth when she saw the wound dealt by the sword. This was her fault.

The Hunter's head cocked as he looked at the knight. Did he really want to go through the trouble of healing him? At least one of the injuries was serious enough to threaten his life if it remained untreated. Why did he care? Why should he risk his soul?

"Well?" Addy pressed.

"You realize what this is going to take from me if I do this, right?" Strider asked.

Her gaze dropped, unable to meet his. She'd seen him nearly die in The Ways. He'd told her the risk of using magic. Did she still want him to risk his life to save this man? It'd terrified her when she thought she was going to lose both him and Greer. Could she really ask him to risk his life again, for someone he didn't know?

"We don't need him."

Addy gave a disbelieving look. Then she remembered who she was dealing with and instead uttered an exasperated huff. "You don't help someone just because you think they'll be useful. Seriously, how did you get this way?"

Strider stared off over her shoulder, not saying anything for several heartbeats as he seemed lost in thought. "That is a long and bloody story."

"He was hurt... protecting me." She locked eyes with Strider. "Which is your job, as I recall."

He didn't have to heal him completely. She didn't want him to risk ending up so close to death like before. But she couldn't let Tevin die.

"Don't go as far as you did with Greer, just enough to save him."

"If he attacks me when he wakes up, I'll kill him."

"He won't," Addy said firmly. "And you won't. Now. Heal. Him."

Strider looked at her for a long, quiet moment. She felt responsible for this man. His death would weigh heavily on her. Shrugging, he placed a hand on Tevin's chest. The magic filled his body with its familiar warmth as it flowed through him and into Tevin. It homed in on the injury as it set to work repairing the damage.

Tevin took a sharp intake of breath as his body reacted to the magic. Strider's eyes flicked to his face, but the man didn't show any signs of waking, so he returned to his task. He felt the strain on his soul as he drew on more magic, funneling the vast well through a small line. His chest felt tight almost immediately, a warning that his soul was weary. He kept the magic flowing steadily, the warmth in his blood growing hot as the tightness in his chest turned to pain.

His soul burned, unable to handle the stress for much longer. He pulled away, his breath heavy as he severed the connection. The heat and pain faded, leaving behind a severe cold that made him shiver. Sucking in a breath, he closed his eyes as the fresh pain stabbed through his chest. He could feel a dull ache forming in the back of his skull, and he found it difficult to catch his breath. It felt like his lungs were half frozen. The earth beneath him swayed like the deck of a ship tossed at sea. Further warning that his soul couldn't take much more.

"Strider?" Addy asked, concerned.

He opened his eyes to see that she'd moved closer to him, a hand outstretched as if she had meant to reach for his shoulder. She withdrew it quickly. But he'd seen.

He sat back, his voice harsh and breathless. "I'm fine. Bandage him back up."

Addy looked down at Tevin. His wounds were not completely healed, but they didn't look like they would threaten his life.

"You couldn't heal him more?"

Strider shook his head. "Healing takes the most power to perform." He could cause quite a bit of damage with the magic he had access to without breaking a sweat. But healing such an injury left him completely drained. "Even if I had that much power, I wouldn't heal him completely."

"Why not?"

"It is good to let the body heal itself when able," he explained. "This will also make it difficult for him to misbehave."

Addy frowned at him. "He won't attack you once I explain to him what is really going on."

Strider gave a scoff. "If he behaves, you can practice learning healing magic on him."

Addy's eyes lit up. "You're going to teach me how to heal people?"

"It'd be a waste not to try; you've found your connection to magic," Strider muttered. "Plus, we have someone for you to practice on." He'd have to slip something in the knight's drink to knock him out each night. Though his sleeping powder had no side effects, the knight may notice his wound healing abnormally fast. Blaming that on the poultice he used should be enough to deflect any questions; such items were sold to the public, albeit at an exorbitant price.

Addy placed her hand over Strider's, her brown eyes gazing into his. "Thank you."

He reclaimed his hand, giving a dismissive shrug. "You need to learn."

"I meant thank you for healing Tevin," she amended.

Strider gave a slow nod. "You're welcome."

Chapter 34

Question Everything

Tevin stirred shortly after Addy finished bandaging him. Strider left them to start a fire. As he left, Addy noticed he moved differently, like he was unsteady on his feet. Her brow knit together in concern. Had he used more magic than he'd told her? She would've asked him, but the waking knight stole her attention.

Tevin's eyes fluttered open to stare up at her in confusion. "Lady Fenforde?" he mumbled, as he tried to sit up, wincing when his injury protested.

She put a hand on his shoulder to stop him from rising. "Don't move yet," she urged. "You need to rest."

"What happened? The ambush..." he trailed off, as he remembered what happened. "You escaped and came back for me?"

Addy gave a small smile and shook her head. "I escaped, but I didn't come back for you."

"Then some of us survived the ambush. They rescued me?"

Addy looked away, unable to meet his gaze.

Puzzled by her actions, Tevin propped himself up onto his elbows to look around for more of his comrades in arms. Addy moved in front of him, blocking his view of the firepit for a moment longer.

"No," Addy said, shaking her head. She bit her lip, trying to figure out how to explain what had happened. "I don't think there were any other survivors."

"Then how am I still here?" Tevin asked, growing more confused. "Did the gods spare me?"

Strider scoffed, as he struck his knife against some flint. "The gods had nothing to do with it."

Addy made a face as she turned to Strider. "You're not helping."

"I wasn't trying to."

Tevin shifted, trying to peer around Addy to see who she was talking to, but she moved to block his view once more.

He gave her a frustrated look. "Who is that?"

Addy let out a controlled breath before saying, "He's the one who saved us."

She shifted out of the way so Tevin could see who had spoken. He took in the dark cloak, curved blade, and the cloth masking the lower half of the stranger's face where the hood didn't currently cast it in shadow. His gaze trailed to the recurve bow with the felaris feather tied to the tip before shifting to look at Greer sitting not very far away. Tevin tensed. Pushing himself up further, he reached for a sword that wasn't there. Cursing quietly, he tried position himself between the man and Addy but his body wouldn't respond.

"Did he hurt you?" he hissed, as he eyed Strider.

"No more than usual," Strider muttered.

Tevin's eyes flashed with anger, and he tried to stand.

Addy gave Strider an exasperated gesture as she tried to keep Tevin down. He didn't have the strength to fight her. His jaw tightened.

"No, he hasn't hurt me." She glared at Strider. "Stop antagonizing him!"

Strider shrugged and placed more wood on the fire.

"You need to get out of here," Tevin ordered her, as he glared at Strider.

Addy didn't appreciate being bossed around by the knight, and her tone indicated as much when she replied, "No, I don't. You need to listen."

His eyes briefly flicked her way before returning to the threat of the cloaked figure. Addy didn't wait for him to reply as she began.

"Strider is not the enemy. Though he does a good job of acting like it," she mumbled the last sentence as she glared at Strider.

"He's the Dark Ranger," Tevin argued. "He kidnapped you."

"I'm not a 'Dark' Ranger," growled Strider, tired of hearing people call him any sort of Ranger.

"He isn't the one who kidnapped me," Addy interjected before Tevin could respond. "I hired him to protect me from those who did."

Disbelief pulled at his features. "He tricked you somehow! Made you believe you were in danger and that he is the only one who could protect you."

"You did a mighty fine job protecting her," Strider piped up irritably.

"Shut up!" Addy yelled.

Strider flinched as the sound made the pain in his head worsen.

"Not so loud," he hissed. He leaned back against a fallen tree that he hadn't bothered to clear and pinched the bridge of his nose between his thumb and forefinger.

"Stop antagonizing him, and I'll not yell! What has gotten into you? You're even more moody than normal."

"That tends to happen when you push too hard using magic," Strider said under his breath. He'd meant to say it quietly, but Addy heard.

Addy's anger faded. "Did it really drain you that much?"

Strider grunted, his eyes remaining closed. "That kid better be worth it."

"I am not a kid," Tevin said. "And what are you talking about?"

Strider let out a heavy breath, not in the mood to explain. He heaved himself to his feet and walked over to Copper to fetch a pot. His head throbbed as a wave of dizziness washed over him. Placing a hand on the horse's saddle for the support, he closed his eyes. He stood there until the worst had passed, continuing to ignore the knight as he fished out dried pork, some potatoes, and other supplies to make a small stew.

Tevin watched him closely. Addy took Tevin's hands in hers. This caused him to focus on her.

"You were hurt badly in the ambush. Strider found you while coming to rescue me. He was the one who bound your wounds and brought you with him. He saved me from the men who ambushed us, and he used his magic to save your life. He didn't need to do any of that. But he did."

Tevin found it hard to meet Addy's gaze. He looked away, finding his eyes resting on Strider as he prepared a meal for them.

"He never kidnapped me, Tevin. I know. I escaped the men that did in Denmahr."

She went on to tell him about that night. The storm, the landslide, about how the men who had her bore the Denmahr crest. She spoke about having to survive in Altia. Told him how Strider helped her when Gen and his men had first cornered her in the alley.

She left out the part where she'd first stolen from him and how he'd left her to die as a result, figuring it would be best not to tell Tevin of the crimes the Hunter had committed against her. She also left out how she'd tried to steal Greer as she ran away, and omitted The Ways or the other pieces of secret information Strider had shared with her.

"If he is truly as innocent as you say, then why did he attack your father's men in Fair Fork?"

"They attacked me," Strider cut in dryly. "I merely finished the fight."

"Why didn't you try to explain yourself?"

"Would you have listened?" Strider asked pointedly, fixing Tevin with an even stare. It was the first time Strider had really looked at him since he'd woken up and the knight met his gaze defiantly. But Tevin couldn't hold the stare for long and shrank back as he looked away.

"I don't know," he finally answered.

Strider turned back to scoop stew into two cups.

Addy cocked her head and frowned as she left the knight's side to retrieve a bowl.

"Tevin needs one too."

Strider gave Tevin a sidelong glance. "Have you asked him?"

Addy made a point of exaggerating her movements as she turned around. "Tevin, would you like some stew?"

Tevin nodded, though his face looked unconvincing.

"Are you sure?" Addy asked, seeing the expression.

"You don't have to accept it just because she is offering," Strider told him. "We don't need you reopening your wound by vomiting after forcing your body to eat."

Tevin scowled at Strider, who sat unaffected.

"Can that happen?" Addy asked Strider, now concerned for the knight.

Strider nodded. "His body has experienced a lot of shock and blood loss. In that state, it tends to reject anything you try to force into it."

He could see something click in Addy's mind. "In Altia you…"

"Yes," Strider cut in sharply. That had been why he'd given his mutton to Greer and had only sipped at his soup.

"I am fine to eat the soup," Tevin piped up angrily. "Though I should probably expect it to be poisoned."

"It's not poisoned, but it tastes terrible," Strider said casually.

"I could've cooked," Addy interjected.

"You were busy."

Tevin looked aghast. "You make Lady Fenforde cook for you?"

Addy smiled, and Strider looked to the sky before bending over his cup of soup. He ignored the knight as he ate, done dealing with the man. Addy grabbed another cup for Tevin and returned to the fire. She poured a small amount from the pot and brought it to the knight before sitting beside him.

"Don't eat it if you think you will throw it back up," she said, before handing Tevin his cup.

He looked at the stew, the scent of it made him feel nauseous. He quietly handed it back to her, and she took it without comment. She ate her own meal in silence. Strider had already finished his food. Taking the pot from the fire, he set it aside to let it cool. Addy paid no mind as she ate.

The food wasn't bad. But it left much to be desired, and she knew she could've made it taste better. Especially now that she'd learned how to locate different edible plants she could use to add more flavor.

Strider hadn't bothered to add anything more than what was necessary for survival.

Greer let out a sneeze as he padded over to the fire. The Hunter stroked the di'horvith's head before fetching a bowl from Greer's packs and pouring soup into it. The large canine eagerly lapped up the dinner, snorting and snuffling in his rush to devour everything. Addy caught Tevin eyeing Greer like a rabbit might eye a starving fox.

"That is Greer," Addy told him.

Greer's ears perked at the mention of his name. His tail wagged in a friendly manner as he trotted toward Addy and Tevin.

"Ho there," Tevin warned, holding up a hand. "Stay back!"

"He won't hurt you," Addy assured him.

Greer ignored the man's orders as he lumbered over. He came up beside Addy and gave her ear a kiss. She giggled and swatted him away playfully. This only encouraged Greer, and he pressed in again, stealing another kiss before flopping down next to her, his great head laying on her lap. He sniffed at Tevin, and his fluffy tail wagged harder as he looked at him.

"See?" Addy said, looking at Tevin as she rubbed the wolf's fluffy cheeks and ears. Greer grumbled his appreciation.

Tevin had heard the stories about how this vicious wolf had ripped men apart as they tried to rescue Addy, how he was like a demon who thirsted for blood. He was a large, light-colored wolf and because of that, intimidating. But he didn't act like a bloodthirsty monster as he lay there, accepting the affections of Lady Fenforde. He looked like a big, friendly dog.

Tentatively, he reached out. The wolf watched him, his eyes kind and happy as he wiggled closer so Tevin could reach him easily. Carefully, the knight began petting the massive wolf's head, and he heard the thump of the animal's tail increase in speed as he leaned into the touch.

Addy smiled, which Tevin returned. Greer inched closer, savoring the attention being given to him by the two ummanie.

"Alright, Greer, leave them be," Strider said, from his spot by the fire. "You have a job to do."

Greer huffed before pulling away. The giant wolf padded over to the resting Hunter, who had moved to lie by the fire, using the packs he'd removed from Greer as a pillow. He lay wrapped in his cloak like a lumpy shadow on the ground. With another heavy huff, the di'horvith flopped on top of the Hunter, who grunted in surprise as the air was knocked out of him.

"Greer!" Strider gasped, the pounding in his head increasing. He clutched his chest as pain exploded within it. He took several breaths, trying to regain it, but couldn't seem to find enough air. Seeing this, Greer wiggled forward and began licking his chin. Strider pushed his face away, and the di'horvith pressed the attack until both wolf and Hunter were wrestling on the ground. The Hunter grabbed Greer, using his shoulder, back, and leg muscles, he rolled over, taking his brother with him. Strider straddled the half di'horvith, pinning the wiggling animal. Greer smiled up at him, tongue lolling from the corner of his jaws.

"Are you done now?" Strider panted.

Greer gave a small sneeze, and Strider playfully cuffed him behind the ear before letting him up. He sat back, taking a deep breath for the first time since he'd healed Tevin. Strider noticed his chest and head no longer hurt, and he frowned in puzzlement. He also noticed the sound of Addy laughing. Tevin didn't join in as he stared at him, eyes narrowed.

In his tussle with Greer, his hood had fallen back, revealing his pointed ears. Strider returned Tevin's glare with a cold one of his own as he pulled his hood back over his head and laid back down. Greer had taken up his post, sitting in the same spot as earlier.

"Addy, you take first watch," Strider said, as he rolled over, turning his back on the two.

"Seriously?" Addy asked. "Why?"

"Because, aside from your knight, you're the only one here who has slept in the last two days."

Addy narrowed her eyes suspiciously. "You've never let me keep watch before."

Strider waved his hand dismissively. "First time for everything. Greer will stay up with you if you're worried."

"I'm not worried," Addy shot back. "Just suspicious."

"Good, you're learning."

Chapter 35

First Watch

Addy wrapped herself in a blanket Strider had retrieved from the horses, doing her best not to think about the man it once belonged to. She wasn't sure how long she'd slept in the saddle, but it had left her sore and stiff. Strider appeared to have fallen asleep. Wrapped up in his cloak, he looked like a pool of shadow in the uneven firelight. Tevin sat at her side, and she guessed he would likely stay up with her despite his own weariness.

Addy had never watched the camp before, though Strider had already taught her how to keep a lookout in the darkness. She wouldn't have believed someone if they'd told her she'd one day learn magic, swordplay, survival skills, and more from a man she'd tried to steal from.

She used one of those skills tonight while she kept watch, doing her best to never let her gaze linger in one area for long, never looking directly into the shadows when something caught her eye, but used her peripheral vision instead to catch shapes and movements she otherwise couldn't see. Tevin stirred beside her, and she looked back at him. He grimaced as he moved in closer to her and whispered, "We need to get you out of here."

Addy frowned, her gaze shifting to the sky in annoyance. "No, you need to rest."

"I am well enough to ride."

Addy doubted that very much. "We're not going anywhere," she told him, her voice taking on the old air of someone used to having her words obeyed.

Tevin frowned, his voice rising slightly. "I understand if you're afraid. If he has hurt you or threatened you into staying…"

"He's done nothing!" Addy hissed, barely remembering to keep her voice down so as not to wake Strider. "I told you what really happened. He is helping me!"

"You told me, but it could all be a lie he has made you believe. Where is the proof?"

"And where is your proof of what transpired?" Addy challenged.

"King Elias-"

"You're trusting the words of another country's king?"

"He has been an ally of Myvara for many years. He's given no reason-"

"Just because he pretends to be our ally doesn't mean he is one."

"He killed King Elias's men!" Tevin said, jerking a thumb toward Strider.

"To protect me when they tried to take me again!" Addy countered.

"Or so Strider wants you to believe! My lady, he has been lying to you."

Addy looked at him, taking a moment to formulate her response. "You think he infiltrated castle Timara, came into my room"— her eyebrows raised—"kidnapped me, smuggled me across the border, and put me in a carriage escorted by soldiers bearing King Elias's crest. Only to send a mudslide that could've killed me down onto the carriage, killing his men.

All so I could escape and live in Altia for two moons before he came and *rescued me*, then waited for me to ask him for help before agreeing to take me home?" Sarcasm bordering on exasperation laced her words. "That is a rather complicated plan. To do what? Win my father's favor?"

Tevin opened his mouth to reply, but said nothing, as his face took on a look of consideration. His jaw worked before tensing as he pressed on.

"He is still dangerous, my lady."

"You're right, he is," Addy agreed. "Dangerous to those trying to take me."

"And what is to stop him from turning on you once your father has paid him?"

Addy paused for a long time, her gaze shifting to Strider.

"I don't think he expects to get paid," Addy said somberly. "I honestly think he was hoping you would take me home safely."

Tevin's brows knitted at her words. "Because he is a yulie?"

Addy's gaze snapped back to him, a look of shock on her face.

"I saw when his hood fell while he played with Greer."

"Everyone believes he is responsible. My father and brothers will try to kill him if he comes close to my home, and if they don't kill him, they'll imprison him. In doing so, they'll find out what he is and kill him, anyway. If Strider fights back..." she trailed off.

"He will confirm all the lies that were told about him," Tevin finished for her.

"That is why he left me with you."

She had been thinking about it ever since she'd learned the truth about Strider's parentage. Before, the act of him returning her home safely would've been enough to convince her father to show the Hunter his gratitude. He'd likely never learn Strider was part yulie, because he always kept his hood up.

But now things were much more complicated. If she'd considered it, surely Strider had, and came to the same conclusion. Her father likely would repay his efforts with a noose around his neck or a sword through the gut. She wasn't sure if her mother could stop him, even if she wanted to.

Tevin rubbed the back of his neck as he looked over at the sleeping form of the Hunter. Addy could tell that he didn't trust the Hunter. She knew Strider hadn't given Tevin any reason to suspect that she was being mistreated. But the rumors, combined with Strider's lineage, clouded his judgement. Addy knew that it'd take time for Tevin to see past his prejudices.

She yawned, stretching her arms over her head. "Strider told me something once," she sighed, as she relished the stretch. She lowered her arms, re-wrapping the blanket around herself. "Actions speak more truth than words ever will." She cocked her head as she looked back at him, her brown hair glowing amber in the firelight. "Watch him and decide for yourself."

"I will," Tevin agreed.

Addy didn't like the way Tevin eyed Strider. She fixed him with a hard look learned from her mother.

"You're not to try to harm him," she told him. "That is an order."

Tevin gave her a frustrated look, but he remembered his place and didn't argue. Instead, he bowed his head and said three simple words that would bind him to her wishes. "Yes, my lady."

Greer arrived then, nudging Addy to tell her that her watch had ended. She yawned again and stood.

"You're welcome by the fire," she offered.

Tevin shook his head, unwilling to be so close to Strider.

Addy shrugged and went to find a spot near the fire's warmth. Greer returned to his position as he took his turn at watch, leaving Tevin alone with his thoughts.

Chapter 36
The Trouble With Knights

Tevin stood slowly. His head swam, and he felt nauseous as he shakily began walking toward the horses. Neither Addy nor Strider stirred. He hated to leave Addy behind with Strider. But he was in no condition to fight the man. If he could steal the horses and ride to the next town, he'd be able to gather more men to hunt them down. Without the horses, their travel would be slower. More men would bring hounds and use the items inside the saddlebags to track their scent. They would free Addy of Strider, and he would see that she returned safely to her home, or he would die trying.

A form appeared before him, forcing him to stop. Large brown eyes looked at him, framed by Greer's furry face. The wolf stared up at him with a worried look. He whined quietly.

"Move," Tevin whispered, as he tried to step around the di'horvith.

But Greer barred his path. Tevin raised a hand and advanced on Greer threateningly, but Greer stood firm. The di'horvith's soulful eyes bore into him, soft and pleading. Tevin let his hand fall, unwilling to harm the animal. Instead, he tried to push Greer aside with both hands. He didn't budge. Tevin pushed harder before letting out a gasp as the pain in his side and nausea in his head brought him to his knees.

He still had his hands on Greer's shoulder as he knelt before the wolf, head bowed in pain. He felt the hot breath of Greer on his forehead. Slowly lifting his gaze, Tevin forgot the horses as he locked eyes with Greer's. Those dark brown eyes were like deep pools that drew him in. As he peered into them, Tevin felt a sense of calm grow within him. He felt a powerful pull to stay to protect Addy.

Greer pulled away, and Tevin blinked, confusion fogging his mind for a moment. Finally, he sighed in defeat, no longer possessing the strength to pull himself into the saddle. He would stay, if only to make sure Strider didn't harm Lady Fenforde. He didn't have the strength to fight Greer, nor could he bring himself to hurt him.

Slowly he got to his feet, and with Greer offering his support, he stumbled back to the blanket. He collapsed onto the makeshift bed and felt Greer snuggle up next to him. As he drifted off to sleep, Tevin was unaware of golden eyes watching him from underneath a dark hood.

Strider loosened his grip on his bow as he watched Tevin return to his blanket with Greer. He would've shot the knight had he attempted to ride off with the horses. He almost shot him when he raised a hand to strike Greer. But to the knight's credit, he didn't follow through with his threat, instead opting to shove Greer aside rather than hurt him.

But the di'horvith didn't move, and Strider had the sense that Greer had won a battle without dealing a single blow as he led Tevin back to his bed. They were now both asleep, cuddled close, and snoring softly. Strider silently got to his feet. He moved beyond the dying fire, melting into the shadows, like a spirit from the abyss.

Selecting a place where he could watch the camp without being seen, he settled in. His soul was exhausted, and it still hadn't recovered from the damage he'd done to it when he saved Greer's life. The cold never truly left him now. It ate at his soul and made his limbs feel slow and heavy.

The ice had spread within him with new strength, its frigid claws encircling his soul, threatening to drag him down as it always did. It whispered sweet words of oblivion and rest. The fire popped and sizzled, casting sparks into the air, but Strider was beyond its warmth.

The Hunter's eyes closed, his breathing growing shallow. He was being drawn deeper into the cold, the blackness. It would give him rest, it would give him peace, and he would see his loved ones again. But something kept him from leaving.

He looked down at his wrist to see a silver thread wrapped firmly around it, intertwined with a new thread. One of fiery orange. Both shook with the strain of keeping him from slipping closer to death. He looked back toward the fire's dying light to see Addy and Greer's sleeping forms.

He'd made a promise to return her home. He was many things, but he didn't break his word when he gave it. His gaze returned to the darkness one last time before moving back toward the image of Addy and Greer. Strider took a deep breath as he opened his eyes. He'd slumped against a tree whose shadow he'd sought shelter under. All was still, filled with the sound of the fire, accompanied by the forest's night songs. Strider rubbed a hand down his face as he tried to fend off the coldness that still lingered within him.

As he did so, he felt eyes on him. Looking back to camp, he met the gaze of Greer. The di'horvith was watching him from where he lay beside Tevin. His intense expression slowly softened as he seemed to see something that assured him. He thumped his tail once before laying back down and going to sleep. Strider was struck for the hundredth time by how the wolf made him feel as if he were seeing into his soul.

His gaze shifted to the prisoner, who'd begun to stir. Strider watched the man as he slowly came to and realized the situation he was in. The Hunter's head cocked as he observed the man as he tried to get free.

As he worked, he found Strider had positioned the knots so that they faced up toward his elbows and out of the reach of his fingers. The man stopped, seeming to sense someone watching him. But he didn't notice Strider hidden in the darkness. Deciding that no one was there, the man went back to work trying to get loose as he glanced warily toward camp.

The prisoner felt, more than saw, a presence to his left as a low, menacing voice, like the growl of a wolf, spoke out of the darkness.

"Keep still, keep quiet, or I'll do more than just knock you out," the dark voice threatened, causing the man's heart to freeze.

He looked to his left, but no one was there. Only darkness greeted his searching gaze. But he couldn't deny the terror that filled him at the sound of that voice. The man spent the rest of the night trying to keep still as the sensation of being watched by a vicious predator kept him on edge.

Strider remained hidden, even as the sun rose, and Addy stirred. She began going about setting a pot on the fire, and soon the scent of coffee filled the air.

Tevin awoke, and Greer stood up with a stretch. He pranced around the camp, tail wagging, before disappearing into the forest. He reappeared a short time later to take up his position watching the prisoner, who remained completely still and silent. In the daylight, Tevin could see the man tied to the tree. He gestured toward him.

"Is this one of them who attacked us and took you?"

"It is," Addy confirmed.

Tevin's expression grew dark.

"I kept him alive to question him," Strider said, causing the prisoner to jump as he appeared next to him. The Hunter fixed his prey with a cold, pitiless look. "I plan to skin him if he doesn't answer my questions."

Addy handed Strider a cup of coffee, her face growing stone cold. "You're not dressing him up like a deer."

The Hunter peered out at her from behind the mug as he drank.

"Seeing as it was your men he killed," Strider said, eyeing Tevin. "What would you like to do with him, Noble Knight?"

Tevin, who'd been staring at the thug, now focused on Strider. He had to work his jaw loose when he realized he'd been clenching it.

"I want him brought to the next town and publicly executed," Tevin answered harshly.

"It will be a pain and a risk to bring him along. Why wait?" Strider asked, his expression and tone casual. "I have a rope to hang him, or if you prefer beheading, my yulie blade can easily cleave a man's neck. Though I won't promise that I could cut it off with one strike."

Tevin fixed Strider with a measured stare, his eyes a hard as flint. "I won't have you killing him."

"Then I'll let you send the horse out from underneath him, and he can dangle from a tree."

"No."

"It is within your power, Noble Knight," Strider pointed out, his voice dripping with sarcasm as he uttered the title.

"I am not going to exact justice here," Tevin said flatly. "He will be tried publicly, and executed, publicly. I want people to know the price for attacking a knight of Myvara."

Strider's head dipped to one side as he accepted this answer. "No killing then."

Addy looked back and forth between the two men. Tevin's face was flushed. She could tell that the conversation had disturbed him. Strider was as calm and collected as ever. Casually discussing this man's life as if he were going over a shopping list. The Hunter turned his attention back to the prisoner.

"The knight has been kind enough to let you live a little longer. But I am not. There are ways to make you suffer without killing you," he said, his voice low. "You will answer my questions with a simple yes or no. Only elaborate if I ask. Respond in silence and you'll regret it." He drew his knife and tilted his head as he regarded Addy.

"You might want to take your knight for a walk."

Addy frowned at him, and Tevin stepped forward, as if to stop Strider. But Greer barred their way.

"You want to know who betrayed your family," Strider said to Addy. "Who killed your father's men? Then let me do my job."

Addy sat down on the log, her arms folded and back straight. "I want to hear what he has to say," she said with resolve. "He attacked my father's men. He took me. I have a right to hear."

Tevin placed a hand on her shoulder. "Lady Fenforde, this is not something a woman of your standing should witness."

The Hunter's gaze was as cold and emotionless as the metal they resembled.

Addy shrugged him off and lifted her chin in defiance. "I'm not a child that needs coddling. I'm staying here."

Strider gave his own shrug of indifference, then turned back to the man. "You understand my instructions?"

The man nodded, then remembered to utter a shaky. "Y-yes."

Strider nodded and Greer came to sit on the prisoner's right. With a coffee cup in one hand, knife in the other, Strider asked a series of questions. "Did you know who it was you were kidnapping?"

"I swear on K'yarie's-"

The edge of Strider's dagger flashed up and pressed against the man's cheek, stopping him cold.

"Yes, or no," Strider cut in, his voice and gaze as sharp as the dagger's edge.

"No," the man answered.

Greer let out a low growl, fangs bared in what looked like a vicious smile. Strider's blade slid softly to the man's ear.

"Lie to me again, and I'll take your ear."

The thug tried to move his head away, but the dagger followed, pressing harder against the section where the top of his ear and skull met, biting into the flesh. He froze and gulped.

"Do you know who hired you?"

"N-no."

This time Greer remained silent, his lips curling back over his long fangs.

Strider withdrew the knife with a small nod. The prisoner visibly relaxed.

"That wasn't so hard." He took another sip of his coffee before asking his next question. "You didn't know who hired you, did your boss?"

"No."

Strider gestured with the knife for him to elaborate.

"He had a go-between, but I don't know who it was. Tatcher never brought me when he went to meet him. Never said where he was going, either."

"Did you know how Tatcher intended to hand the Lady over?"

The prisoner eyed Greer before answering. "Yes."

Greer remained silent once more, gazing intently at the man.

"Tell me." Strider's head cocked to one side, brow raised.

The scoundrel licked his lips as he looked away. Greer let out another low growl as he sensed the man considering lying to Strider. Strider tilted the dagger, so it caught a bit of sunlight, flashing silver light into the man's eyes. He flinched.

"We were to hold Lady Fenforde at the old keep until more men arrived to take her," he answered.

"How were you to alert your employer when you had her?"

"The messenger, the one who led the knight and his men into the ambush; he left to deliver the message. I'm not sure how he planned to get it to whoever hired us."

Greer remained silent, though Strider's eyes narrowed at this news.

"I'm telling the truth!" the thug urged, noticing the look.

"Those men still wouldn't have arrived at the old keep yet," Strider mused, as he turned to eye Addy.

"I am not going to be your bait," Addy said firmly.

Strider's head tilted, and she could tell by his eyes that he was smiling softly under the mask. She finally realized part of his reason for leaving her with the knight and his men.

"You wouldn't need to stay in the keep; they will assume you're already inside. We have a chance to catch someone who might have valuable information."

"No, we are not going back there," she said, with finality, and Strider could tell she wouldn't budge on the matter.

"I won't let you put Lady Fenforde's life in danger," Tevin interjected.

Strider ignored him as he eyed Addy for a long moment. He saw a haunted look flicker across her face and let the topic drop.

"Do either of you two want to ask a question?" Strider asked. Finishing his coffee, he tossed the dregs into a nearby bush.

"How much did they pay you?" Addy asked, her tone curious.

Both Greer and Strider's heads canted to the right in curiosity as they looked at the man. The thug licked his lips again as he looked at the young woman, who met his gaze steadily. Tevin stood at attention behind her, his face as hard as stone. The man hesitated a moment longer before finally answering.

"Two-thousand crowns," he muttered softly.

Strider let out a low whistle.

"For that price, I may consider switching sides."

Addy could feel Tevin tense behind her at Strider's comment, and she rolled her eyes. "You'd have gotten more money ransoming me in Denmahr."

Strider scratched his chin in thought. "True." He glanced at Greer. "Seeing as this was your bright idea, I'm taking the loss out of your cut."

The di'horvith cocked his head and let out a low woof.

"Do you know how many more people were hired around here?" she noted the look of approval Strider gave her when she asked the question. A flash of pleasure sparked within her, only tempered by the grim nature of her question.

"I don't," the man replied. "But I'm sure we weren't the only ones hired. Plenty of people would love to get their hands on that much coin."

Addy hesitated to ask her next question, scared to hear the answer. "Do you know anything about my family? Are they safe?"

"No one's heard of anyone dying, if that's what you want to know."

Relief washed over her. They were safe, for now. "Did Tatcher talk of any plans to take Timara castle, or did the messenger?"

"They hired us to catch you, not siege a castle," the man retorted, earning a growl from Greer. But it was the malicious looks from both Strider and Tevin that had the man backpedaling in a panic. "I-I mean, no, my Lady. They didn't mention any plans for the castle or its people."

Addy's moment of relief was replaced by a large knot in her stomach. Denmahr had gone through a lot of trouble to not only kidnap her but reclaim her as well. She wasn't sure what their plan was, and it terrified her to think that it might not just involve holding her for ransom. Addy stood, done with the conversation.

Strider caught sight of her hands shaking before she hid them in front of her as she turned away. His eyes flicked to Tevin, who didn't seem interested in asking the prisoner questions. He continued to stare at the man tied to the tree.

"Are you sure you don't want to kill him?" Strider asked, not liking the idea of keeping the useless man around.

Tevin blinked, seeming to be drawn from a trance. He looked at Strider, his gaze hardening.

"I told you all I know!" the man shouted. "I cooperated with you!"

"We are not killing him," Tevin reiterated.

"Pretend he is a yulie, ummanie tend to find killing them easier," Strider jabbed.

"Yulie, tahrvin, or a Chaos-ridden demon, it doesn't matter! The man will be tried publicly for his crimes."

Strider shook his head slowly. "Then you can guard the deadweight." Standing, he sheathed his dagger and left the prisoner.

"You should let me go!" the prisoner bellowed. "I've told you everything!"

"And in exchange for telling us, I will not be removing body parts," Strider stated flatly. "That was our agreement."

The man thrashed and strained against his bindings in fury.

"Of course, you'd think that was fair, you son of Chaos," he spat. "You were the one who killed the others. The demon in the fog."

Strider paused to look back at him, regarding him with a single golden eye.

"I was," he answered simply.

The man's eyes narrowed at him. "They warned Tatcher about you. Offered an additional two thousand crowns if we could kill you." He let out an ironic laugh. "Like we could kill a Ranger. Demons, the lot of you."

"I am a Hunter," Strider corrected with a growl, as he shot an annoyed glance Addy's way. "We're deadlier than Rangers."

"It doesn't matter what you call yourself, there is a bounty on your head. Any mercenary and bounty hunter would make a nice profit off you. At this rate, even Urserith Femiera will take an interest."

When Strider spoke, his voice was like ice. "They better be prepared to die then." He fingered the yulie saber as he turned away.

The thug noticed the blade for the first time. Recognition flashed across his face before it grew deathly white, his eyes widening in terror. A menacing glare from the Hunter compelled the man to hold his tongue.

Chapter 37
Swords & Magic

They broke camp shortly after having a cold breakfast. Tevin tried to help, but his injuries prevented him from being useful, and Addy ordered him to rest while she helped pack up, much to the knight's displeasure. Without a word between them, she and Strider packed up and loaded the horses with an efficiency born from repetition. Addy had first complained about helping as she fumbled through the jobs Strider assigned her. Now, she worked quickly and efficiently.

Finished, Strider swung into Copper's saddle, sticking with the familiar horse despite there being newer and better-looking coursers. He had his bow out, an arrow already knocked, as the weapon rested across his lap. He motioned for Tevin to tend to the prisoner, who'd remained tied to the tree while they broke camp.

Tevin could feel the Hunter watching him as he untied the ropes securing the thug to the tree. The man didn't attempt to escape, his gaze flicking toward the Hunter nervously as Tevin escorted him toward the horses.

Addy stood before Su'lris, his reins in her hand. She spoke to her horse as she softly stroked his forehead and nose. The animal blew in her face and nibbled gently at her hair with his lips. She laughed and offered him apple slices from their supplies. The horse gratefully munched on the treat while she pulled herself into the saddle to wait for Tevin.

She watched warily as Tevin gestured for her kidnapper to get into the saddle of a horse before tying his hands to the saddle. Taking the animal's reins, he secured them to his own horse, preventing the prisoner from grabbing them should he break free. Finished tending to the prisoner, Tevin went to mount his horse before hesitating.

"Need help?" Strider asked casually.

Tevin's jaw tightened, but he didn't reply. With a grunt he pulled himself up into the saddle. Addy shot him a worried look; his face had grown pale and sweat beaded his brow. It looked like a stiff breeze would blow him out of the saddle. But he didn't complain. Addy guessed he didn't want to show Strider any weakness. She hoped Tevin would learn to trust Strider soon, uncertain how long she could stand the hostility between the two.

Addy urged Su'lris to follow Strider when he sent Copper into an easy trot. The other horses remained untethered, yet they followed obediently behind Greer, who'd taken up position behind the prisoner's horse. They moved back onto the game trail Strider had been using the day before.

Strider took them through forests and plains, once again avoiding well-traveled roads. He kept them moving at a hard pace. Addy soon lost any sense of direction and would constantly have to reference the point of the sun or mountains to regain her bearings. Strider never seemed to need them as he traveled. Picking a path as easily as if he were following a road. Addy continually cast glances behind her, worried about Tevin. The route they took was difficult for even a healthy rider. His face was stoic as he fought to stay atop his mount.

She hoped he could hold on until they made camp. Strider would be determined to avoid any kind of ummanie path or road. Her gaze met Tevin's and she offered him an encouraging smile. He quickly looked away, not returning it. She frowned; he had to be in a lot of pain.

Unable to do anything, but not wanting to spend the entire ride fretting, Addy fished inside her saddle bag. Letting the reins go slack she pulled out a stout branch and began trying to call to her magic. It answered her, but when she tried directing it to make her stronger it fizzled out.

She tapped into her power once more. Though she focused on trying to channel the power, she remained moving with the horse, her body fluid but rigid. Su'lris didn't seem perturbed by being given his head, nor did he wander or stop to eat the foliage. He continued to follow Copper faithfully. Addy's head cocked to the side, her brown hair falling off her shoulder. Finally, she let out a frustrated breath.

"I don't feel any stronger," she said with a vexed huff.

"You won't, if you give up that easily," Strider replied.

Addy let out another heavy breath, then fell quiet again as she seemed focused on the magic once more. They hadn't gone very long before she spoke again.

"It was a lot easier to feel magic back in the cave," she muttered.

"Magic?" Tevin piped up. "You're teaching Lady Fenforde magic?"

It was Strider's turn to sigh as he slowly shook his head.

Addy stiffened at the slip of her tongue. Swearing softly under her breath, she answered, "He is."

"My lady, I must request you stop. Magic practiced outside of the Syliceon Church is dark magic, dangerous."

"Magic is magic, no matter what practice you follow," Strider interjected. "There is no right or wrong way."

"Without the guidance offered by Syliceon, magic becomes evil."

"Is a sword evil?" Strider asked, his tone calm.

"No, a sword is an object," Tevin replied slowly, clearly suspicious of where Strider was leading the conversation.

"Magic is like a sword; it's the person wielding it that is good or evil."

"Then why are certain spells created with evil designs?"

"Man took a sword and made it sharp. He took magic and made spells. Neither the sword nor magic had a say in the matter."

Tevin fell silent. Before he could figure out some sort of remark or retort, Addy asked a question.

"So, it was man who made the evil magic?"

Strider's head tilted to one side. "Is it really evil?"

"Yes," both Addy and Tevin said in unison.

The knight flushed and looked away. It was impolite to cut off Lady Fenforde.

Addy watched him for a moment before continuing.

"Some spells are designed to hurt others, while others save lives," Addy pointed out.

"I have seen people use healing spells to prolong a prisoner's life so they could torture them further, while another man used a spell designed to inflict pain to save an innocent life," Strider countered. "Which is the evil one then?"

Addy frowned; her head hurt, like it always did when she got into these conversations with Strider. Silence filled the air, and she knew he was waiting for her to answer. He would wait in silence as long as it took for her to either answer or grow frustrated with the question.

"It all comes down to the intent and end result?"

Strider nodded his confirmation, and she let out another breath. "My head always hurts when you talk like this."

"Use it more and it'll hurt less."

Addy teasingly stuck her tongue out at him. She realized Tevin had grown silent and suspected he'd made a tactical retreat from the conversation. She looked back to check on him when Su'lris' gait became choppy as they descended into a dry ravine. He was still stubbornly clinging to his saddle.

"You sound like such an old man," Addy remarked.

"I sound like a man who's experienced far too much of this world," Strider responded, in a world-weary tone. "Age plays but a little part."

"You never told me how old you were."

Strider gave a soft snort. "You never asked."

"Well, I am asking now," Addy said haughtily.

Silence followed her words. She waited, having learned that Strider would speak when he was ready, not when she wanted him to.

"How old do you think I am?"

Addy squinted her eyes at him. She was terrible at guessing people's ages. "I think you look like you're in your late twenties, maybe early thirties. But you act like you are at least sixty."

"Try sixty, plus forty."

Addy's mouth dropped open out in shock. "You're one hundred years old?"

"It isn't all that surprising. I'm half yulie."

"You really are an old man," Addy laughed.

"And yet I somehow doubt you'll respect your elder," Strider said, as he steered Copper out of the ravine.

Addy called for a stop when she noticed Tevin's state deteriorating. He didn't respond to her when she called to him and he held a death grip on the saddle. His skin was waxy and beaded with sweat, his sides heaved from the pain and strain it took to stay in the saddle. She slipped off Su'lris and hurried toward him, gently touching his knee to get his attention. He blinked like he'd entered sunlight after a dark room, jerked back into reality by her touch.

"We're stopping here for the night. You need to rest," she said, as she led his horse into camp.

Tevin didn't dismount nearly as gracefully as Addy, and would have crumpled to the ground, had it not been for her and his horse.

"Put out a blanket," she said to Strider.

Tevin wasn't lucid and it was like steering a severely drunk man as she helped him toward the blanket. She grunted under the strain of his weight before she lost her grip and he fell onto the blanket.

"Sorry!" she said, but Tevin was already unconscious.

Buckles jingled as Kyre hefted the saddle onto the chestnut mule's back. He worked his frustration out on the straps and buckles. Every person he'd questioned in Addy's kidnapping had led nowhere. Whoever had organized the job had taken care to ensure none of the pieces were truly aware of one another.

No one could name who was in charge. It was a fragmented web, and he'd reached the last broken strand with nothing to show for it. He'd never cared for difficult quarries who hid themselves behind schemes and misdirection. Elyphain had the patience to untangle their plans. He came in at the end when things got exciting.

The mule snorted as he gave a jerk on the cinch. He patted his stomach. "I'm sorry Maple, I'll be gentle." Maple shook his head before lowering it in relaxation. Kyre gave him another pat, double checking that the saddle was secure before picking up his bridle. True to his word, he was more careful as he slipped it over his nose. He was fastening the last buckle when he heard footsteps entering the barn.

Turning, he spotted both Curthis and Renard. Both looked careworn and Curthis had clearly lost weight, like his mother. Dark rings hung under both men's eyes and their shoulders appeared to be bearing a great invisible weight. They both looked at him pleadingly.

"Have you heard any news?" Curthis asked.

Kyre gave the young man an understanding look. While the loss of their charge harrowed the two men, Curthis bore the brunt of the blame. He'd been guarding Addy the night she'd been taken. The guilt was taking a toll on the young man.

Kyre hadn't completely cleared his doubts of either of them, even if he felt pity for them. Normally he'd lie or provide a non-answer to suspects, to lull them into a false sense of security, or unbalance them and reveal their hand. It just so happened that telling the truth would work this time. If one was guilty, they'd feel comfortable that they weren't close to being caught and grow careless.

"I'm afraid we've got a heap of nothing," Kyre said, with an open handed shrug.

"Can we help you search?" Renard asked.

Kyre regarded him with an even gaze. Like Curthis, he'd grown into the role of Addy's guardian, brought to the castle under the recommendation of Bishop Markane when he was twelve. His parents had given him to the Syliceon. Unlike commoners, whose orphans and unwanted children often found their way into the Ranger's hands, many of the ummanie nobility entrusted their excess sons and daughters to the Syliceon to raise.

Kyre knew he had little trust for Rangers and their 'dark' magic due to his Syliceon upbringing. Despite that, he'd always been cordial when they did speak. He'd shown nothing but dedication and loyalty toward Lady Adelin. Adelin was close with both her guards, whom she'd grown up with, which made their potential betrayal all the more heartbreaking.

Kyre put a hand on each man's shoulder. "You can help by going and getting some rest."

"We're fine," Curthis argued.

"You look like you'd lose a fight to a feather! Go rest, you're useless to Adelin in this state."

"He's right," Renard admitted, his gaze downcast. "I wouldn't trust me to help anyone right now."

Curthis bit his lip as he blinked several times. Kyre waited until his shoulders slumped in defeat.

"Go and sleep, and grab something to eat afterward," he said, swinging up into the saddle. "You better not look half dead when I get back, or I'll lock you both up."

He sent Maple trotting out of the stable into the sunlight, leaving the men behind.

Chapter 38
Burning Bridges

Addy lifted Tevin's shirt as she inspected the bandaged wounds on his side. The white of the cloth was light pink in some places where the blood had seeped through.

"Why didn't you tell us you needed to stop?" she chided the unconscious knight. She didn't dare remove the bandages for fear of causing the injuries to bleed more. Looking up in search of Strider, she spotted the Hunter tying their prisoner to a new tree, having already taken care of the horses.

"Can you heal him again?" she asked.

Strider shook his head as he retrieved the materials he used to make his snares and traps. His body protested every movement, but he pushed through the exhaustion, knowing that if he stopped, the cold would set in. They didn't have time for him to give in. They didn't have time to waste on Tevin. The longer they took to reach the castle, the higher their chances were of getting caught. But he knew Addy wouldn't leave the knight behind.

Addy fetched a blanket from the horses. She knelt beside Tevin, draping the blanket over him. Worry laced her voice when she spoke again. "Can you do something?"

"I've done what I can."

Addy wrapped her arms around her knees, her gaze never straying from Tevin.

"You said you would teach me healing magic," she uttered softly. "Do you think I could heal him?"

"Not yet," Strider answered.

"Not even if I could connect with the magic again?"

"Can you connect with it?"

Addy's brow creased as she concentrated for a moment, trying to call to the inner well of magic. He waited, knowing the outcome. She opened her inner channel and could call to her power, but she couldn't focus it. He'd not shown her how; she needed to build up her proverbial muscles first and reaching out to her inner well did that. He still allowed her to try; she needed to see it wasn't possible, or else she'd fight him over it. Finally, Addy let out a frustrated sigh, shaking her head in defeat.

"Then no." Strider patted her softly on the shoulder before leaving.

Addy's shoulders drooped as she hugged her knees tighter.

Strider watched her as she kept a silent vigil over Tevin, her face shadowed with worry. Greer had come over to join her, keeping her company, even though it was his job to watch the prisoner in Tevin's absence. Strider didn't scold him. The girl needed him. The Hunter sat down and began making more snares and traps, keeping himself busy to fend off the ice in his veins.

His gaze flicked to the annoying knight, who'd done little to prove his worth. He couldn't even properly protect one girl with an entire unit of soldiers. But Addy felt responsible for him. Which meant she'd expect him to make him healthy again. Something she knew he didn't want. Healthy meant Tevin could cause a problem.

The Hunter wanted to keep him well enough not to slow them down a considerable amount. Like he'd done today. He'd have slipped something into the knight's drink already, but he knew Addy would feel responsible for the young man's death. As she did the others who died protecting her. He couldn't bring himself to add to her burden.

His gaze shifted to the prisoner, who was far too well behaved, considering he was heading to his death. Strider briefly considered breaking one of the man's knees to prevent him from getting away, but the moaning and cries of pain he'd end up making as they rode would give them away. Letting him escape and shooting him in the back was a far more favorable option.

Strider felt eyes watching him. He looked over to find Greer fixing him with a hard look. When their eyes locked, that look changed to one that Strider interpreted as, *You know better*, or *Don't even try it*. Strider shook his head, stood, then returned the traps and material to the pack before walking over.

"Watch the prisoner," he told Greer.

The wolf gave him one final look before padding over to sit before the thug. Strider sat next to a tree near where Tevin lay. Wrapping his cloak around himself, he settled into a comfortable position before closing his eyes to rest.

"I can heal him tomorrow," he told Addy. "Not completely, but enough that he shouldn't keep passing out every few miles."

"Thank you," Addy whispered.

Strider merely grunted his response. Wrapping his cloak tighter, he pulled his hood down over his eyes. The warm cloak did nothing to help fend off the frigid feeling in his blood. He glanced over at Greer, who was eyeing him closely, a new expression darkening his face. A look of warning. Strider disregarded it. The Hunter already knew. He felt it within his soul. He was killing himself.

"No, I'm not going to let you do it!" Tevin barked angrily. "You're not using magic on me again!"

"Then we leave you here to die," Strider replied, his tone dangerously calm.

"Tevin," Addy said, her tone hard. "I am ordering you to let Strider heal you. You can't protect me in this state."

Tevin looked like he wanted to argue, but held his tongue. Unable to fight with Addy, he instead glared at Strider, who remained unfazed. Finally, he gave a curt nod before removing his arm that he'd placed protectively over his injury.

Strider regarded the knight for a long moment before quietly crouching beside him. He hid his annoyance at having to heal Tevin for Addy's sake. The young man was aware of Addy's own endeavours to use magic. He'd intended to have her practice while Tevin was unconscious. It'd have been easy enough to knock him out with a bit of sleeping draught. But there was no need for secrecy now. He'd have to deal with Tevin discreetly before they reached the castle in order to protect her secret.

Strider motioned for Addy to sit beside him. He waited to speak until she was next to him.

"Your hand." He held out his own hand to her.

She looked puzzled, but placed her hand in his. Taking it, he pressed it against Tevin's side, his own splayed on top. Both knight and lady froze.

"You're not going to use me to teach her magic!" Tevin exclaimed, pushing away from them.

Strider sighed.

Addy gave Tevin an exasperated look as she spread her hands. "How am I supposed to learn to heal people?"

"You can learn herbs and medicine, not magic."

Addy gave him a look as she fought the urge to smack him on the side of the head. "I am learning magic to help people, and to protect myself, Tevin." She met his indignant glare with one of her own. "You're helping protect me by doing this."

Tevin gave her a disbelieving look. "I'd be condemning you to death if anyone else finds out!" He kept himself propped up with his hands, ready to crab-walk away from her should she try anything.

"Are you going to tell?" she challenged.

Shock and disgust flashed across the knight's face, before taking on a somber expression, as he realized for the first time that he held Addy's life in his hands. "No," he said, his voice grave.

She placed a hand over his as she said in a soft voice, "Then please, let me learn."

A flurry of emotions played across Tevin's face, before he finally slumped down in defeat against the packs Addy had piled behind him. "Just do it quickly," he sighed.

"Thank you."

Strider, who'd sat quietly observing their exchange, moved forward. Taking her hand, he once again placed it on Tevin's injured side, his own resting over it.

"Focus on the magic, listen to it, feel what it is doing as I heal," he said coarsely.

Addy nodded and forced herself to relax. She focused on trying to sense the magic. Strider gave a small nod before channeling healing power into his hand, through Addy's hand, and into Tevin.

Addy could feel the heartbeat of the magic as it passed through her hand. It felt the same as the power from The Ways and the Well she had been trapped in. As she focused on it, she felt it move through her and into Tevin as it repaired the damage. She could feel the intent of the magic and feel her own heartbeat fall into rhythm with it.

The longer she sat, the more she realized that Strider's magic was different. It held its own inner song. While the magic in The Ways was steady and unyielding, Strider's magic was quiet and calculated; hard, yet soft. An unassuming accompaniment to the magic surrounding them.

She forgot to breathe, astounded by this new discovery. Not only did she finally hear Strider's magic, she experienced how he directed it. He wasn't trying to strangle it and force it to do what he wanted. Micromanaging the power until he silenced its song. He used his will to direct it but did not seek to dominate it. He was the conductor; the magic his symphony.

"Reach out to your own magic; picture it joining mine in the task of healing," Strider instructed.

Addy licked her lips and nodded before closing her eyes. She reached inwards, toward her magic, envisioning it like a stream she was dipping her hand into. The magic met her, drawn out by the presence of Strider's magic. Its beat grew stronger as it coursed through her. Its own rhythm eluded her, but she gently directed it with her desire to heal Tevin. The channel in which it flowed through her was small, much smaller than what she felt coming from Strider. But it came to her more readily.

She savored the sensation of power warming her body before picturing it traveling down to her hand to join Strider's magic in healing Tevin. She pictured the wound mending, and the magic responded. The sensation of her magic merging with Strider's, like a stringed quartet adding their voice to the melody, caused her breath to catch in her throat as excitement filled her.

The tension in Tevin's body eased as the magic warmed his body. Swallowing the pain and weariness in its embrace. The knight slumped gratefully against their packs.

"I don't feel any pain," he said gratefully. "This is amazing!"

Addy gave a thin smile as she continued to channel her magic. A strange tug pulled at Addy's soul as she continued to pour magic into Tevin. The tug grew stronger, and she had to strain to keep the magic flowing. She fought against the pull, trying to reach for more magic. A tightness grew within her chest.

Strider jerked his hand away, breaking off the connection. Snatching Addy's wrist, he pulled her hand away from Tevin. Her gaze snapped to him.

"Why did you do that?" she snapped.

"You're at your limit," he responded calmly.

"No—" she began, but a fierce shiver cut her off as an icy cold entered her soul with vicious intent. She hugged herself, looking up at Strider wide-eyed. "Do you always feel so cold after?"

"You hit your limit," Strider said, his voice remaining level as he assured her. "It will pass. Don't dwell on it."

The dark cold was like a blizzard trying to envelop her. How could she not dwell on it? It whispered words to her that cut her deep. She wasn't good enough. She wasn't strong enough. Her family didn't want someone as useless as her back.

Her gaze fell, and she hugged herself tighter, trying to fend off the shivering. Strider stood, but she didn't look to see where he went as she drowned in the frigid presence. If she curled up and let it take her, she wouldn't feel like this anymore. The cold would cease. Something popped her on the head, snapping her out of her trance. Her hands shot up to massage the pain away.

"Ow!" she whined, looking up to see Strider holding her sparring stick out to her.

"Listen to me when I speak. Get up and move," Strider told her, his voice firm. "Don't sit and dwell on what you are thinking."

She didn't feel like moving. She didn't feel like doing anything but curling up and letting the darkness take her.

"I'm not going to use the sword anymore," she said solemnly. She was terrible at it, anyway.

"You're okay with those who've betrayed you harming you and your family?"

Addy's eyes lit with fury. "No! But I'm not going to use the sword to kill anyone!"

"Then you forfeit your life and the lives of those you love," Strider told her pointedly, as he held the handle of the makeshift sword out to her.

"I'll learn to use magic to stop them."

"Magic can be blocked or canceled. Only fools rely on it entirely."

"And if someone takes my sword, I am defenseless," Addy argued, her anger flaring as the cold still gripped her.

"That is why I have been teaching you to fight with more than just a sword," Strider explained, the volume of his voice never rising.

Addy's own voice became louder as she spoke, "I can't beat a man in a hand-to-hand fight, or with a sword!"

"You don't have to beat someone. Your goal is to survive, not win," Strider told her.

"I hate to say it, but I agree with Strider," Tevin cut in. "You need to be able to defend yourself, my lady."

Addy shook her head, her jaw set.

"Even a deer doesn't lay down to die when beasts hunt it," Strider told her. "It will fight until its last breath to survive."

"A deer doesn't feel guilty for killing a beast!" Addy snapped, her anger continuing to build.

"If you won't fight for yourself, then fight to protect your family," Strider said, his voice soft, even tired.

Addy lifted her chin as she glared at Strider, who met her fiery gaze with a steady one of his own.

"My father and brothers are capable of protecting themselves, and we have plenty of guards."

"None of them could stop you from being kidnapped. Your enemy will bide their time, then strike. Next time, it could be your mother. Next time, they may decide to kill."

Addy was quiet as she glared at him, the ice in her soul unwilling to break loose, even as fury heated her cheeks.

"You'd know, wouldn't you!" she shouted. "You've probably done the same thing!"

Strider regarded her for a moment.

"I have had it done to me, and I have done it to others." His voice remained measured, but it held an undertone of warning that Addy didn't notice.

"Whoever did it to you didn't do it well enough!" she hissed. "You're still alive."

"They were not trying to kill me at the time." Strider's voice took on a sharper edge, the warning clearer now. "That is the point. They will go after others you care about, Addy."

"Like you care about anyone!" she hurled the words at him like a dagger. "If someone like you loved them, they probably deserved what they got!"

Strider gripped the wooden sword tighter, and Addy saw pain flash across his face. Before being replaced by an icy fury. His eyes hardened and narrowed. There was a coldness there she'd never seen before. It held more intensity than the harshest of winters, yet there was a familiarity to it. It felt like the ice currently freezing her own soul.

Had she had her wits about her, she would've fled, fearing for her life. But she didn't care. She'd finally struck a blow that hurt him, and that was what mattered!

Strider raised the wooden stick as if to strike her.

Tevin lunged, placing himself between Strider and Addy to shield her from the blow.

It never came. Strider dropped the wooden sword before walking away. Addy continued to glare at him as he grabbed the packs he'd removed from Copper before heading toward the horses.

"What are you doing?" she demanded.

"Leaving," he hissed, as he secured the saddlebags to Copper and began tightening the cinch on his saddle.

"You can't leave! I paid you to take me home!"

"I won't risk my life for someone content to die."

"I am not content to die!"

He turned his withering gaze on her. "Then you're a coward, unwilling to protect what you cherish."

That was it! Addy grabbed the wooden sword and stood.

Tevin grabbed for her cloak but missed.

Shaking with fury, Addy rushed at Strider, who had his back turned to her. Gripping the wooden sword in both hands, she raised it high above her head, aiming to deal a damaging blow to the back of his skull.

Without a word, Strider stepped aside, dodging the overhead swing with ease. Addy stumbled, the force of her attack throwing her off-balance. Flailing her arms, she tried to stabilize herself. Strider moved in. Grabbing her wrist, he yanked it into an awkward angle, forcing her to let go of the weapon as she cried out.

With the same motion, he thrust her aside. Already off-balance, Addy fell on her face in the dirt. She cursed as she rolled onto her back to find the point of her wooden sword pressed to her neck. Strider looked down at her, his expression dark. They glared at each other for several heartbeats.

Strider breathed heavily, struggling to stay in control of his own anger, of the ice raging through his veins, screaming at him to kill her. She deserved it after all she'd put him through. After what she'd said.

The end of the weapon shook as Strider wrestled with murderous intent. He felt Greer's presence beside him, watching him. He let out a shaky breath before tossing the stick aside with contempt. The Hunter turned his back on Addy.

Swinging into the saddle, he sent Copper into a swift canter with a kick. He left without uttering a single word. Greer passed by Addy. He paused to give her a look of concern before padding after the disappearing Hunter.

Addy screamed after them, dissolving into tears as she hugged herself. She'd never felt so cold and alone in her life.

Chapter 39
On The Edge

Addy's outburst left Tevin speechless. Her anger shocked him. He'd encountered unstable nobles before, but Addy hadn't struck him as the type to fly off the handle in such a spectacular way.

He approached Addy slowly, as if he were closing in on a furious tiger. He held the blanket she'd given him spread out before him, like a flimsy shield, as he came closer. Carefully, he draped the blanket over her shoulders. Her screaming had quieted, dissolving into heavy sobs. She didn't look up when she felt the blanket fall across her shoulders. Grabbing the edges of it, she pulled it tightly around her.

"Come on, let's get you warm," Tevin whispered, softly coaxing her over to sit on a log.

Though the injury in his side protested as he set about building a fire, the pain was more irritating than debilitating. He felt energetic and full of life, awkwardly so, given the tense atmosphere around him. He'd heard of people within the Syliceon who possessed the power to heal, but he'd never seen anyone healed before. It was incredible how magic could reverse such damage.

Like most people, Tevin didn't completely trust what he didn't understand. But he believed that magic was indeed a gift from the goddess K'yarie. Though he questioned why certain souls were gifted while others clearly more worthy weren't. Was there a purpose behind it, or did it have to do with bloodlines and nothing more? The fire spat as it took hold, its orange flames spreading across the logs like hungry fingers grasping for food. Tevin stepped back, sitting next to Addy on the log.

Addy continued to shiver under the blanket, the warmth of the fire doing nothing to fend off the chill within. She didn't acknowledge Tevin as she stared into the dancing flames, lost in the sea of darkness invading her soul.

Tevin wanted to say something to make her feel better. But he had no idea what to say, nor was it his place to address the noblewoman in such a casual manner. Even as a king's knight, he was of lower rank and status than Lady Fenforde. His position and status would eventually increase with time served, but that was the future, not the present. So, he sat quietly beside her, aware that such an action could be considered disrespectful, but he was unwilling to leave her alone.

Addy was the first to break the silence, her voice a hoarse whisper. "I'm a coward."

"I don't think being unwilling to take a life makes you a coward," Tevin stated. Taking a moment to collect his thoughts, he added, "But I also don't believe you should stop learning how to defend yourself."

Addy didn't respond, so he pressed on, very aware of her outburst moments ago.

"I think you should learn, if only to ensure that you can act if you choose to do so. If you don't, you forfeit your ability to choose." He spoke softly, gently reasoning with her. "You're powerless to stop something, even if you want to."

"I don't want to talk about this right now," Addy rasped, her tone hollow as she withdrew further into herself. She sat there, arms wrapped around her knees, eyes distant.

Tevin could tell he was losing her. He didn't know how, but he knew, and it terrified him. He felt powerless to help her. Strider had said she needed to move, to distract herself from her thoughts. But he doubted he could get her to walk about the camp. He looked around, trying to figure out something he could do to draw her out of herself. His gaze fell on something he knew was close to her heart.

"Tell me about your horse, then," he urged. "Have you named him?"

Addy blinked, her own gaze traveling to the shaggy bay.

"Su'lris." The name tumbled from her lips like a quiet song. The large horse looked at her, ears perked forward as he caught mention of his name.

"Su'lris," Tevin repeated, testing the name on his tongue. "That is a beautiful name. Is it yulie?"

Addy offered a ghost of a smile and nodded as she continued to stare at her horse.

Tevin hurried on, not wanting to lose her attention again. "How did you acquire him?" If he could keep her talking, then maybe things would be alright. He felt like he was talking to an injured soldier who was fighting to keep awake, knowing that if he let the man fall asleep, he would never wake up.

"Strider stole him from one of King Elias's men when he saved me..." she muttered, her voice trailing off.

He was losing her again and scrambled for something else to ask her.

"Your home! Tell me about Timara Castle. I saw it when I was younger but don't remember much of it. I hear it is beautiful."

Addy's head tilted to one side. "It is beautiful," she agreed, vacantly. "It sits beside the Tahl river that supplies the water for the great moats. The walls are a soft cream that glows pink when the sun rises and sets. There are vineyards, orchards, and farmlands around it. My brothers and I would go for rides in the countryside. My mother has a beautiful garden inside the walls that I used to play in as a kid. I still like to sit in there and read. It is always peaceful there."

She drifted off again, though this time she seemed to be dwelling on the memories of her life rather than whatever dark thoughts were plaguing her.

"Will you ride Su'Iris through the countryside when you get back?"

She smiled softly. "Yes, I think he would enjoy that."

Tevin spent the entire evening asking Addy question after question, never letting her linger in silence for too long. Neither one noticed the prisoner carefully working his restraints free.

Chapter 40

Pinned By A Pooch

"None of our men have reported seeing Lady Fenforde or her protector at Bayvar Pass," Bishop Markane said, as he sat in a large, lavish chair, sipping wine in King Elias's study.

The king sat in his own chair, far more extravagant than the bishop's, by a crackling fire. He frowned, saying, "Which means they found another way through the mountains. That should be impossible."

"Impossible or not, it is safe to assume they've already entered Myvara."

Taking a large draught from his own glass, the king leaned back in his seat with a heavy sigh. "In which case, we have no way of capturing them."

"Perhaps not, though the entire kingdom will be out to kill this Dark Ranger. If they somehow make it to Timara castle, our men in place there will know what to do."

Elias's voice took on a severe tone. "It was your man that suggested this confounded scheme to kidnap Lady Fenforde in the first place. It was risky and could undermine everything we have worked toward. Who's to say he won't do something brash?"

"Calm yourself, your highness," Bishop Markane said in a soothing tone. "Our man is more skilled than you give him credit for. He has a far tighter hold on the castle Timara than Lord Fenforde and his king's addled knight, Sir Tamous, realize. Even the Rangers have been unable to uncover who orchestrated Lady Fenforde's disappearance. He will not fail us."

"He better not, Tochure," King Elias warned, using the bishop's first name.

"We have already placed evidence to frame Lord Villock, for any action taken against Lady Fenforde and her family," Bishop Markane assured him. "He has always spoken boldly against our alliance with Myvara. None of this will connect back to us. Lord Fenforde has no doubt sent his Rangers to investigate the matter. What they find will incriminate the lord."

The king seemed appeased as he took another drink from his glass.

Putting down his glass, Bishop Markane stood before bowing. "I leave for Myvara tonight. I have other business to attend to there."

Perched on the windowsill outside the king's study was a large bird of prey. Elyphain watched the forms of king Elias and Bishop Markane through windows of the study, her feathers fluffed up to fend off the chilly wind. The flight over the Tahlrin Mountains had been an arduous one, leaving her tired and sore as she slowly infiltrated king Elias's lands. She'd first gone to Newman to gather information before making her way toward the king's castle at Dovern.

She'd entered the castle grounds at nightfall. No one had noticed. The guards watched the grounds, not the skies. Neither man inside the study saw the large, red-breasted buzzard. The glow of the fire and candlelight turned the great window into a one-way mirror, hiding the dark world outside from view while it peered in with envy.

Her keen eyes picked out the movement of Markane's lips whenever he turned his head to look at the king, allowing her to catch snippets of his side of the conversation regarding a mole within castle Timara. The man turned his head back to the fire, and she missed the information about Lord Villock. She observed as the bishop bid the king farewell, remaining still as she sat in the darkness. She stayed perched on the windowsill long after King Elias retired for the evening.

The castle grew dark and quiet. Shifting, Elyphain's buzzard form dissolved into smoke, replaced by a lithe, anumie woman. Drawing a knife, she carefully positioned herself in the middle of the window before working to undo the window's inner latch. She made quick work of the window before slipping into the study, as silent as a shadow.

Alone in the darkness, she began searching through the stacks of papers, books, and drawers, careful to place things back in the exact position they'd been in. She paused whenever she found any documents she deemed useful. Pulling several blank sheets of paper out of her bag, she placed one over a document before channeling magic into it.

A perfect copy of the document traced itself onto the blank sheet, leaving the original free to return to its hiding place. No one stirred or took notice of the intruder as she meticulously tore the study apart. Come morning, there'd be no sign she'd ever set foot in the room.

Anger coursed through Strider's body like cold fire. A flame still burned within him as he steered Copper in a wide loop around their camp. The Hunter sought to run out the anger fueling the ice in his soul until his chest burned like frostbite. For decades, anger and hate had kept him going, as he hunted down the assassin who had killed his father and Kinri. But now he fought it down.

But his soul, unbalanced and exhausted, made controlling the emotion as difficult as wrangling an oiled snake. He wouldn't let himself do or say something to Addy that he'd regret. So, he'd distanced himself from her in order to regain control or else risk that snake harming the only person he cared about.

Copper jerked to a stop, catching the Hunter by surprise. He tried to right himself, but his strength failed him, and he tumbled from the saddle.

He hit the earth hard, doing his best to roll with the fall before landing on his back, his head striking the ground. His vision went white before changing to flashing lights. He lay there stunned for a moment, when a weight suddenly lay on top of him, pinning one arm underneath him. Strider coughed out curses at Greer, who perched atop him. The di'horvith rumbled and whined at him. The snake within him found something to strike out against.

"Get off me!" Strider ordered, his vision clearing as he struggled. He grabbed Greer's scruff with his free hand, trying to pull the enormous wolf off, but his grip failed him. His hand was too weak to keep hold.

With a bark of defiance, Greer snatched Strider's wrist in his mouth, preventing him from trying to dislodge him further. He met the man's gaze with a fierce one of his own.

"This isn't helping!"

Greer let out a low rumbling growl accompanied by barking chatter, muffled by Strider's arm in his mouth as he stared at the Hunter.

Strider glared back, still struggling feebly to get free. But the cold had robbed him of everything. Only ice and anger remained. His labored breathing was made worse by the weight of Greer laying on top of him. Their eyes remained locked in a silent contest of wills.

Finally, thoroughly exhausted, Strider let his head fall back against the ground in defeat. He lay there in silence, breathing hard, while Greer gazed at him intently. Strider ignored him, instead focusing on the fury within himself.

He knew it was foolish. Addy had attacked him because of the void that invaded all magic users after reaching their limit. It was an experience she needed to have in order to understand the dangers of using magic. He knew it would likely cause her to lash out irrationally, as her emotions became unstable. It was normal.

He shouldn't have reacted the way he had. His own soul was in turmoil. Her words cut far deeper than they should've.

His own words had been equally cutting and he realized he'd failed at leaving the situation before he'd said things he'd regret. It had been his own guilt stabbing him in the back, used by the cold to push him closer to breaking. He knew he'd overreacted. But unlike Addy, he should've been able to control himself. His anger faded, replaced with remorse. He shouldn't have spoken to her that way.

What did you expect would happen? A dark voice in the back of his mind said. *You only ever managed to hurt those you care about. You'll do it again if you go back.*

He sucked in a deep breath through his nose, smelling the normally comforting scent of the forest floor. The familiar scent did nothing to soothe him as he stared up at the canopy of leaves. He wished nothing more than to sink into the soil, to lay and rot among the roots of the trees. Maybe then he'd be able to escape this crushing guilt and devouring cold that weighed on him like a silent iceberg.

"She could go on by herself," he said. "It'll be better that way."

Greer gave a huff, clearly unconvinced.

"I trained her to handle herself. Her knight is healed; if he has two coins worth of sense, he'll keep her away from the cities and roads."

A gentle breeze stirred the surrounding trees, mingling with night sounds and the quiet munching noises coming from where Copper stood a few paces away.

"If I go with them, I will end up executed by her father or dying from overuse of magic. You know this. Why do you insist on continuing?"

Greer let out a low rumbling noise that resonated in Strider's chest. He gazed deeply into the Hunter's eyes and Strider found it hard to meet them. He knew their job wasn't done. Addy wasn't truly safe. She never would be, until those who betrayed her were found.

They'd been skilled enough to avoid being caught by the Rangers. They wouldn't be able to hide from Greer. Strider breathed for several minutes as his guilt seeped away, leaving him feeling nothing but empty and deflated. He was too exhausted to feel anything more. He closed his eyes.

"I'm tired, Greer," he admitted softly, his voice weighed with a weariness beyond a thousand lifetimes. "I'm tired and I'm dying." He uttered the next few words in a weak whisper. "I can't do this anymore."

He didn't want to be here. He didn't want to keep fighting to stay in this god-forsaken world. He couldn't help Addy in this state. He'd end up failing her like he failed everyone else. It'd be so much easier if he let go. The pain would stop, the cold would stop. Strider looked into Greer's eyes, finding his own pain reflected there.

"So why do I stay?" Strider asked him, searching for the answer in those deep brown eyes.

Letting out a soft whine, Greer leaned forward and licked his chin.

Strider placed his hand on the wolf's cheek, stroking it softly. He didn't have the strength to keep fighting, and yet he couldn't bring himself to let go. Was he scared of dying? No, everyone died. Death would be his release. If only he'd let it take him.

But despite accepting and even welcoming the idea of death, a part of him still wanted to live. This part of him had been growing since traveling with Greer and Addy. It was the part that remembered the good times he'd had with his mother, his father, and Kinri. The side that craved warmth.

He'd thought that side of him had died. But it'd resurfaced, slowly. He hadn't even noticed until the night he found himself staying, not just for Greer, but Addy, too. Now it held him here, surprising him with how strongly it fought to stay in this world. It held him here with a fierce conviction to see Addy home, and he hated it for that. He didn't want to be responsible for another life, another attachment. He was as dangerous to her as the traitors in her castle.

Strider couldn't look away from Greer's intense gaze. He could feel the warmth within them. Feel the pain and worry Greer held in his soul. As Strider continued staring into Greer's eyes, he felt that loving warmth enter him, soothing him, and Strider realized he would live a little longer. For them. Until he ensured Addy was safe, he'd be unable to find peace. He wouldn't fail her. After that, he could rest. Letting out another breath, he tapped Greer's side.

"Get up, you big lard. We need to go back."

Greer sprang off Strider with a low woof, wagging his tail furiously.

Strider groaned as his ribcage expanded after being crushed under the heavy wolf. He gingerly pushed himself to his feet. His body felt weak; his bones were like iron and his muscles felt like jelly, but he pulled himself back into the saddle despite feeling like he was going to break apart. Taking a moment to orient himself, he turned Copper around. Greer took off ahead. Copper plodded steadily after him as the di'horvith hurried back to camp.

Addy didn't know how long Tevin sat with her. He never left her side as he asked her question after question, gently prompting her to talk. As she answered his questions, her mind focusing on each topic, she found that the winter inside her soul began to thaw. The less she focused on the cold, the less power it held over her. She slowly emerged from her shell as Tevin asked her about each member of her family, what she liked to do with them, and so many other questions.

He never let her slip back into the icy darkness that dwelled inside her. When the conversation waned, even if it seemed like he was grasping at straws, he always had an additional question to ask her. She answered, hollowly at first, hardly considering her words. Her mind was a scattered mess as she rambled. But he listened and waited for her to finish before asking something else.

Slowly, she found herself moving away from the darkness inside to be more present. Her numbness faded as her emotions ricocheted inside her like trapped cats overloading her until even the touch of the blanket put her on edge. She let it fall from her shoulders.

The dull thump of hooves against dirt caught her attention. Strider rode into camp from the opposite direction he'd left. Greer walked in front of Copper, his tail raised like a fluffy flag bouncing with each step. Tevin stood up and walked toward them, blocking Strider from coming closer.

"You shouldn't have come back," Tevin said, grabbing Copper's reins, forcing the horse to stop.

The Hunter didn't reply as he slid out of the saddle, keeping an arm across the horse's back, his eyes fixed on Addy.

Her anger flared once more, colliding and entangling with the guilt that tied her insides into knots. She couldn't stand looking at him! Addy stood and rushed toward Su'lris, unable to face him. She reached him, and with practiced ease had the cinch tightened on the saddle and Su'lris free, inadvertently untying another of their horses. She heard Tevin yell, but she was in the saddle and galloping away before he could stop her.

Strider grabbed Tevin's shoulder before he could chase after Addy.

"Let her go," he said, his voice far too calm for the situation.

Tevin whirled on him, his face twisted in anger, as he knocked Strider's hand away. "She can't be alone right now!"

"She'll be fine."

"No, she won't!" Fear flashed across the young knight's face. "You didn't see her. She was so close to slipping away. You weren't here!"

"But you were," Strider said, his voice firm as he locked eyes with Tevin. "You kept her here. She's past the worst part now. She needs space to calm down and reclaim control."

Tevin turned away, and Strider seized his arm. Tevin rounded on him, trying to backhand the Hunter. Strider stepped back, dodging the blow. Greer appeared between them, forcing the two apart. Strider didn't pay him any mind, returning Tevin's glare with a steady one of his own.

Movement behind the knight caught Strider's eye. The prisoner was escaping!

"Move!" he ordered.

Strider's bow was in his hand, an arrow knocked in a heartbeat. Tevin jumped aside, looking to see what Strider was aiming at. He spotted the man they'd left tied to the tree, as he finished tightening the saddle straps.

Strider drew back on the bowstring, his gaze locked on the man. His vision went dark as his strength failed him. He lost his grip on the arrow and half knocked, it shot off at a wide angle, before slamming into the dirt. Strider's head spun and his legs failed him. Tevin instinctively grabbed him by the arm, keeping him from hitting the ground as he fell to one knee.

The fleeing man whirled the horse around, whipping it with the ends of the reins as he shouted. "Ya!" The horse let out a shrill cry before it bolted off into the forest.

Tevin let go of The Hunter, intent on following. But Strider grabbed his arm.

"Leave him," he said, gritting his teeth as he fought back the bile rising in his throat.

"We can't let him go!" Tevin looked between Strider and where the man had disappeared.

"Him or Addy?" Strider said, releasing Tevin's arm as he bowed his head. Ice crept into his brain, stabbing painfully behind his eyes. "You can't chase both."

Greer let out a whine as he touched his nose to Strider's cheek. The Hunter patted the di'horvith's head. He breathed deeply, fending off the darkness and nausea as strength slowly crept back into his limbs.

Tevin let out a frustrated sigh. Strider could see his feet as he paced back and forth a few steps before they stopped before him. He dropped his free hand to the hilt of his sword, prepared for the knight to attack while he was down. Instead, the man asked.

"Are you alright?"

"I'm fine, it'll pass," Strider grunted, as he used his bow to pull himself to his feet.

"What happened?"

"Nothing."

"Right," Tevin drawled, shooting Strider an annoyed look. "Can you ride?"

"Put out the fire and get the horses."

Tevin gave him a dubious look. Strider returned it with an even stare of his own until the knight walked away. Strider turned back to

Copper, eyeing the saddle. He absentmindedly stroked Greer's head as he collected himself. He gave his body a moment longer before gathering the strength to haul himself into the saddle.

Every muscle shrieked as he strained against the weight of his own body. His boots were like lead as he clumsily swung a leg over Copper's back. With a labored grunt, he righted himself. His head swam from the exertion, and it took several deep breaths before the sensation dissipated.

Greer let out a concerned whine as he looked up at Strider.

"I'll be fine," Strider told him. They both knew it was a lie.

Chapter 41
Tenuous Cooperation

Strider led them through the night, slowly tracing Addy's path. She'd recklessly let Su'Iris gallop through the forest, choosing his own route through the trees. He couldn't increase his pace to match Addy's. It was hard enough staying in the saddle as his soul teetered within him, barely held in place by the thin threads tethering him to this world.

Greer trotted beside Copper, ever watchful as he kept one ear on the woods, the other angled toward his brother. He was worrying his brother, Strider knew. He could lie to the others about the state he was in, but not Greer, who remained close, unwilling to let him out of his sight.

Strider's strength gradually returned as they rode. Tevin had remained blessedly quiet, forced to follow the Hunter through the darkness. Strider kept an eye on him. While the knight hadn't taken advantage of his weakened state, he didn't trust him to ride at his back. The only thing uniting them was their desire to locate Addy. Though Tevin was more urgent, Strider could feel the man's frustration. But Strider didn't push himself. He couldn't.

Eventually, the pace proved too much for the knight. "Can't we move faster?" he urged, frustrated.

"Do you want to do the tracking?" Strider replied, as he followed a set of Su'Iris' tracks with his eyes.

"I can't see in the dark."

"Then we're moving at the speed I choose."

"Lady Fenforde is increasing her lead." Tevin waved a hand ahead in a general direction they'd been riding. "At this rate, we won't ever catch up with her."

"She can't keep this pace the entire time." Strider steered Copper around a cluster of trees.

"She's being hunted. She needs to be protected."

Strider looked back at Tevin, allowing Copper to slow a stop as he munched on a clump of wild grass. "She won't thank you for coming to her rescue."

"I don't need to be thanked for doing my job," Tevin growled, glaring at Strider. "I don't need to be paid to bring Lady Fenforde home, either."

"More gold for me then," Strider grunted.

"You're an honorless son of Chaos."

"Honor doesn't pay for supplies." Strider clicked his tongue to urge Copper forward again.

"You know the Fenfordes will kill you the moment they find out what you are," Tevin said.

"And you'd think them justified. Death to all yulie, their existence is a crime, and tripe like that," Strider shot back, leveling his gaze on Tevin.

"And why wouldn't I feel that way after all that was done to us?"

"How noble of you to give a known kidnapper a fair trial for their actions while the man who saved Addy, and you, is condemned because of his heritage. Truly, you are a noble knight."

Tevin's ears grew red, as he grabbed for his sword, but he stopped, because he remembered his promise to Addy. He physically held himself back as if someone had barked an order for him to freeze. The Hunter knew he'd promised Addy that he'd not attack him, but he hadn't expected him to keep his word. Strider pointedly followed Tevin's hands with his eyes before returning to meet the knight's furious stare. He afforded the knight a small glimmer of respect for his self-control.

"Once you find Addy, leave," Tevin ordered. "I'll take her the rest of the way."

"I already tried letting you take her home, and look how that turned out," Strider retorted, his newfound respect not dampening his bite. "You're lucky Addy escaped, and I was there to drag your half-dead carcass along."

Tevin flinched, and Strider knew he'd struck a cord. The knight was very young, though he'd likely had led men before in skirmishes at the borders. It was probably the first time he'd lost an entire outfit.

If he were a different person, he'd have felt bad for dealing such a low blow.

But life had made him calloused, and he couldn't muster the energy. A tense silence lingered in the air. He didn't try to breach it, allowing the knight to linger in his thoughts while he kept an eye on him. He'd stopped himself from openly attacking an armed enemy, but even knights weren't above taking an opponent by surprise.

In his physical state Strider wasn't sure he'd be able to best the younger man. It took everything he had to hide how difficult it was to stay on his horse. Waves of weakness wracked his body, chased by shocks of frigid electricity. And he was keenly aware of how many joints he had as each one protested their use with stabs of pain. Worst was the void within him, bordered by glaciers that pressed against his ribs, sapping his will and energy.

An owl's soft hoots joined the sounds of the night. The gentle breeze whisked away the scent of horse sweat, replacing it will the cool scent of the forest. Copper snorted, letting out the tension within his ribs. Cricket chirps wavered in the air like a musical heat wave. The closest cricket's song cut short when they road by, before picking up again with renewed vigor.

A fox barked in the distance, causing Copper a moment of concern, but Strider was able to settle him down. But the effort left his muscles quivering and weak. His stomach threatened to unload its contents onto the courser's neck. He focused on breathing deeply through his nose to try to keep from being ill. It took several beats before the lightness left his head and he felt steady once more.

Even if Copper didn't care for them, the Hunter preferred the noises of the night over Tevin's yammering. But the peace wouldn't last as Tevin's voice drifted through the darkness, calmer than before. "Addy said you saved her."

"She rescued herself." Strider couldn't help the pride that entered his voice. "I helped tie up the loose ends."

"You trained her then. Why?"

"She needed it with how she attracts trouble. She learns quickly, when willing." Though he'd never suggest it, she'd make a decent Ranger if given the chance. He didn't need another person hunting him. Especially not one he helped train. "Would you prefer I kept her helpless?"

"No, I just didn't expect you to."

"Neither did she."

His answer sent Tevin retreating back into his own mind and Strider was granted his wish for the return of silence.

Chapter 42

Wolves & Lambs

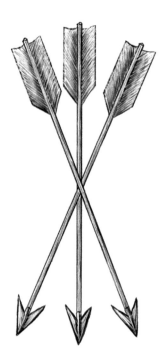

Strider let his gaze trail up and down the riverbank. They'd followed Su'lris' tracks through the night, arriving at the water's edge as golden threads of sunlight peaked through the forest canopy. The earthy scent of decaying leaves, wet stone, moss, and earth mingled with the fresher scent of water. The river was small and fast running, but shallow.

It babbled and chattered, filling the air with its endless murmur. The constant churning current made it difficult to see the rocks below, preventing Strider from picking out any disturbed moss on the rocks while the fast-flowing waters had smoothed over any prints left in the sand.

A cursory glance toward the opposite bank told him that Addy hadn't crossed directly. She'd used the river to hide her trail. He couldn't help the proud half smile that tugged at the corner of his lips. She was learning.

"It'd be best to split up." Strider pointed downriver. "You head that way and look for tracks. She won't be able to hide the trail of water her horse leaves behind." He hadn't taught her how to draw the moisture from the soil, so she couldn't completely mask her trail.

Tevin shook his head. "No, I'm not letting you run off with Addy the moment you find her."

Strider gave an annoyed grunt. "Then you go upriver, and I'll go down."

"We both go the same direction."

"You could find Addy and run off with her as well," Strider pointed out. "Why does it matter if we split up?"

"I don't trust you. That's why it matters."

"Take Greer with you then." Strider gestured at the di'horvith, who looked up from drinking from the river. Water dripped from his chin.

"No."

"Is everyone from Myvara as stubborn as you and Addy?"

"Is everyone from Roxbi an ill-tempered boor like you?"

The two men glared at each other until a loud splash drew their attention. They looked to see Greer on the opposite bank making his way downriver. He stopped to look back at them, then upriver before tossing his head and bounding off through the shallows.

Strider turned Copper upriver and sent him walking with a click of his tongue and pressure from his knees. "Come on, knight," he growled.

"We're not following him?" Tevin asked, looking back toward Greer.

"He'll tell us if he finds anything," Strider said over his shoulder.

Strider didn't bother to cross the river. He could clearly see any signs Su'lris had left on the other riverbank. He wouldn't make Copper cross until he had to. It would become more difficult to track Addy now that she was actively trying to hide her trail. The river would confuse Greer's nose until Su'lris left its waters. But like Strider, Greer had experience in the art of tracking those who didn't want to be found.

Some strength had returned to Strider's body, but he didn't rush. He made a point of maintaining the same speed as the night before. He could see by the tensing of Tevin's posture, and the occasional deep slow breath to relieve tension, that he was getting under his skin again.

"How about you move faster?" Tevin said, and Strider had to hide the slight curl of his lips at the mounting irritation in the knight's voice. "I know you can track faster than this."

"You're welcome to go on ahead," Strider said, his tone level. "Unless you can't track."

"I can track. I can also tell when someone is trying to get rid of me."

Strider stayed relaxed in the saddle as they rode. "I'm not moving faster."

"You're insufferable."

"Compliments won't make me move faster."

Strider took pleasure in the knight's agitation. Making him even less inclined to pick up the pace. He wasn't worried about catching up with Addy. She'd have to give Su'lris a rest, given the pace she'd pushed him the night before. They'd be able to make up time then. He'd let her be alone with her thoughts a little longer.

The fact that she was hiding her tracks meant she either needed more space, or she'd decided to go on without them. Given more time, she'd change her mind and come back, or she would tell them to shove off when they caught up with her. In either case, they'd both be more collected than they'd been during their fight. It was a plus that it also irritated Tevin. The string of curses he could hear him muttering under his breath made him smile.

"What will you do if Addy decides not to return home?" he asked, catching Tevin off guard.

"Of course, she wants to go back," he said incredulously. "Her family is worried about her, and she's a lady of the court."

"And what if she doesn't? Will you force her to?"

Enough silence elapsed between them that Strider glanced Tevin's way to see if he'd fallen off his horse. But he was there, his brows furrowed as he debated between fulfilling his job and honoring Addy's wishes. "My job is to return Lady Fenforde home safely. What she chooses to do after that is her business," he concluded.

"Even if you have to force her against her will?"

"It would be hard. And she'd never forgive me. But yes," he added with conviction. "But I don't believe Lady Fenforde would abandon her family."

"You'd be surprised what people will do when the threat of death hangs over them," Strider said grimly. He'd seen mothers abandon their children to save their own skin, fathers selling their family if it meant another bottle of liquor.

Nobility was a cesspool of backstabbing and betrayal. And though Addy appeared to love her family very much, her desire to live a day longer could outweigh that love. He hoped the strength he saw in her eyes wouldn't fail her in the critical hour, like it had so many others. Most of all, he hoped her own family hadn't betrayed her.

"Who exactly are you?" Tevin's voice cut through his thoughts. "I can tell you're from Roxbi by the accent. It's one of the few places that'd let a yulie live. But you're equipped with a Ranger's bow and are called the Dark Ranger."

"Addy called me that in Denmahr; seems the soldiers she insisted we let live spread the word. I should've killed them, regardless."

Tevin refused to be distracted from his line of questioning. "You still have a Ranger's bow. Did you kill one to get it?"

"No."

"Steal it?"

Strider let out a low chuckle. "I don't have a death wish."

"You bought it then?"

"No."

"They gave it to you, or you inherited it?"

"Also, no."

Tevin's voice changed to exasperation as he exhausted every avenue he could think of. "Then how did you get one?"

Strider titled his head as he asked. "What makes you think I have one?"

"You have a felaris feather," Tevin said, gesturing to the color shifting feather secure to Strider's bow.

"That doesn't make it a Ranger's bow, only that I have a feather that Rangers happen to use as a symbol." He jerked a thumb over his shoulder to his quiver. Raven feathers and one blue jay feather lined the rim, a string of animal teeth and beads sat hidden beneath them. "Rangers also decorate their quivers with other feathers. Does that make my quiver a Ranger's quiver?"

"How did you get the felaris feather, then?"

"It was given to me."

"By whom?"

"Someone who wanted me to have it."

"By K'yarie," Tevin cursed. "If you don't want to answer the question, just say so."

"Alright," Strider said, keeping his amusement from reaching his voice. "I don't want to answer your questions."

Tevin collected himself, rebounding quickly into a different topic. "I understand why you are staying with Addy, but it'd be better for the both of you if you left her."

Strider gave him a sidelong glance. "And why is that?"

"Because Lady Fenforde doesn't need to see you being punished, nor does she need your kind of protection."

"My kind of protection?" Strider repeated flatly. He knew where this was going. It was the same dance everyone performed.

"Forgetting the fact that mere association with you is enough to earn the ire of the Syliceon. Entrusting her to you is like trusting a wild wolf to guard a lamb," Tevin said, trying to keep his tone businesslike.

"Does the wolf consider the lamb its pack?" Strider asked coolly.

"What? No!" Tevin said in a quiet exclamation.

"Pity," Strider commented, scratching his chin absently. "If it did, that lamb would have a fearsome guardian that the Syliceon would have reason to fear."

Tevin scowled at the Hunter. "Is that what you think you are? Her guardian?"

Strider gave a scornful scoff. "I'm nothing so noble. I'm more like the demon upholding his end of a deal."

"And once that deal is complete, what do you intend to do?" Tevin challenged.

Strider slowed Copper to fix Tevin with a steady stare, then he cocked his head and looked away as he contemplated the question. He hadn't considered what he would do after returning Addy. Honestly, he was expecting to die before all of this was through. But if he didn't, what would he do? He looked out into the trees thoughtfully.

"I'll return quietly to my lair, so long as no annoyingly noble knights provoke me."

"Stop calling me that!" Tevin snarled. "And stop making light of this!"

"I am being serious," said the Hunter, his voice low. "And I won't be leaving. I'll have to trust her parents to keep Addy safe once she's home." The Fenfordes were high enough in the noble pecking order that the church couldn't risk creating an enemy of them. If Addy could keep a lid on her temper, and hide her magic, she'd likely go unpunished for being associated with him.

"She won't just have her parents," Tevin stated. "I'll do what I can to help."

"You don't think I've tainted her, by teaching her 'dark' magic?"

Again, there was a pause of consideration from the knight. "You simply gave Addy another sword to use. I don't believe Addy would use it for dark purposes."

Tevin was more thoughtful than many of the knights Strider had met. Young, brash nobles who thought their title earned them the world. Their codes of honor merely a decorative gilding on their otherwise rusted souls. Their names and faces had faded into obscurity, but the ones who lived by that code, he remembered. It was easy to claim you lived honorably. It was much harder to actually do so. He suspected Tevin would be among those he remembered.

Chapter 43
Regret

The tired horse stumbled to a halt. Foam dripped from its lips and its sweat soaked sides heaved with each gasping breath. Steam rolled off its skin in wispy curls. The world was silent, save for the horse's laborious breaths. The rider forced the animal onward with a hard kick, sending it into a slow walk as it entered the broken remains of a forgotten town.

Trees hemmed in around them like a dark wall, its depths a black void in the night. No crickets chirped, not even the wind stirred. The rider pulled the horse to a halt beside a relatively intact home before sliding off. He looked about, expecting to hear sounds of pursuit. But the forest remained deathly still. He'd clearly lost Lady Fenforde and the knight. Still, the man everyone called the 'Dark Ranger' was loose. He'd watched him leave after he and her ladyship fought.

He and his wolf could be anywhere in the forest. Tying his horse to a rotting fence, the escaped prisoner rummaged through the saddlebags. He cursed when he found them empty, raided by the three travelers. With no food and no means to build a fire, the mercenary turned away from the horse. The dark, slumped form of the house stood before him.

One wall had caved in, and the roof was missing, but it was better than sleeping out in the open. He didn't like the quiet. The forest was supposed to have sounds, even at night. But nothing stirred. Pulling his cloak tighter around himself, he hunched his shoulders against the growing chill. The mercenary couldn't shake the feeling that something wasn't right.

The horse let out a shrill scream; it bucked and pulled against its tether. The man backed away, narrowly avoiding being kicked.

"What the Tarn has gotten into you?" he spat at the horse.

The courser continued trying to break free, forcing the mercenary to move into the street as he tried to reach its head without being pinned against the wall of the house or kicked. His unease grew, as the horse's cries of terror replaced the unnatural silence. He sensed something behind him. The man whirled, fists raised. Nothing was there. Only the forms of dark trees looming over collapsed homes. Then the darkness moved.

He watched an inky form detached itself from the shadows in fascinated horror. Its long, clawed hands brushed against a pile of dead leaves, but they made no noise as they moved, each brittle leaf breaking against the ground without a sound. It was as if the gods had stolen the sound but left the world moving as it should. The shadowy form grew less certain when it entered the moonlight, though that did nothing more than increase the mercenary's terror.

He backed away, his eyes never leaving the lanky creature. It crept toward him, unaware that the ummanie could see it. The man increased his speed backward, ignoring the horse as it resumed its struggles with more fervor. The creature cocked its triangular head, seeming to realize the man saw it for the first time. It paused, as if it wasn't sure what to make of it. The monster and mercenary stared at each other for several heartbeats. One moved closer, the other moved back.

The beast lazily dragged its long ebony claws through the leaf litter, generating no noise, before lunging forward with startling speed. The man turned to flee. He ran toward the house, trying to use the horse as a shield. A scream had barely reached his throat before the creature was upon him, its dark claws tearing into his neck as its weight landed on his back.

The two tumbled into the crooked doorway of the home. Silence filled the night, quickly replaced by the sound of snapping wood and galloping hooves as the horse bolted into the forest. The shadow exploded from the home, loping after the horse in a long, awkward gate. Nothing else stirred within the dead town. Not even the insects dared show themselves at the scent of blood and death.

Addy had let Su'lris crash blindly through the forest. Branches whipped her face and snatched at her clothes. But she didn't stop or slow him in her desperation to flee the situation, to escape her guilt. Her tears freely fell, stinging her cheeks where salt touched small cuts left by the branches.

Tucking her head, she held onto Su'lris, letting the horse run. He needed no further urging, holding the original pace she set him to. The horse's nostrils flared as spittle and foam soaked his chest. His coat, covered in sweat, glistened in the scattered rays of moonlight filtering through the canopy.

He'd have run forever, never slowing until asked by his rider. Carrying her away from her problems upon swift hooves. But a horse could not run forever, nor could a person outrun the guilt about a mistake made in anger, and his gallop eventually slowed to a canter, then a trot. Addy didn't berate him or press him to speed up. She didn't notice when they'd slowed to a walk. Her mind was replaying everything she'd said, and what she'd tried to do.

She still didn't understand where the broiling anger had come from. Her temper had always run hot, but that'd been on another level. Irrational and uncontrollable, she'd wanted to hurt Strider and took pleasure in seeing him wounded. A shudder ran through her body, as she remembered how satisfied she'd felt. She'd brought up his father's murder!

Addy rested her forehead against Su'lris' mane. "What did I do?" she said, her voice tight, as she struggled to hold back tears of regret. "He's never going to forgive me." Su'lris plodded on in silence.

Addy wiped away residual tears, as she took deep breaths to calm herself. It did little to help. That terrible ice within her chest had all but dissipated, leaving her drained. The void it left behind was filled with regret. She couldn't face Strider, not after what was said between them. But what was she supposed to do? Su'lris halted and the sound of him drinking deeply snapped her back to the surrounding forest.

The moonlight was strong enough for her to see the river they'd come to. It hissed and burbled, sparkling in the darkness. She let the horse drink for a moment before pulling him away from the water's edge. Not wanting him to fill his stomach and slow himself down. She looked up and down the river, uncertain where to go.

She couldn't turn around. Strider was no doubt tracking her. If he wasn't, Greer had to be. The river would provide cover for her tracks and would wash away their scent trail. The others would have to split up or pick a random direction. Her eyes followed the water's flow down the river. Most likely she'd find a road or town if she followed it. She'd learned from Strider that when lost in the mountain to follow the water, as it always ran toward the lowlands, and people built settlements near a water source.

But Strider would know that, and he would he expect her to go that route? Towns were not her friend right now and she didn't know who to trust. It'd make more sense to ride upriver, then move parallel to the mountain. She'd eventually reach the Denam Plains and from there she could find her way home.

Home.

A lump formed in her throat. Every day, she drew closer to her family, as well as her enemy. People had betrayed the Fenforde household; people who were likely still there. The king of Denmahr had somehow planted snakes within their walls.

Did she really want to go home?

The thought surprised her. But she let it linger. While she loved her family, the pretty dresses, and shoes back at home, she found she loved the freedom she'd had while traveling. Maybe it'd be safer for everyone if she faked her death and went off to live somewhere else. She could become a trapper, save up some money and buy a home within The Wilds, where no one would recognize her.

Images of her parents and siblings crying over an empty grave brought fresh tears to her eyes. She couldn't put them through that kind of pain. She needed to return to them, to show them she was safe and warn them of the danger.

Strider also needed to have his name cleared. She'd dragged him into this situation. Addy knew it was cowardly to run and not face the

Hunter and own up to her mistakes. If she could exonerate him of her kidnapping, then maybe he would forgive her?

"Okay, Su'Iris," she said, straightening in her saddle, her brow furrowing in determination. "We're going to set things right."

With pressure from her legs and a small flick of the reins, Addy sent Su'Iris walking into the river. The muffled, gritty thud of his hooves on sodden sand changed to splashing as he entered the river. He tossed his head at the water's cold touch but didn't balk. Addy gasped as the glacial runoff splashed onto her legs and hips.

The two quickly became accustomed to the water's temperature and they set off upriver. Addy kept the pace slow, allowing Su'Iris to place each hoof with careful precision. The riverbed was thankfully not too rough and Su'Iris made his way upriver without too much difficulty.

As he waded, Addy monitored the banks. Her heart leapt in her throat, as a sound like a hoarse, screeching bark, pierced the lull of crickets and night birds. Su'Iris barely lifted his head, ears swiveling toward the sound. Otherwise, he seemed unbothered. "Why do foxes sound so terrifying?" Addy said with a shiver.

Addy once again let Su'Iris pick his path through the river. Whoever trained him had taken the time to teach him to maintain the pace his rider asked, resulting in Addy only ever having to ask him once to walk. The surefooted courser plowed on through the water. The rhythmic splashes and the sway of the horse's stride a disjointed song amongst the nightly serenade unfolding around them. Scents of horse sweat, water, and damp horse's hair filled Addy's nose, drowning out the fresh scent of the forest.

She'd need to stop and give Su'Iris a rest after his hard run. Trudging through the water would exhaust the rest of his energy. She hoped that Strider and the others had been slow to start after her. They had the prisoner to drag along, and the two men didn't get along. Tevin would keep his word to not hurt Strider, but Addy hadn't gotten such a promise from the Hunter. Hopefully Greer kept them both in check.

After traveling upriver for some time, Addy eased Su'Iris onto the bank. She scowled at the trails of water that streamed down his legs, and the dark stains left on the stones. She had made sure not to come out on a bank with soft soil and mud, but a rocky section of the river, to avoid leaving deep hoofprints in the mud. Hopefully, the stones would dry before Strider found them. Addy sighed. It would be difficult, but she had to try to hide their trail.

She steered Su'Iris deeper into the forest before stopping to ease herself out of the saddle. Securing his reins to a tree, she pulled out a shirt left by Su'Iris' previous owner. Ripping it apart, she secured the fabric to the bottom of her boots in order to break up the outline of her footprint. As she backtracked, she looked for any other signs of her passage.

She did her best to cover up Su'Iris' tracks. They'd avoided the dense parts of the forest to prevent them from damaging bushes and trees. But Su'Iris didn't care about stepping on grass and plants, making it impossible for Addy to completely erase signs of his passage.

Reaching the riverbank, she looked at the dark, shining stones. Maybe she could spread them about intermixing them with dry stones? No, that'd make it look even more irregular. Magic could probably dry up the water. The thought of trying to use magic after what had happened left a sour taste in Addy's mouth. She didn't want to feel that cold ever again. Experimenting with magic was out. She opted instead to do something manual.

She removed her cloak, socks, and any items she didn't want to get wet and tucked them behind a tree. Working her way down the river, she kept to the rocky ground, careful not to overturn any stones. Addy unwrapped her shoes and held the fabric in a ball above her head as she walked into the water. Again, she gasped, as the cold water came up to her bellybutton. The current pulled at her, and she let it angle her path in a diagonal route rather that fighting to cut straight across.

She slowly applied her weight to each step, never fully committing to shifting her weight to that foot until she was certain the rocks beneath wouldn't shift unexpectedly. Any misstep and the current would sweep her legs out from under her. Once she reached the other side, she tossed her fabric straps onto the dry bank while staying in the rocky shallows. She had picked another spot lined with rocks instead of soft soil.

Bending down, she scooped up a handful and water, then walked out onto the rocks. Her dripping clothes aided her as she splashed onto the shore. After several trips, the wet path mimicked the amount Su'Iris had left behind. She even disturbed the stones like he had. Addy surveyed the shore, glistening in the moonlight with a sense of satisfaction.

She grabbed the fabric and wrapped them around her feet once more before heading into the forest. Here she disturbed a plant here and there, leaving strands of her hair on higher branches. Crouching down, she outlined a faint trace of a hoofprint that looked like she'd rushed to cover it up. Making it look like she'd tried to hide a trail leading into the forest.

It might not deceive Strider, but she hoped it'd give him enough pause, or trick Tevin if he was the only one following her. With more time, she'd have gone deeper into the woods with this false path, but she didn't have the luxury, so she stopped at a hard packed section of the forest to hide her trail and began carefully working her way back upriver on land.

When she crossed the river again, she did so above where Su'Iris had exited. Waiting in the shallows until her clothes stopped dripping, she used the now very dirty old shirt as a dry place to stand. Keeping her shoes off, she picked her way up the rocky shore into the tree line, where she put her boots back on and grabbed her things before returning to Su'Iris.

Chapter 44

To Track An Addy

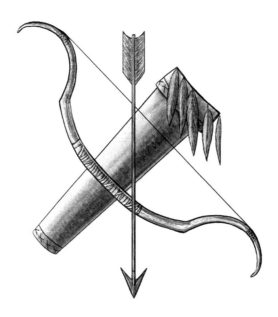

"Why do you think it's a false trail?" Tevin said, gesturing toward the riverbank in front of him, where one could clearly see a wet path left across the stones.

"Because I taught her how to make them," Strider replied.

Tevin gave him a look of irritated befuddlement. "Why did you teach her that?"

Strider met his gaze with a half-raised eyebrow, like a teacher unimpressed with his student for not finding the obvious answer. "For her protection."

Tevin gestured around them as if to point out Addy's. "You're doing such a great job protecting her."

"I try."

"That wasn't a compliment."

"I know," Strider said, resting his hands on his thighs as he held the reins loosely. He wouldn't admit it but having the knight around to needle served as a good distraction against the pain and exhaustion. It had eased, and the bouts of weakness were lessening, but he still didn't feel right. Like he wasn't quite inside his own body anymore.

"Enough of this," Tevin said, in exasperation. "Maybe, knowing you, she expects you to think her first trail is fake and left it obvious on purpose?"

"She isn't that devious yet. That mindset is harder to teach in some than in others."

"It's not a matter of training," Tevin argued. "She's been with you long enough to understand how you think."

"Follow the trail," Strider said, with a slow wave toward the path. "If I'm wrong and you reach Addy, I'll give you my war sword and leave without a word."

This piqued Tevin's interest. "And if I'm wrong?"

"You leave."

"No."

The two men stared at each other for a moment, before Strider clucked to Copper and the horse started forward. The Hunter could hear Tevin's frustration mounting behind him.

"You're seriously so dead set on being right you're unwilling to at least check the trail."

Strider brought Copper back around so he could look at Tevin. "We have two people. It makes no sense to have us searching the same route."

Tevin hadn't moved from his spot beside the trail Addy had left. "And once I'm out of sight, you'll vanish without a trace. Find Addy and carry on without me."

Strider was growing tired of Tevin's attitude and overall bullheadedness. If anything, he was the one wasting their time. "I won't be wasting my time hiding my tracks," Strider said, whirling Copper about to continue their walk upriver. "Follow them."

"You expect me to believe you?"

Strider let out a weary sigh, but he didn't stop Copper to offer an irritated reply. "Greer should be headed back by now. He'll find you first, then lead you straight to me."

Tevin paused his arguing long enough to consider this before nodding. "Alright," he said. "Search further upriver. I'll check this trail."

Strider almost praised the gods. Finally, they were getting somewhere! He offered Tevin a flippant wave of acknowledgement. The Hunter waited until he was sure Tevin was out of earshot before picking up his pace. He knew he could catch up to Addy.

Her efforts to conceal her path would've eaten away at her time and stamina. Su'Iris had also been working hard; running full speed before being forced to walk against the current, while Copper was still relatively fresh. The two would tire before him, and he could see in the dark.

He spotted where she and Su'Iris had exited the water further upriver and soon he and Copper crossed to the other side. The efforts she'd put into hiding her actual trail and laying a fake one would've confused other trackers. Strider couldn't keep a smile of approval from appearing as he carefully tracked his quarry.

She'd remembered her training. Practice would only improve it. He'd have to hope the Rangers at Timara castle wouldn't take notice of her budding skills. He quickly realized she was a potential weapon he didn't have a defense against. That still didn't stop him from feeling proud of her as he steadily closed the gap between them.

Chapter 45

Unsavory Types

The soft touch of morning light dancing on the forest floor couldn't chase away the melancholy within Addy's soul. She had a purpose, but remorse still clung to her like a bitter taste in the back of her mouth. She accepted that the feeling wouldn't go away and now used the task of hiding her trail and navigating to help distract from it.

The Tahlrin Mountains were visible in the growing daylight, and she kept track of them through breaks in the trees, using them as a constant landmark. She knew to keep them to her left, ensuring she was going the right way. Either she'd find the Denam Plains or travel far enough that she'd reach the Tahl River. Either way, she could navigate home, though cutting across the great chasm in Denam Plains would shorten her trip considerably. She just had to stay ahead of the others.

Su'lris walked out onto a road. Addy reined him in, her heart rate spiking, as she looked to either side in panic. No one was there. She let out a pent-up breath, her shoulders relaxing. On closer inspection, she realized the road was old and overgrown. It'd not seen use in a while. Still, the ground was hard where wagon wheels and horse hooves packed the earth, perfect for hiding hoofprints.

"This must be an old logging road," she said aloud.

Su'lris lent an ear to his rider as he waited for instruction.

"Or maybe a quarry." Either way, the money must've dried up as no one appeared to use the road anymore. It lay forgotten and abandoned.

"There might be some old buildings we could shelter in as we give the others the slip." Going toward the mountain instead of away from it wouldn't make sense if one thought logically. Like going upriver, Addy hoped it'd mislead the Hunter.

Still, she took a moment to make it look like she went the other way, leading Su'lris down the road before doubling back. It wouldn't confuse Greer's nose for long, but any moment of delay on their part could prove vital. She knew she couldn't do much more of these feints herself, as it cost her precious time. From the ghost town, she'd make a straight shot for home.

Addy spent the rest of the day following the old road to its source. Dilapidated waddle and daub buildings made up the remains of the desolate town. The small homes were falling apart, their roofs long since rotted away or caved in. Sections of walls had fallen in on many of the houses, leaving gaping wounds in the buildings.

Doors and windows looked like the hollow eyes and mouths of skulls, dark and lifeless. Off in the distance, on a small rise, stood the remains of an old manor house where the presiding mayor may have once lived. From where she was, it looked like a fire had turned the great wooden building into a burned-out shell left to collapse in on itself. The blackened beams and supports jutted out of the rubble, like dark bones protruding from the dead husk of a monster.

Other parts of the town looked to have suffered from the fire, while others appeared to have simply succumbed to years of neglect. The town held a depressed, haunted air about it. Addy's skin crawled in unease. Something didn't feel right, though she didn't know why. The feeling went beyond being spooked by the ghost town. There was something dark here; she could feel it.

"We shouldn't stop here," she said, all hope of setting up camp gone. She didn't want to be near the town when night fell.

Su'lris made no complaints.

They stopped only when darkness forced them too. They'd left the town far behind them. Dejected, she busied herself tending to Su'lris, going more by feel than sight as she fumbled through the dark. It brought back memories of the first night Strider had helped her tend to Su'lris. How he'd taken her hand and led her around the camp so she could safely cool Su'lris down, and then guided her hands when it was too dark for her to see as he taught her how to rub the horse down.

Addy wished she had Strider's eyes. If she did, they could've continued traveling well into the night. She rested her head against Su'lris' great shoulder, seeking comfort in his presence. The horse stood steady, providing the stability she needed to stand against the wave of guilt that crashed over her.

She hated having to stop; at least while she was moving, she could busy herself. But it was too dark to continue, and both she and Su'lris needed to rest. Though her muscles ached from the hard ride, he'd worked the hardest. Which left her nothing to do but try to keep busy, at night, when she could hardly see.

Fumbling for her sleeping roll, she unrolled the first layer designed to protect against moisture and groaned as her back complained. Once she finished setting everything up, she laid down. She didn't dare start a fire, so darkness surrounded her. Before she'd begun traveling with Strider, the thought of spending a night in the forest with no light terrified her. Now it felt comfortable in its familiarity. Her exhaustion won out over the spiraling thoughts of her argument with Strider. And after three slow blinks, Addy slipped into sleep.

The scent of wood smoke and coffee woke her in the morning. Addy sat up and stretched, blearily wondering why Strider hadn't woken her up sooner. It took her a moment for the memories to return. When they did, her back stiffened and her heart found a new home in her throat.

"You fell asleep without setting a perimeter alarm," a stern voice said, from somewhere behind her. "You're lucky no unsavory types decided to drop by during the night and slit your throat."

Addy whirled around, fully awake now as a single word leaped from her lips.

"Strider!"

Chapter 46
Promises & Apologies

Addy gaped in shock as she took in the image of Strider crouched before the fire, drinking a cup of coffee. His hood was up, as usual, casting half his face in shadow, though he no longer wore his mask.

"You also took all the coffee," he noted flatly, shaking his head.

"Strider!" Addy repeated even louder.

"That is my name."

Addy bit her lip and blinked rapidly, fighting back tears. Now face to face with him, she couldn't run anymore.

"Strider I-" she began, before choking on her words.

Unable to speak, she instead rushed toward the man, who held up a warning hand. She stopped before his hand, eyes shining, face red. She bit her lip; her face twisted by the torrent of emotions that whirled inside of her.

"I am so sorry!" she choked out. She bowed her head, unable to meet his gaze. The act of apologizing uncorked whatever was holding her words back as she said in quick succession. "I said such terrible things. I don't know what came over me. I just- I don't- I'm so, so sorry!" The tears were back, streaming down her face. She hated it. But she couldn't help but cry as she finally said what she wanted.

"It was so cold and dark," she hugged herself as she shook. "I was so scared, I felt so empty and alone, and I-" *I wanted someone to hurt as much as I did*, she thought, as her throat closed off again and she couldn't find her voice. Her eyes were beseeching as they lifted to Strider. He had remained silent the entire time she'd spoken. He didn't move, as he drank his coffee thoughtfully. When she looked at him, he gave a nod of understanding, as if he knew what she'd left unsaid.

"Now you truly understand the cost of magic," he told her.

"So, everyone feels like that?" Why did anyone want to use magic if the price of overuse was that they had to endure something so terrible?

"Yes," he answered softly. "I should've expected you to lash out the way you did. People tend to hurt others when they themselves are hurting."

"That is still no excuse for what I did."

"I never said it was," Strider answered simply, talking into his mug.

"How do you deal with it? How do you keep the cold at bay?"

Tossing the dregs of his coffee aside, he poured another cup for himself. He eyed the trees for a moment before pouring one for Addy. He offered her the cup and Addy took it with a quiet thank you.

"On the first night I healed Tevin, what did you see me do?"

"You were extremely irritable and sarcastic. You wouldn't stop verbally poking Tevin."

"Not what did I say. What did I do?" he repeated patiently.

Addy thought about this for a moment before saying, "You kept busy."

Strider nodded his approval. "Do not dwell on the cold or the thoughts it brings. Always keep busy, never let yourself be alone, and if you ever find yourself alone, remember the things that keep you here. Be that a person, a place, or a goal. Remember it; cling to it."

It occurred to Addy that the ice began to thaw when she spoke to Tevin about her family. Then another thought struck her.

"You've been alone. Every time you've overtaxed your magic. We've left you alone; *I* left you alone."

Other than the time he'd nearly died after healing Greer, she'd never made any effort to reach out to him after he used his magic.

"Who said I was ever alone?" Strider asked.

It didn't take Addy long to realize who he was referring to.

"Greer is your grounding force." She should've been able to guess that, with the way Strider treated the di'horvith. The way he'd been willing to give up his own life to save Greer when he was dying under the mountain.

He nodded.

"Why did you come back?" she asked. "After what I said, I wouldn't fault you for leaving me."

"I promised to take you home," he said, holding her gaze. "And I also needed to apologize for what I said. We were not ourselves that night."

Addy glanced down at the mug in her hands. She sniffed, holding back more tears. "It's alright; we were both terrible that night."

The conversation devolved into nothing, leaving the sound of the crackling fire and morning birdsong. Addy couldn't believe she'd slept through the construction of the fire. The image of the Hunter carefully placing each piece as softly as possible nearly made her spit up her drink when it randomly popped into her head. Coughing, she wiped her mouth on the back of her hand. Embarrassed, she fought to say through her coughing fit, "Where's Greer and Tevin?"

Strider tossed the remaining dregs of his coffee into the fire before fetching his bedroll from Copper. "Tevin insisted on following your fake trail. They'll be along, eventually."

"Oh," Addy said, biting her lower lip. "I'm sorry about running."

"It's in the past," Strider said, laying down on his blanket. "Keep watch and we'll call it even."

Addy smiled. "Deal."

Tevin scowled at Strider over his mug of coffee. The Hunter paid him no mind as he drew out a rough map in the dirt. Tevin and Greer had arrived later in the day; Tevin was weary and irritated. Addy had tried to make amends by making a fresh batch of coffee. They now huddled around the rough drawing, steaming mugs in hand.

"We're going to lose the cover of the forest before we reach the plains," Strider said.

"They have to know Addy is still free," Tevin said, as he eyed the map. "They'll likely have people watching the roads."

"They won't have to invest in many." Strider pointed toward an open part of the map with a line snaking parallel to the mountains cutting through it. "The fastest route to Timara is across the chasm. They likely have an ambush waiting on the other side."

"If we go around, it'll take at least half a moon to reach home," Addy said despondently, as she hugged Greer for reassurance.

"We don't have that kind of time," Tevin said in frustration. "The longer it takes to reach the castle, the more forces the enemy can enlist to track us down and trap us."

Strider didn't want to get into unnecessary battles, especially now with his soul already strained and draining him.

"It would be better if we avoided their trap," he muttered. "But time is not our friend." Finishing his coffee, Strider looked into the distance where he knew the bridge to be, his head tilting to one side. If they left the horses, and it was only him and Addy, they'd likely be able to sneak by.

"We'll decide what to do closer to the bridge," he determined. He'd be able to scout the area once they'd gotten there. With nothing else to do, he wrapped his cloak around himself and laid back on his bedroll, pulling his hood down over his eyes.

"You're going to sleep again?" Addy asked, still sitting with Greer, who had laid his head across her lap.

Upon seeing Strider lay down, the di'horvith left her and nestled next to the Hunter, using the man's stomach as a pillow.

"I am," he told her. "Rest while you can. We travel hard and fast tonight."

Chapter 47

Pages of Memories

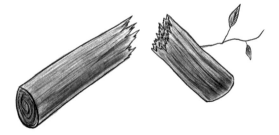

Night fell and the little party continued their travels. After a few hours, the forest fell away, as Strider led them onto the road. Out in the open, he opted to use the clear path, then navigate the fields and fences that littered the landscape. Those who hunted them likely used the light of the sun to aid in their search. Their enemy knew where they had to go. They had no choice but to reach the bridge, and the road provided the quickest way at this point.

Strider glimpsed a figure vanishing behind a windmill one night while they rode by a small farming village. The time for farmwork was long past. There shouldn't be people out doing honest work. His suspicions proved right when he saw the same figure spurring a horse back the way they'd come. Their pursuers would now know exactly where they were.

The flatlands provided no effective area to lay an ambush between their current location and the Denam bridge, but that meant there were no places to hide, either. The bulk of their pursuers were likely behind them, pressuring them toward the chokepoint. No doubt confident they had their prey cornered.

The darkness covered their swift travel, though Strider knew the shadows were as merciless as the sun to those who let their guard down. Sun or moon, both shone while wicked creatures had their way. Though the darkness favored one such as he, it hindered the ummanie hunting them.

He expected there to be a couple anumi among them to aid in the night hunts, so he watched for animals behaving out of the ordinary. Each day, when they stopped, Strider had Addy heal Tevin's wounds, careful to watch and make sure she didn't overextend her magic. The process was slow, but bit by bit, his injuries healed, until they sealed completely. At night, he had her focus on connecting to her inner well while they rode, keeping her busy and silent for several hours, as she practiced calling to her magic.

Addy attempted to channel magic into her body as they moved through the darkness. She held a thick branch in her hands, far thicker than she could break using her normal strength. She visualized the branch breaking before trying to snap it in two. The wood held firm. Addy let out a breath in frustration. She didn't understand. Her magic usually responded to her will, only needing a gentle prompting. Was it because she was asking it to perform more than one thing?

"Stop focusing on the branch," Strider told her. "Focus on the act, your muscles. The way they feel when you exert yourself, the strength you need. Picture your magic flowing into your muscles and bones, fusing with them, strengthening them."

"Isn't there some sort of spell you could tell me that'd do that?" she asked. "Don't mages usually use magic words?"

"Words help to shape the magic to a task they're trying to perform. But it is unwise to become reliant on those words," Strider told her. "The mages you've seen couldn't will the wind to do as they wished, without using verbal commands or spells. They can't alter the spell, either, as the word invokes a static response each time. Nor can they strengthen their body in the middle of a sword fight without breaking concentration to utter an incantation. Take away their ability to speak, and you take away their power. Speaking magical words also makes it obvious you're using magic."

Addy nodded with a sigh, and tried to focus on her muscles instead of the wood. She imagined the magic flowing into her, extending through her body and seeping into bone and marrow before creeping out to saturate her muscles. She could feel her magic tugging at her soul as it moved through her.

It ran through her blood before burrowing deep within her bones. They felt warm. That warmth bled into her muscles and tissue. Addy couldn't explain how she knew when she had enough strength to break the branch. It was an instinctual understanding that compelled her to try. The branch cracked loudly, snapping in two.

"I did it!" she exclaimed in excitement, holding the two pieces up victoriously.

Strider gave a small nod. "Now practice until you barely have to think about it."

Addy spent the rest of the travel trying to break more branches from their stash of firewood. Now that she knew what to ask of her magic, it amazed her how it answered her so easily. This sort of internal magic came easier to her than the external healing magic. It wasn't the quietest form of practicing, but the enemy already knew where they were going.

Addy continued to work until she felt the warning tugs on her soul, telling her she was reaching her limit. Not wanting to feel that terrible cold ever again, Addy stopped practicing, and tossed a recently snapped log back into the bag. She'd have to rest and try again the next night.

"How did you learn magic?" she asked Strider.

She didn't expect him to answer; he'd hardly spoken to her since he returned. It had taken him three days before he'd begun teaching her magic again. Beyond that, he said little, having retreated into himself. It surprised her when he answered.

"My mother."

"What was she like?" Addy continued, tentatively. She'd been curious to learn more about the yulie woman. She could feel him eyeing her, though she couldn't see his eyes. The darkness cast by his hood hid his face. He fished in his satchel and pulled out the worn book she saw him drawing in from time to time.

With one hand on the reins, he used the other to open the book to the first page before handing it to her. She took the book but could barely see the pages as she squinted.

Strider flicked a hand in her direction and a small silver orb the size of a coin materialized from his fingertips. It danced and drifted toward her like a dandelion seed in the wind. It hovered over the book, its soft moonlight barely bright enough for her to see the picture it illuminated on the page.

Addy held the book with reverence. Other than his sword, Strider had never given her anything of his before. The hairbrush didn't count; it was Greer's. By the way he handled it, Addy knew the book was special to him and she didn't dare drop it as she looked at the drawing on the page.

The image was of a breathtakingly beautiful, dark-haired yulie woman. She was smiling softly in the image. Her face radiated a warm inner light of love. Even from the picture, Addy could tell she was a kind person. Her kind smile reminded Addy of her own mother.

While she could be stern and quick to correct, she was also quick to show her love for her children. She'd heard that not all nobles took time for their children, preferring to let the tutors raise them. But Addy's parents had always tried to be in their children's lives. She knew they loved her and they were worried about her.

She brushed her thumb along the edge of the book cover. The care taken in drawing every detail perfectly preserved the moment in time, as if she were staring through the magical doors of The Ways, leaving a perfect black and white image in its place. Great care, attention to detail, and devotion, was put into this picture dedicated to preserving the vibrant life of this lovely woman.

Addy found she hadn't taken a breath, stunned by the beauty of the picture. This was nothing like the normal sketches she'd seen Strider draw, which were beautiful in their own right, but were far looser and more fluid in nature.

"She's beautiful," she breathed. "What is her name?"

"Her name was Sephyra."

Strider's voice was stoic, and Addy wished she could see his face and eyes as he spoke. The tone did not match the care taken to create this piece of art; it was far too cold, too distant.

"I'm sorry," she told him, remembering what he had told her in the tunnels. She handed him the book back and the little light died.

"You didn't kill her," Strider said, matter-of-factly.

"I know," Addy responded, before growing silent; her face took on a serious expression as she thought. "Was she the one the assassin killed?"

"No," Strider answered, after a long pause.

Addy narrowed her eyes at him. The answer had been far too long in coming, and it made her suspicious. "Who was it then?"

"If I tell you, you will feel guilty all over again," Strider told her flatly.

Addy knew that was true. She already felt a fresh wave of guilt rising inside her like a coming storm.

"What you said is in the past," he told her. "Leave it there, learn from it, and move on. I already have." With a swift kick, he sent Copper into a trot, pulling further ahead of Addy and ending the conversation.

They didn't make camp until the sky was blushing a soft pink over rows of wheat and lines of apple trees. They had to move far from the road to find a secluded area, behind an apple orchard, nestled against a small hill. The crisp, sweet scent of apples accompanied the pastel light of dawn. The land was growing flatter and more orchards and fields hedged in around them. Addy groaned, as she placed her hands against the small of her back and stretched.

"I feel like an old woman," she moaned, easing her shoulders and neck of stiffness as she rolled them. Su'Iris moved away from her, and she looked over, startled. He'd never wandered off before. She looked puzzled when she saw Strider leading the large animal around alongside Copper.

"What are you doing?" she asked him.

"Sit down and rest," he told her. "We don't need you breaking a hip."

"Don't make me hit you with my cane," she threatened, good-naturedly. "Us old people are dangerous when we want to be."

"I don't doubt it," he said in amusement.

Having nothing else to do, Addy tried to help Tevin with the other horses. He refused to let her, saying in an aghast tone.

"I would never make an elderly woman tend to the horses! Go sit down. Do you need a blanket to keep warm?"

Addy swatted him playfully on the arm. He laughed and Addy paused as she heard a low soft chuckle come from Strider. She wasn't sure she could remember the last time she'd heard him laugh. Had he ever laughed before, other than cynically?

"The nerve of the kids these days!" she said, shaking her head much in the same way old people did when bemoaning the state of the youth.

Grabbing Greer, she pulled him over to the center of the camp and began rummaging through his packs, looking for some dried food to set out for everyone. Strider and Tevin soon joined her in eating a cold meal. Free of his harness, Greer rushed off to hunt down a meal for himself. They were only a day away from Denam Chasm, and Addy felt restless anxiety forming inside her stomach. Unable to sit still, she got up and went over to Su'lris to fetch something.

Strider had pulled out his sketchbook as he lounged on the grass, back propped against an old oak. A piece of jerky protruded from between his lips, like a meaty cigar, as he sketched. No one started a fire for fear of alerting the enemy to their exact position. The Hunter heard footsteps approaching and looked up from his sketch to see Addy standing over him. Her eyes shifted from him to the ground like a puppy who knew it had done something wrong as she rocked on her feet. Her arms were behind her back, and he could see the two wooden swords he'd made poking out from behind her.

"I know I told you I didn't want to use the sword anymore. But would you still teach me?" she asked sheepishly, holding out a crudely crafted sword. "Please?"

He closed his book, studying her for a moment. While he'd been adamant she should learn before, he hadn't pressed her to pick up the blade after their fight. Before, she'd been hesitant, because she'd been told she couldn't. Now she could, but she'd decided not to continue learning the art of the blade. He respected her choice, even if he didn't agree with it. But decisions made in the height of emotions often changed when a calmer mind ruled.

Addy continued to look sheepish, but she mustered the courage to meet his gaze.

Strider put the book in his satchel without a word, and took the offered weapon.

Chapter 48

Tevin Gets A Stick

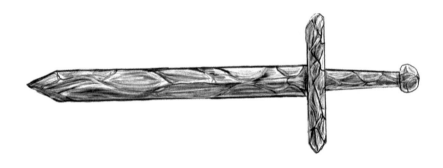

"Forward thrust, right, left; move that back leg!" Strider called out each move, never settling into a specific pattern, as he struck with his wooden blade.

Addy did her best to answer each attack with her own counters, parries, and dodges.

Strider abruptly stopped calling out his strikes as he moved in closer, picking up the pace and forcing Addy to work harder.

"Stop. Staying. On. The. Defensive!" he told her, punctuating his words with skillful strikes.

Addy barely avoided being hit. Growing frustrated, she lashed out at him with a clumsy slash, earning a painful welt on her hip, as Strider knocked her blade aside and smacked her with his sword.

He pressed in harder, his blade moving even faster as it collided with hers again.

"Stop holding yourself back!" he ordered firmly.

She saw an opening that would allow her to strike his right side and went for it, only to find that it had been a trap as her blade clacked against the wood. Strider pivoted, a hand grasping the wooden blade where the tang met the cross-guard. He jerked her toward him, his own blade coming up to press against her throat.

"I've told you before," he scolded. "Do not attack in frustration or anger. If you become angry, you die."

She let out a breath full of frustration. She pulled her blade free of Strider's grip before backing away. "I'm never going to beat you!"

"If that's what you believe, you're right," he agreed, earning a glare from her as she massaged her throbbing hip.

"You are doing well, my lady," Tevin said in encouragement. He'd been watching their training match closely. "Though you need to watch your opponent; learn to read their body to predict their moves."

Addy looked over at him thoughtfully. "Maybe I need a change in sparring partners?" she suggested, looking up at Strider innocently. "So I can learn how to read different fighting styles."

Strider's head tilted in consideration. "Maybe you're right," he conceded, before tossing his blade to Tevin, who caught it easily. Strider stood at the edge of the area they'd designated for sparring, arms folded across his chest. He watched as Tevin took up a loose fighting stance.

"Come at me, my lady," Tevin said, smiling like an excited kid.

Addy came at him, aiming for a downward slice at his left side. Tevin parried the move, but with not nearly the same amount of force as Strider would have. He didn't completely knock her weapon away, allowing her to redirect it into a strike aimed at his head.

Tevin blocked the move again. The two wooden blades cracked together sharply. With her sword on the outside of his, he had an open shot at her, and she swiftly withdrew, trying to put up a guard. But he gave only a half-hearted attempt at an attack.

"Don't go easy on her," Strider admonished. "You're not doing her any favors."

Tevin glowered at him but turned his attention back to Addy when she came at him again. This time she attempted an upward strike, or so she wanted him to think. There wasn't any commitment to the attack as she suddenly shifted at the last second to deliver a thrust aimed at his stomach inside the guard he would've put up.

He once again stopped her attack, surprised at the move. Had he been any less skilled at observing an opponent, he might have fallen for her feint. Strider easily rebuffed her attacks, but that didn't mean she wasn't skilled. Only that he was a master and had learned to predict her moves before she made them.

"She can handle a few bruises," Strider interjected again. "Attack her, or she'll never learn to defend herself."

Addy was panting from exertion, her eyes completely focused on him. "Stop babying me and come at me!" she ordered him, with fire in her eyes.

Tevin rushed forward, aiming a thrust at her stomach much in the same way she'd done earlier. Addy danced aside, her feet shuffling on the ground as she used her sword to redirect the attack. She moved to answer with her own slice to his gut. Tevin jumped back, barely avoiding being struck hard, and Addy grunted in frustration as she brought her sword up to block an overhead slash Tevin launched when she left herself open.

Wood met wood again, but this time Addy's arms failed her, and she ended up barely deflecting the attack. Tevin's blade struck her arm below the shoulder instead. She yelped in pain and Tevin instantly balked, jerking backward and forward again as if he couldn't decide if he should distance himself from her, or come closer to see if she was seriously injured.

"I'm so sorry, my lady!"

"You're not dead yet," Strider called to her. "Keep fighting."

"No, we're done!" Tevin said, stepping away from Addy before she could raise her sword again.

"No, we're not!" Addy said haughtily. "I can still fight!"

"Your arms are too tired to handle any more blows from me," he told her.

"No, they're not!" she insisted, though no one believed her.

Strider sighed, as he moved to take the sword from Tevin. The knight backed away from him, raising the tip of the blade to the Hunter's chest.

"Do you still plan to spar with her?" he challenged Strider.

"If she wants to keep trying, then yes," Strider told him.

"I do," Addy said, still breathing heavily as she brushed strands of brown hair out of her face. "I want to get better."

"You will," Tevin told her. "But you shouldn't push yourself. You don't need this man to teach you either."

Strider narrowed his eyes at him. "You think you can do better?"

Tevin met Strider's gaze with a defiant one of his own. "I do."

Strider held out a hand to Addy, motioning for her to give him the wooden sword.

She wasted no time handing it to him before stepping away. She sat cross-legged in the dirt, watching intently.

Raising the blade, Strider tapped it against Tevin's weapon as he canted his head to the side, a brow raised in a silent challenge. Tevin frowned at him and tried to push Strider's weapon aside. He was met with equal force, the wooden shafts clicking together as both men answered each other's challenge.

The two circled for a moment, swords presented to their opponent. Tevin moved first, aiming to dictate the momentum of the fight as he thrust outward, only to have his move deflected and the strike answered with a thrust of equal force. He swatted the attack away as they continued to circle, their shuffling feet kicking up a cloud of dust as each man tested the other with strikes, counters, parries, and dodges. Each blow became faster, harder as the two warriors fell into their rhythm.

Addy watched as blow after blow rained down, her eyes unable to keep up with the flashing wood that cracked together like whips, or hissed, as a blow was deflected. As she watched the fight grow more heated, she realized that this match was about more than just a disagreement about training.

If any of those attacks actually hit, they could break bones, or worse. Greer padded up to sit beside her as he, too, watched the fight. Addy let out a sigh and shook her head, as she looked at Greer.

"Why can't all men be as amiable as you?" she asked the di'horvith. Greer cocked his head and Addy wondered if he'd gotten the habit from Strider, or if it was the other way around.

Strider predicted the attack aimed at his head. His own sword flashed, as he swept it in an upward arc. It caught Tevin's blade and knocked it up and to the right as he continued the arc of his own blade. He circled it around Tevin's sword, forcing it downward, trying to trap the blade. Tevin broke his sword free and answered with a thrust. Strider brought his sword up again, preventing the attack from getting through his guard as the two fell into another dance of blades. For every attack, the other had an answer. Then the momentum began to change as Strider applied pressure.

Addy watched as Strider went on the attack, his blows becoming even more focused, seeming to move faster. She still couldn't recognize the skill and timing that was truly lending the Hunter speed. Strider took the lead in their ballet, forcing the knight on the defensive.

Tevin's blade was knocked aside again, as Strider circled around the back of the knight, where he aimed a hard slice at his back. Tevin barely regained control of his blade as he pivoted enough to bring it around, using the momentum to block the attack. The wood cried out once more with a resounding thwack! Strider pushed back against Tevin's sword, almost knocking him off balance, but Tevin kept his footing and the two broke apart.

Addy sneezed due to the dust being kicked up by the dueling swordsmen. Neither man gave a sign that they noticed, though Greer gave her nose a kiss as if that would make it better.

Strider didn't relent as he pressed forward, forcing Tevin to defend himself once more as the pressure increased. Tevin struggled to keep up as blow after blow came, and he found fewer chances to answer with his own attack. He found an opening and offered a counter but realized that Strider had baited him with the same move he'd used on Addy earlier. Sword met sword. Tevin felt his wrist being grabbed, a thumb pressing hard on a pressure point, causing him to let go of his blade as Strider thrust his own sword toward Tevin's stomach. It stopped before impact, the tip poking painfully into his gut.

Both men locked eyes; deep blue met steady gold as they stood there in the final stage of the fight. Strider waited as realization dawned on the knight, melting through the fog of battle. He waited for Tevin to step back before releasing his wrist. He had won.

Tevin collapsed to the ground, gasping for breath, exhausted.

Strider brushed his hair that had plastered to his forehead out of his eyes, as he held the gaze of the ummanie, who looked up at him in shock that quickly changed to anger, then acceptance.

"Why?" Tevin gasped, his voice barely loud enough for Strider to hear. "Why do you insist on coming with us? Why risk your life like this?"

Strider offered him a hand, his face as stoic as usual.

Tevin eyed the hand for a moment before accepting the help.

Strider gave a hard yank, pulling Tevin to his feet. He stepped in close; his lips were barely an inch from Tevin's ear as he spoke. "She has proved her loyalty. I will prove mine."

Strider pulled back, locking eyes for a moment before Tevin looked away. He dusted himself off as Strider observed quietly.

"That was incredible," Addy breathed, as she leaned back on her palms. Both men looked at her, finally remembering she was there.

Addy leaned forward, resting her elbows on her knees. "Now that you both got that out of your system, do you think we can work together?"

Tevin gave Strider a long, hard look. Addy knew he did not care for the man and wanted him gone, but Strider had made it clear he wasn't leaving. He let out a deep breath.

"At least until we get you home," he told her.

Strider gave a small smile and offered a barely perceptible nod as his answer.

"Good," she said, then smiled. "I'm glad I am not the only one to get beaten by an old man."

Strider shot her a narrowed-eyed look. "I didn't get this old by chance, remember that." He walked back to the tree he'd been sitting against. Wrapping his cloak around himself, he sat back down, pulling his hood over his eyes.

"I'll take the last watch," he told them.

"Wait!" Addy protested. "I wasn't done training!"

"I'm done teaching," he told her. "If you're still eager to train, Greer can take the first watch while you run through your drills again. Practice using your magic to enhance your endurance while you're at it."

Tevin collapsed in a bundled heap near Greer, not bothering to layout a bedroll to keep the moisture at bay, as he fell asleep. Like any warrior, he'd mastered the art of catching sleep when the moment presented itself.

"Great," Addy said, holding up both hands in exasperation. "Well Greer, it looks like it's just the two of us." She looked at the fluffy canine. "Do you know how to use a sword?"

Greer gave her a clueless look before kissing her on the cheek.

"I didn't think so."

Chapter 49

Schemes & Stories

Addy, Strider, and Tevin stared across the Denam Plains. A flat expanse of rough grassland stretched out before them. Tall yellow and green grass carved out a life in the rocky soil, hedging the roads created by countless feet over the decades. While unfit for farmland, grazing herds of sheep and cattle dotted the plains, lazily milling about, before being called back home by their owner's songs.

A great chasm cut through the land like a jagged scar. Below them sat a covered bridge spanning the great canyon. On the other side of the bridge lay another forest, its trees old and thick. It stood out of place with a single mountain peak behind it. Strider laid on his stomach beside Addy at the top of one of the taller outlaying hills, surveying the land.

"You think they have set up an ambush on the other side?" Addy asked, her tone less than hopeful.

"Unless they're dumber than a sack of rocks," Strider stated flatly. "They'll know we have to cross."

Addy sighed. "We can't go around. I need to get home."

Both Tevin and Strider nodded, but neither looked happy about it.

"Tell me, knight," Strider began, gesturing to the chasm and the forest beyond. "How would you set up an ambush?"

Tevin, lying on Addy's other side, studied the land. "I would set up camp deeper into the trees to prevent any fires from being spotted. Then post men to watch the bridge from the cover of the forest while having an additional unit behind the target to herd the enemy into my trap and flank them when the trap has sprung."

He looked up the road that followed the chasm on their side of the bridge; he could see the smoke of cook fires in the distance indicating a large camp. "If I had the manpower, I'd ensure another unit was waiting in that direction to surround the enemy."

Strider scratched his chin thoughtfully. "I'd be inclined to rig the bridge to fall as well."

"Of course, you would." Addy rolled her eyes, exasperated by Strider's willingness to go to extremes. "But I think these people want me alive."

"It's safer to assume they now want you dead and be wrong than to put our faith in the chance they value your life," Strider countered.

"It'd be nice if we could take the bridge out from under them," Tevin mused.

Strider gave Tevin a sidelong look. "I can arrange that."

"You can?"

"That's surprising to you?"

"You realize that's the king's bridge, right?" Addy interjected. "You'd be hanged for destroying it."

"By the time anyone hears about it, I'll be long gone, or dead."

"Always looking on the bright side, aren't you?" Addy said, with a sigh.

"He's a regular ray of sunshine," Tevin agreed.

Strider ignored them, his gaze traveling up the road back the way he knew the rest of the men would come. The pursuing force couldn't be more than a day or two behind. They'd burned a day to allow him to rest and shift to a nightly travel routine, regaining a day in their travels. They could rest for the remainder of the day. Come night, he could prepare his trap.

"I'll scout the bridge tonight. Come tomorrow, I say we prepare to spring their trap."

"I want to come with you," Addy said, as Strider secured Greer's harness.

"No!" he and Tevin said in unison.

Addy threw her hands up in frustration. "I am not waiting here in camp while you go investigate the bridge." She folded her arms across her chest, her jaw set stubbornly. "I won't get in the way."

"I refuse to let you put yourself at risk like that," Tevin argued. "If something were to happen to you, this entire mission would be futile."

"Listen to your knight, Addy," Strider urged, as he moved to Copper and began rummaging through the packs for something. "I can't work and keep an eye on you at the same time."

"You won't need to keep an eye on me! I can handle myself!"

Strider gave her a hard look. "You let yourself be beaten before. You've shown me that you'll hold yourself back. This means I do have to watch you because you refuse to handle yourself."

Addy looked at him in shock. He turned away from her as he messed with Copper's saddlebags. She felt a slight stir in the air before he turned around. He held an arming sword in his hand; one she didn't recognize.

Strider still didn't acknowledge Addy as he walked over to Tevin, who'd been securing the other horses. The knight looked up when Strider approached. He spotted the sword, a look of shocked confusion flashed across his face.

"That's my sword!" he exclaimed, snatching the offered blade from Strider's outstretched hand.

"It is," Strider agreed, stating the obvious. "Try not to lose it."

Strider eyed Tevin as he drew the blade to inspect it, his hand coming to rest on the handle of his yulie saber.

Seeing no visible damage or wear, Tevin sheathed the blade, his own gaze locking on Strider as he belted the weapon on. Neither one made a move to attack the other, despite the tension between them.

"Where did you hide that?" Addy asked. "I removed Copper's saddle myself and never saw that sword there."

Strider looked over at her. "I have a few tricks you aren't aware of."

"You'll have to show me that one when we get back from scouting," she commented.

"You're not coming," Strider told her, his tone hard.

"I need to test myself somehow! I doubt any of them have ears or eyes as good as yours. I've already snuck up on Tevin several times!"

"You're under the assumption they haven't hired any anumi. You're staying. I'll tie you to a tree if I have to. Or you can sit with Tevin and Greer nicely until I get back."

Addy grumbled a curse under her breath.

"So, you're ready to fight to survive?" Strider challenged; his tone doubtful. "If I'm not there to do it, you're willing to injure or even kill to ensure you make it home alive?"

"Fine, I'll stay!" she folded her arms and sat down on a log with an angry curse. "Stupid Hunter."

He ignored her as she pouted, looked at Greer, and then at Tevin. "Watch her closely."

Tevin replied with a determined nod, and Strider vanished into the darkness.

They had made camp in a small thicket of trees too stubborn to be uprooted by farmers. The poor soil however, left their leaves yellowed and trunks thin, as they struggled to live on the edge of the plains. They provided a poor screen, but the shadows would hide the camp well enough. Stopping before morning, they'd set up camp and watched the chasm, but saw no signs of life on or around the covered bridge.

Denam Chasm was no natural formation. Addy had learned of the old legend that spoke of a great tahrvin mage who'd sacrificed their life, during their wars with the yulie, consuming their soul and body to split the earth with a massive force of magic causing a small mountain to rise and a forest to sprout at its base, impaling the enemy army on their branches. Their act cut off the yulie's pursuit, allowing the defeated tahrvin army to escape into the Tahlrin Mountains.

The story had given her nightmares when she was young, as she dreamed of trees springing out of the ground, whisking her family high into the air, their bodies hanging limp suspended by branches. It was an old legend told before the ummanie had appeared in the world, and while the landscape corroborated it, Addy wondered how much of it was true. Looking at the forest now, it was nothing like she'd imagined. The trees weren't dark and twisted, their thick old trunks looked like the wooded areas she'd traversed with Strider. Life beneath the trees wasn't as intimidating as before, now that she understood how to survive in them.

With nothing left to do, Addy decided to finish setting up camp. She checked Su'lris' saddle, making sure he was comfortable. Clouds swallowed the moon, dipping the world into darkness. Addy heard Tevin curse as he tripped over something. She smiled when he uttered a hasty apology.

"You're fine," she laughed softly. "I'm not so frail a lady that I can't handle a curse word or two. K'yarie knows Strider never holds back."

"I noticed," he commented.

She could hear the smile in Tevin's voice when he spoke.

"I expected he'd swear in yulie, not tahrvin. What is the story behind that?"

"I asked him once," Addy grunted, as she pulled her bedroll off of Su'lris. Placing it on the ground beside her, she continued to ensure that Su'lris was settled. "He told me he doesn't swear in yulie because everything you say sounds like a Chaos ridden compliment, and ummanie words aren't as potent."

Tevin laughed, drawing a smile from Addy. Happy to have something to distract her, Addy spoke about other funny things she'd learned or experienced while traveling with the Hunter. She and Tevin tended to the horses, paying special attention to the horse he'd been riding. Addy had named her Tulie.

Tevin chuckled as he made his way toward her, his own bedroll under his arm.

Addy was unaware of what he was doing as she finished caring for Su'lris. She turned around to say something to him and ran right into him. She squeaked in surprise, stumbling backward.

Tevin grabbed her, steadying her.

"I'm sorry, my lady!" he apologized profusely. "I didn't mean to startle you."

Addy held up a hand to silence him, though he probably didn't see it, given the darkness.

"It's alright," she giggled. "It was my fault. I should've paid more attention."

"No, it was mine. I should've alerted you to my presence."

Addy shook her head. She'd forgotten how people treated a noblewoman of her status. Strider never bent over backward for her or waited on her. He expected her to carry her own weight and held her responsible for her own stupidity.

"You don't have to treat me so formally. I'd feel more comfortable if you wouldn't."

It was odd saying that. While she did like the perks that came with being a noblewoman, she didn't like Tevin treating her like she was infallible and made of glass at the same time. Others, maybe, but not Tevin. She also didn't like the lies, two-faced people, sycophants, and other characters that came with living as a noble. Strider had been frustrating, but at least he didn't put on airs.

Tevin realized he was still holding onto her arms and let go, swiftly stepping aside.

"I'm not sure I have done a very good job of treating you formally," Tevin admitted.

"Continue to fail miserably," Addy said, with a bright smile. "That is an order, good knight."

Tevin unknowingly returned the smile.

"Yes, my lady," he said, struggling to keep a straight face as he said it.

Addy laughed lightly, and Tevin's smile grew wider as he set down his bed for the night.

Addy placed hers to the left of where she heard Tevin.

"Where are you from, Tevin?" she asked, as she curled up in her blanket. Greer appeared and curled up next to her.

Tevin didn't lay down on his own bedding, instead taking up his position as the first watch.

"I am from the Laygo fiefdom," he told her. "My father is the presiding Lord Ulwick."

"You're a long way from home." Laygo was on the border of Myvara. Tevin was likely not in line to inherit his father's fiefdom, and so had been apprenticed to a knight.

"I am."

"Do you miss your home?"

"Sometimes; though I doubt my father notices that I'm gone." A touch of bitterness entered the knight's voice.

"How did you end up a king's knight posted in my father's regiment?"

"I am the sixth son in my family. Having no inheritance, I decided to choose what I wanted to become rather than waiting for my father to ship me off to Syliceon or another monastery. That year we hosted The King's Tournament. Knights from all of Myvara had gathered to take part. I sought an apprenticeship with one of them. I watched knight after knight in the tournament that day, and the one who stood out to me the most was Sir Tamous."

Addy smiled when she recognized the name. Sir Tamous was one of her father's oldest and most trusted friends. Though he'd never formally retired as a king's knight, he'd taken up a role as an advisor to her father. Traveling less and less as his age increased.

"I approached him and asked him to apprentice me. I expected him to laugh and tell me to get lost. But he told me that if he was to accept me, I'd have to prove myself."

"What did he ask you to do?" Addy asked from beneath the folds of the blanket she'd cocooned herself in, snuggling closer to Greer in order to stave off the chill in the air.

"He grabbed a couple of training swords, tossed me one, and told me to take a stance." Tevin gave a light bark of laughter. "I had trained ever since I could carry a sword, and he beat me soundly. Despite not being able to land a single hit, Sir Tamous agreed to teach me and spoke with my father regarding the matter after the tournament."

Addy's smile transformed into a grin. She'd watched old Tamous do the same to her older brothers. They always challenged the old knight, seeking to one day beat him in a sparring match. None of them ever had. She didn't recall ever seeing Tevin at the castle, though she'd hardly paid any attention to the knight's squires.

"It takes a lot to impress Sir Tamous. He must've seen promise in you."

Tevin was glad for the darkness that hid the red that colored his ear. "If so, I've done a poor job living up to his belief. I should've known that we were being led into a trap."

Addy sat up. "I was the one who made the call. If it was anyone's fault, it was mine."

"I am a knight, trained to spot such obvious traps and deception."

"You are also bound by duty to obey my words. I said to follow the messenger, even though I felt that something was amiss. Even if you had insisted that we not follow them, I would've overruled you and you still would've had to go."

"I should've spoken up. Maybe if I had, you would've thought better of it."

"Maybe, maybe not. I'd made up my mind, and that is not something easily changed. If you won't blame me entirely for what happened, at least let me share the blame with you."

Or blame Strider for all of this, she thought. He'd been the one who'd left her in Tevin's care. She pushed the thought away as soon as it entered her mind. He may have had an idea that something like the ambush might happen. In fact, she knew he'd used her as bait to draw out the people responsible for her kidnapping.

But she'd ultimately been the one to agree to follow the enemy into their trap. Her guilt returned as silence fell between them. She buried herself deeper into her blanket, as if it would allow her to escape the feeling that filled her stomach with acid.

"Alright," Tevin sighed into the darkness. "We can share the blame."

Though she'd said it to help Tevin, she didn't want to share the blame, but she suspected that despite what he said, he would still try to bear the full weight of it on his own.

"How did you really meet?" Tevin asked. "I could tell you left parts out of your story." Addy wasn't sure if she was happy with the direction the conversation changed to.

She toyed with the corner of her blanket as the moon peaked out from behind the clouds. "Oh, well, I," Addy began, her tone sheepish. "I stole from him."

"You did what?"

Addy pulled the blanket over her head to hide her embarrassment. "I stole from him. I'm not proud of it!"

"And he didn't kill you."

Addy fell silent for a long moment, unsure how to answer. She risked angering Tevin again and undoing what little progress the two men had made. Maybe if she stayed hiding under the covers, he'd forget about it?

"Did he try to kill you?"

No such luck. Addy pulled the blanket off of her head. "No, but he probably would have, if he didn't think he could leave me to die instead," she finally answered, before hurriedly explaining. "Greer knocked me into a magic hole, called a Well. I was stuck in the center of this sand-like magic that was slowly sucking me under."

"And he decided to leave you there to die after getting whatever you stole from him back," Tevin growled.

She wished Strider hadn't given Tevin his sword back. "Yes, but then he came back and helped me. And then later in Altia, he protected me from some men who'd cornered me in an alleyway."

"Why?" Tevin gave her a puzzled look.

Addy offered a shrug. Strider's fickleness had confused her then, but now that she had spent time with the Hunter and Greer, she understood. "Greer wanted him to."

Tevin uttered a laugh of disbelief. "So, he used the wolf as a scapegoat?"

Again, Addy shrugged, a habit she'd picked up from Strider. "Greer isn't a normal wolf. You've experienced that much."

Tevin fell silent as he seemed to think about something.

"I've done a lot that would make anyone else abandon the job," Addy admitted. "But Strider has risked a lot to get me home. For that, I am grateful."

Tevin frowned. "What did you steal from him?"

"The yulie saber," she told him, guiltily. "He was asleep. It had fallen to the side of him and I picked it up. He woke up and tried to grab me, but I think I kicked his injured side and got away. Greer was the one who caught up to me."

"He was injured?" That was new information. "By what?"

Though she knew the answer, Addy gave a frustrated sigh as she remembered their first conversation. He had been insufferable! "He wasn't very forthcoming with that information at the time."

"Did he tell you where he got his yulie blade?"

"Yes, but that isn't my story to tell. You'll have to ask him," she told him, unwilling to share the personal information Strider had entrusted to her, not after she'd taken the information and used it against him.

Tevin scoffed. "I doubt he'd tell me where he bought his boots, let alone how he came by such a blade."

"You might be surprised," Addy suggested. "He may not regale you with a grand story or offer every detail. But if you think to ask, you might get enough of an answer to your question to piece things together."

Tevin thought about this for a moment before offering a nod of confirmation.

"I'll try asking him sometime," he told her.

Chapter 50
Sabotage

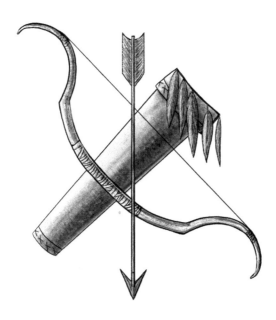

Strider surveyed the bridge as he crouched at the edge of the chasm. A work of ummanie craftsmanship, the covered bridge was the only route across the rift in the earth. Wooden beams provided a lattice work of supports for the wooden bridge resting atop it. It had been around since before Strider was born, commissioned by a late king of Myvara, to shorten trade routes within the area.

Despite the active trade, no town had cropped up on either end of the bridge, and he wondered if it was due to lack of water, or the haunting wind that constantly blew through the Denam Chasm, screaming like thousands of lost souls, rising and lowering in pitch as the wind ebbed and surged. It could be rather maddening, listening to the sound day and night.

Gauging the distance between the cliff edge and the closest beam, Strider jumped. He landed on the lowest beam, the wind buffeting against him, threatening to push him off, if he wasn't careful. Unbothered, he made his way across the framework. He moved upwards, having to jump the span between the wooden beams to get up to a cross-section held together by iron joints.

As he climbed, he searched for signs of tampering. He sensed no magical traps that might destroy the bridge when people crossed it. Nor did he see any signs of physical rigging. The construction felt sturdy, as he leaped from one cross-section to another, as agile as a squirrel.

Pausing at key joints, he withdrew one of his pencils he used for sketching. Channeling a small amount of magic through his hands into the pencil, he sketched a symbol into the metal. The charcoal embedded itself into the metal as he drew on the intersecting wooden beams before moving on.

The wind howled around him, attempting to knock him off balance, as he climbed sideways along the great bridge, leaving strange symbols as he went. He looked down, as he mapped out his next several moves. The chasm dropped far below him, swallowed by a darkness so deep even he couldn't see the bottom. It was a fall he wouldn't be able to survive.

He crouched there for a moment, feeling the wind's breath on his face. The wind came and went like a fitful heartbeat; its wails rang in his ears.

The wooden latticework arched until there was only a single line of the beams at the highest point. He paused like a cat perched on a ledge. He breathed in the chilly night air, trying to center himself. His body didn't feel right, like his bones and muscles were not his own. They were heavier, more sluggish.

But for now, they didn't prevent him from completing his task, though he moved slower than he'd have liked. Taking a breath, he waited for the wind to calm, then jumped. A gust of wind roared through the chasm, snatching at his cloak and hood like vicious claws, throwing him off course mid-jump.

His chest slammed into the wooden beam, knocking the breath from his lungs. He grabbed the rough timber, saving himself from falling into the darkness. He paused a moment to catch his breath, before he lifted himself back onto the girder and getting back to work.

He moved quickly and efficiently, as agile as a spider, as he swarmed up and down the supports. But he knew he was moving half as fast as he should be. He couldn't push his body any harder, however, as his wounded soul drained it of energy. Reaching the cliff face, he left the frame and began climbing sideways along the rough stone.

Like a shadow, he seemed to glide across the wall to reach the other section of wooden struts and supports as he repeated the same process on his return trip. Each time he stopped to mark the beams and metal, he'd look and listen for any sign that people had taken notice of him. But only phantom screams wailed.

Strider heard the thud of boots on the wood as he'd returned to the side of the bridge where he'd started. He moved under the bridge, taking up a spot behind a beam secured to the side of the cliff. He used foot and handholds in the stone, avoiding placing his hands on the edge of the beam in case a brave soul ventured down.

"I thought I saw something on the bridge," a man said.

"On the bottom of the bridge?" another snorted derisively.

"I'm telling you I saw something!"

"Ain't no one on or under the bridge!" a third person said. "By Chaos, it's freezing! I shouldn't of let you drag me out here!"

"You're an anumi. Don't you see or smell anything?" the first man asked.

"I'm a woodpecker anumi, not a cat or dog."

"What's the point of having you around, then?"

"He's only good at sending messages," the second one jabbed.

"An' scout'n the area!" the anumi man shouted. "If it weren't for me, you'd have been spotted by the soldiers the other day."

"Fly down and check under the bridge, then," second suggested.

"Did slugs go'n eat your brain?" the anumi exclaimed. "That there wind down there would tear me to shreds! Go look yurself."

The other two grumbled as they fanned out. One of them approached the edge of the canyon to look at the wooden latticework. Nothing was there. Only darkness and the howling of the wind.

"There's nothing here," the first guy said. "Anything on your side?"

"Nothing!" the anumi yelled over the wind. "I told you, you was crazy. I'm going back to camp. You can finish up your watch with the ghosts you're seeing."

Strider could hardly hear the man's response as the wind hit a new crescendo, but the men began making their way back across the bridge. As the wind slowed again, he could hear the other giving the watchman a hard time as they moved further away. For a moment, Strider thought of going and scouting out the enemy encampment but thought better of it. He didn't have the time to waste. The sun would be up in an hour. With the bridge covered, the men wouldn't be able to see him, as he climbed back over the cliff and began working his way toward camp.

Chapter 51
Burning Bridges, Literally this time

They'd ridden halfway across the Denam Plains when Addy first spotted their pursuers.

"Here they come!" she warned.

Over twenty men on horseback came around the bend. They were a ragtag group of men. Mercenaries and sellswords, united under the promise of profit. A cry went out when they spotted the small party. Whipping their horses into a gallop, they charged down into the plains.

Addy sent Su'lris into a headlong run, close on the heels of Copper. Greer fell back a pace behind the horses, settling into an easy stride. Addy heard Tevin and the pack horses galloping behind her as they raced toward the covered bridge.

The enemy split into three groups, fanning out to catch the party if they changed directions. It was clear they were herding them toward the covered bridge. Strider didn't change course as he leaned over Copper's neck, his cloak billowing out behind him.

The last time Su'lris ran, Addy hadn't noticed how powerful he was. He surprised her. She'd grown so accustomed to the steady, easy-going nature of the animal that she'd formed a mental picture of him being rather ponderous. His speed was startling. The horse's powerful legs ate up the ground beneath him. His breath came in snorting puffs as he plowed down the road. The feeling was exhilarating!

The thunder of hooves clattered around them, as the half-circle of pursuing horsemen closed in. Their enemy pushed their horses harder to close the gap. Addy resisted the impulse to push Su'lris in response to their speed and instead followed Strider's lead as per their plan.

Strider's hood flew back as he rode, his dark hair tangling in the wind. He took in the surrounding force as they edged closer, the distance they had until the bridge, but didn't urge Copper to go faster. The bridge loomed before them, a gaping maw seeking to swallow them. Beyond it lay the forest. He caught sight of movement in the trees. Vague shapes that were not of the forest and its creatures as men on horseback emerged from its dark shelter.

The sound of hoofbeats on dirt changed to a clattering cacophony of hooves against solid wood when Copper barreled onto the bridge—followed closely by the rest of the group.

Their pursuers closed the distance with startling speed. They surged onto the bridge as the men shouted triumphantly. Strider gestured for Addy to take the lead, falling behind the party before they'd reached the halfway mark. Greer didn't join him, following the others across the bridge. Leaning down, Strider drew upon his magic as he extended his right hand down so it hovered inches above the wooden floor. He held onto the power, waiting. His chest tightened in warning.

The leading horsemen reached the center of the bridge. Strider released his magic. With a powerful burst of red light, the power attacked the bridge. A wave of energy rippled across the bridge like an orange nova, passing around the horsemen, chasing them until it reached the end of the bridge behind them. The entire structure shuttered. The air grew still, while magic channeled into the symbols he'd drawn onto the supports. Nothing happened for several heartbeats.

Wood and metal violently exploded with a roar like a thousand thunderclaps as fire erupted along the far end of the bridge, breaking it free of the cliff side. The magical wave rushed back toward the men in a blazing inferno. Timber groaned, and the bridge wavered and sway as the support beams collapsed in quick succession, blown apart by further explosions before plummeting into the chasm. Straightening in the saddle, Strider kicked Copper, sending him running even faster to catch up with the others who were exiting the other end of the bridge.

Men and horses screamed as the lattice bridge collapsed beneath them, sending them falling to their deaths. Flaming energy spread across the beams, exploding each time it encountered the symbols Strider had drawn. Strider could feel the ground beneath him shuddering and swaying as the chain reaction and the weight of the bridge began pulling it free of the other side of the canyon where it remained anchored. Copper ran harder, sensing the danger.

The bridge separated from the wall, creating a gap as it tilted down into the chasm. Strider felt Copper tense a split second before the horse leaped into the air as the rest of the bridge fell away, erupting into flame and explosions as the last of the symbols ignited. The two hung suspended in the air for a moment before Copper's hooves slammed into the ground. Snorting heavily, he galloped away from the ledge to join the others.

Strider heard shouts from the men in the forest. At first shocked, then enraged, as they came pouring out of the woods.

"Shoot the mage!" someone bellowed.

Bowmen stepped out from the tree line. They drew back their bows, letting loose a slew of arrows. A great wall of wind erupted from the ground at Strider's command, rising between them and the enemy. The wind caught the arrows and sent them flying into the sky before clattering to the ground. The enemy's horses spooked, bucking and trying to bolt from the display of power. Addy and Tevin had taken a hard left, following the length of the chasm. They slowed enough to allow Copper to catch up before resuming their mad dash.

Their would-be ambushers quickly regained control of their horses. With angry shouts, they raced along the wall of wind, soon reaching its end before falling behind their fleeing targets. There were still at least thirty men chasing them. Their fresh horses gained on the party despite their lead.

Strider reached back and sent another blast of energy toward the ground in front of the leading riders, earning a sharp stab between his ribs as a reward. Roots shot up from the earth, entangling the legs of ten of the horses. They cried out in alarm as they fell, sending their riders flying.

Several more tripped over their fallen comrades. The other riders swerved, narrowly avoiding the trap. Only half the group of men remained. They kicked and whipped their horses, trying to close the distance Strider had given them with his stunt.

He'd hoped to fell more than he had, or at least scare them away with his use of power, but these men were driven by self-interest. The Hunter shrugged off his bow. He hated to use arrows, his supply being limited, but he didn't want these men getting any closer. Tevin had pulled back to join him, sword drawn. Strider drew back his bow. He hesitated, feeling the rhythm of Copper's gate. Copper's gallop was ill suited for archery, having never been trained for the task. The Hunter waited until the horse was mid-stride, when he was the steadiest, before letting an arrow fly.

A man was thrown from his saddle, an arrow protruding from his chest. The horse he'd been riding reared, panicked by the sudden loss of its rider. Others had to swerve to avoid the startled horse as it whirled and cantered away. The horsemen continued their pursuit. Another man fell, transfixed by another arrow. They still kept coming, closing the gap rapidly.

Strider felled a third man before slinging his bow over his shoulder. He drew his saber as the riders drew too close for comfort. The first man caught up with Tevin. Their blades flashed and sang as metal struck metal. The engagement didn't last long. Tevin's sword shot in under the man's guard and he fell from his saddle with a cry.

Strider sent the first man to meet him, crashing to the earth with a deft stroke, the man's scream silenced by his own horse's hooves. A heartbeat later, Strider blocked another strike as another man drew up beside him. He knocked his attacker's blade aside and took the opening to slash his stomach. He heard someone cry out in Tevin's direction, but he didn't have time to check on the knight as three horses closed in. Strider sent a blast of energy slamming into the chest of the man on his right as he blocked a blow coming from the rider to his left.

The rider behind him took the place of the man that'd been to his right. He aimed for the Hunter's exposed side. Clang! Strider's warsword knocked aside the man's sword while his yulie blade remained locked with the other opponent.

Strider ducked another strike from his left, fending off blows as best he could. Mounted combat had never been his forte, given his luck with horses, and he had to remain conscious of Copper to ensure he didn't accidentally harm his steed. It also reduced his maneuverability.

Knocking one of the men's blades aside with a powerful blow, he was able to send the man tumbling to the earth with a swift kick. As he fell, he reached out, grabbing Strider's leg nearly pulling him from the saddle. Strider kicked the man away, fighting to stay on Copper. Seeing his enemy thrown off balance, the other rider launched another attack.

Strider's blade was too slow. He knew he'd not be able to block it in time. He instinctively called to his magic, prepared to blast the man back when the rider suddenly went rigid, his eyes glazing over before he slumped in the saddle before tumbling off of the horse.

Tevin sat atop Tulie on the other side of the attacker's mount, his blade stained with crimson. The two locked eyes and Strider gave a nod, sheathing his longsword. The knight swiveled around, blocking another thrust from a sword, while Strider shifted to the side to dodge a spear being thrust at him.

Grabbing the shaft, he yanked hard, pulling the attacker off balance. She hit the dirt, one of her feet getting caught in the stirrup. The spooked horse veered away, dragging the screaming woman behind him.

Flipping the spear around, he threw it at another man aiming to attack Tevin on the left opposite of his sword hand. The horse reared as the attacker jerked back on the reins when the spear pierced him. It was Tevin's turn to offer a nod, after dispatching another swordswoman.

Not liking how close the men were, Strider sent a rippling blast of red energy that slammed into the remaining pursuers. The horses stumbled, some fell, the rest panicked. Riders hit the dirt. The other horsemen who stayed in their saddles slowed. They stopped to watch the small band disappear into the forest.

Tevin glanced at Strider, wary of the power the Hunter displayed. The horses slowed as the riders eased their pace, their chests and sides stained with froth. They puffed and gasped for breath as they plodded through the underbrush.

"I didn't know you had that much power," Addy breathed,

"That's because you've only ever seen me heal," Strider panted. "That takes far more magic than what I did today."

Despite what he said, he felt a stab in his chest that made it hard to breathe. He hadn't used nearly all his power, but the act of calling any at all caused him serious pain these days. His soul couldn't take much more.

Addy remembered him telling her something to that effect, but she'd never witnessed the difference. Then she scowled at him. "You realize you destroyed the king's property."

Strider gave a dismissive shrug. "That's never stopped me before."

"Because that is going to console him when you try to explain yourself," Addy sighed.

"I won't be around to explain anything," Strider told her grimly, as he took the lead once more.

"Of course, you won't," Addy muttered in exasperation.

"If you don't say anything, no one will find out about the bridge for a while."

"You left witnesses, though; they'll tell people about what happened."

"You're the one who said she didn't want me killing everyone," Strider pointed out dryly.

"It was my idea," Tevin replied. "Such a tactical move is well within my rights as a king's knight."

"Let's hope your king agrees," Strider said.

"Which means I have to convince my father, brothers, the Rangers, and now the king, not to kill you and Tevin." Addy let out a defeated sigh. "Who do you plan to anger next? The gods themselves?"

Strider gave her a roguish smile. "Perhaps."

Chapter 52

Wolves In The Mist

"Can all Rangers use such powerful magic?" Tevin asked, as he pulled up alongside Addy, still watching Strider like he might suddenly explode.

Strider looked at him with a measured gaze. "I'm fairly average for a Ranger in terms of power," he informed Tevin, before Addy could reply. "Dedicated magic users can out-power a Ranger easily enough, though they often struggle to defend themselves physically."

Addy and Tevin thought he was powerful, because they had no one to compare him to. Fully realized magic-users were rare, having died out long ago, after the fall of the Devian Empire. His display would've looked rather pitiful compared to such a being, like a star trying to compete with the sun.

The Syliceon church had a dedicated force of mages and other magic users, though their adherence to vocal spells limited their abilities. Rangers in the field opted to use will-based magic as a complement to their skills, aiding them in fighting magical beings more powerful than themselves.

The Sanctuary, the home of the Rangers, held powerful mages not bound by the arbitrary rules of the church, but they didn't venture beyond the borders of The Wilds often. Other small sects and groups practiced their own magic, but they were dwindling in numbers, thanks to the preaching and prosecution of the Syliceon church.

Most of the ummanie had turned their back on magic after the Devian Empire fell. Many were revolted by the power that connected them to the yulie. The Syliceon nurtured that mistrust until the ummanie believed magic outside of the teaching of the church was evil.

Gone were the days of ummanie mages, capable of splitting earth and raising mountains, like the power used to create the Denam Chasm. According to those he knew, even the tahrvin, whose mage had altered the land so, lost most of their ties to magic. He knew nothing of the ravack and their ways. His mother had once been a powerful mage before her illness. She had spoken of schools where her people attended to learn and grow closer to their magic. Given their pitiful state, it was a wonder the ummanie hadn't fallen under the rule of the yulie once more.

They stopped to water the horses at a stream. Strider checked Copper's legs and hooves, picking out a stone from the horse's hoof that had caused him to limp. Greer came up beside him as he stooped, his wet nose connecting with Strider's cheek. Strider glanced at him, meeting Greer's worried gaze. He rubbed Greer between the ears, doing nothing to ease the di'horvith's worries, before reaching up to climb into the saddle.

His strength vanished, and he had to lean on Copper to stop himself from collapsing. His chest seized with pain and his breath caught in his throat. The episode lasted for only a moment before he found he could breathe again. He found the strength enough to pull himself back up into the saddle, though the idea of dropping to the ground like a bundle of limp rags was far more preferable.

Neither Addy nor Tevin noticed what happened, too preoccupied with inspecting the other horses. Greer watched Strider, the worry in his face deepening. With a huff, he padded off, grumbling to himself in a low, whining tone.

They didn't allow the horses to drink their fill of water in case their pursuers renewed their chase. So far, they'd seen no signs that they were being followed, but they remained vigilant. As the threat died down, they dismounted and walked the horses, allowing them to catch their breath. After a time, Strider handed Copper's reins to Addy. Instructing her to follow a game trail, he disappeared to cover their tracks. Greer diligently followed him. He'd fallen silent, but he continued to watch the Hunter closely.

Strider didn't attempt to ease Greer's fears; he couldn't do or say anything to put him at ease. Anything he said would be an obvious lie. So, he remained silent as he slowly covered their tracks, stopping from time to time to catch his breath. Normally, one could recover from such magical exhaustion with a good night's rest. But a wounded soul was another story.

The first few days after using his magic were always the worst, though the fog of weariness and gloom had never truly left since saving Greer. The sun could occasionally pierce the winter chill that haggard his spirit and froze his blood. The grip of death was growing stronger, however, and he was finding it increasingly difficult to stay warm. But he pressed on, too stubborn to give in.

A light rain began falling when the pair reappeared, rejoining the group as they continued following the game trail. Fog rolled in, seeping up from the ground like the exhaled breath of the earth on a frosty morning. Returning to riding their horses rather than walking, the little group made better time, since Strider could move them at a faster pace than what he could manage while walking under his own power.

Tevin noticed forms moving in the shadows of the trees as they rode. He looked harder, trying to pick out the shapes as they came closer. The shadows changed course, moving parallel to them. His eyes widened, and he gripped the hilt of his sword in alarm. A large pack of wolves surrounded them, keeping pace with the horses.

"Easy," Strider said, when he heard the scrape of Tevin's sword on its sheath. "They won't harm us."

"How do you know that?"

"If they were hunting us, you wouldn't have seen them until they'd attacked. They're here for Greer, not us."

Greer detached himself from the group. He trotted forward to greet several of the wolves. He dwarfed them, showing Strider how much he'd actually grown during their travels. Greer tossed his head and pranced in a playful dance with the wild wolves, who happily yipped and howled greetings. Greer played with them for a time before falling back into an easy lope in front of Copper. The wolves continued to escort them through the forest, dancing around them in their excitement.

Tevin eventually sheathed his sword, no longer concerned with the wolves, but he remained watchful. Normally horses and wolves didn't get along. Legend said that the horse and the wolf were jealous of each other. Like two children fighting over the attention of their parents, they desired to gain the di'horvith's favor. The wolves envied the horse for their size and speed, while the horse envied the wolf for its fangs and cunning.

Neither the horse nor the wolf could stand the other's presence. But none of their horses had spooked or shied away from the wolves, and the wolves didn't seek to harm the horses as they milled about them. All were calm. Tevin looked at Greer, wondering if all the old stories were actually true.

After a time, they came to a halt at the edge of a large clearing. Before them sat a small settlement, where ten short houses crouched amidst sown fields, wreathed in growing fog. Copper tossed his head when Strider pulled him to a stop. Greer came to stand beside him while the wolves continued to pace. A brightly colored banner caught the Hunter's eye as men and women shouted in protest and fear. Armed men were forcing people out of their homes, gathering them before a man sitting on a large white horse, the banner shifting in the wind as a page boy stood beside him.

"Those are knights under the king," Addy said, confused and mortified. "Why are they treating the king's people like this?"

"Not all knights are honorable," Tevin told her grimly, as he also watched the families being ripped from their homes while the men ransacked the town.

"Let's go," Strider ordered, turning Copper away.

"We can't leave them!" Addy protested, as Strider began riding away. "They're looking for me. If I show myself, they'll be forced to stop."

"Or they'll kill you," Strider pointed out, his voice low. "Even if they aren't your enemy, they'll try to kill me."

"That's fine with me," Tevin muttered.

Strider ignored him.

Addy looked to Tevin beseechingly. "We have to do something. This isn't right."

Screams erupted from the townspeople gathered together at the edge of town. Both Addy and Tevin looked. But Strider didn't. He instead ordered Copper to walk back the way they'd come. He didn't watch, but he knew what was happening as he listened to mothers and fathers begging, the threats of the soldiers, and the sobs of the daughters, young women, and some boys, as they were dragged away.

Payment for the knight and his men's services, they'd call it. He'd seen it all before. Strider's jaw clenched as the cries grew more desperate. Copper only plodded a couple more paces before Strider had enough. The ice within him flared like frozen fire, and he swung Copper around, his hand reaching for his bow.

Chapter 53
Judgement

Addy watched in horror as the soldiers began dragging the daughters and sons away from their families. They struck down anyone who tried to stop them. Her hands went to her mouth as if to block a silent scream of horror. Two men dragged one woman away, laughing at her terror.

Fwish, thwack! An arrow sprouted from one of her assailant's chests, and he tumbled to the ground without a sound. The second looked over, dumbfounded, before he, too, fell to an arrow. Arrow after arrow appeared, slamming into men as they panicked. The villagers broke and ran for the cover of their homes, dragging their freed family members with them. Anyone who tried to go after them found themselves struck by an arrow.

Addy looked over her shoulder at Strider as he fired arrow after arrow. The look in his golden eyes was terrifying. He muttered something under his breath and Greer sprang forward, following behind the path of an arrow. As he ran, the pack of wolves joined him in his charge toward the frightened men at arms. The knight atop his white steed shouted orders, trying to gain control of his unit. An arrow slammed into his helmet, splintering with the force as it sent him tumbling from the saddle.

Tevin spurred Tulie, sending her rushing after the wolf pack, sword drawn. Addy watched the scene unfold, unable to help. Her kidnappers had taken her sword, and she'd never gone back to retrieve it. Could she have been able to help, even if she had her sword? Could she strike down those men to defend others? The idea sickened her.

The panicked foot soldiers turned to look toward the sound of pounding hooves. They saw, to their horror, a warrior charging toward them his sword drawn, led by a pack of snarling wolves, one of which was massive. White or light gray wolves were demons or minor gods in the eyes of the ummanie, because of the rarity of their coloring.

Unlike a white horse that was coveted by man, people feared a light furred wolf. Like a demon from local legends, the giant wolf bore down on them, followed by the rider brandishing his weapon. They still hadn't seen Strider. But his hail of arrows left them rattled. Upon the sight of the wolves and Tevin, they cracked.

With cries of alarm, they ran, tripping over themselves as they fled toward the other side of the small valley. Tevin reined in Tulie, who slowed to a stop outside the village. Greer and the wolves continued chasing the men, until they reached the edge of the forest, before looping back. Greer ran the way he'd come, leading the wolves as he joined Strider, who had appeared at the edge of the forest, bow in hand.

Addy and Su'Iris sidled up next to him.

"Don't do what I did," Strider told her, the fury within him ebbing, leaving behind a frosty emptiness.

"Don't save people?" she asked, incredulously.

"Don't get involved in needless battles."

She cocked her head as she studied him. There were still remnants of the hard look that had been in his eyes as he fired on the soldiers. "You wanted to leave quickly because you knew what they were going to do, and you knew you'd retaliate if they did."

Strider didn't respond, as he fingered the string in his bow, eyes scanning the opposite edge of the valley for any sign of the soldiers. He'd used all but three of his arrows, each one having dealt death to their intended target.

"I really don't understand you."

Strider looked at her, head cocked to one side. "I'm not that difficult to understand. You just make it that way."

She was about to retort when Tevin hailed them from the village.

"We have injured!" he shouted, waving an arm for them to come, as the settlers gathered around him.

At his call, they turned to look toward the area he was shouting and saw Addy riding toward them. Behind her, still hanging near the fringes of the forest, sat a hooded figure on a red-tinted horse. Around him milled the wolf pack, their presence calm, yet menacing. The largest light-colored wolf stood next to him; the physical representation of a monster born from stories.

Fog hung around them like ghostly waifs, swallowing the animal's legs until they appeared to be phantoms floating through a smokey veil. The dark forest stood imposing and silent behind them. The mounted rider blended into the surroundings as if he were an incorporeal being, his face shrouded in shadow. It was clear this rider had been the archer who killed their attackers with unnatural accuracy. A being befitting the old tales told around the fire.

The townsfolk watched as the hooded figure leaned over and patted the enormous wolf on the head before sending him off. The massive creature took off, easily catching up to and matching the pace of the beautiful woman riding toward them. They'd been told of the Dark Ranger, and like all tales spread by word of mouth, the story had blown out of proportion.

But on that day, the people of this village believed them all to be true. All, save for the stories about him being a cold-blooded monster. He'd saved their loved ones, and likely their entire settlement. Soon, new tales of this strange figure and his companions would spread, much to Strider's displeasure.

Addy leaped off of Su'Iris and followed Tevin toward a group of injured people. Their family members were tending to their wounds the best they could as they wept. Other townsfolk were tearfully laying the bodies of the slain further down the street. Addy couldn't bring herself to look at them.

A daughter was bandaging the arm of her mother. A man sat on the ground, unable to move because of an injury to his leg as his own family fussed over him. No one appeared to have any mortal injuries. Some wouldn't be able to work, however, and that was easily a death sentence for people who had to work to survive.

"Do you think you can heal the worst of them?" Tevin asked.

"I can try," Addy said, her face pale. She turned back the way she'd come. "Strider, get over here and help me!"

The Hunter shook his head.

"I need you!"

He shook his head again, before sending Copper in a slow trot toward the town. The wolf pack dispersed, running off after the fleeing soldiers, their excited howls filling the air as they resumed their hunt.

A murmur sprang up from the people as they watched the hooded figure riding toward them. Their gaze shifted to Addy, and the murmuring continued, as they marveled at how their lady, for she could only be Lady Fenforde, could command the Dark Ranger. They watched the hooded figure dismount his horse, stepping back as he neared Addy. Greer appeared before him, dropping the arrows at Strider's feet. Addy's face grew pale at the gruesome sight, and she quickly turned back to the injured people.

"Only the seriously injured," Strider told her, as he reached into Greer's packs and pulled out a jar of his strange poultice. He offered the jar to a woman who'd been helping to care for the others.

"Use this on the rest."

She took a tentative step forward, accepting the offered jar with shaking hands. She offered a tight 'thank you' before scurrying off to tend to the wounded.

Addy gestured toward two men and a woman, the only ones to receive serious wounds, who were still alive. Strider scanned them with indifferent golden eyes before he followed Addy to the first man with a broken arm. She knelt before him, and Strider placed a hand on her shoulder as he breathed.

"You're revealing that you can use magic if you do this."

"I know," Addy whispered. "But they need my help."

"I can't offer a lot of magic this time. Don't heal him completely, only to the point where it moves again."

He waited for Addy to nod in understanding, before crouching before the man. Like he'd told her, Addy had to use most of her own magic to help the afflicted. She couldn't fully heal anyone, but they were out of immediate danger. With everyone tended to, the woman who Strider had given the medicine to, offered the jar back. He shook his head.

"Keep it," he told her. "It'll fend off infection and speed up healing."

Tevin had left Addy and Strider with the injured people as he moved toward the still form of the knight. He recognized the personal emblem of the knight as Sir Gregor Willen Conlin. His form was still; he'd never risen from the ground after being struck in the helmet by Strider's arrow. Tevin drew his sword. He approached slowly, careful to remain out of reach of the knight's hands or legs.

Reaching over, he tapped the helmet with the tip of his sword. The action elicited a groan from the older knight. Keeping a careful watch, Tevin relieved the man of his weapons and helmet. The knight's eyes fluttered open as the cold air touched his face. They widened, when the fog of confusion cleared, and he found a sword pointed at his throat with a very grim-looking warrior on the other end of it.

He didn't recognize Tevin for a knight. Strider hadn't bothered to save the young man's armor or emblem, though he'd left him with the signet ring all the king's knights were given by king Ranmous. Sir Conlin couldn't see the ring and assumed he was looking up at some brigand or mercenary.

"Get up," Tevin ordered.

The knight complied, wobbling unsteadily as his head swam. "Do you know who I am?" the knight began.

"Yes, and that's what makes your crime worse," Tevin said, roughly shoving the knight forward. "Move."

The entire village spotted Tevin as he forced Sir Conlin, who'd been the source of their terror moments ago, to kneel before them. Strider tossed Tevin a coil of rope, and he bound the knight's hands behind his back.

Greer padded over to stand watch. The bound prisoner eyed the massive canine with clear unease.

"I am Sir Gregor Willen Conlin. I serve directly under king Ranmous," he said in a superior tone, despite being forced to kneel in the dirt. "Your treatment of me is considered treason. If-"

Tevin's blade made a metallic clanging noise as it slapped down on the pauldron protecting the man's shoulder, abruptly cutting off the knight.

"And I am Sir Tevin Ulwick, sworn under king Ranmous, in service to Lord Fenforde. You have committed treason against your king by violating the oaths you took before him." His voice shook with barely suppressed rage. "I am hereby revoking your status as a knight. These people, who you attacked, will decide and carry out your fate, as a traitor to the kingdom."

"You have no power to make such claims," the knight spat. This was true. Tevin, though a king's knight, ranked lower than this man in both age and social status. Their noble families were leagues apart. He had no authority to revoke the man's rank or title.

"Maybe not," Addy said, stepping forward, shoulders straight, her chin raised with noble pride. "But I, Lady Adelin Roselia Fenforde, have that right."

The entire village broke into another wave of murmurs as their suspicions were confirmed. Many offered hasty bows to the young lady. She graciously waved them to their feet as she continued to stare at the knight kneeling before her, eyes blazing.

"I witnessed you and your men breaking the oaths made to our great king and his people. You're no knight, and you'll suffer a fate befitting a traitor."

"I am the king's knight, girl," Sir Conlin spat. "Your father couldn't strip me of my rank, let alone his insolent little daughter. Keep quiet and know your place, or it will be your father who suffers."

"Enough!" Tevin roared, his blade kissing the knight's neck. "I will not have you speaking ill of the lady!"

Strider, who'd left the people to clean the arrows Greer had retrieved, moved forward. Tevin fell silent as he watched the man casually crouch before the knight, removing his hood with his free hand. An audible ripple of surprise ran through the crowd gathered around. The knight's own eyes widened in shock upon seeing the pointed ears.

"You're a-"

A rumbling growl from Greer cut the knight off.

Strider continued to clean the gore from the arrow tip with casual indifference.

"You could be the chosen herald of K'yarie herself," he began, his baleful tone sending shivers down everyone's spine. His eyes flicked up to meet the knight's gaze. "That still wouldn't stop me from shoving this arrow down your throat the next time you speak to the lady like that."

The noble tried to meet the Hunter's piercing gaze, but what he saw in those eyes caused him to look away.

"Thank you," Addy said, taken aback by the display. "But I am perfectly capable of jamming pointed weapons down people's throats on my own behalf."

A devious idea struck her. "Tell me, Ranger. Do you think Sir Conlin deserves to hold his rank as a knight after betraying his oath?"

Strider cast her a sidelong glance, easily figuring out where this was going. He didn't like it. Cocking his head, he studied the knight for a long moment. He knew the consequences of playing along with Addy's plan. The danger of encouraging others to believe that he was a Ranger would likely lead to his death. On the other hand, they already believed him to be one. Albeit a 'Dark' Ranger, whatever that meant.

He couldn't deny it publicly, though that hadn't stopped him from doing so back in Denmahr. But here, the people were not looking at him as an enemy, or a Ranger who'd betrayed his oath. Here, these people saw him as their protector. He quietly cursed the

Rangers and their council before cursing himself for agreeing to their terms all those years ago.

"So, am I a knight or not, Ranger?" Sir Conlin taunted.

Strider had an overwhelming desire to light the man on fire. But he'd depleted his magic, helping to heal the villagers' wounds. The cold within him filled him, tugging at his soul, feeding the desire to watch the man burn, if only to bask in the warmth. He was sure he could find other means to set the man ablaze. The people of this village would likely aid in burning him alive. The idea was extremely tempting, and he toyed with it for a moment longer before dismissing it.

"Who is the leader of this village?" Strider asked, his eyes never leaving the knight.

An elderly woman stepped forward, a solemn look upon her face. "My husband was the head of our village. A foot soldier cut him down when he tried to stop them from forcing us out of our homes." Her voice shook with loss as she spoke. "I... am the head now."

Strider gave a slow nod. "It would seem you have a traitor to execute." He stepped away, allowing the villagers to surge forward, grabbing the knight roughly as they began tearing away his armor.

"Stop! I command you!" the knight ordered. "He is no Ranger! He is a traitor!"

"He is as much a Ranger as I'm a woman!" the village head snapped. "He defended this village from you and your vile men. He is a Ranger if ever I saw one!"

"He has no authority!" Sir Conlin roared.

"Only the king is above a Ranger," Tevin said, over the chaos.

The words were carried through the crowd like a ripple on a lake until it was chanted like a dark mantra. Shouts to hang the dishonored knight rang out, soon replacing the chant as they dragged the man away, kicking and screaming, to a solitary barn at the edge of town. None of the three travelers followed, as the mob set off to complete their grim task.

Strider returned his arrows to his quiver. With a sigh, he walked over to Copper. He pulled himself up into the saddle before looking down at Addy. She had no idea the danger she was putting him in. He'd walked a fine line with the Rangers for decades. This would be enough to send them over the edge. He accepted it, but Addy was creating an image of someone he wasn't. She was forming a far too high opinion of him. The cold had moved into his bones again, weaving through his veins as it traveled to his soul. He doubted he could live through much more of this, nor would he ever live up to the reputation she was crafting.

He kicked Copper and sent him into a canter, distancing himself from the other two before they could ask any questions.

Chapter 54
The Touch Of Death

The elderly woman stepped out from behind a small house a little way in front of Copper. She raised a hand to hail the Hunter. Strider brought Copper to a stop instead of riding past her.

"I can tell you're eager to leave, but won't you stay and allow us to express our thanks?" she asked him.

Strider shook his head. "We will leave you to bury your dead in peace."

"The dead will be buried, but it will not be in peace. Your presence will make no difference to them, but it will to us. We don't like leaving debts unpaid."

Strider's gaze drifted to the forest, unconvinced.

"You look exhausted," she continued. "I'm not so old and blind that I couldn't see what healing those folks took from you and the young lady. Rest here for the night and regain your strength."

Strider couldn't deny the weariness that tugged at him. He was tired, they all were. Finally, he gave a small nod of ascent before dismounting.

The elderly woman led them to her house, the largest in the village. As they walked, she introduced herself as Wylla. People were returning from the barn; many uttered their thanks to the trio, before returning to their own homes or tending to their dead. As the day faded to night, people began appearing at Wylla's home, bringing cheese, pottage, pies, bread, and other meals as they gathered to thank those who helped them.

People sat on the floor as they ate and visited with one another, their cheerful mood laced with an undertone of mourning for those they'd lost that day. Addy regaled them with the story of their travels to Myvara, once again excluding information about the tahrvin tunnels or Strider's darker deeds. When asked, she offered a knowing smile before saying,

"Rangers have a few useful tricks."

Strider hung back from the rest of the crowd, seeking to preserve as much personal space as possible. The room felt small and suffocating. His chest grew tighter as the irrational need to escape threatened to overwhelm him. The icy touch in his soul only amplified the feeling, making it harder than normal to deal with the noise and chaos that came with too many people being crammed into too small a space.

As usual, he forced himself to remain calm and composed, though he couldn't completely hide the tightness in his shoulders as his eyes roamed the room, never seeming to settle on any one thing.

It was always easier to ignore the feeling when he had a purpose for being in a crowded space, but tonight he had none. The only comfort was in the fact that he still had room to stretch his arms and move about if he chose. It did little to help distract him from the cold that touched his soul and sought to fan the flames of his irrational desire to escape. The feeling of being trapped by this crowd eventually drove the Hunter out of the warmth of the house as he sought refuge in the open air outside.

He stood in the shadows near the doorway, breathing in deeply as he calmed himself. The chilly night air helped to clear his head as he collected his thoughts. The constriction in his chest lessened. He could breathe again, enabling him to fend off the frost that coated his insides.

He closed his eyes, letting out a long, heavy breath as he leaned against the wall, soaking in the sounds of the night. Feeling the openness of the air, the darkness on his skin, the forest around him, as the wind sighed through the trees. This was where he belonged. Not back in the light and warmth. Not among the happy chaos inside this house. But here, alone in the darkest shadows of the night. The sound of the door opening caused him to open his eyes as an elderly voice spoke out into the darkness from the safety of the light.

"Not one for crowds, I see."

Strider looked down at the hunched figure of their hostess.

"No," he told her, seeing no reason to lie.

Wylla nodded and wrapped a threadbare shawl around her

shoulders, before stepping out to join him in the darkness, leaving the door open a crack to allow herself enough light to see by. She smiled up at him before gesturing toward two chairs set up together outside of her home. "Come, sit with me." She hobbled over to a chair and eased herself into it.

Strider followed but remained standing as she sat.

"Do you have something against chairs?"

"Not particularly," Strider said, eyeing her.

"Then sit down, young'n!" she ordered, with all the authority of an elderly woman. The kind one didn't argue with.

A small, amused smile touched Strider's lips at the woman's gumption. He didn't inform her he was older than her as he pulled up a seat. She gave an approving nod at his compliance.

"You care deeply for our Lady Fenforde," she commented, gazing out into the darkness.

Strider gave her a sidelong look, and she smiled.

"My husband was a lot like you. He never had much to say. But he spoke volumes. You just needed to pay attention. You could see his love in his actions, the way he moved or looked at you. I see the same with you as you watch over Lady Fenforde. You have the same look my husband did when he watched our children as they grew." She patted Strider on the knee in a knowing and comforting fashion. "She doesn't know, does she?"

Strider said nothing as he sat there, elbows resting on his knees, hands steepled between his legs. He continued to watch the old woman, eyes narrowing. She nodded in understanding, and he looked away.

"I doubt you will tell her, but you should let her know you care."

"She doesn't need to know," Strider stated. He didn't need her to find out. It would be better for both of them if she thought of him as nothing more than the hired help.

The woman patted his shoulder as if trying to console him, before shivering. "It is freezing out here!" She pulled her shawl tighter around her.

Strider moved to undo his cloak when she stopped him with a raise of her hand.

"I'm much obliged, young man. But I think I'll go inside and warm up. I'll toss the rest of the town out while I am at it. They're liable to start breaking things if I don't." She stood and hobbled toward the door, then paused and looked back at him with a motherly expression.

It had been a long time since someone looked at Strider like that. Despite the long, hard years, he found that he missed having someone look at him that way. To regard him with the same warmth in their eyes as his mother once had.

"Be sure to come back inside where it is warm when they're gone." She shuffled back inside, taking her kind gaze and the last of the light with her as the door swung shut.

It didn't take long for the muffled hum of voices to be cut off by the crow of the old woman as she brought their celebration to an end. The villagers filed out, laughing and talking. One man nearly jumped out of his skin when he took notice of the Hunter silently sitting in the darkness. The man brought everyone's attention to him, and they began casting their goodnights, thanks, and well wishes to Strider as they passed him.

Strider offered small nods to the villagers, regarding them with the same quiet, steady stare he always seemed to have. No one appeared afraid despite the dark. What would dare attack a town that held a Ranger after all? The streets soon grew quiet, as the people returned to their homes, leaving Strider alone again. The sounds of the night enveloped him once more, and the Hunter let his head drop as he closed his eyes.

Weariness made his bones feel like stone. His muscles protested as they held him up. But it wasn't the physical exhaustion that made him want to disappear. It was the weariness in his soul that dragged him down and threatened to sap the rest of his strength.

The rest of his resolve. He was tired of this world and the ice inside his body sought that weakness, that darkness, and gave it strength. It sought to use it against him as a weapon to break the threads he used to keep himself bound to this world.

He loved and hated using magic, hated the heaviness he felt, the dark thoughts that he had to fight against every waking moment. He'd seriously injured his soul, a wound he continued to widen each time he called on magic. It filled him with an almost debilitating amount of exhaustion and agony that left him too depleted to care about what his soul and body were telling him.

The Hunter knew he was dying, and he was the one responsible. He knew, with a solemn resolution, that he likely wouldn't survive getting Addy home, and he was okay with it. He deserved death as his reward after all he'd done.

The door opened again, but he didn't have the strength to see who it was, or care. The chair next to him shifted closer.

"Weren't you the one who told me never to be alone?" Addy scolded softly, as she leaned forward to peer at him. Unlike him, she'd been wise today not to use magic beyond what she was capable of.

Strider glanced at her, not bothering to raise his head. He didn't even have the strength to muster a wry smile. She pulled back, and he felt the weight of her head on his shoulder. They sat there quietly, listening to the songs of the night.

He focused on her, the sound of her breathing, the pressure of her head against his shoulder. Like with Greer, he pushed everything aside as he focused on the things he clung to this world for. She didn't know it, but she'd become one of those reasons. His promise to her bound him in more ways than she could imagine. It kept him tied here. One more thread to keep him from drifting away.

His mother had always told him that strong ties could make a difference between life and death for those who walked the path of magic. He remembered asking her as a child who she had that tied her to this world. He could still feel the warmth of her in her voice, the love, as she told him that it was him.

On that day, he'd felt like he was the most special person in the world, because it was he who kept his mother here when the aching cold tried to steal her soul. And it always tried. Every day since he'd been alive, it tried to take her from him. It ate at her. Sapped her strength. When she was told her husband was dead, it nearly took her. He sat at her bedside for three days, praying to any god who would listen, pleading with them to help his mom survive.

She'd come back to him. She'd stayed for him. She stayed for him every day until the day she was killed. Because of him. His head drooped lower as the cold whispered to him. Blamed him for her death. He never should have agreed to be Mink's apprentice. If he hadn't, Minkus never would've felt compelled to take action. She'd still be here.

Arms slipped around his forearm as Addy embraced it, her head still weighing heavily on his shoulder. She didn't say anything, seeming to sense that he wouldn't speak. But she wouldn't leave him alone. He had told her the dangers, after all. Tonight, it was her tie that kept him here.

He didn't know how long they sat there until he found the strength to speak. Time was a concept his mind couldn't grasp.

"I need you to promise me something," he whispered.

Addy lifted her head to look at him. "Anything."

"Don't agree to something without first hearing the person out," he told her tiredly, still finding the strength to lecture her.

"You're not just anyone, Strider," she told him. "I trust you."

That did little to comfort him, and he let out a heavy sigh. "Promise me that if something happens to me, you'll care for Greer."

Addy frowned. "You know I'd always take care of Greer; I'll take care of Copper too. But nothing is going to happen to you, so stop talking like that."

The Hunter didn't respond; he found himself unable to tell her he knew he wouldn't survive this endeavor. He didn't have the heart to tell her; to saddle her with the weight of that knowledge.

"Let's go back inside," she suggested.

He didn't argue, and Addy cradled his arm, guiding him back into the warmth and light. Both Tevin and Wylla looked up when they entered. Both had waited up for them, despite the late hour. Greer let out a low woof as he plodded toward Strider, a worried expression on his face. He knew. Strider could see it in his eyes. But he had always known and could only watch in silence as his brother slowly destroyed himself. Unable to do anything to stop him.

He'd have to apologize to Greer for that, for the burden he placed on him. But right now, he didn't have the strength. Greer stuck to the Hunter like glue, as he moved toward an empty corner. Someone had placed empty canvas sacks over a small pile of hay to form a temporary bed for the village's guests.

He collapsed onto it and Greer plowed into him, snuggling up close and offering his comfort. Somehow, being close to the di'horvith eased the cold that still lingered in his bones. Draping an arm over Greer, Strider closed his eyes and let the warmth of the room sink into him.

No one said anything as they, too, prepared for bed. Strider could hear them moving about. The candles were snuffed out and soon the rhythmic breathing of people sleeping filled the room. Strider laid awake, despite his exhaustion, kept up by a deep ache in his bones. He held onto Greer as he listened to the others sleep.

Over time, another noise invaded the night. The sound of soft sobs coming from the area Strider knew the bed to be. It was Wylla, finally crying for the loss of her husband, now that she thought no one was awake to hear her. Strider quietly retracted his arm from Greer, who'd also remained awake. The wolf looked at him and the Hunter gave a small nod before rolling over.

Wylla hugged her blankets close to her as she tried to cry quietly. The empty space next to her felt cold, empty, alien. Devoid of the life that should have occupied it. She had remained strong for the people of the village, for those who'd saved them. But that barren space had broken her, and she couldn't stop herself from letting the pain out.

A soft whine caused her to start, and she pulled her blankets closer as she looked toward the edge of her bed. She could barely make out the face of the Hunter's wolf across that terrible, empty space. He whined at her again, and she couldn't deny the empathy she saw in those dark eyes. He moved closer, first his shoulders, then his legs, then his entire body occupied the wretched space.

The weight of his body caused the mattress to shift like it always did when her husband got into bed at night. He wiggled closer to her, his head coming near hers. She reached out and stroked his fur as she continued to cry.

"You're such a sweet boy," she whispered between sobs. "Such a sweet boy."

Addy awoke the next morning to find Strider gone and Greer asleep next to Wylla. She scrambled out of bed in alarm.

"Tevin!" she whispered urgently.

"Wha...?" the knight mumbled, as he sat up, hand reaching for his sword.

"Did you see Strider leave?" Addy asked, as she slipped on her boots.

"He said he's preparing the horses." Tevin yawned, not sure why she was so concerned. It wasn't uncommon for the man to disappear in the morning.

"You let him go out alone?"

"Yes? He's with the horses. Why are you so upset?" he spoke the last sentence in annoyance.

"Because he used all of his magic last night," she said in exasperation. "You remember what happened to me when I did that? We have to find him."

He did remember, and the memory disturbed him enough that he got up. "Do all magic users go through that when they use too much magic?" Tevin asked, pulling on his boots.

"Yes," Addy said, as she opened the door to find their horses tacked and ready to go.

Strider stood among them, inspecting their hooves and legs. Addy slumped against the door frame in relief. That relief quickly turned to annoyance. Her head cocked in concern as she watched the Hunter. He looked tired. Addy had traveled with him long enough to know that Strider hid his injuries or weaknesses. Until last night, she'd never seen him show any sign of weariness since the night he'd passed out outside of Altia.

Tevin appeared in the doorway. Spotting Strider, he said, "I found him."

"You're a master tracker," Addy said sarcastically.

Pushing off the doorframe Addy approached Strider, who was fiddling with a piece of Copper's saddle, doing busy work to keep himself occupied. She now recognized the actions.

"You know you could have slept in for once," Addy said, as she came up to pet Copper's neck.

"The longer we stay, the tighter our enemy closes their net," Strider told her, finishing his task.

"You should still rest."

"I'll rest while we ride."

Greer let out a low woof as he bounded out of the house. Tevin followed after him, toting the di'horvith's harness. Strider took it from him and began putting it on Greer. Once again, the new straps were tight, and Strider frowned at Greer.

"You got bigger," he said accusingly to the di'horvith. Greer looked at him innocently.

"How big do half di'horviths get?" Addy asked.

Strider shrugged. "I don't know. He's the first one I've ever met."

Seeing that the harness would no longer fit, Strider gave up and secured it to Copper's saddle. He would make a new one when this was all over. He paused, realizing that day might never come, before pushing it to the back of his mind.

"Leaving already?" Wylla asked.

They all turned to see their hostess standing in the doorway, her shawl wrapped tightly around her.

"Looks like it," Addy told her. "Someone is anxious to leave." She gave Strider a pointed look, but he didn't respond, as he finished securing Greer's harness to the back of his saddle.

"Thank you for letting us stay with you and please thank the villagers for us for the food last night."

"We only wish we could do more to thank you all for helping us," Wylla told her.

"It'd be best if you and your people didn't mention that Lady Fenforde was here," Strider told her. "Or that you witnessed her use magic."

Wylla nodded her agreement. "We will not tell a soul," she promised, before asking them to wait as she returned to her home. Returning moments later with a bundle wrapped in cloth, she handed it to Tevin.

"Food for your travels," she told him. "It isn't much, but it'll be something more than the jerky and dried supplies you've no doubt been eating."

They thanked her before mounting their horses and setting off again. They rode through the town and passed the paddock where Addy had seen two dead horses the night before. Her brow furrowed when she saw two brown horses grazing in the paddock. Two horses that looked very familiar. She swiveled in her saddle to count the animals following behind them. Only the knight's white horse followed behind Tulie. The other two were missing.

"You gave them two of our horses!" Addy declared.

Strider looked at the paddock with his usual catlike stare.

"I gave them two of *my* horses. They needed them, I didn't," he said, dismissively. "I expect your father to compensate me for the loss."

"Of course, you do," Addy said, with a knowing smile.

Chapter 55

Usereth Femiera

The group made camp later that afternoon. Addy waited until Strider sat down to eat before jumping him. "You're not taking a watch today," Addy said firmly. She stared down at Strider, her arms crossed.

Strider raised a brow as he looked up at her. He held her gaze, waiting for her to look away, but she stood firm.

"You're going to sleep while the rest of us keep watch."

"I'm fine, Addy," Strider told her, but that only caused her jaw to set in determination.

"No, you're not," she snapped back. "And you'll get me killed if you're not, so rest!"

Strider continued eyeing her. He was tempted to argue with her; he'd pushed through worse before. But he kept his mouth shut. He wouldn't try to explain to her that his weariness was not physical. Sleep wouldn't change it. But she hadn't experienced enough magical fatigue to know that. No amount of physical sleep would mend a magically fractured soul. It took time. His magic would return with rest, but his soul wouldn't heal that quickly. He let out a breath and gave a dismissive shrug of his shoulders.

"Alright," he yielded.

"Alright?" Addy parroted in surprise. She'd been expecting Strider to put up more of a fight. She smiled, pleased with her victory. "Good." She turned to Greer. "Greer, you'll take the second watch. Sit on Strider, if he tries to do anything other than rest."

Greer gave a low chuff of confirmation. He sat next to Strider, watching him closely.

Strider gave a small shake of his head before returning to his meal. He knew he wouldn't win against their united front.

Tevin volunteered for the third watch, leaving Addy to take the first. She kept one eye on Strider the entire time to make sure he didn't try anything. It looked like he actually was asleep, though she didn't trust it. Strider's voice echoed in her head, saying two words that often drove her nuts. 'You're learning.' The afternoon was quiet.

Birds and other forest creatures went about their day, uninterested in the group of people camped out in their home. It was peaceful in the shade of the towering trees, and Addy enjoyed her time at watch. The forest wasn't as scary to her as it had once been.

In Altia, she'd only entered the woods to avoid discovery and potentially find some food. She had vowed never to go back into those trees again, only to follow Strider right back into them the following night. Back then, she didn't know how to survive within the forest, but now, thanks to Strider, she was more prepared.

Her eyes drifted toward Strider's sleeping form. She bit the inside of her lower lip. Memories of last night played in her mind. She'd never seen him look so worn down, so defeated. He'd gone through a lot to get her this far, and she was afraid he couldn't take much more. But she didn't know how to help him beyond insisting he rest. Only her worries troubled her during her shift, following her to bed when Greer relieved her.

Tevin was on watch when Strider finally stirred. Tevin hadn't heard him get up, but Greer's soft, incredulous whine caught his attention. He watched the Hunter wave the di'horvith back to sleep. Greer gave him another look before laying his head back down with a huff. He didn't go back to sleep, his brown eyes never straying from the Hunter's form. Strider quietly moved across the camp toward the horses near where Tevin sat.

Tevin watched Strider prepare Copper for the night's ride. He looked down at his clasped hands, as he recalled what Addy had said earlier that day. It had stuck with him, along with a nagging feeling that wouldn't go away. He had something he needed to say to the Hunter. Words he never wanted to utter to the man, but he knew he should.

It had taken him most of his watch to chain down his pride and throttle his dislike for the Hunter long enough to say it. Now that

Strider was up and standing before him, both emotions fought to bind his tongue. Letting out a breath, Tevin uttered the two words he'd been rehearsing in his head all day.

"Thank you," he said, not looking at Strider.

Strider paused what he was doing to look at the knight, head cocking to the side. He shrugged and returned to tacking Copper. "For what?" he asked.

"For helping Addy, for healing me, for saving my life," Tevin told him, each word forced from his lips. He willed himself to relax as he remembered what Addy had told him. "I know what happens when you exhaust your magic. You risked your own life to heal me."

It hadn't struck him as hard as it did now, how much Strider risked for the both of them. Strider, despite his dislike for him, had risked himself to heal him. For Addy's sake. Tevin hated it.

Strider offered another indifferent shrug. "You're welcome."

"Knowing the dangers of using your magic, why do you still use it?"

"Because if it comes down to dying now, or later, I tend to pick later."

"So, you knowingly put yourself at the risk of dying, to prevent yourself from dying." That made sense to him. Tevin stood and walked over to Tulie. He secured her cinch before checking her other tack.

"You're only at risk of dying from the cold if you give in to it." Strider moved from Copper to Su'lris and began preparing him for their travels. "Eventually, you learn not to listen to what you tell yourself when in that state. You learn not to give in."

Tevin paused what he was doing to look at Strider incredulously. "You seemed to be listening to it last night."

Strider sighed, as he rested his elbows on Su'lris' saddle. He peered at Tevin across the horse's back. "Even masters make mistakes." He stepped away from the bay and began checking the other animal, leaving Tevin be.

The knight grew quiet as he thought. He realized Strider had answered his questions. Shrugging, he figured now would be a good time to follow through with Addy's suggestion to inquire about his sword.

"How did you get that saber?"

Strider's gaze flicked up from his task before looking back down at what he was doing. He continued to work for a moment longer before speaking. "I took it from the man who killed my father and Kinri, a panther who I considered a friend," Strider told him, jerking on the buckle he'd fastened to make sure it was secure. He stepped around the horse and began making sure the saddlebags were secure, putting him close to Tulie, and parallel with Tevin.

"Did a yulie kill them?"

"No, he was half ravack," Strider answered again. He offered no further explanation, keeping his answers short and to the point.

Tevin was surprised that Strider answered at all. All this time, he'd thought the man to be rather tight-lipped and uncooperative. But Addy had been right. So long as he paid attention and didn't push further than Strider was comfortable, he'd answer questions. So, he kept asking, not in a way that previously provoked sarcastic or hostile remarks. But with genuine curiosity.

"Do you know how he got a yulie blade?"

Strider eyed him again and Tevin half expected a sharp or sarcastic quip, but Strider once again gave a simple answer. "I do."

"Really?" Tevin was interested in knowing. People rarely possessed a yulie blade. The weapons were rare and difficult to come by these days.

"How?"

"It was given to him."

Tevin resisted the urge to punch Strider, who'd gone from being semi-cooperative to downright difficult. Instead, he kept his tone civil and slow. "By whom?"

Again, Strider regarded him. He stepped away from the horse and drew the sword in question. Tevin stepped back, his hand going to his own sword. But Strider made no move to attack him. Instead, he held out the blade to him. Tevin looked at it, then at Strider skeptically, before taking the sword.

He was amazed by how light it was. It weighed less than half the weight of his own sword, yet the blade was a good deal longer. It was perfectly balanced. He stepped away from Tulie and twirled the sword, flicking his wrist to test the feel of the weapon.

It hummed as it sliced through the air with a deadly swish. He stopped and held it, looking down the silver-blue blade. It was considerably thinner than a normal armingsword. It should've shattered when pitted against any of the ummanie swords it came into contact with. As he held it, Tevin became aware of the sword. It didn't just look different; it felt different. As if it were searching for something within him.

It felt empty. But that had to be in his mind. He turned the sword this way and that, allowing it to catch the light of the dying sun. As he did so, he saw something on the tang before the hilt. Bringing it closer, he inspected the markings. It was a design of thirteen snakes intertwined to create the shape of a tree.

Their bodies formed a tangled trunk, their tails spanned out like roots, their heads fanned out to form the canopy of the tree. Surrounding the tree in a circle were words he couldn't read. He thought he remembered seeing this design before but couldn't remember.

"Thank you for letting me test the sword, but that didn't answer my question," Tevin said, offering the weapon back to Strider.

"You really are green." Strider let out a breath before taking back the blade. He sheathed it and fixed Tevin with a hard stare. "That is the mark of Ursereth Femiera. I hope you know who they are, at least."

"The crime syndicate?"

"The very same."

Tevin had only heard of the name in passing, spoken in hushed undertones. The Ursereth Femiera were said to rule the underworld of the ummanie kingdoms, in all of Fareldin. They had a hand in every black market and outlaw network, taking payment from the local groups of thieves and brigands that always wallowed in the backwater of towns and cities.

Rumor had it, their reach even extended into the noble households, and even some royalty had dealings with them. Like the Rangers, they had spread throughout the ummanie kingdoms, as the first empire collapsed and the land fractured into the kingdoms that stood today.

While the Rangers helped to maintain order as the empire fell, Usereth Femiera moved to increase their power, feeding off of the other criminal groups that had been weakened by the chaos. Now, only they had any real footing in the underworld.

Yet they remained in the shadows, elusive and cunning, to the point that most people didn't know they existed. Rangers especially, were on bad terms with the Usereth Femiera. They'd waged a silent war for years, neither side making any progress against the other.

"Your father and friend were killed by one of the Usereth Femiera?" Tevin asked skeptically.

Strider nodded, as he checked the new horse's legs and hooves.

Tevin followed Strider as he moved about the horse, more concerned with this story than preparing to leave. "But why?"

Strider remained silent for a long time, moving from one horse to the next, as he checked them again, paying close attention to their legs and hooves.

Tevin continued to follow him, not sure if he should press for an answer or wait. Strider often was slow to answer things he'd learned while observing him speak with Addy. It was like he always considered whether he wanted to share that information with her or not.

That was exactly what Strider was doing now as he checked each horse for any injury or stones in their hooves. "He was sending a message. To me."

Tevin sensed more, so remained silent for Strider to find the words.

"He was hunting me but found my father instead. My friend

was protecting him." There was another long pause. "He was an eighty-year-old man, but he still managed to put up a fight." Strider smiled bitterly. "Rangers, even old ones, don't die easily. I found him hanging from the eves over the entry to his cabin, a note pinned to his chest. It was written in his own blood. Kinri was dead inside."

He put down the hoof he'd been removing a stone from and stayed there as the emotions of that day flooded back to him. The anguish that had ripped through his chest at seeing his father hanging there like a piece of meat at a butcher's shop. The anger, the grief at knowing he was the reason the assassin had come.

Like his mother, he'd been the reason his father and Kinri had died. That grief had increased when he walked into the cabin, the home he had known for twenty years, to see the panther he'd raised skinned and laying on the ground. His precious Kinri, skinned and defanged like a common beast. It all slammed into him like a horse kicking him in the chest. Ice flooded through his body like a frigid poison.

His soul burned like salt was being poured into an open wound. He wanted nothing more than to curl in on himself and disappear, if only to escape the pain. But he wouldn't. He continued to fight stubbornly against the frigid weariness of his own soul. Given time, he knew he would recover, his soul would heal. Not completely. It had never recovered from being broken so long ago. But he could survive it. He always did.

"I hunted that man for decades. It was a game for him," Strider said through gritted teeth. He wiped the knife blade he'd used to tend to the horse's hooves on the grass before sheathing it. "A game I eventually won."

His body felt heavy when he rose, sluggish; not his own. He set about slowly finishing his preparations to leave.

Tevin stood there in shocked silence. Strider didn't seem to notice as he stared at him, unsure what to say. He couldn't fathom the pain the Hunter had gone through. The life he'd lived. He felt as if this were something Strider had not shared with anyone in a long time. If ever. He didn't understand why the man had chosen to tell him.

But he appreciated it, even if it left him with more questions. Questions he couldn't bring himself to ask. He'd heard the pain in the man's voice, as he spoke of that day, and he found that he didn't want to hurt Strider further. But he had a question he needed to ask.

"Will they send others after you?" If they'd attacked his loved ones to get at him, they may also attack Addy.

Strider seemed to read his thoughts, and he made a dismissive gesture. "She is in no danger from them. They don't know where I am. And the Father would have to learn about and approve any additional lives taken beyond that of my own. Especially if it meant provoking the hostility of a powerful noble. There would be no profit in it. That is, assuming they piece together the fact that I am this 'Dark Ranger' everyone is talking about before I get Addy home." Strider turned to wake Addy. "They have also learned something after killing my family that will give them pause."

"What's that?" Tevin asked.

"They learned how deeply I can hurt them when provoked." Strider's tone resembled that of a snarling dragon. His eyes burned like their flame as he looked back at Tevin.

Chapter 56
Going Through The Front Door

Addy, Tevin, and Strider looked out over the valley to the castle town of Timara. The old city lay nestled in the crook of the Tahl river, its waters sparkling in the noonday sun. Like Fair Fork, the castle town of Timara had grown significantly since Strider had seen it last. The city was broken into four sections, by towering walls that spanned out from the original central keep, like ripples on a lake.

The rest of the town had grown beyond the walls, surrounded by farmland and orchards. Years ago, the great river had been used to create a large moat around the city. Now, new channels created four separate moats for each wall, making the castle look like a section of walled islands connected by bridges.

Addy's chest tightened with relief and joy when she saw her home. Her eyes watered with barely suppressed tears. All she wanted to do was kick Su'lris into a run and get there as quickly as possible.

"I never thought I'd see it again," she said, her voice tight.

"Your undying faith in me is heartwarming," Strider muttered, eyes following the outline of the walls.

Addy frowned at him. "You know what I mean."

"Now that we're here," Tevin cut in, looking at Strider. "I can take her the rest of the way. You don't need to risk being caught."

"I want him to come with us," Addy interjected.

"My lady, we don't need him anymore."

"He is coming with us," Addy snapped. She looked at Strider. "Your name will be cleared, and you'll be paid for your trouble."

Strider let out a deep, resigned breath. "I figured you'd say that. You're going to be the death of me."

"You've been trying to figure out how to get in there anyway," Addy said, with a knowing smile. "You know the enemy is still inside, and your work would be for nothing if I got kidnapped or killed."

"My job was to get you home, not hunt down the rats in your castle."

"I'll make sure you get paid for it."

"You always assume I'll take the job." Strider gave a small smile, though it didn't reach his eyes.

"You haven't turned me down yet."

"I tried the first time. It didn't work out." He studied the castle for a moment, before voicing his plan. "If you want me to come with you, we might as well walk through the front door."

"You'll be arrested the moment you approach the gate," Tevin pointed out, before sarcastically amending, "No, I like this plan. Let's do it."

"Tevin," Addy warned.

"Not if I am already in your custody," Strider said, ignoring Tevin.

"They'll still want to take you and throw you in prison," Tevin reminded him.

"Not if I have anything to say about it," Addy piped up. "I can insist on taking him with us to present to my father. The garrison won't be able to refuse an order from me or a knight of the king."

"And what if your father tries to kill him?" Tevin countered.

"My hands won't really be bound. They'll find I'm a hard person to imprison," Strider told him. "Addy will hold my weapons."

Greer let out a low whine as he looked up at Strider, giving him a warning look.

Strider ignored him. He knew he was already pushing too far, but he wasn't inclined to stop. Either he could rest after they found Addy's enemies, or her father would kill him, and he'd find peace. It really didn't matter to him, as long as Addy was safe.

"They won't let Greer into the city," Tevin said. "Everyone thinks he's a demon at this point."

Strider smiled. "They aren't wrong." Pulling out the pendant from underneath his shirt, he fingered it for a moment before looking at Greer. "In you go, brother."

Tevin watched in wary fascination as Greer dissolved into mist before vanishing. "Where did he go?"

"Into the pendant," Addy informed him. "Are you going to hide your Felaris feather as well? To avoid drawing attention."

Strider nodded as he tucked his pendant away and reached for his bow. Brushing the feather down against the bow, the feather folded into the wood, becoming nothing more than a decorative design.

Tevin shook his head in amazement. "You really are full of tricks."

Strider gave a brief smile. "You have no idea."

"Hopefully, you won't have to use your magic," Addy said. "I just need to talk to my father, tell him what happened. I'll tell him you surrendered. It could make my parents more willing to hear what we have to say, if he knew you came willingly."

Strider gave a nod in agreement, before looking at Tevin and nodding toward the white horse he had taken. He had strapped the dead knight's armor to it. Neither Tevin nor Addy cared to think about how he had gotten it.

"Take that knight's armor and put in on. You were about the same build. It'll make you more believable and presentable."

Tevin frowned. He didn't like the thought of wearing the dead man's armor, but he knew that beyond his signet ring, he didn't look like a person of his station.

"The two of you are crazy," he relented.

Both Addy and Strider grinned.

Addy took time to wash and comb her hair as best she could, using a stream running toward the river. Strider had offered a strange poultice to her that helped get the worst of the debris out. Apparently, it was a mixture most commoners knew how to make. She always had her brushes and beauty supplies given to her and didn't realize it was so common a product.

Strider had given her a wonderful gift, and she held it like it had been a magical potion. After washing her hair, she tried to braid it but only succeeded in knotting it. Frustrated, she worked out the new mess she'd created and tried again with an annoyed huff. Her hair tangled for a second time. Irritated, she once again brushed the tangles out of her hair.

"Here," Strider said, touching her hand.

She gave him a puzzled look when he took the brush from her. Still confused, she turned her back on him when her gestured for her to do so with a wave of the brush. She felt him take her hair and begin working. His hands were gentle, as he braided her hair with surprising skill.

"I didn't know you could do hair," she teased.

"I used to do my mother's hair when she was too sick to do so," he told her, his tone soft. "It wasn't much, but it made her happy."

"Oh." Addy looked down at her hands, feeling foolish for teasing him. "That was very kind of you."

He tied off the end with a bit of string, ensuring the braid wouldn't come undone. Straightening, he moved away to prepare for their venture into town.

"Thank you," Addy said, stroking the new braid with her hands.

"You're welcome."

They fell in step with the crowd of traders and workers filing down the main thoroughfare toward the first wall. Plastered white like the castle and town, the walls reflected the morning sun onto those seeking entry into the first sector. Addy kept her hood up while Tevin led the way. She rode next to Strider, who kept his unbound hands hidden within the folds of his cloak.

He held his reins, per Addy's request. She wanted to show her father that he'd come in under his own power. His hood was up, his head bowed. Addy knew, despite appearances, that he was aware of everything going on around him.

Ushered along with the rest of the crowd, the guards at the gate gave them only a cursory glance, only stopping those with carts and trade goods to question their business.

The market before the main gate was bustling with throngs of people who scampered out of the way of the three riders.

Addy took in the familiar sights and sounds of her home, her heart filling with excitement and anxiety. Tears welled in her eyes, but she wiped them away, reminding herself that she wasn't safe yet. She and her family wouldn't be until they found who had betrayed her. For that, she needed Strider and Greer. But first, they'd have to convince her father and brothers not to kill them. She worked on her argument in her head as they rode.

The guards at the second gate let them through, uninterested in the little group moving with the carts into the second market square. White wattle and daub buildings lined the road as it twisted and turned through the city. Like other castles, the main street did not take a direct path to each gate, making it more difficult for invading forces to conquer each section.

The next two guards questioned Tevin, but upon seeing his ring with the symbol of a lion over two crossed lances, identifying him as a king's knight, they gave them no trouble. He didn't reveal who his traveling companions were. They didn't want news of Addy and Strider to spread before they reached the keep.

The crowd soon fell away as they approached the final gate. Addy's heart hammered as she looked at the white walls slowly growing closer. They guarded the keep, encircling her home in a protective layer of mortar and stone. Only those with permission or rank could enter within. Despite knowing this, Addy's heart spiked when the guards stepped forward and called out.

"Halt!"

Tevin drew in his reins, bringing their group to a stop.

"State your name and business."

"I'm Sir Ulwick, king's knight. I currently serve under Lord Fenforde," Tevin answered. "I'm escorting Lady Adelin Roselia Fenforde home."

At the mention of her name, Addy urged Su'lris forward, drawing down her hood. She'd not bothered to send Tevin into town to buy a dress for her. Though it'd been suggested. Her cloak hid most of her attire from view.

The guard bowed to her, easily recognizing her. "Your Ladyship!" the man cried out, in relief and astonishment. "Thank K'yarie you're safe. We feared the worst."

Addy motioned for him to stand, her chin raised, her back straight, as she'd always been taught. "Yes, thank the goddess I am safe," she agreed. "I wish to return home after this long hardship. You do not need to send word ahead. I wish to surprise my father with the good news."

She gestured for him to step aside.

The man straightened and hurriedly stepped aside. "Yes, my lady!"

Addy kept Su'lris in front of the man, trying to block his view as Tevin led the way into the fourth tier of the castle through the gate leading to the keep's courtyard. But the guard spotted the dark, hooded figure riding quietly on the scruffy varnish roan. His eyes narrowed.

"My lady, is that?" His hand went to the hilt of his sword, only stayed from drawing it by a firm glare from Addy.

"Yes, that is who you think it is," she told him firmly. "And I will not have you raising a hand against him."

"But my lady, he-"

She snapped, her voice curt and full of arrogant authority, befitting of a high-ranking noblewoman. "He is innocent of the crime he was accused and has come willingly and peacefully, under the guard of Sir Ulwick, to plead his innocence before my father."

The guard bowed again, offering a hurried apology before stepping further back. He eyed the hooded man, who hadn't glanced his way as he rode by. No one followed them as they passed through the gate. It was only when they were out of sight that the guard remembered that he should have sent an escort with them.

The guard at the other end of the gatehouse was not so forgetful. He managed to draw his weapon when he saw Strider before a sharp order from Addy had him backing down. More soldiers followed them into the courtyard. Despite her orders, word spread of her arrival and the appearance of the Dark Ranger. Other soldiers filed out of barracks, surrounding them.

Strider waited for Addy to dismount before slowly and carefully getting off Copper. He took care to keep the horse's body between him and the line of men to his left. With Su'lris to his right, he was sheltered from surprise attacks on either side, though that did little to protect him against the dozen archers he saw gathered on the walkways, arrows aimed directly at him.

He kept still, not wanting to agitate the situation any further. All these men were ready and willing to die for their Lady. A crime must be avenged, and he was the target of that vengeance. Strider could only imagine the look Greer would give him as he felt for the magic within. It responded, but it immediately brought a tightness to his chest. If all went well, he'd not have to use magic. But he was never one to rely on a plan going well. Rely on a plan too much, and you leave no room for flexibility. Hopefully, he didn't have to see how flexible he really could be in this state. His body still felt heavy, tired, and so cold. It was a weariness no amount of physical rest could heal.

He watched the surrounding men noting their positions. How many there were. The general skill they showed by how they held themselves, and the routes he could take to escape should he need to. He had no desire to fight, but he would if they attempted to follow through with their desire to kill him. He was tired and dying, but that didn't mean he wouldn't fight like a demon to keep them from killing him.

Tevin had moved Tulie to stand on the other side of Su'lris, placing Addy between them.

A young man not much older than Tevin stepped toward Strider, sword drawn.

"How dare you come here after kidnapping my sister!" he yelled.

Strider leveled his gaze on the young noble, steady, and unyielding.

"Put away the sword, Elayis!" Addy ordered, as she came to stand next to Strider. "Strider didn't kidnap me, and he's come here willingly, under my protection, to prove it."

Elayis looked at her as if she'd gone mad before turning back to glare at Strider. "What kind of spell did you put on her?" he snarled.

"Obviously the wrong one," Strider answered. "She insists on hiring me for difficult jobs rather than leaving me be."

Elayis advanced further, but Addy stepped between him and Strider. She grabbed her brother's blade and moved inside of his guard so quickly he didn't have time to react. Had she held a blade of her own, he would've been dead.

Strider's lips twitched in a ghost of a smile.

"He is under *my protection*, Elayis," she reiterated, her tone hard. "And he is to be treated with respect while I tell mother and father what really happened."

Elayis looked her dead in the eye. The two siblings locked gazes in a silent battle with one another. Finally, Elayis sheathed his sword, though the look he gave Strider could've cut through steel.

"Put him in a cell while we sort this out."

"Elayis!" Addy said, about to argue.

Strider put a hand on her shoulder, and she looked back at him.

"Don't you touch her!" Elayis ordered.

Strider dropped his hand, but he remained focused on Addy, who nodded before turning back to her brother.

"Sir Ulwick," she said, her gaze locked on her brother. "Escort Strider to a cell and watch him until he is summoned."

She turned to look at Tevin, a message clear in her gaze.

Tevin gave an understanding nod and a bow. "Yes, my lady."

"Don't forget his weapons. They're on my horse."

She looked pointedly at her brother then, who suddenly noticed that Strider was unarmed.

Elayis frowned and turned away to signal to several men to escort Strider to a cell.

Tevin slung the Hunter's weapons over his shoulder before taking up a position next to Strider, his hand gripping the hilt of his sword as they followed the men down to the dungeon.

Chapter 57
Cells & Secrets

"Take off your cloak and shirt," the prison guard barked at Strider, after they'd passed beyond a heavy locked door and entered a small room separated from the main dungeon by an equally formidable door. "We'll be taking your boots as well."

"He keeps them," Tevin ordered.

"Prisoners aren't allowed these items." the soldier argued. "Those are the rules."

"He keeps them," Tevin repeated in a harder tone. "Or would you like to explain to Lady Adelin why the man under her protection was deprived of his clothes and boots?"

The man gave no further protest, not wishing to incur the wrath of her ladyship. He could always blame the knight who stood before him. He was the one who gave the order. Who was he to argue? With a growl, he unlocked the door and led them inside. Despite its size, the dungeon was surprisingly vacant. Tevin could see only a handful of people locked away in dark cells. They jeered at Strider as he passed, who ignored them.

The hallway outside of the cells was well lit, dispelling any shadows from providing cover to escaped prisoners. Even if they escaped, the only way out was through two thick doors. If they broke through the first door, they'd crowd into a small room as they attempted to break through the second door.

Tevin had noticed the grate in the roof of the small room that would allow men from the room above to pour down hot sand, boiling water, or shoot down into the little room as the prisoners attempted to escape. This would be a difficult prison to break free from.

Tevin watched the four men who escorted them, wary of what they might try down here, where the sound of screams wouldn't be heard. Addy had been smart to have him accompany Strider. Though she may have insisted that he was under her protection, Tevin doubted that would have stopped the men from trying to beat the Hunter bloody. Lady Adelin was much loved in the castle, and anyone accused of kidnapping her would be treated harshly. He honestly wasn't sure they'd be able to restrain themselves, even in the presence of a king's knight.

His hand never left the hilt of his sword as he watched them. He knew if these men did attack, Strider would have no qualms about fighting back. The Hunter was here to prove he was innocent. That didn't mean he wouldn't defend himself if attacked. He knew Strider was also aware of what may happen. Yet he stepped into that dark cell without a glance backward. The man who had tried to take his clothes and boots made to follow. Tevin promptly grabbed the door and shut it.

The man stepped back, disgruntled.

"He needs to be chained to the wall!" the soldier barked. "If he isn't, he could attack anyone who might enter."

"He will only attack those who attack him," Tevin growled. "Now lock it and be gone."

The man grumbled under his breath and locked the door.

Tevin stared him and the other soldiers down as they lingered. Eventually, they turned and left. They were unwilling to risk their lives by attacking a king's knight, no matter how badly they wanted to hurt the man inside that cell.

Tevin watched them until the door closed and the lock slid into place with a loud thunk. Certain they were not coming back, he retrieved a stool and set it directly outside Strider's door. He had clung stubbornly to Strider's weapons. Another thing the guard had tried to argue over. Tevin leaned them against the door as he sat with a sigh. Pressing his own back against the door, he looked up and down the lonely hallway.

"Well, this place is nice," he said, sarcastically.

He couldn't hear Strider moving around inside the cell, but he couldn't recall a time where he had heard the man moving about the entire time they traveled together.

"It's better than most prisons I've seen." Strider's voice echoed from inside of the cell.

"Seen a lot of prisons, have you?"

"A few. Though never for very long."

Tevin smiled as he rested his head against the door.

"Thank you." The words drifted through the small, barred window in the wooden door, catching Tevin by surprise.

"For what?" he asked, confused. "Making sure they didn't take your things? Lady Fenforde is the one you should thank for that."

Strider's voice didn't immediately answer, but it eventually drifted to him. "She wanted you to prevent anyone from trying to get even. The rest was your doing."

Tevin considered that for a moment before replying, "You're welcome."

Strider paced around the room. It was twice as wide as his arm's length, and at least six feet deep. He paced like a caged tiger, as the same feeling of being trapped caused his throat to constrict. The Hunter worked to calm his breathing, reminding himself that the walls were not closing in on him. He could still move, could still stretch his arms out. He wasn't trapped and could escape this room at any time. His breathing steadied, but he kept pacing, unable to work out the nervous energy building up within his chest. His fight or flight instinct was a step away from triggering an all-out panic attack.

He had to move to prove to his stupid brain he wasn't trapped; the room was still as large as it had been two seconds ago. Clean straw covered the floor and only a bucket in the corner occupied the room other than the chains on the wall. The place was cool and slightly damp. But as far as dungeons went, it was clean and not entirely unpleasant.

Aside from the fact that he was locked in a small room under the hulking weight of a castle. He let out a deep breath, forcing his mind to focus on something else as he made another short lap around the room. Normally, it would've taken him a lot longer before he descended into this level of agitation. But the instability of his soul had launched him into a near state of panic the moment the guards left. He cursed under his breath, hoping that in the pit of Tarn, the soul of Minkus would feel the anger he directed at him.

"Are you alright?" Tevin's voice called through the door.

Strider resisted the urge to curse again. He hadn't meant to speak so loudly the first time. "I'm fine."

"You don't sound it," Tevin said. He'd been with Strider long enough to pick up on his change in tone. "You sound like you want to murder something."

Strider let out a deep breath as he continued pacing. "Maybe I do."

"I'd suggest not admitting to that in the presence of Lord Fenforde," Tevin added lightly.

Strider let out a growl as he moved up to the small window. Looking out didn't help. The view only showed him the door on the other side. He moved to the side of the door and could see a couple of other doors, but nothing more.

"I thought you said you've been locked up before," Tevin began.

"I have."

"It doesn't seem like it. I'm actually hearing you move around in there as you pace."

Strider growled again before returning to his pacing. He continued to walk around the room for several laps before returning to the door.

"It's not normally this bad," Strider answered.

"I thought you said this place was better than most dungeons?"

"Not the dungeon, or the cell," Strider snapped, his tone low.

"Then what is it?" Tevin prodded.

Strider lapped the room again, muscles growing taught like wound springs. He had to work to loosen them. Finally, he returned to the door.

"It's the space," he admitted.

"You're afraid of tight spaces?" Tevin scoffed. "Seriously?"

"Have someone tie you up, lock you in a trunk for two days, and tell me how you feel about tight spaces afterward," Strider hissed.

"Who locked you in a trunk?"

Strider took a deep breath. Instead of deflecting with sarcasm, he gave Tevin an honest answer. "My mentor. I was ten."

"Your mentor doesn't sound like a nice person."

"He wasn't." Strider stopped at the door again.

They sat in silence for a while.

"I'm afraid of heights," Tevin revealed. "Terrified of them."

"You must love the castle wall, then."

"I can't go near the edge. I always walk in the middle, or as close to it as I can manage. Sir Tamous, my mentor, always told me that fear was a choice. Clearly, he never felt what I did when looking out over the battlements. It is irrational, I know, but I can't seem to stop it."

Strider grunted his understanding. He'd gone back to walking circles. Fending off the walls that were closing in on him.

"It normally isn't this bad, though," Strider muttered. "I've been in smaller places and kept control for days."

"What's different?" Tevin asked.

Silence answered him. Strider considered not telling Tevin. What good would it do? Despite knowing it'd do nothing to relieve the growing panic, he found himself moving toward the door. "If I tell you, you must swear to me you won't tell Addy."

"Are you really that worried about her?"

"Swear to it, knight," Strider growled.

"On my honor, unless it endangers or brings harm to Lady Fenforde, I will not tell a soul."

Strider let out another heavy sigh, and it struck Tevin how tired he sounded. If he didn't know any better, he could have sworn he sounded defeated.

Chapter 58
The "Dark Ranger"

"**A**delin!" Lord Fenforde cried, as he scooped his daughter into his arms. "Thank K'yarie you're safe!"

Addy laughed, tears staining her father's shirt as she hugged him fiercely. An older gentleman, dressed in plate armor, approached and bowed to her. "Lady Fenforde, it is good to have you home."

She smiled at the kindly old knight. "Thank you. It is good to be home, Sir Tamous."

"Where is mother?" she asked, pulling away from her father. "I want her to know that I am okay."

The doors to her father's study burst open. A woman dressed in red, with dark brown hair tinged with streaks of gray, rushed into the room like a crimson hurricane.

"Adelin!" she cried, engulfing her daughter with a hug so tight the young girl couldn't breathe as her mother's red dress folded around her.

"Mother!" she sobbed, returning the tight embrace.

Her mother held her for a long moment, as if she were afraid to let go. Finally, Addy had to pull free as she wiped tears from her cheeks.

"What are you wearing?!" her mother gasped, as she registered details beyond that of her daughter being home.

Her mother spread out her cloak, holding onto the hem as if it were poisonous. She studied the clothes her daughter was wearing with a look of sheer horror.

"Who dressed you like, like, a boy?" disgust filled her voice.

Addy looked down sheepishly, wishing she'd sent Tevin to buy her a dress after all.

Addy scuffed her boot against the carpet. "People were looking for a noble girl, so..."

"So that filthy Dark Ranger forced you to dress as a man." Her mother cupped a hand over her mouth in shock. She looked as if she were about to faint.

"No!" Addy said, her head shooting up. "He didn't force me, and he is not filthy! He did it to protect me!"

"Protect you?" her father cut in, outraged. "He was the one who stole you! And now I hear you brought him here, asking that he be pardoned!"

"He is here?" her mother gasped.

Her father turned to Elayis. "Where is he now?"

"My men escorted him to the dungeon. He is currently under the guard of a knight that accompanied Addy. Sir Ulwick, I believe, is his name."

"I want preparation made for gallows to be built. We will hang him as soon as it is finished."

"No!" Addy yelled, causing everyone to stop. "You won't hang him!" Addy shot back, returning her father's gaze with equal amounts of fire. "He came here willingly, unarmed, because I asked him to! You will clear his name and pay him for his troubles."

"You will not speak to your father in that manner," her mother scolded her.

Addy balled her hands into fists as she shouted, "I will speak however I want, and you will listen to me!"

"Adelin-" her mother began, but Addy cut her off.

"No mother, you will listen, or I will leave this castle and take Strider with me!"

Her mother looked taken aback by the threat but said no more.

Addy took a deep breath to keep her temper under control. She couldn't let it run away with her like it so often did.

"I don't-" her father began, before a look from his wife cut him off. He let out a controlled breath, motioning for her to begin.

Addy began from the beginning, once again leaving out the part about how Strider had left her to die. Though this time she pointed out that she'd stolen from him, and he'd let her go despite that.

News of her daughter living on the streets and stealing like a beggar left her mother visibly shaken. But neither she nor her husband spoke beyond asking clarifying questions as Addy told them her story.

"But how did you get past the border and arrive in Myvara so quickly?" her father asked, when she skipped their travels through The Ways.

Addy frowned. "That is something you will have to ask Strider."

She moved on, unwilling to answer the question when prodded again later. She spoke of encountering the soldiers in Fair Fork and how Strider hadn't killed them, even though they had intended to kill him.

She spoke of him then, placing her in the care of Sir Ulwick and his men, hoping they'd bring her home safely. With a bitter taste in her mouth, she described to her parents how she'd fallen for the false messenger and was led into a trap before being kidnapped again. She had to pause for a moment to find her voice as the memories of her escape, of stabbing that man, hit her again.

She told them everything about that night. How Strider had been following them the entire time to make sure she got home safely, how he'd tracked down her kidnappers and rescued her at the last second. She even told them she'd only escaped and defended herself because Strider had taken the time to teach her, in case something like that happened.

Her mother placed her hand over her mouth again upon hearing how her daughter had moved about like a thief, forced to pick locks and engage in battles to the death. But she said nothing as she listened respectfully, tears staining her cheeks. She listened to the ordeals her daughter had been through, her heart breaking with each word.

Addy told them that Tevin had been the only survivor, and that Strider had tended to his wounds. She stressed that Sir Ulwick wouldn't be alive had Strider not come in time.

She left out the ambush at the bridge, unsure how to explain it away without revealing Strider's magic. He'd likely be executed for that alone, and she hoped it would be at least another month before anyone found out about the bridge. Tevin claimed the king would pardon such an act because he'd deemed it necessary. But she couldn't put her faith in that. Sir Tamous might get away with such a call, but his rank and reputation preceded him.

She grew sober as she talked about the knights raiding the village. She began by describing how the men had begun taking people away. Her mother reached over to comfort her, telling her that she didn't have to say more. But she shook her head.

"Strider saved them," she told her. "He killed every man that tried to touch them. He stopped them from-"

This time she stopped and took a deep breath as she blinked away tears. Again, she left out any mention of magic, knowing how her parents would react.

"And now I am here," she finished, after regaining her voice. "Strider would've let Sir Ulwick take me the rest of the way home, had I not asked him to stay. I asked him to come here. I offered him my word and protection. He trusted me and came here unarmed as proof of that trust. Please don't make me a liar. Please don't make the reason he dies, be because he trusted the word of someone he risked everything to protect."

Her parents sat silently for a moment. Addy looked at them pleadingly, her gaze searching their faces for any sign that they believed her. Both of their features had softened.

"He saved you and Sir Ulwick," her mother said. "Then he is a hero, not a kidnapper."

Addy nodded. "Yes. Tevin would've died had he not healed him."

"Healed him, with magic?" her father asked, and Addy knew she'd slipped up. She cursed herself internally for being so stupid.

After a pause, she replied, "Yes, with Ranger magic."

She could see her parents shift, their posture stiffening once more as their earlier acceptance vanished.

"You have been through a lot," he told her. "You're confused, or under some kind of spell."

"I am not under a spell!" Addy insisted. "It is ridiculous to think he was responsible. Why would someone who can clearly sneak between the borders ever enlist the help of a carriage, or armed men to bring me to Denmahr? Why not take me there himself?"

her anger reddened her cheeks as her voice raised. "Why wait two months before appearing again, in a forest where he didn't know I'd be, and wait for me to steal from him before rescuing me twice and having to be paid to take me home. For what? What does he get out of this? He knew if he came here, he'd be executed. He gains nothing! It. Makes. No. Sense!"

She took a deep breath before adding, "Ask Sir Ulwick; he will tell you."

She looked at her mother pleadingly, begging her with her eyes to realize that what she said was true. Her mother frowned softly, as she considered Addy's words. Her frown deepened when she saw the clothes Addy was wearing again. Finally, she placed a hand on her husband's arm.

"Perhaps we should take a moment and consider what our daughter has to say," she suggested. "We're all emotional from the ordeal. Let us take a moment to allow calmer minds to rule."

Her father looked at her, the same fire in his hazel eyes that Addy inherited blazed within them. The same fire that lent well to irrational decisions led by pure emotion. His jaw tightened as he considered his wife, then looked to Elayis.

"What did you think of Sir Ulwick?"

Elayis, who'd been standing off to the side of the room, thought a moment. "He looked trustworthy enough, though I cannot say for sure. I didn't speak with the man."

Sir Tamous stepped forward then, having taken position behind Addy's father.

"If I may, my lord?" he inquired.

Her father waved for him to speak.

"I trained Sir Ulwick and have known him for many years. He is not the type to abandon his oaths to the king or this kingdom. If he has offered his support to this 'Dark Ranger', then I'm inclined to give the man the benefit of the doubt, especially after hearing the story your daughter has told."

The fire in her father's eyes died then. Sir Tamous was his oldest friend. He'd always been steady and calm, and her father trusted his counsel, even if he didn't always like to hear it.

"His name is Strider," Addy said, her tone sheepish. "He is a Hunter, not a Ranger. I sort of started that rumor in Denmahr, to spite him."

Both Sir Tamous and her father raised a brow.

"He isn't a Ranger and yet he holds a felaris feather?" Sir Tamous questioned.

Addy nodded. "He was furious when I told the soldiers of Denmahr he was one."

Her father let out a deep breath. "Very well," he said, signaling to Elayis. "Bring Strider to the study."

Chapter 59
Bothersome Brothers

"You're serious?" Tevin said in disbelief, sitting back against the wooden door. He'd heard old tales of magic users spending their own lives to perform near god-like feats of magic, but he'd thought those were specific spells and not the price one had to pay if they overtaxed their magical reserves and soul.

Strider answered with a resigned, "Yes."

Tevin remembered how unsteady Strider was, each time he'd used magic; at the time he'd thought it was simply exhaustion, like when one overworked themselves. Knowing what he did now added new weight behind the man's actions, as well as some words he'd said.

"You need to tell her," Tevin said, getting to his feet so he could face the small window. Two golden eyes peered out at him from the darkness. "She is expecting you to use magic to get away if you need to. She needs to know it'll kill you."

"No," Strider stated firmly.

"Do you know what it'll do to her if you die?"

"Do you know what it'll do to her if she knows? If I die and she knows, she will blame herself. I know that if I have to, I can get away. She'd never see me again and assume I've escaped."

"So, you plan to escape and go off and die somewhere alone?"

"If I can't walk out of here as a free man."

"You're ridiculous, you know that?"

"Maybe, but I'd rather die out there than be hanged or beheaded before a crowd like some spectacle."

Tevin's look of disbelief changed to one of exasperation as he spoke. "So, you'd rather go off and die in some ditch, then be put on display."

"I'd rather go off and die in a ditch than have Addy watch me get killed, knowing she was responsible for it," Strider snarled.

"She'd figure it out, eventually."

"I'd simply disappear. She'd never know I died. Even if she heard news of my death, people die on the road all the time. She can assume something else killed me."

"You are not a normal person."

"I've killed plenty of people not considered normal," Strider growled through the bars. "Keep your word, knight. This won't harm or endanger Addy."

Strider's resignation to his death took Tevin aback. He'd expected him to fight to stay alive. He clenched his jaw as he glared at Strider. How did this make sense in Strider's mind? To him, he was protecting Addy by potentially going off to die alone. While it would prevent her from hurting now, and she might believe he decided to never return, she would ultimately end up getting hurt. Which Strider knew and was taking measures to at least try to ensure that guilt didn't couple with her pain. It was all insane! But he'd always believed the Hunter was a bit Chaos Touched.

Tevin was about to comment further, when the loud thunk of the lock cut him off. Someone had opened the first door and was approaching the second. He kicked the stool aside so it wouldn't trip him in case he had to fight. He watched the door as someone unlocked it. It opened with a loud creak. This was also another security feature. Quiet doors made for quiet exits. A loud door was not so obliging.

Two young men stepped into the hall, dressed in practical attire of loose-fitting white shirts and tan trousers. Only the material revealed their wealth. Both men wore fine swords at their side. They looked very similar to Elayis and Tevin guessed they were Tymott and Curthis, Addy's elder brothers.

Elayis was the eldest, Tymott was younger by a year, and Curthis was only a year older than Addy. Like their siblings and parents, they had brown hair. Despite being the youngest son, Curthis had managed not to be sent to Syliceon, and Tevin wondered what he'd done to convince his father to let him stay.

They both strode purposefully toward Tevin.

"Is this the cell where the Dark Ranger is being held?" Tymott asked, his voice soft despite the edge it carried.

"It is," Tevin said, his voice level, as he looked from one noble to the other. He didn't like the look in their eyes.

"Step aside then," Curthis ordered, louder and more forceful than his softer spoken brother, as he pulled out the key from his pocket. "And wait outside."

"I am afraid I cannot do that," Tevin told them. "I am under orders to remain here, guarding the man to whom Lady Fenforde offered protection."

"Protection?" Tymott said in surprise, looking to Curthis for clarification. His younger brother's connection to the guards had afforded him more information than himself.

Curthis glowered at Tevin, for once not caring to be formal to a man of higher rank. "She was likely scared into saying that. The devil just wants to get out of being hanged, so he forced her to promise to protect him."

Tevin frowned, finding that he didn't like hearing the young nobleman speak ill of Strider. How ironic, considering he'd said similar things when he'd first encountered the man.

"That may be," Tevin said, his tone hard, as he kept his composer. "But I gave my word to her ladyship."

"And I am saying you're no longer bound to that promise," Tymott replied, before Curthis did or said anything that could get him strung up beside the Hunter. "Or will you go against my orders?"

"Let them in, knight." Strider's voice came from inside. Like the growl of a caged wolf. "No sense in risking your position."

Tevin didn't like the sound of Strider's voice. He knew what would happen if he let these men pass, and it wouldn't help to clear the Hunter's name.

"He is right," Curthis agreed. "There is no sense in risking your rank to defend a monster like him."

Tevin didn't move as he stared Tymott directly in the eyes. Of the two brothers, his rank and title protected him from punishment. If he backed down, Curthis would be forced to as well, or risk offending a king's knight. His hand had moved to grip the handle of his sword and the two nobles copied him.

"I will not move until Lady Fenforde herself orders it."

The brothers took a step back to offer themselves more room as they drew their swords.

"You can move, Tevin." Addy's voice cut through the tension like a knife, her tone just as sharp.

They all looked to see Addy standing in the doorway, having walked through the door the brothers had left open. Behind her stood Elayis, who scowled at both of his brothers.

"What are you two doing?" he asked.

"We were just-" Tymott began, all the gusto evaporating in the face of Elayis and Addy's disapproving stares.

"We wanted to speak with the prisoner, but the knight refused us," Curthis cut in, his tone cool, his face unreadable.

"So, you drew your swords?" Elayis asked. "On one of the king's knights?"

"We uh..." Tymott trailed off, as he sheathed his sword and looked at the ground. Curthis followed suit, though he looked far less sheepish than his brother. Neither one could meet Addy's furious glare.

She walked over to them, snatching the key from Tymott, who uttered a quiet apology.

"I'll yell at you both, then hug you later," she said, before turning to Tevin.

She beamed at him. "Thank you for watching him. I'm sure he wasn't very good company."

Tevin offered a thin smile, though it didn't reach his eyes. "He was as terrible as to be expected. Worse, actually, since he didn't have you or Greer to tell him to behave."

Addy laughed softly, as she motioned for Tevin to move aside. As he did, several more guards appeared.

"Addy, let them-" Elayis began, but she'd already unlocked the door and opened it.

Two golden eyes peered at her from the darkness. She stepped back, and the room watched as what appeared to be a shadow melted out of the dark doorway. Both Curthis and Tymott placed their hands back on their swords as Strider met their gazes. Tevin did his best to hide a smile as both young men took a step back as they sensed they were in the presence of something dangerous. Strider looked down at Addy, the glint in his eyes softening like hard frost before summer sunlight.

"My father wants to speak with you." She smiled up at him, then frowned. "Behave yourself. You have no idea how hard it was to convince my father to listen to your side of the story."

"You mean how a noble girl lied to me about who she was, then expected me to protect her against the kingdom hunting her, while trying not to be killed by the one trying to save her?" Strider offered a small smile that was anything but reassuring.

"Something like that."

He glanced at his weapons, sitting within easy reach. Elayis and the guards put their hands on their swords. Strider merely gestured to them. Tevin picked them up again. Both knew that a prisoner's valuables tended to vanish. Strider nodded his thanks. A guard stepped forward, holding a pair of manacles. He eyed them, and Addy gave him an apologetic shrug.

"It was part of the deal."

Strider nodded, and let the man shackle him. Tevin took up his position beside Strider, as the soldiers surrounded him once more. Addy and her brothers led the procession out of the dungeon and toward her father's study. It was difficult for the Hunter to walk patiently behind them when all he wanted to do was run from the dungeon as quickly as his legs could carry him. The open sky called to him like liquor called to a drunkard. It had taken every ounce of willpower not to launch himself out of that cell the instant Addy opened the door.

He hid his anxiety well, however, as he followed them from the cramped dungeon back to the courtyard. The tightness in his chest and the need to escape subsided. He bowed his head, face hidden under his hood. Strider took a moment to close his eyes, savoring the smell of fresh air and the feeling of being under the sky.

They moved swiftly across the courtyard and into the keep, ushering him toward the study, where Addy's parents waited to meet the man she claimed saved her life. As they walked, Strider watched, soaking in every detail. Every turn they made, every nook, crevice, and cranny of the keep. His trained eyes searching out hiding places, escape routes, everything he'd need if he were to have to escape. It didn't take long for them to reach the study, where Elayis excused the guards before they entered. Addy's brothers took up the position of guard around Strider alongside Tevin as Addy led the way inside.

Chapter 60
The Meeting

The study was one of the largest rooms within the keep. Bookshelves lined the walls, filled with colorfully bound books. A large table, with a map of the known world upon it, stood in the center of the room. Smaller maps and papers lay scattered around the main map. Cut into the back wall behind her father's desk, stood two tall glass pane doors, set in between two equally large windows leading out onto a small balcony. A great, dark-stained desk, sat before the bay windows; the desk where Addy's parents waited. Sir Tamous stood at attention behind them. Both husband and wife watched Strider with a mix of different emotions as he entered.

Addy stepped forward, offering a small curtsy.

"Father, mother, this is Strider. The man who brought me home safely," she reiterated. "Strider, these are my parents. Lady Felice Rolandi-Fenforde and Lord Tylin Fenforde."

Strider offered a nod, drawing a frown from the two nobles.

"You've already met my brothers Elayis, Tymott, and Curthis. Behind my father stands Sir Rishurd Tamous."

The brothers remained standing at attention around their prisoner. Tevin stood off to the side until Addy introduced him.

"This is Sir Ulwick, the knight who helped to bring me home."

He offered a low bow to the two nobles, who returned his bow with small nods.

"Tell me, Sir Ulwick," Lord Fenforde began, not acknowledging Strider. "What are your thoughts regarding this Dark Ranger?"

Tevin remained silent for a moment, collecting his thoughts, as he looked at Strider.

Addy watched him closely. Strider merely cocked his head to listen to what the knight had to say.

"He is an extremely dangerous man," Tevin answered. "And extremely loyal to your daughter. He has shown time and time again that he is willing to die, if it meant she arrived home safely."

Strider lifted his gaze to look at the knight, who met his steadily, as he added, "I have never seen a fiercer guardian."

They kept their gaze locked on each other. Strider dipped his head in thanks and Tevin returned the gesture.

Addy let out her breath slowly, in relief. She remembered what Tevin had said the first night when he tried to get her to run away with him and couldn't help but smile at seeing how much things had changed.

"High praise, coming from a knight of the king," her father said, drawing her attention.

"He has earned it, my lord," Tevin admitted, with a bow of his head.

"You are not merely saying this because he saved your life?"

"Father!" Addy protested, but he raised a hand to stop any further argument.

"It must be said," he told her, watching Tevin closely.

Tevin shook his head. "No, my lord. Had I been able to at the time, I would've tried to slay him. I believed the charges against him. Even after Lady Fenforde told me her story, presenting a convincing argument, I likely would've attacked him."

"So, what brought about this change?"

"I watched him. Upon Lady Fenforde's request, I observed Strider while recovering my strength. In doing so, I was convinced he wasn't the one who'd taken her."

Lord Fenforde remained silent for a moment, before excusing Tevin with a nod and a thank you. His hazel gaze locked on Strider then, growing hard as he looked at the man whose face was half-covered in shadow.

"You'd do well to remove your hood while in the presence of a noble," he said.

Strider once against tilted his head, saying nothing.

Before anyone could react, Addy stepped forward, her eyes on her father.

"His visage tends to startle or offend," she informed him. "First promise that you'll not react rashly or on impulse if he does."

Her father narrowed his eyes suspiciously. "What is he hiding that you are so worried about?"

"Father, please," she urged him.

He sighed. "Very well."

"That is one way of saying I am ugly," Strider joked, as he reached up and pulled down his hood. Only Tevin and Addy didn't react.

"A *yulie* has been traveling with our daughter?" Addy's mother gasped. She turned pale again.

Strider sighed at the overreaction. Addy's father clenched his fist as he glared at Strider.

"You gave your word," Addy reminded him, before he could speak.

He looked at her before looking at Tevin. "You knew what he was?" he accused.

Tevin nodded.

"And you still let him near my daughter?"

"It isn't illegal for a half-breed to risk their life to help someone," Strider stated. "I don't recall it being a crime for a full-blooded yulie, either."

Her father's eyes flared with rage, and he clenched his jaw, shooting daggers at the Hunter.

"My lord," Sir Tamous interjected softly. "Despite what he is, he has earned the respect of a king's knight and proven his loyalty to your daughter. I trust Sir Ulwick's judgment."

"Tell me then, Strider," Addy's father said curtly. "Tell me your side of this story and why you helped my daughter."

Strider cocked his head again. "You mean why did I decide to help someone who stole from me?" he offered a dismissive shrug. "I really don't know. But your daughter paid me one silver coin up front, promising further compensation, and later a cleared name, upon getting her home." He looked at Addy. "You still owe me the remaining money you promised me."

"You haven't finished your job yet."

"I got you home."

"And payment for that is something you should work out with my father. Our other arrangement has not been met."

"I'm starting to think that you should've been the one accused of holding me hostage," Strider growled, though he didn't sound upset.

"You can leave at any time."

Strider gave the manacles a light shake, making the chains clank together as he and Addy glared at one another.

"You didn't have to come with me."

"You asked me to."

"I figured you'd like to have your name cleared and get paid!"

"Are they always like this?" Sir Tamous asked Tevin, as he observed the two.

"This is actually rather mild," he answered with a shrug. "They're usually much worse."

"Enough!" Lord Fenforde snapped, interrupting Addy and Strider's bickering.

Both stopped to look at him.

"You will not speak to my daughter so casually," he warned Strider, who regarded him with a cool stare.

"It'd be nice to hear you call me lady for once," Addy teased.

"And it'd be nice if I could go back in time and tell a certain young noblewoman no, when she insisted I take her home," Strider shot back. "We don't always get what we want."

Addy huffed. "You're such a stubborn old man!"

"And you're a rash young woman."

"Better than a grouchy stick in the mud! I still don't know how Greer puts up with you."

"For the same reason he insisted on helping you, I'd imagine."

"I said that is *enough!*" her father bellowed.

The door behind them flung open. A tall man dressed in brightly colored clothes of yellow and scarlet came rushing in. He looked around the room wildly, before locking his gaze on Addy.

"Lady Fenforde!" he cried out, rushing to her and falling on his knees. "I came as soon as I heard you'd returned safely to us."

He panted heavily, clearly having run the entire way to the study in his haste.

Addy beamed down at him. "It is good to see you, Renard."

He looked up at her, tears streaming down his face. "I do not deserve such kindness after failing to protect you. I beg your forgiveness."

Addy noticed Curthis glance down at his feet, no longer able to look at her. He'd been the one guarding her that night, not Renard. She placed a hand on his shoulder. "You didn't fail me. You don't need to ask my forgiveness." She directed her words at both her retainer and her brother, but she couldn't read Curthis' expression.

Renard wiped away his tears on a scarlet cuff. "Thank you, my lady!"

"Are you well?" he asked, launching into a rapid fire of questions. "Did your kidnapper hurt you? By K'yarie, *what are you wearing?*"

Her father gave an annoyed sound, and Renard turned to him, still on his knees.

"My apologies for interrupting, my lord," he said. "I was overcome with relief upon hearing of Lady Fenforde's safe return. I couldn't help myself."

Lord Fenforde waved the man away. "While I appreciate your dedication to serving my daughter, I would warn you not to interrupt a meeting ever again, Renard." There was a bite in his words that sent the man back into a corner as he uttered an apology.

Addy frowned at her father.

Strider cocked his head, as he watched the colorful man, with a steady, unreadable gaze.

"That is Renard," Addy explained. "My steward. He has served me for as long as I can remember."

Renard finally took notice of the Hunter, and he started with a gasp.

"Is that the man?" he asked. Seeming to be far too comfortable speaking out to be a mere servant. "Is he the one who stole you, my lady?"

"No," Addy said, curtly. "He was falsely accused and has been helping me this entire time."

Renard regarded Strider with a haughty and suspicious eye. The Hunter returned his look with a silent and unwavering stare. He held the man's gaze until Renard finally looked away, clearly uncomfortable.

"Back to the matter at hand," Addy's father announced, regaining everyone's attention. "I've listened to both my daughter and Sir Ulwick. Both of whom speak highly of you. Though I do not see why," he added the last bit under his breath, as he looked disapprovingly at the Hunter.

"I do admit that my daughter's argument has valid points. If what she said is also true about the knights of Denmahr, that implicates King Elias, who has been this kingdom's ally for many years."

Strider gave an indifferent gesture with his hands. "I'd wait to hear what your Rangers conclude before doing that."

"And yet you were reported to have fought off his men."

"Uniforms are easily stolen."

"That is true," her father agreed. "What is to stop me from believing that you orchestrated the entire thing to frame Denmahr and walk away with a reward?"

"Because that is an overcomplicated and tedious plan," Strider said, with a heavy breath. "If I was looking for money, I'd have not gone through the trouble of bringing her back and would have simply sold her in Winlotte. There are people there who would pay a king's ransom to get their hands on a noble girl."

"It's disturbing that you know that," Addy muttered.

Strider shrugged. "You learn a lot of things when you've lived as long as I have. Most are unpleasant."

"And what if it wasn't money you were after?" Renard suggested. "Perhaps you are after land, or Lady Fenforde herself."

Addy, Tevin, and Strider scoffed at the idea.

"I already have land, and I'd sooner slit my own throat than marry Addy."

"Assuming I didn't kill you first," Addy told him.

He smiled. "Actually, land a blow during training first, before making such a threat."

"I came close last time."

"Close means nothing in a fight."

"You never told me you had land," Addy redirected.

"You never asked."

Again, her father interrupted them. "Despite all of this, it is possible that you arranged the whole thing; a possibility I am not inclined to overlook."

"Have your Rangers dig deeper, then. I know they're combing Denmahr as we speak. Assuming they aren't spending their time trying to find this Dark Ranger, they're more than capable of figuring out the truth."

"So, you admit you're not a Ranger."

"I have never claimed to be one."

"Then how did you come by a felaris feather and keep it?"

"There is no law against someone carrying a felaris feather unless they're a Ranger. Though Rangers are inclined to challenge you for it. They seem to think they have a claim to them."

"You have a Ranger's bow."

"A felaris feather doesn't make a Ranger's bow. Though there is no law stating I cannot use one."

"How did you get the bow?"

"I made it."

"How?"

"A Ranger taught me."

"Why?"

"I imagine he felt like it."

"Seriously, Strider?" Addy huffed. "You told me, why won't you tell him?"

"Because I don't trust him," Strider answered flatly, still meeting the irritated gaze of her father.

Addy was taken aback by Strider's straightforward answer, and it took her a moment to formulate a response. Which was something neither parent had seen her do before. Their daughter was normally belligerent and hot-headed; quick to respond, slow to think. It was rare for her to stop and consider what she'd say next.

"He is my father, and I trust him, along with those in this room. Please answer him."

Strider looked at her for a long moment. "My father taught me how to make the bow, and the ways of a Ranger. The felaris feather was also his until he gave it to me."

"I didn't know Rangers were now training yulie."

"He was ummanie, though Rangers accept anyone willing to follow their code." His tone was flat and cold. "Though they don't send anyone of clear yulie decent to work for the kingdoms."

"You say he was a Ranger."

Strider's voice was devoid of emotion when he replied, "He died fifty years ago."

"What was his name?"

"If you want to verify my story, ask the Rangers. They're quite familiar with it. They've been trying to take his feather back for decades, after all. It's somewhat of a sore spot for them."

"So, they were already aware of you before the allegation brought against you?"

Strider nodded, flashing a crooked smile. "If you ever want to annoy a Ranger, mention my name."

"If they consider you such a black spot on their record, why haven't they done anything about you?"

"They've tried," Strider said, grimly. "And they've failed."

Of course, he'd never ticked them off as much as he had now. The rumor of the Dark Ranger would be the final straw. He'd broken his contract with them. They would be out for blood. The entire room was silent for a time, as they considered the weight of Strider's words. Rangers weren't known for failing to accomplish a goal they set their mind on. To fail to retrieve a feather for so long was unheard of. It gave the entire room pause, and made them look at the half yulie standing before them with a great deal more caution.

"I have one last question," her father went on. "How did you bypass the defenses at Bayvar and cross into our kingdom?"

Strider considered the question, his head tilting to the left. "There are ways."

Everyone but Addy frowned at his vague answer. Slowly, it dawned on Sir Tamous, and his face grew pale. "You used The Ways."

Addy watched her father's face drain of color at the gravity of the situation, then redden.

"How did you enter The Ways?" he bellowed. "Do you realize you could've started a war if the tahrvin discovered you?!"

Strider shrugged. "Their High Priestess didn't seem too concerned with my using them."

"Their High-" He couldn't speak out of disbelief. His glare snapped to Addy.

"He took you through The Ways, and you refused to tell me? You knew that was a breach of our treaty with the tahrvin!"

Addy didn't shrink back, as she faced her father. "The tahrvin High Priestess allowed us to pass with no repercussions."

"And what did you have to promise her in exchange?"

"I didn't promise her anything. She bartered with Strider, not me."

All eyes turned to Strider.

"What did she require of you?" Lord Fenforde demanded.

"Nothing that concerns the ummanie kingdoms," Strider informed him. "If the Priestess wanted war, you'd have it by now."

"I still want to know what the terms were."

"So would I," Strider sighed, annoyed. He was growing tired of all the talking.

"You mean you don't know?"

"The deal was I'd owe her a favor. She never gave specifics."

"You didn't think to ask?"

"My concern was getting Addy home. I didn't care to argue the point."

Her father thought about that for a moment before finally sighing. "My daughter is home safe. That's what matters. And despite everything, she has presented a sound argument. You're to wait here until the Rangers return with further information, but for now, you won't be charged for the crime of kidnapping."

"My lord!" Renard sputtered. "You're a merciful man, but what proof does this... this... *yulie* have that he is innocent? Lady Fenforde, forgive my boldness, could be under some sort of spell. The knight, as well. Ranger and yulie magic is truly unknown and powerful dark magic. All we have are the words of these three, one being that of the criminal himself!"

"And that is why he is to remain in the castle, until I receive word from the Rangers we sent to gather information," Lord Fenforde said, his tone hard.

"Do you intend to confine him to a cell?"

"No!" Addy argued. "We can sequester him in one of the guest rooms. There is no need for him to be locked up. He hasn't tried to escape, and he won't."

"He hasn't tried to escape, because he is shackled and surrounded by skilled and well-armed noblemen," Renard said, in a placating tone.

Addy looked pointedly at her steward. "He could've slipped those manacles off at any time, and I have seen what his magic can do. He'd be out of the castle and gone before anyone could stop him."

"I have to agree with Addy," Sir Tamous spoke. "Other than his uncultured tongue, he has cooperated with us fully."

"Who is to say he will continue to do so when let loose?" Renard shot back. "He could be biding his time, waiting for us to let our guard down before striking. He is the Dark Ranger. He doesn't follow the same code of honor that the Rangers do. He's abandoned it."

"He isn't a lawless animal, Renard," Addy snapped. "He won't attack the moment he is unchained, nor is he here to harm me, or any of us."

"How can you be sure he wouldn't try to escape the moment we leave him alone?" Addy's mother finally said. She'd been quietly listening to the conversations in the room, observing each person as they spoke. "A cell is better equipped to handle dangerous people."

Addy looked at Strider, who'd remained completely quiet throughout the entire debate. Eyes watching, observing everyone in his silent manner.

"You won't run, will you?"

"You said you still had a job for me. I have no reason to leave until it is done," he told her. His gaze shifted to Addy's mother. "And if I were here to kill you, my lady, I would've done it long ago rather than stand here wasting my breath and listening to you all discuss my fate as if I weren't here."

She balked at the comment, but didn't stop meeting his gaze as she lifted her chin in the same defiant way Addy did. He couldn't help the small, crooked smile that touched his lips at the sight. He saw Addy in both of them.

His tone was softer when he spoke again. "I am only here because your daughter asked me to come. I will stay here, because your daughter has hired me to complete a job. And I will only kill if someone tries to kill me or those I am protecting. And I suspect the job she hired me for includes protecting you."

"You agreed to a job without knowing its terms?" Renard said.

"Even if I knew them and disagreed, I'd still be here doing it."

"You make it sound as if someone would force you into it."

Tevin, Addy, and Strider all said in unison.

"There is."

Chapter 61

The Ranger

"Who is this person?" Lord Fenforde asked.

"His di'horvith," Tevin offered.

"A dire wolf? You didn't tell me his wolf was a dire wolf," Addy's father said in shock. Addy was surprised he knew what the word meant. She'd opted to call Greer a wolf during her retelling.

"He's only half di'horvith. That's why I called him a wolf," Addy corrected. "But he's able to tell when a person is lying. I've seen him do it before. He could help figure out who helped in my kidnapping."

"And the wolf is the one who'd force Strider to help you in this hunt?"

"Yes," Addy said, with a barely suppressed smile. "Greer can force Strider to do anything."

"You're telling me the wolf controls the hunter?"

"He doesn't control anyone," Strider growled.

Even Addy's parents couldn't hide their amused smiles at the absurdity.

"Still, how can a dire wolf detect lies?" Lady Fenforde asked.

"Di'horviths are magical beasts," Addy said. Many legends surrounded the animals, so it wasn't much of a stretch to believe they could detect a lie. "And he has an almost white pelt like the ones in the stories. I think that's why."

"His abilities are not infallible," Strider told her.

"But he's able to detect when someone is lying?" Addy's mother inquired.

Strider nodded.

"Have you seen this too?" She turned to Tevin.

"Yes," Tevin answered. "He used Greer to interrogate a man he'd captured, who had been involved in ambushing my men and me, while we escorted your daughter home."

"I'd like to see this wolf," Lady Fenforde said, determinedly. "I would like to see his abilities tested. Where is he? We'll send Sir Ulwick to fetch him."

"He isn't anywhere Tevin can get him," Strider answered. "Only I can retrieve him."

"You cannot leave this castle," Lord Fenforde reminded him. "How do you intend to fetch him?"

Strider gave him a dark smile, knowing the noble wouldn't like his answer. "Magic."

The frown Lord Fenforde gave rivaled his wife's but he did not protest. "We don't need your protection. You're not working for my daughter."

"Father! At least hear me out!" Addy interjected. "We need him and Greer to find those responsible for taking me!"

"We haven't found the leader responsible for your kidnapping, and until I know for certain this man isn't responsible, I'm not going to consider hiring him." He raised a hand before Addy could protest. "We will discuss this later."

Despite the circus that'd become his study, and his misgivings and dislike for the Hunter, Addy's father decided not to lock him in the dungeon. He motioned for Elayis to unshackle Strider's wrists. When the noble stepped closer, Strider promptly handed the young man the unlocked manacles. Everyone gave him a startled look. No one had seen him remove them, or how he'd done it. Elayis took the manacles with a look of wonder and suspicion.

Tevin walked over and offered him his weapons back. Strider accepted them and began buckling them back on.

"While I am letting you roam the lower quarter of the keep and the courtyard, you're required to have an escort during the day, at night you're not to leave your room, and you're not to step foot outside the gate," Lord Fenforde told him. "My men will be watching you, with orders to kill if you attempt to leave without my permission."

Strider nodded his understanding as Lord Fenforde ordered. "Bring your wolf here."

They allowed him to go to the barn to summon Greer under escort. Sir Tamous volunteered, while Addy and Tevin stayed behind for more questioning. The man walked behind Strider, offering verbal directions on how to reach the stables.

"Lady Fenforde said that you were teaching her the ways of the sword," Sir Tamous said casually.

Strider tilted his head to glance back at him before nodding.

"I am glad."

"You wanted her to learn?"

Tamous nodded. "I always thought it wise for a young lady to know how to defend herself. Her mother forbade it, of course, saying it was unbefitting of a lady."

Strider scoffed. "Plenty of noblewomen in Myvara know how to handle a sword."

"Not in the kingdom of Rachia, where Lady Fenforde is from. She has adopted many of Myvara's ways, but some things she still insists on. Though now, she may re-evaluate her beliefs, given what has happened."

Strider nodded his understanding. Each ummanie kingdom varied a surprising amount. Two kingdoms that shared borders could have vastly different views on things.

"Lady Adelin has grown quite a bit," Sir Tamous observed. "I am sure that is in part due to the ordeal she has gone through, though I suspect most of it has come from the company she kept."

Again, Strider angled his head to look at the man, unsure of what to make of him. He was an older knight and his sandy-colored hair was faded with streaks of gray. He had a strong face with kind eyes, and he carried himself with quiet confidence and authority. Sir

Tamous had been far more cool-headed than Addy's father, who appeared to take his word in high regard.

"She's been through a lot," Strider agreed.

"And she says you watched over her through all of it. For that, you have my thanks."

"You don't think I was the one to kidnap her?"

"No. I don't believe her parents think so either. Like me, they're not blind, and they know their daughter well. They saw how she interacted with you, and you with her. Lord Fenforde, as well as I, have been around long enough to know a dangerous man when we see one. Yet she speaks boldly to you, without fear. I sense not many people get away with such a thing around you."

"I suspect she'd speak the same way to a dragon as it held her captive," Strider said, smiling.

Sir Tamous laughed. "You're likely right. But the dragon would've eaten her for doing so."

They stepped into the courtyard, and Strider had the sense that he was being watched. Keeping the movement of his head subtle, he searched his surroundings for anyone of interest. The wall guards paid them no mind, and he couldn't sense the exact presence that watched him. Hiding any sign that he'd noticed, he continued toward the barn.

Sir Tamous stopped once they'd reached the stable door. "I will let you enter alone," he said, with a dip of his head.

Strider returned the gesture before entering, closing the door behind him. He wandered down the hall, his gaze drifting from stall to stall, ever watchful for danger. All he found were horses, hay, and dust. But he now felt someone was nearby. Eventually, he spotted a familiar long face staring at him.

Copper let out a sound of greeting, and Strider stroked the animal's nose and neck. He spotted Tulie, Su'lris, and the white horse he'd claimed, a few stalls over. He didn't see their saddles or gear, but all were well-groomed and had plenty of feed and water. Turning his back to the faded roan, Strider pulled out his pendant.

Silver mist swirled before him and out emerged Greer. Every horse nickered in delight, greeting the di'horvith, who shook his pelt gratefully, before bouncing around the stable to meet each horse. Strider watched him, amused by Greer's happy prance.

A figure burst from the shadows of the stable. A blade flashed in the dim light, aiming for Strider. The Hunter drew his saber. Metal sang as the two blades collided, and Hunter found himself staring into furious hazel eyes.

"I was wondering when you'd show yourself," he said. "Ranger."

Chapter 62
Magic Happy

T he Ranger pushed back, slashing with his sword as he launched a flurry of attacks. Strider shuffled away from Copper's stall, fending off the onslaught. Moving out into the hall, he knocked the man's blade aside. The Ranger took a hurried step back, expecting Strider to capitalize upon the opening he'd created. But Strider retreated instead, falling into a defensive stance. The Ranger hesitated. He'd been expecting the Hunter to press the attack, not back off.

Greer let out a low woof. He bounded over, tail wagging. He didn't approach the Ranger who now stood in front of Copper's stall. The massive canine gave the man even more pause.

"Lower your sword, Ranger," Strider said. "I'm not your enemy today."

The man scoffed. "You made yourself our enemy the day you broke your oath, Hunter."

Strider cocked his head. "I left The Wilds fifty years ago. None of you complained when I did so."

"That's because you remained in the shadows while you hunted the man who killed your father," Kyre growled. "We allowed you to seek justice for one of our own, as long as you kept the rest of your oath. But you've gone back on every promise. Now you're fair game."

The man shifted his grip on his sword.

"It was the lady who began the rumors about a Dark Ranger," Strider informed him. "And it was your oath that had me keeping quiet about it."

The man scowled. He, like any Ranger, knew the strange conditions of Strider's oath. Do not leave The Wilds. Do nothing to reflect badly upon the Rangers. Tell no one that you're not a Ranger. While in The Wilds, if someone were to come to him for help, he was to do so, assuming they found him. In return, the Rangers would only formally challenge him for his feather, rather than resort to other tactics. Though that hadn't stopped everyone from trying more underhanded methods to best the Hunter.

"It doesn't matter who started the rumor," Kyre snapped. "People know about you, and we have to set an example."

He lunged forward, blade glinting in the dim light.

Strider shuffled back again as he parried, blocked, and dodged each attack. He moved back toward the closed stable door. Frustrated at being met at every turn, the Ranger launched a blast of magic aimed at Strider's chest.

Strider crossed his arms, enforcing himself with magic as he took the hit. The force of the impact sent him flying. His back slammed into the barn door and the dried wood splintered with a resounding crack as it gave way. He flew out the stable door and into the courtyard. His back hit the brick road, and he rolled, flipping with the momentum until he was on his feet again.

He'd taken no damage from the attack, thanks to his quick reaction, but pain spiked in his chest. Kyre rushed toward him and Strider raised his sword in time to block another attack. The two resumed their deadly dance of blades in the center of the courtyard.

Sir Tamous, who'd been standing off to the side of the door when it suddenly exploded, leaped aside as Strider flew by. He reached for his sword, expecting an attack. Another form rushed past him, and he recognized the familiar figure of Kyre, their resident Ranger, as his sword crashed against Strider's. Their weapons sang as they moved about the courtyard.

Sir Tamous watched them, his initial surprise subsiding. He looked at the ruined door and let out a heavy breath. Noticing movement in the darkness, he held onto his blade as a massive canine came trotting out. He saw no malice in the creature's posture as the large animal casually trotted over to sit beside the head knight. Sir Tamous looked down at what he assumed was the half di'horvith called Greer. He slowly released his grip on his sword.

Greer smiled up at him before turning to watch the Ranger and Hunter fight, his attention focused on Strider. Sir Tamous also returned to watching the display. He'd never seen Kyre so worked up. He was a cocky fellow, but like most Rangers, he didn't rush to attack.

But he went after the Hunter like he'd murdered his mother. It was the first time he'd seen a Ranger face one of his own. They never trained where others could see them. Sir Tamous let curiosity get the better of him, so didn't stop the two from fighting.

Strider parried another one of Kyre's attacks, as he moved through the courtyard. He felt himself being backed up toward a wall. Metal sang harshly as the blades slid against one another. Neither swordsman gave an inch. As the two weapons met once more, Strider sensed the Ranger's magic-like electricity in the air.

Strider did the same out of instinct. Magic met magic, and the two were thrown apart. Both Ranger and Hunter flipped and rolled with the force that blew them back. With the grace of a cat, Strider was on his feet and moving again.

Kyre cursed as he sent another blast of energy at him.

Strider danced aside. The magic slammed into the ground, kicking up dust, as it shattered the neatly laid brickwork. Strider didn't answer with a magical attack of his own.

Kyre continued his assault as he rushed forward, sending bolts of violet magic out with one hand. Strider cartwheeled away from another destructive attack aimed at shattering bones. He ran, not allowing the Ranger to close the gap easily.

The noise of ringing blades drew the attention of the garrison. Men on the walls pointed and called, while others stepped out of the barracks to see what was happening. No one tried to stop the fight. Everyone was curious to see who would win, and bets were soon started. They shouted and jeered, egging the fighters on. Neither one seemed to notice them as they fought. A tremendous cheer went up at the display of power from the Ranger, and more bets were placed as soldiers shouted encouragements to the fighter they'd chosen to win, goading him on.

Strider leaped out of the way of another bolt of magic, kicked off the castle's stone wall, and vaulted onto the roof of one of the buildings that lined the wall. Kyre ran on the ground below, parallel to Strider, as he moved to close the distance. He sent a burst of magic aimed to cut off the Hunter as he moved across the roof toward another building. The roof exploded in a shower of splinters, dust, and thatch. Strider sheathed his sword and kept running as he leaped over the massive hole. He vanished into a cloud of dust before reappearing on the other side, bow in hand.

Another shot came as he landed on the edge of the new building, demolishing the other roof. Strider flipped backward off it to avoid being taken out by the explosion. As he did, he drew an arrow from his quiver, knocked it in his bow, and fired mid flip. He felt the magic warm his body as the arrow slid from his fingertips. It shot from the bow. The arrow hissed through the air, aimed directly at the Ranger's chest. Kyre stepped aside, using his sword to slap the projectile away. The arrow exploded the moment the blade made contact. The violent burst of power sent Kyre flying, knocking his weapon out of his hand.

Strider landed on the courtyard ground. Ignoring the burning in his chest, he moved with startling speed. The Ranger had rolled across the ground, clumsily finding his feet and drawing his own bow. Like Strider's quiver, it held onto the arrows despite its owner being tossed around. He nocked an arrow before releasing it from his bow.

Strider sidestepped the arrow, never bringing his own sword up to deflect it as he closed the gap. He sensed no magic from it. Another arrow shot his way. He twisted aside again, plucked the arrow from the air, and fired it right back at the Ranger. Kyre had to dive to the side to avoid the arrow at such close range, hardly noticing the pain as it sliced into his leg.

Strider's chest constricted with the magical strain and his body grew heavier. He put his bow back on his shoulder and rushed toward Kyre, who had dived toward his sword, his own bow forgotten.

Again, Strider drew his yulie saber. The blue metal flashed savagely in the sunlight.

Rolling on the ground, Kyre barely grabbed his sword in time to block Strider's blade. He parried, slashing at the Hunter's face.

Strider jerked back. He felt wetness on his cheek, though he hadn't felt the sting of the actual cut. He smelled and felt the blood, though. The scent snapped him to attention, and for a moment, the cold found itself unable to hold him down as it fought to make his limbs tired and slow.

Sir Tamous saw a change come over the Hunter. The old knight had watched the two men battle closely. Both fought with great skill, yet he felt something was off with Strider. His speed astonished the knight. He seemed to glide across the courtyard as he avoided Kyre's magic. But it felt as if he were fighting against something unseen at the same time.

Still, he met every attack of Kyre's with a precise answer and avoided every magical blow. The knight felt his hair stand on end when the spells began; he was uneasy watching the display and when the Ranger destroyed two rooftops, he stepped forward. What he hadn't expected was Strider to fire an arrow laced with magic. Neither had Kyre, apparently.

It was the first show of magic Sir Tamous had seen Strider display since the two fighters had sent each other flying in the first half of the battle. Even as Strider closed the gap, Sir Tamous had a strange feeling that something wasn't right with the Hunter. It was only when his own blood was spilled that he snapped to attention. The change was terrifying as the man finally broke free of the invisible force holding him down. His sword moved with far more precision and speed as he fell into a flurry of attacks.

Rangers were known for their skill in using defensive moves to line up a counter-attack. But Kyre was struggling to keep up with the new pace the half-yulie now set. The rhythm of the battle had changed and even the cheering men had grown quiet, silenced by the aura of the Hunter. Sir Tamous glanced down when he sensed movement at his side. Greer had gotten to his feet, ears forward, eyes locked on Strider. Without a sound, he padded toward them.

Strider pressed Kyre back as he rained down blow after blow. He continued pressing the Ranger to keep him off balance so he couldn't regain his own rhythm and answer any attack effectively. Kyre sent another wave of magic, taking care to keep his hand well within the guard of his sword to keep it from being cut off. Strider redirected the attack with a swipe of his blade, channeling his own power to deflect it as he stepped closer. The yulie blade seemed to cry out in anger, the metal ringing low and sharp.

Kyre brought his sword down in an attack aimed at the side Strider had exposed while deflecting his magic. Only to find the blueish yulie weapon appearing to counter his strike with surprising strength. The two blades rang out as they met, and the Ranger's was knocked aside as Strider's came up with more force.

The Hunter's blade struck out as fast as a snake. Kyre stumbled back, attempting to avoid the blow. He called his magic to bring up a guard and increase his speed. The yulie saber didn't bounce off of his shield. It slid through his barrier as if it weren't there. Metal found flesh. It cut through his side rather than piercing up under his ribs like it would have had he not used magic to make himself move faster. The cost of avoiding the mortal blow threw him off balance. He aimed a clumsy overhead strike as he stumbled.

Strider caught his wrist and squeezed, forcing Kyre to drop his sword, as he swept the only leg holding the Ranger upright out from underneath him. Kyre landed hard on his back.

Strider's blade sang as it slashed down at his throat, aiming to slice it open.

A low woof boomed. The blade stopped short, kissing the Ranger's neck enough to cause him to bleed as it rested against the side of his throat. He was alive. Strider stood over him, golden eyes flashing like cold coins.

"Why don't you kill me?" Kyre challenged, glaring up at Strider.

"I don't care to start a war with the Rangers," he told him.

They glowered at each other, and Kyre really looked into the Hunter's eyes as the battle drained from his blood. His eyes narrowed in suspicion. He saw something off in Strider's eyes. Something only those touched by magic could learn to see.

He let out a breath of disbelief, his eyes widening when he realized what it was he saw. "You're a Chaos Touched idiot. You pushed too far, didn't you?"

The blade bit into his neck harder. He stopped talking, as he stared up at the Hunter.

"Tell anyone and I'll kill you," Strider threatened. "No one is to know."

For the first time, both men became aware of the cheering men. A shadow fell over Kyre, and he glanced up to see the face of an enormous wolf staring down at him, smiling.

"Hello there," Kyre said, very aware of how large Greer's teeth were. "Nice doggy."

Greer cocked his head at him before planting a wet kiss on his face.

Kyre spluttered, not expecting the sudden show of affection.

Greer looked up at Strider, offering a low woof. He stepped over Kyre as he moved closer to Strider, who looked like he was reconsidering the idea of killing Kyre, forcing him to back away from the Ranger. Sheathing his sword, Strider stepped away from the defeated man. He calmly walked back toward Sir Tamous.

"I think we kept the Fenfordes waiting long enough," he growled.

Greer let out a low, long whine, as he watched Strider walk toward the keep. He looked worried as he watched his Hunter.

"Looks like I'm not the only one who knows," Kyre said, as he stood and dusted himself off. Picking up his sword, he sheathed it, grabbed his bow, and walked briskly after the others. Greer snorted before taking off after Strider and Sir Tamous, easily passing Kyre to catch up with his brother.

Chapter 63

Truth Or Lies

The Fenfordes eyed both Strider and Kyre standing on either side of Sir Tamous. Kyre favored his injured leg. His hand clutched his side where his shirt was stained crimson. Blood oozed down his neck from where Strider's blade had cut it. He looked far worse for wear compared to Strider, who only had a cut on his cheek that had already stopped bleeding. Dried blood smudged his face where he'd tried to wipe it away. Both men were coated in dust and sweat, and Strider had stray stems of thatch and splinters poking out of his messy hair and cloak.

"What happened?" Lord Fenforde demanded.

"It would seem our Ranger found the Hunter," Sir Tamous said, barely hiding an amused smile.

"Did you win?" Addy asked Strider.

"I still have my feather," the Hunter answered simply, and she smiled.

"Wait, two Rangers fought, and we missed it?" Elayis asked, disappointed.

"He's not a Ranger," Kyre said.

"He's skilled enough to beat one!" Tymott interjected, as he looked to Sir Tamous, his face eager. "How was the fight? Was it amazing?"

The head knight nodded. "They're extremely skilled."

Such a compliment sent a ripple of excitement and disappointment through Tymott and Elayis. Curthis remained grim faced and quiet. They'd never heard such high praise from the old knight.

Addy's father glowered at the two men. "I hope you didn't cause too much of a scene."

"The Ranger has already offered to pay for the damages," Sir Tamous answered for them.

"Damages? What damages?"

"He owes you a couple of roofs," Strider said, brushing some dust from his shoulder. "The Ranger got a little magic happy."

"A couple roofs!" Lord Fenforde's gaze snapped to Kyre. "You destroyed two buildings?"

The Ranger glared at Strider. "*We* will cover the cost of the repairs. No one was hurt in the fight."

"That's because I stopped you before you could go blowing up another building," Strider interjected. "Are all Rangers so quick to blast magic everywhere these days?"

"You used magic too."

"I didn't destroy a single brick or building."

"That's because you attached it your arrow!" the Ranger argued.

"Fused with an arrow or not, the magic was more precise than what you were recklessly lobbing around."

"Ruther shouldn't have showed you how to bind magic to an object. He should've taught the Rangers, not his son."

"My mother taught him, and he wasn't inclined to share the skill outside of the family. If you want to learn so badly, then you should ask a yulie to teach you."

"You know they don't teach their ways to the Rangers. Your father was a special case."

"Maybe you should try marrying one, then?"

"*Enough!*" Addy's father boomed. "We will sort this out later. Do you have your wolf?"

Strider looked toward the door that still stood open. "Greer."

The di'horvith mutt trotted through the door, having waited outside while the three men went in.

"You sure that isn't a horse?" Elayis said, putting words to the ripple of alarm that ran through the room.

Greer's tail never stopped wagging as he padded into the room. He spotted Addy and his tail wagged faster. She held out her arms as the giant wolf went up to her. Her brothers stood around her, hands on their swords as they watched her rub Greer's cheeks and ears in disbelief. Greer let out a groan of appreciation, leaning into the affection and nearly knocking Addy over. Addy laughed and pushed him back.

"This is your wolf?" her mother asked in shock. "The one that can detect lies?"

"It is," Addy confirmed. "Mother, meet Greer."

Addy's brothers gathered around the di'horvith and were petting him, made confident by their sister, as she lavished Greer with affection. Their added attention caused Greer to make more sounds of appreciation. They laughed at his goofy expression and noises. He melted onto the ground in pleasure, accepting belly rubs.

"I've never seen a dog or wolf so big," Curthis said, drawn from his brooding by the cheerful brute.

"Do you think we could get one?" Tymott asked.

"I think not," their mother said, as she looked at Greer. "He's a wild animal."

"I've never met a nicer, more well-behaved animal in my life," Addy said, defending Greer. "He's far more civil than Strider."

Kyre laughed, and Strider shot him a warning look. The Hunter couldn't deny her words, however. He watched the siblings succumb to his brother's charms, quietly amazed at how easily Greer made friends.

"Let's get this over with, then," Strider grunted. "Who are we using for this test?"

The three brothers straightened.

"That'll be us," Elayis said.

"I will ask the questions we agreed upon," their father spoke. "We know who is lying, but will your wolf?"

"We'll see," Strider replied, watching Greer as he lay on his back, limp with gratification. "You will ask them questions, and your sons will answer yes or no. Nothing more. Greer will know if they're lying."

"How will we know if he has detected a lie?" Addy's mother questioned, while the three brothers pulled up chairs from the table sitting in the center of the room.

"I'll know," Strider answered.

"Alright, let's get this over with then," Elayis said, placing his feet up on the table, disturbing several maps. He leaned back in the chair, waiting. "I want to spar with the Hunter after this."

Tymott voiced his agreement while Curthis quietly took a seat.

Addy's mother stood, as if to say something, but her husband cut her off with his hand.

"Order your wolf," he told Strider.

"Greer," Strider called, gesturing for him to come over. The massive canine got to his feet and plodded over to Strider, who stole a chair for himself. Greer sat between his legs, as Strider rubbed his neck. The Hunter leaned forward to speak in his ear.

"Tell us who is lying."

Greer focused on the three brothers intently. Their father stood behind his desk and asked the first question.

"Are you three brothers?"

All three answered yes.

Greer did not react, and Strider declared, "Truth."

"Tymott, did you take and lose my fine riding crop last year?" Addy cut in.

"That wasn't me, that was Curthis!"

Greer's lips twitched downward in a ghost of a snarl.

"Lie," Strider said cooly.

"I knew it!"

Tymott went red. "I thought you said it only worked if I said yes or no?"

"I said it works best if you answer with simple answers, not that it doesn't work at all."

Addy's father cleared his throat. "I'd appreciate it if you didn't hijack the trial, Adelin."

"Sorry, father," she said, though her tone wasn't apologetic.

Her father went through a series of questions to which Strider would pronounce who was lying or telling the truth based on what he saw in Greer. The brothers grew increasingly more astonished as Greer accurately pointed out every lie.

"Incredible," Lady Fenforde said. "How much do you want for him?"

"He isn't for sale," Strider told her, with a flat growl.

Greer's ear swiveled back to catch his words, but otherwise, he looked clueless.

"Surely there is a price you'd be willing to take for him."

"I wouldn't give him to the goddess K'yarie if she offered me the world."

"Are his abilities passed down through blood?" she asked, trying a different tactic. "If so, we could pay you for a litter."

This time Greer cocked his head.

"I don't know if they are," Strider admitted. "That is something you'd have to ask the Ravack."

"I don't think it would be a good idea to buy a litter of dire wolf puppies," Lord Fenforde said. "The Ravack have been the only ones capable of taming them."

"Strider clearly tamed this one," Elayis pointed out.

"More like Greer tamed him," Addy coughed.

Strider scowled. "Greer isn't a typical di'horvith. He is a half-breed and was never born with the instincts and size that make most di'horviths so difficult to handle. Though he comes with his own challenges."

"Even still, I am interested in seeing if his abilities could be inherited by one of his puppies. If so, I'd be willing to pay handsomely for one," Lady Fenforde went on.

Strider sighed. "I'll think about it."

"Please do."

"We will gather the staff tomorrow," Addy's father stated, reclaiming the conversation. "Until then, you and Greer will remain locked in a room on the main floor. Guards will be posted outside to ensure you remain. If you're caught wandering the halls, or trying to escape, my men have orders to stop you with lethal force. You'll be allowed to roam the lower quarter and courtyard under escort come morning.

"Tymott, Curthis, escort him to his room and arrange for the guards to be stationed there."

"Yes, father," the brothers said, getting to their feet.

"Ranger Kyre, you will stay. The rest of you can go." Lord Fenforde dismissed the gathering with a wave of his hand.

The Ranger nodded at his words, though he eyed Strider as the Hunter followed Curthis and Tymott.

Addy followed Strider to the door, but a word from her mother stopped her.

"Adelin, go with Renard and see about getting yourself out of those clothes and into proper attire."

"I'll do that after I am done speaking with Strider."

"Tymott and Curthis can see that he is comfortable. You need to take care of your image. A lady shouldn't be running around in trousers!"

"Ranger women run around in them."

"You're not a Ranger, you're a noblewoman of the Fenforde house! It is already scandalous that you were seen riding into your home wearing such immodest clothing!"

Renard stepped forward and placed a hand on her shoulder. He smiled down at her. "You'll see him tomorrow. For now, let's get you cleaned up and taken care of," he said kindly.

Addy let out a sigh. "Very well."

"I'll escort you to your room and then find Tyra. She'll draw a bath for you."

The sound of a hot bath was tempting. Any thought of arguing or slipping away after they left the study vanished. She let Renard direct her down the hall, in the opposite direction Strider and Greer now walked.

Chapter 64

Growing Tension

Addy told Renard a condensed version of how she met Strider and their travels together.

"He is part yulie, and has questionable morals," Addy finished. "But he isn't all bad."

"He saw a way to make money. Holding you for ransom would've gotten him a sizable amount," Renard said, his lips set into a perpetual frown at the thought of Strider.

Addy returned the frown with one of her own. "And yet I'm here, not ransomed off."

"That's because he had to take you home. You forced his hand when you proclaimed he was the Dark Ranger," Renard said, his tone bordering on exasperation and disbelief that Addy didn't grasp what truly happened. "Don't you understand? He needed to clear his name. It wasn't to help you."

Addy bristled at his words, and she jumped to defend the Hunter. "You don't know Strider; he's not like that."

Renard patted her on the shoulder like he was comforting a wayward child, causing Addy's back to stiffen.

"You've been sheltered, so I don't expect you to see it. Creatures like him are cunning. Every action was calculated, designed to earn your trust and sympathy. He needed you to care for him or else you wouldn't fight so admirably for him." He gave her a reassuring look. "You'll come to see it once you've spent time away from him."

Addy pulled away from Renard, her cheeks flushing as her temper grew. Renard had an answer for everything, twisting Strider's words and actions into self-serving calculations. When had he become so condescending? What happened to the man who always told her how smart and mature she was and listened to her problems?

"You wouldn't say that if you'd seen what I've seen! He taught me to defend myself and survive! He took care of me!"

"You don't know what you're talking about." Renard's tone had shifted again to a patronizing drawl. "You're young and naive. That's why I'm here, to protect you from those seeking to take advantage of you."

"I'm not naive! And you're barely older than me, Renard."

"I am trained to spot these things. You're not. He showed a sheltered, lost young woman some useful skills, blinding her with the allure of adventure, safety, and a promise of returning home." Renard countered. His demeanor was placating, as if he were trying to reason with an irrational child. Which drew Addy's ire even more. "You got to live out one of your stories, but he isn't a charming prince come to save you."

"I wasn't blind to anything!" Addy yelled, stopping outside her door to face Renard. "He's no prince, but he's my friend, and he earned that trust through blood!"

Renard stepped back as if struck. He gave her a pained look. "How can you not see it? He's really gotten to you," he said, his voice thick with sadness. "Adelin, this isn't you. You used to be so sweet. You never used to talk to me this way. What happened to you?"

Addy opened the door and entered her room. She turned to face him, a hand on the door as she looked Renard in the eye. "She went through living Tahrn and back, that's what. And it wasn't you who risked his life to bring me out of it!" She slammed the door, causing her lady in waiting, Tyra, and two other girls who'd been preparing her bath, to jump. With a furious twist of the iron key left in the lock, she locked the door and stormed to her bed. She pressed her face into one of the many pillows crowded against the headboard and screamed.

Chapter 65

The Fluff Always Wins

"Sir Tamous, please see to it that Sir Ulwick is taken care of," Lord Fenforde said, after Addy and Strider left.

"Yes, my lord."

Both knights bowed and left. Addy's mother excused herself as well, while Elayis stayed to listen to the conversation held between the Ranger and his father. As the heir, it was common for him to sit in on such meetings, to better learn the role he was expected to fill.

When the doors closed behind Lady Fenforde, Lord Fenforde leaned forward, fingers steepling as he rested his elbows on the table.

"We have known each other for many years now, Kyre," he began. "I trust your skills and your candid nature when giving me information and I ask that you continue to show that same level of professionalism now."

"You want to know about Strider," Kyre said. He'd expected Lord Fenforde to lay into him for destroying the buildings in the courtyard, so the change of subject was welcome.

"Yes. Tell me everything you know about him."

Kyre pulled up a chair and sat in it, propping his feet up on the corner of the study desk.

"I only know what has been told over the years," he began. "Not all of it is entirely reliable. But the heart of the story hasn't changed."

Lord Fenforde waited for him to go on, eyes watching him like a hawk.

"His father was Ruther Longstride, one of the many ummanie orphans taken in by The Sanctuary. He grew up to be an exceptional Ranger. One of our best at the time. The story goes that he ended up marrying a yulie woman he'd been asked to guard, who acted as an ambassador for her people.

"Strider was their only child. I don't know what happened after that. The three vanished for almost three decades before Ruther and his son returned to The Wilds. Ruther had a cabin there before he left and ultimately married. He trained Strider as his apprentice, giving the man his felaris feather when he completed his training.

Though he has a felaris feather, he isn't a Ranger. He never took the oath binding him to our secrets. He's registered as our oldest apprentice, though."

"And the leaders at the time let him get away with not taking your oath?"

"They worked out a deal with the council after aiding the Rangers in defeating a powerful threat. A contract that, if broken, would allow us to seek retribution."

"And what were the terms?"

"Strider was never to leave The Wilds. He was never to do anything to dishonor the Ranger name. He was not to allow anyone to learn that he isn't a Ranger, and if someone did call him a Ranger, he was to act as if he were one and assist them in any way he could, as Rangers are expected to."

"And he's broken every one of those oaths?"

"He claims it was your daughter who started the rumor of him being a Dark Ranger. Though it really doesn't matter. Our leaders were willing to look the other way when he left The Wilds because he was tracking the man who killed his father. But now they want him brought in and tried."

"If it's true that he helped my daughter, he hasn't gone back on his word to act in the capacity of a Ranger. And Adelin admitted to starting the rumor to spite him," Lord Fenforde remarked. "It would seem whoever constructed the oath bound his tongue as well. He wouldn't have been able to deny these rumors about him being a Dark Ranger without breaking at least one more oath. Whoever did this wanted him to fail."

"It wouldn't have mattered, had he remained in The Wilds."

"But your leaders knew he had and left him to wander."

"Because he'd been keeping to the shadows this entire time."

"And had he not been helping my daughter, he never would have been outed."

Kyre gave an exasperated sigh. Like most Rangers, he cared little for the dealings of nobles and their politics.

"The contract was designed specifically to encourage him to remain in The Wilds, away from people. He knew what he was agreeing to. He knowingly broke that contract, and he will answer for his crimes."

"And what would his punishment be?"

Kyre waved the comment away dismissively. "That'll be for the council to decide. The fact that he risked so much to help your daughter will probably convince them to be more lenient, but he won't be allowed to continue as he has."

"Do you believe he is innocent of these allegations?"

"I do. From the stories I have been told of Strider, he isn't one to go back on a job he agreed to do." Kyre leaned back in his chair, hands clasped behind his head. "He was a tolver, Usereth Famiera's word for assassin, and was ruthlessly efficient. He'd racked up quite the kill count, probably would've become one of their generals had he not had a falling out with them when he'd rescued his father. Thank Ky'arie that never happened." — Kyre paused as he scratched at the scab forming over the cut on his neck —

"Even still, he refused to reveal their secrets to us when he returned with his father. The fact he'd rescued one of our own, and his father's reputation, kept him from being imprisoned and questioned. If he was your daughter's kidnapper, she wouldn't be here right now. I don't know how your daughter managed it, but she's earned his loyalty. He did everything within his power to get her home."

"Which leaves me in the uncomfortable position of explaining to our king that King Elias has probably betrayed us." Lord Fenforde sighed. "Have you heard anything from Elyphain or the others yet?"

Kyre shook his head. "They've no doubt been investigating King Elias' claim. We Rangers aren't the most trusting bunch. We like to know where and how people have come by their information. Good old Elias dismissed the Rangers in the same section of Denmahr that they took Adelin through. An odd coincidence, isn't it? No one was to know of the Rangers leaving the kingdom yet. It lines up too perfectly."

"Maybe you should be the one to tell King Ranmous," Lord Fenforde suggested, with a wry smile. "He can't do anything to you, beyond requesting you be removed from his kingdom."

Kyre laughed. "We Rangers are used to delivering bad news. I figure the king expects it at this point whenever one of us pops in to have a little chat."

Then his face grew serious. "After all of this is over, I will need to take Strider back to The Sanctuary to stand trial. You'll need to ensure Addy doesn't cause any trouble."

"I'll be sure to keep her out of your way."

Kyre leaned forward in his seat, a mischievous smile tugging at the corners of his lips. "Speaking of trouble, we might've kicked a hornet's nest by letting so many people learn of Greer's abilities."

Lord Fenforde leaned back in his chair. "That was the plan. Someone in that meeting is our traitor. The wolf's abilities will force them to show their hand, or they'll be discovered come tomorrow."

"You expect them to go after Greer and Strider?"

"I do."

Kyre stood, wincing as his injuries protested. "I pity the person who tries to attack that man."

"High praise coming from you."

Kyre gave a wry smile. "It wasn't a compliment."

Strider followed Tymott and Curthis, as they led him and Greer down the hall, committing each turn to memory. They passed decorative tapestries depicting scenes of legends or ancestors performing heroic acts. Armor and heirlooms perched atop ornate wooden displays sat in alcoves. The metal gleamed in the candlelight, polished to a mirror finish by dedicated servants.

As noble households went, the Fenforde's boasted a rich array of items. But nothing looked new. The styles reflected older generations. The decor would've been out of style when he was a part of the Userith Femiera. Either the Fenfordes hadn't bothered to keep up with the latest fashion, or things had circled back around.

Weariness creeped into his bones, like a starved animal circling a dying fire, waiting for the last spark to die before pouncing. The keep was relatively warm, but the sensation of frost prickled across his skin, sending the sensation of thousands of needles up and down his body.

He fought against the desire to collapse on the spot. Using the distraction of memorizing their path through the halls to keep him focused, he caught Tymott and Curthis casting quick glances over their shoulders as they walked. He'd not bothered to pull up his hood after leaving the study.

"Do you have something you want to say?" Strider said, when he caught Tymott trying to sneak another look.

The young man stiffened. "I do have a question, actually," he said tentatively.

Strider gave a dismissive gesture, his elbow protesting the movement. "Then ask instead of stealing glances like I'm an outcast meant to be shunned."

Tymott didn't rise to the bait. "Is it true yulie can meld into trees?"

"Meld into trees?" Strider parroted. He hadn't heard that one before. He looked down at Greer who smiled up at him. The ummanie had many myths about yulie, many of them derogatory, all meant to breed further distrust and hatred for their captors. Strider likely wouldn't have cared, had they not directed the same vitriol toward him and his mother. He preferred to be hated for what he'd done. His mother never deserved a thing.

"Yes; sort of like how one would slip into a pool of water, but a tree," Tymott clarified. "It was in an old book about yulie I found. I take it from your reaction, that's incorrect?"

Tymott's tone wasn't condescending, and Strider didn't sense any intent to insult or demean. He was a curious ummanie trying to navigate and understand a sensitive topic. Strider decided to humor him.

"The author probably meant *liely'pine* and misunderstood what the yulie were doing," he explained. Unsurprised that the ummanie author didn't bother to research or seek to understand the magic being performed. They likely never thought to ask a yulie, though depending on the time the author was alive that might not have been possible. However, speaking with the ravack or even the Rangers would've provided a clearer understanding of the practice. "In yulie, *liely'pine* loosely means 'to walk unseen paths.'"

"Unseen paths?" Curthis asked, entering the conversation for the first time.

"Some people call them the trails of the gods, or god trails, and believe they are places where the gods have walked. They're, for lack of a better word, paths that one can slip into, traveling great distances in a short time, unseen by others." Strider stopped to observe a painting depicting a man on horseback pursuing a buck across a field, bow drawn. The artist's brushstrokes were hardly noticeable, lost in the soft pink and gold hues of twilight among field and flower. He didn't show it, but he needed to gather himself again as that lurking weariness tested the boundaries of his will.

"Some people. Does that mean others are able to use these trails?" Tymott said, drawing Strider's attention away from the painting. He'd come to stand beside Greer, stroking the di'horvith's head.

Strider considered Tymott for a moment as they began walking again. He was quick to catch things. "If a magic user who knows the art stays in an area long enough, they can discover and use them. Those without magic, do occasionally fall into them by accident."

Curthis slowed to walk beside Strider. "Can people use these trails to enter our keep?"

Strider recalled Addy mentioning that he was one of her guards. Like him, Curthis had a mind geared toward spotting potential dangers. It made sense that he'd be concerned about the risk of enemies popping up unannounced, or escaping before Greer outed them. Though she was adamant her brother wouldn't betray her, Strider was less trusting. Greer was at ease around the brothers, but that did little to prove innocence.

"Those who originally built old castles like these wove spells and wards into their walls preventing paths from forming. They're also resistant to most magic." It'd take a group focusing their magic together to trouble this castle's walls. Defending against physical attacks was a different matter. Most didn't want to risk placing more enchantments into the walls. Having all your hard work crumble to ash, or worse explode, was too great a gamble. So, they relied upon their design to fend off physical attacks.

"It's incredible the allied armies were able to defeat the yulie in the Liberating Wars," Curthis said. "Knowing the yulie could appear at any time, attacking without warning before retreating."

"It helped that they had yulie who sided with them," Strider grunted. It was becoming difficult to keep up the energy required to continue the conversation. His mind and body were reaching their limit. His thoughts drifted as he became aware of the fact he needed to walk. Needed to put one foot in front of the other. He was content to let the two brothers carry on the conversation without him.

"Yulie didn't side against their own people," Curthis argued.

It was Tymott who answered, sparing Strider the energy needed to make a scathing remark. "They did, actually." He'd stayed walking ahead of Strider but now slowed to better engage in the conversation. "Many were helping ummanie escape slavery before the war started; in secret, of course."

"I don't remember being taught that," Curthis said, his brow knitting in confusion.

"You weren't," Tymott said. "I learned it by going through the old history books in the library."

Curthis shook his head, as if he couldn't quite come to terms with the idea that information would've been altered or hidden from them. "Why wouldn't our tutors teach us this?"

"To erase it from history," Strider cut in. The group paused in the hall before a thick wooden door. He guessed it was their destination, by the way the brothers turned toward it. Greer sat watching them, as they continued their conversation.

"He's right. Not only do they not teach that yulie helped, but they also erased all the ummanie that sided against us from history," Tymott said, his tone bordering on excitement as he spoke about the obscure history he'd learned. "I can't pronounce his yulie name, but in the books I read, there was an ummanie man who we called The Butcher. His treatment of captured allies was so horrible, men would rather die upon their own sword than be taken alive by him."

Curthis looked mortified. "Why would an ummanie fight for the yulie?"

"He had a good life, from what I could find," Tymott said, his earlier cheer replaced with disgust. "He bred some of the finest slave stock, as they called it, to sell to the well-to-do yulie families."

"By Takari, that is..." Curthis said, invoking the life god's name as he searched for a word to express his disdain. "Monstrous."

Silence enveloped the three, as the two younger men dwelled upon the horrors of the past. Strider was impressed with Tymott's knowledge. Many people didn't take the time to delve through dusty old tomes, learning unpleasant truths about where their people came from. His earlier curiosity, though potentially insulting, had been in good faith. He wanted to learn what was true and what was false.

"As much as I'd like to ask more questions," Tymott said, gesturing toward the door they'd stopped before. "We're here, and Curthis and I have other duties to attend to."

Curthis opened the door for Strider just as two guards walked into view.

"If you need anything, ask the guards," Tymott said, as Strider passed him and entered the room. "They'll be instructed to ensure you get whatever you need."

The Hunter gave a curt nod of acknowledgement before Curthis shut the door behind him. He listened as the bolt of the lock slid into place with a thud. He could hear Tymott and Curthis giving instructions to the men set to guard his door before leaving. Tymott hadn't followed through with his desire to spar with him and for that he was grateful. He didn't have the strength to fight either of them. Their earlier conversation had drained a lot out of him.

Turning his back to the door, Strider took in the room. It was a modest space. Ten feet by ten feet with a small bed against the wall and a couple of armoires and dressers for storage. The room was either a privileged servant's quarters or a room reserved for less distinguished guests. It made little difference to him. All that mattered was that it was bigger than the cell. Two small windows sat on either side of the fireplace, carved from the thick stone wall. They were too small for an adult to squeeze through, however. The only way out was the locked door behind him.

The lock was sturdy, but it wouldn't pose a problem. The guards didn't worry him either. What kept him here was Addy. She still wasn't safe, despite being behind the walls of her castle. There were still people that posed a threat to her, and he wouldn't leave until he was certain they were dealt with. He just needed to get out of this room. Placing his quiver and bow beside the bed, he casually walked about the room, checking the drawers and armoires. They were empty. He moved to the windows, inspecting them. Running a hand down the stone, his head canted to one side as he considered using magic to widen it.

A low, unhappy rumbling sound came from behind him. He turned to see Greer watching him, a knowing look on his face.

"How do you suggest we get out?" Strider asked him softly. "We can't get rid of the guards. They'll be relieved of their post. It'd be rather suspicious if the men weren't there."

Greer gave a sniff and shook his head so hard his entire body shook. He steadied himself before padding toward the bed. The di'horvith stopped before it and looked back at Strider expectantly. The Hunter shook his head.

"Now isn't the time to sleep."

Greer gave a low chuff and a groan. He turned back to face the

Hunter before bouncing toward the bed, giving him another meaningful look.

"You realize they're likely planning to use us as bait to draw out the traitors."

Greer cocked his head before flicking it back toward the bed, much like a horse or dog would flick their head in play. Strider sighed.

"Of course, you don't care. You could learn Chaos himself was coming to kill you and you'd still be stupidly happy about everything."

Greer snapped his jaws together, letting out a string of yowling barks as he walked halfway to Strider, then bounded back toward the bed. He stopped and looked at him pleadingly.

"Sleep if you want," Strider told him, turning back to the window. "I'm going to see about making sure we survive the night."

The fireplace flu was too small for a man to fit through, and that amount of stone would be too much to manipulate quietly. Leaving the window as his best option. He could manipulate the stone so it was wide enough for him and Greer to escape through, should things go south. The Hunter would arm the door with physical or magical traps if he weren't afraid Addy might decide to barge in.

He'd taught her well enough to devise a way inside this room after she snuck away from her supervisors. His eyes drifted to the fireplace again. If he didn't arm the door, he could- his cloak jerked back violently. He stumbled backward, nearly being pulled off his feet, as his cloak strangled him.

"Greer!" he choked out, as the massive wolf continued to tug furiously, using his increased weight and strength to pull the spluttering Hunter toward the bed.

Strider grasped at the clasp of his cloak, struggling to undo it as he staggered backward. Then, with a hard jerk, Greer leaped onto the bed, yanking Strider down on the comforter. Gasping for breath, the man finally undid the clasp, freeing himself. He coughed as he propped himself up on his elbows before being forced back down as a large furry weight lay across his chest.

"Get off!" Strider growled weakly, as his breath was forced from his lungs. "Chaos ridden mutt."

His arms were pinned beneath Greer, who merely dug in further with a groan. Strider cursed at him again as he struggled beneath the greater weight of the wolf. But he couldn't get enough leverage to force the animal off him. He had flashbacks of being stuck in the forest and let out another stream of curses.

"I am going to turn you into a cloak!" Strider threatened, his words quickly losing their bite, as exhaustion swept over him like a wave of bricks. "Or maybe just a rug."

Greer let out a grumbling noise as he lay his head down on the bed, one large brown eye watching Strider. The Hunter didn't struggle for long, as the last of his strength failed him. Forced to sit alone with only Greer, Strider lost the will needed to carry on his charade. He found it extremely difficult to lift his head or wiggle his fingers. A terrible chill ran through him, causing him to shudder.

Weariness drained the fight out of him, and he found his mind drifting to nothing as he stared up at the ceiling. He couldn't seem to get it to focus on anything the longer he lay there. His chest still hurt. It hadn't stopped burning since his fight with Kyre. It took everything in him to breathe normally and act as if all was well in front of everyone.

All he'd wanted to do that entire meeting and walk to this room was drop dead. Only his stubbornness kept him moving, kept him acting like all was well. Had Greer not forced him to stop, he would've pushed himself even harder that night. Now, he didn't have the strength left to fight off a butterfly, much less an attacker.

With the amount of ice he felt in his body, he didn't understand why he wasn't drifting toward the darkness. Why the bitter thoughts were absent; all he felt was cold, weak, heavy, and so tired. His thoughts were a muddled mess; a tangle of string dumped into a muddy puddle. Every thought train dissolved quickly after it started, and he was unsure of what it had even been or why he'd thought of whatever it was.

The only thing that remained constant was Greer, a feeling he was vaguely aware of. His body was nothing but a fuzzy haze. He couldn't get it to do anything. Was he even sure it was his body anymore? He didn't know and didn't care. Finally, he decided to lay on the bed for a moment to regain his strength, then sort it all out afterward.

Greer continued to watch Strider closely as he slipped into unconsciousness. The di'horvith gave a worried sigh, unsure of what to do. He fought so hard to keep his brother here, but each time Strider used his magic, he could feel him slipping further away. His soul was fracturing before his eyes, and Greer could do nothing about it. His plan had been to get Strider to form an attachment to Addy, so he'd have another reason to live. But it seemed his plan had worked too well, and the Hunter was determined to destroy himself to ensure her safety.

Greer curled around Strider, trying to get as close as he could to the man, hoping that his presence would be enough to keep him here this time. Though the Hunter hid it well, his soul was extremely weak. His brother was dying, and Greer knew it was his fault.

Chapter 66
Mother & Daughter

"What'd Renard do to make you so angry?" Tyra asked, as she approached Addy, her tan dress swishing around her ankles.

Addy made a frustrated noise as she sat up. "He's being a condescending *chwyte*."

Tyra put her hands on her hips and huffed. "Well, that ain't right, treating her ladyship so when she's just survived a harrowing ordeal." Her lips curled upwards in a mischievous smirk. "Want me to go at him with the bed warmer, milady?"

Addy laughed as she moved toward the edge of the bed. "Oh Tyra, I missed you."

"I missed you as well, milady." The two young women embraced, Tyra giving one of her fiercest hugs that threatened to crack one of Addy's ribs. "The castle hasn't been the same without you."

Tyra was a year older than Addy, though they were practically the same height. Unlike some anumi, she bore no signs of her heritage. Except her hair that started a rich golden brown at the top before darkening to a near black at the ends in a beautiful ombre. She'd told Addy the reason she didn't have ears or a tail, was because she'd completely bonded with her animal spirit that bestowed her with shifting powers.

She didn't fancy announcing to the world she was anumi by keeping her bear's ears on display when she could hide it. "Makes for quite a shock when fellas refuse to leave me alone, it does," she'd laugh. Even her deep brown eyes gave no hint of the animal within; only her bone crushing strength when she wrapped Addy in a hug hinted at the power she held.

"Now, you must regale us with your misadventures while we clean you up," Tyra said, leading Addy to the steaming tub. "Is that man really the one who made off with you?"

"He's the one who saved me," Addy corrected. "Him and Greer."

"Is that *the* wolf he has with 'im?" Tyra asked, having heard the horror stories that ballooned until it spoke of Greer slaughtering a platoon of men. "They passed by me in the halls. Thought I'd walked straight into an old ghost story. 'Bout had a heart attack, I did."

Addy laughed, as she let the maids and Tyra help her undress. "That's Greer, yes. Don't let his size fool you, he's the gentlest creature I've ever met."

"And what of the man with him?" one maid asked, as she helped Addy into the bath. She was a similar age to Addy and Tyra; Wynn, Addy believed her name was. "He looked scarier than Greer."

"I thought he was rather handsome," the other maid said. She was twice as old as Addy and Tyra and had served the Fenfordes for years. Iya, Addy recalled.

The ladies laughed, Addy most of all, as she pictured Iya trying to flirt with the grumpy Hunter. "He's pricklier than a pincushion, but deep down he's also kind."

"Hard to get then," Iya said, as she washed Addy's hair in rose water. "I like a challenge."

"You know he's half yulie, that one?" Tyra reminded her, surprising Addy at how fast the rumors had spread among the staff. A spark of defensiveness for Strider blossomed within her, but it cooled when Iya spoke.

"He rescued our ladyship," Iya said. "Such nobility is hard to find in a man."

"You fancy he'd rescue you from brigands?" Wynn laughed. "Sweep you off your feet like a knight rescuing a princess?"

"If he rescued me from brigands, *I'd* be the one sweeping *him* off his feet."

They all laughed. They helped Addy out of her bath, wrapping her in a large, soft towel. Tyra used a smaller towel to dry her hair while Iya and Wynn brought her sleeping gowns to choose from. She picked a dark blue one made of silk.

She'd forgotten the last time she'd worn such fine material. She savored the smooth, cool feel of it on her skin. At a gesture from Tyra, Addy sat on a cushioned stool before a three-mirrored vanity, while her lady in waiting brushed her hair. Wooden roses and vines framed each mirror, painstakingly carved with vivid detail. Then painted with great care until each yellow petal and green leaf looked like they were plucked from the garden. A knock came at the door.

"Come in." Addy called.

Lady Fenforde entered the room, her crimson dress swishing against the wooden floor.

"Mother!" Addy said, surprised. "You're not in the meeting with father?"

"Your father knows where I stand on the matter," Lady Fenforde said, turning to Tyra and the maids. She gave a soft wave of her hand. "Thank you for tending to my daughter; you're dismissed for the evening."

The three women curtsied and left the room. Lady Fenforde moved to the vanity, picked up the brush Tyra left, and sat at the stool she'd recently occupied. She took her daughter's hair in gentle hands and began brushing. "I wanted to see how you were doing."

"I'm doing okay," Addy told her. "I'm glad to be home."

"We're all glad you're home." Her mother wrapped her arms around her shoulders. "Your father and I have been sick with worry. We were afraid we'd lost you forever." Her voice was thick with barely suppressed tears. Addy placed a hand on her mother's, doing her best not to cry as well.

Lady Fenforde withdrew her arms, patting her daughter on the shoulder before she resumed brushing her hair. "I know everything might be overwhelming right now, but I wanted you to know you can talk to me whenever you're ready."

"Thank you," Addy said. Her chest was tight, making it hard to breathe. Her throat felt constricted, and it took several breaths before she felt at ease once more. They sat in silence. Her mother patiently working tangles from her hair like she'd done when she was a child. They hadn't sat like this for a long time. As she'd grown older, her mother had let her have her space, allowing Tyra and others to take over. She didn't realize how much she'd missed these moments until now.

"Mother, can I ask you something?" she said.

"Of course," Lady Fenforde replied.

"Why didn't you want me to learn to fight?"

"I've told you before-"

"Because fighting is men's work," Addy cut her off. "Why does Rachia think women can't fight? I thought women always held the throne?"

Her mother paused, her hands resting atop the brush as it sat on her lap. "It's not that the people of Rachia think women cannot fight. We were always taught that women were the perfect representation of K'yarie herself. Beings of grace, and if blessed, magic."

"So, women are worshipped?"

"In a way. To dirty our hands by fighting is beneath us. It is the honor of men to lay down their lives to protect us with a blade, and if able, we protect them with spells taught to us by the Syliceon."

"But you don't use magic," Addy said.

"I wasn't gifted in the arts, no," her mother admitted, a whisper of sadness in her voice. "It is why I was permitted to marry outside of Rachia, in order to strengthen the bond between the two kingdoms. They revere women with magic in my old kingdom. They wouldn't be expected to marry lesser men."

Addy felt the heat of anger color her cheeks. "But father isn't lesser."

"No, he isn't. He is a wonderful man. It didn't take me long to realize my people's views were wrong about non-Rachian men." Her mother smiled, her gaze drifting off the side as if she were reliving fond memories.

"Is it possible?" Addy started, turning to face her mother. "That other teachings from your country were also wrong?"

"You mean the belief that a lady shouldn't fight?" her mother smiled. "Perhaps it is a misguided belief. Especially for those unable to use magic."

Addy took her mother's hand, hope and excitement building

within her. "I want to keep learning to fight, and I want you to learn with me."

A look of surprise flashed across her mother's face, chased by a flurry of other emotions as she considered her daughter's request. "I'm alright with you continuing your training," she said finally.

"Will you train with me?" Addy pressed. She didn't want her mother ever put in a situation like what she'd been forced to endure. The gods had smiled upon her and sent Strider to help her, but would her mother be so lucky? It was a risk she didn't want to take.

"I'll have to think about it," Lady Fenforde said, patting her daughter's hand.

Addy smiled as she leaned over to give her mother a hug. "Thank you, mother."

Lady Fenforde returned her daughter's embrace. "You're welcome."

Chapter 67
The Dangers Of A Di'horvith

R enard left Adelin shortly after Lady Fenforde went to bed. He quietly slipped away, unnoticed as usual. He now stood in one of the secluded storerooms of the castle. Another figure stood in the shadows.

"And you believe this 'wolf' can find us, when a Ranger couldn't?" the figure asked skeptically.

"I saw it with my own eyes," Renard said. "Either that wolf is magical, or the man with him has some sort of spell or skill that allows him to see through falsehood. Yulie possess strange, dark magic and he could be pretending the wolf can route lies. Either way, we need to act before we're discovered."

The figure thought for a moment before nodding. "Moving the plan up won't be a problem. My men are ready."

"Be sure to kill the Hunter first. Once that is done, we can see to the family. Make it look like it was the Hunter's doing, and that we subdued him, but not before he killed them."

"I'll send two men to deal with the man and his wolf."

"Make it four."

"And what of the daughter?"

"I'll take care of her. She won't get in the way. Whatever you do, you're not to harm her, or you'll be added to the death count."

The shadowy figure grunted, then turned away.

Renard watched him go, waited several minutes to ensure no one saw them together, then left the storeroom. His heart pounded in his chest as he strode back to wait outside Adelin's room, only to find the door ajar. His heart skipped a beat as he rushed inside to find the room empty. Locating a maid, he questioned her and learned that Addy's mother had dismissed them for the night. Cursing under his breath, he hurried off to catch up with his lady before it was too late.

Greer heard something that caused his lips to twitch in a silent growl. The quiet movement of feet, the sound of steel cutting flesh and bodies being dragged away as the scent of blood tainted the air. He licked Strider's face, trying to rouse him. But the Hunter remained dead to the world. He pressed harder, but still didn't get a response. Finally, he nipped his brother's ear and tugged. Nothing.

The Hunter's mind was too deep into unconsciousness for the pain to reach it. The weariness of his soul dominated his body. Greer let out a quiet whine. Grabbing the Hunter's shirt, Greer dragged him off the bed. Strider fell limply to the floor, still not waking. The di'horvith pulled him into the darkness under the bed.

Greer wiggled out from underneath the bed and crept toward the door. He wrinkled his nose at the powerful stench of blood. Looking back, he could make out the still form of Strider hidden in the shadows beneath the bed. Licking his nose, he took up a position on one side of the door, then waited.

The people outside moved quietly, but not so silently that the di'horvith could not hear them. Their scent came closer, stained with the smell of blood. There were four of them. A key slid into the lock. A soft click filled the room. The intruders eased the door open.

Four men spilled into the room. Their eyes immediately went to the bed, expecting to see a sleeping figure there. None of them saw Strider hidden in the shadows beneath it, their eyes unable to pierce the dark. Seeing the bed empty, they paused.

Greer, having stood where the opened door would hide his presence, attacked. Without a sound, he jumped onto the back of the first man, knocking him to the ground. White fangs flashed as his jaws clamped around the man's neck. His powerful jaws drove his fangs deep into his flesh as he jerked his head to the side and pulled up. Bones snapped and fangs tore through arteries, killing the soldier with shocking speed. He never cried out. The other three men turned in time to watch the massive wolf kill their companion.

The second man barely had time to react as he raised his blade. He struck out at the wolf charging toward him. Metal sliced through the air as the massive animal predicted the attack and ducked aside. In the same motion, Greer spun, his hip slamming into the side of the man's knee. The weight of the enormous wolf caused it to snap unnaturally, buckling the attacker's leg. The soldier screamed in pain as his knee broke. He fell to the other one, his hands grabbing the damaged joint as he sobbed.

Greer darted out of reach of the other men and their swords. He snarled at them as he stood in the doorway, his lips stained crimson, eyes seeming to glow as they reflected the moonlight that filtered through the windows. He let out a booming howl, snapping his fangs together in a challenge.

The traitor with the injured knee couldn't do more than hobble on one leg as he cursed the wolf, tears streaming down his face. Grabbing his sword, he threw it, trying to impale the creature. Greer stepped out of the way and let out another loud howl as the blade clattered uselessly to the floor.

"He'll wake the entire castle!" one of them hissed. "Kill him before he does."

"You two look for the owner," another man ordered. "He couldn't have gotten out. I'll take care of the dog."

Greer continued to snarl. The fighter brandished his weapon and slowly began walking forward. Greer backed up out into the hall, still sounding his howling alarm as he snapped his jaws menacingly. The man and wolf vanished, leaving the two soldiers alone.

"Search the closets," the injured man ordered, through clenched teeth. He clung to the bed frame, tears still streaming down his face as he fought off further sobs of pain.

"You really think someone could hide in one of those?" the other man scoffed. "He's likely cowering under the bed like a scared little girl, hoping his wolf will chase the monsters away. I thought people said he's some sort of terrifying Dark Ranger?"

"Rumors are often wrong. Now hurry up. The boss wants us to kill him quickly."

The uninjured man had stooped to look underneath the bed

when the screaming started. Cries of pure abject terror pierced the night, like the screams of a dying soul, as a demon ripped it to shreds. It stopped, cut off mid-scream, leaving a silent void in its wake.

"Wyath?" the injured man called out.

Click, click, click, click. The sound of something walking across the stone was the only answer. They both waited as the footsteps came closer. Click, click, click, click. The form of the wolf appeared in the doorway, light gray fur dyed crimson, as he snarled low and menacingly. The fur that wasn't soaked red appeared to glimmer with an unnatural blue undertone as the beast stood out against the darkness, eyes glinting silver in the moonlight.

His paws left bloody footprints where he tracked through the blood of his fallen victim. He snarled again at the two men. Only one still held his sword. It shook as he pointed it at the wolf who embodied every tale, every horror story he'd heard of the demons who stalked the night.

As he stood there, staring at Greer, he felt a powerful presence force its way into his soul. It told him to drop his sword and run. He would live if he took his companion and left. If he stayed, he would die. The wolf moved into the room, circling toward the windows, as he left the door open for them to flee. He snarled again, louder, ears pinned back, head lowered as the moonlight silhouetted his great form. He was massive, and he was going to kill them. The traitor's will shattered, and he dropped his blade and fled.

"Oi!" the wounded intruder shouted after him, but his companion didn't stop as he bolted out the door and down the hall. Alone and unable to fight, the final man began trying to drag himself from the room. Fangs clamped down on his remaining good leg, jerking him back inside. He cried out, nails scraping against stone as he flailed uselessly.

Greer growled again. The soldier froze as hot breath brushed against his ear. He could smell the blood on the demon's breath as he growled low, the glint of his fangs visible in his peripheral vision. The soldier tried to move again, but the growl grew louder. He stopped moving, sobbing, as the monster stood over him.

"Please," he begged, whatever god would listen to him. "Please!"

No god answered him. They all stood silent as he prayed.

The sound of Greer's snarls and the quiet crying of someone slowly registered in the mind of the Hunter. As his mind withdrew from the darkness it had hidden within, his consciousness noted the smell. The scent of blood struck Strider like a brick to the nose, and he sat up. His head slammed against the wooden underside of the bed. He cursed and clutched his forehead. Blinking, he looked around him, disoriented.

Memories of the day before came trickling back. He recalled passing out on top of the bed, not underneath it. Greer snarled again and a fresh wave of desperate sobs and mutterings started. The metallic stench of blood was thick in the air. Concerned, Strider peered out from underneath the bed. He saw the lifeless form of a swordsman laying in a pool of blood. Shifting further, he saw another man lying on the ground, and the bloody paws of Greer, as he stood over him.

Loosening his sword from its sheath, he rolled quietly out from under the bed. Sitting up, he attempted to stand, but found that his own legs wouldn't hold him. He felt weak and for a moment he found his vision going dark as he nearly passed out again, his soul nearly losing touch with his body. He was teetering on the edge.

Taking a moment to steady his breathing, Strider eventually found the strength to stand. He crept toward the man Greer was growling at, fangs barely an inch from his ear. Strider took in the bloody scene around him and guessed what had happened. He crouched before the fighter so he could see him. Greer stopped snarling as he eyed Strider with worry.

The soldier, hearing footsteps, risked a glance up to stare into the cold golden eyes of the Hunter.

"Please," he begged, "Get your wolf off of me."

Strider cocked his head to the side, as he regarded the man with the same amount of pity he'd give a rock stuck in Copper's hoof.

"We're going to chat, first."

Chapter 68
A Gut Feeling

Addy's slippered feet made no noise as she padded silently down the corridor of the Keep, taking care to avoid as many eyes as possible. She held in her arms a linen cloth. Inside was a pie, bread, and smoked meat of some sort she'd pilfered from the kitchen. She picked her way quietly through the halls on her way to Strider's room. She suspected no one had thought to offer him and Greer any food after being confined to their room. Even if they had, she was sure Greer would be happy for more, as most dogs usually were.

She hadn't quite worked out how she would get rid of the guards long enough to pick the lock, or what she'd do when she actually wanted to leave. But she'd work that plan out when she came to it. If she were lucky, the men would be ones she could order around, or threaten into doing what she said. No doubt her father would've told them not to let her see Strider, and she was going to his room late in the evening. It'd have been easier to manage if Tevin was the one guarding him. But they wouldn't trust him for such a task.

She'd expected to have to fight Renard as well. But he wasn't at her door like he ought to be. Her anger toward him dulled, when she realized that what she'd said may have hurt him enough that he needed to walk it off. He'd always been sensitive, and she'd dealt a low blow. It wasn't his fault he hadn't been there to protect her. But what he'd said and how he'd treated her was also uncalled for. They'd talk tomorrow, once Greer had rooted out the traitors.

Keeping to the edges of the hall where the shadows were plentiful in the dim candlelight, Addy moved through her home with ease. Few servants wandered the halls, having completed their daily duties. The castle had long since fallen into its nighttime routine.

Still, there were some servants on duty and plenty of guards she had to avoid. She'd worn a dark blue silken nightdress to blend into the shadows more easily than white would. The smooth material felt heavenly against her skin. While she missed some aspects of her trousers, she loved being back in a dress.

Though far simpler than a day dress, she enjoyed the frilly attire. Though it provided some interesting challenges when sneaking about. The fabric liked to flow around her and swish, for instance. If she had to do any sort of jumping or quick movement, she'd find her skirt flying up to an indecent length or tangling around her legs.

She'd have to look into getting some dresses with slits up the side, or at least in a material she could easily rip in a pinch. If she wore more practical undergarments, she could easily run without worrying about showing more skin than she felt comfortable. A petticoat wouldn't suit what she needed. Maybe some trousers…

She smiled. Her mother would probably faint if she knew Addy was thinking of such things. A proper lady would never! Until now, she would've balked at the idea, but she'd changed. For the better, Addy thought. Though it was becoming clear that her parents didn't think so. Though, thanks to her temper, she'd never been quite ladylike enough for her mother, and she was never sure how to amount to this vision her mother had of a proper young lady.

She wasn't sure her mother knew because she could never give her sound advice or guidance other than telling her to try harder or do better. She hoped her mother would agree to train with her and that they might begin to understand each other better.

At least Strider gave guidance on how to do better, as short and prickly as it was. She wondered if he had to try to be the way he was, or if it came naturally. As much as he grated on her nerves, she realized he'd taken far more time and care to teach her than any of her tutors. He never pronounced her a lost cause, though he certainly became irritated with her for giving up easily. He always told her she was the only one holding herself back, not that she was incapable or inept.

When she'd brought up the fact that she couldn't physically surpass a man, he'd offered her ways to work around it by fighting smart, before finally telling her of a magical method, if she'd only try. She'd been kidnapped, and he had taught her how to escape and defend herself. She had a tendency to overlook things and rush headlong into situations.

He constantly made her stop and think, to slow down and observe. For every problem she faced, he taught her a way to overcome it. A way to rescue herself rather than relying on someone else to do the rescuing. Though hopefully now she'd never need to use those skills.

She was home, and she doubted the villains behind her kidnapping would make any rash decisions. She wondered if they even knew where she was at this moment. Her ladies-in-waiting thought she was in her room tending to some business, and she'd taken great care to avoid being seen. She could creep about her home like a quiet house ghost, and no one would be the wiser.

Addy turned and began making her way down the hall that led to Strider's room. She was passing across an open space within an intersecting hallway when the sound of hurried footsteps on stone reached her. She had no time to duck back into the shadows before Renard came barreling around the corner. He spotted her standing in the middle of the intersection.

"Lady Fenforde!" he cried out.

"Chwite!" Addy uttered the tahrvin curse word. She didn't know what it meant, but it was Strider's favorite and seemed fitting for the situation. She straightened as he came closer, her chin held up in the rigid posture of a noblewoman.

"Yes, Renard?"

"Lady Fenforde." Renard came to a stop before her, his breath coming in heavy gasps. "You shouldn't be wandering the halls alone so late at night. The men responsible for your kidnapping are still loose. What if they tried to grab you?"

"I thought you were convinced that Strider was my kidnapper?"

"I am, but he couldn't have possibly worked alone," Renard quickly amended, regaining control of his breathing. "Let me escort you back to your room, where it is safe."

"I will, after I have visited with Strider."

"My lady, that is most unwise, and uncouth. An unmarried noblewoman, meeting with a scoundrel like that in his room at night? Imagine the scandal; the taint on your parent's name!"

"I am his employer," Addy snapped. "It is perfectly fine for an employer to meet with those she has employed. Seeing as he is confined to his room, I can't very well summon him."

She moved down the hall, hastening her steps. Now that her cover was blown, she didn't bother to stay in the shadows. Instead, she walked in the middle of the hall for all to see. Not that there were any eyes to observe her passing. She and Renard were the only two souls in the hallway.

"My lady, he is likely asleep."

"He'll just have to wake up," Addy snapped, shifting the burden in her arms a little.

"What is that, my lady?"

"Dinner."

"There are servants for that. A lady shouldn't be bringing prisoners their meals!"

Addy was growing sick of Renard's tone. He was far too informal. While she'd grown used to having Strider speak to her in this manner, she didn't like that Renard was doing so. Especially after everything he'd said earlier. Had he always been this way? Now that she thought about it, he had, and she had let him.

He was her oldest steward, yet something about the way he spoke to her made her hackles raise. There was some sort of tone hidden under it that disconcerted her. But she couldn't quite put her finger on why.

"I'm not going to bother a servant when I am already going to meet with him," she stated. "Besides, he'll be more trusting of the food if it comes from me rather than some random person."

"My lady, please," he pressed, "You know better than this. Your father will be most displeased."

He moved to stand in front of her, but she ducked aside. Far more nimble than he'd been expecting as he grabbed for her. He actually grabbed for her!

Addy was shocked. Her temper flared, and she gave him a dangerous glare. "I have a right to speak with the man I employ; try to touch me or stop me again, Renard, and I will have you removed from my services."

"Yes, my lady."

Addy didn't see the barely suppressed look of fury and panic, as she rounded the last corner leading to Strider's room. She stopped dead. Darkness shrouded the hallway. But that wasn't what caused her to pause. It was the smell of blood. Clutching her package to her chest, she quietly pressed forward. Renard called after her, but she ignored him. She kept to the side of the hall again.

Her eyes adjusted to the darkness, the candles in the lit part of the keep providing enough light to see. She first came upon the body of the man who'd followed Greer into the hall. His throat was torn open, a look of terror frozen on his face. She looked away, her eyes falling to the sword on the ground at the edge of a pool of blood. She picked it up. Holding the linen parcel in one arm, she moved down the hall. The bodies of the guards were next, tucked away in a dark nook in the wall.

Her steps grew more urgent as she came closer to the door. She had to force herself to stop and take a breath. She could taste the blood in the air like a thick miasma. Standing with her back against the wall, she did her best to steady her breathing. She moved in the way Strider had taught her, working around the doorway, careful to not expose more of her body than she had to. Her sword was in front, ready to block an incoming attack. She'd positioned her feet to allow her to leap back behind the cover of the door frame if someone came at her.

One body lay on the floor, dead. The moonlight revealed it was not Strider. She let out a breath of relief. He wasn't there. But where had he gone? Addy moved into the room to search for clues. She placed the food on the bed and moved around to study the ground.

Bloody paw prints led into and out of the room. Likely Greer following Strider. Renard appeared in the doorway, looking around. He didn't look surprised as he took in the death. His face only grew white when he saw her kneeling on the ground amidst the bloody footprints, near a dead body.

"We must go, my lady!" Renard cried, rushing toward her and ushering her out of the room.

"No! We need to find Strider!"

Renard grabbed her arm and dragged her down the hall, back the way they'd come. She gasped in pain and tried to pull out of his grasp but couldn't break his grip. She was forced to stumble behind him as he dragged her into the large dining hall.

"You're hurting me!" she shouted.

A look of surprise crossed his face, and he immediately let go. "I'm sorry, my lady, but you need to be taken to safety."

"I am fine. It's Strider I'm worried about. If any of the guards find him, they'll attack him. My father needs to be alerted at once, and an alarm needs to be sounded."

"The alarm does need to be raised. That monster is loose and has killed six of our men."

"Strider was protecting himself!" she protested, then stopped. Her eyes narrowed in suspicion. "There were only four men."

"What?"

"There were only four dead," she said; a knot formed in her stomach as her brow furrowed. She knew she hadn't heard wrong but didn't want to believe it. Her mind ran over how Renard had treated her in the hallway, how he tried to undermine Strider and make her doubt herself. She watched him carefully. "Why did you say six?"

"I must've miscounted," Renard backpedaled. "We really must go. And for goodness' sake, put down that sword."

Addy took a step back from him, her chin lifting defiantly. "You weren't outside my door when I left. You didn't seem surprised by the attack or the dead bodies."

"Of course, I was surprised!"

Addy shook her head. Her heart rate quickened as a voice in her head told her to run. "You only grew pale when you saw me crouched near the body."

"That's because I was worried about you being so close to death. A lady of your standing should never have to see such a thing!"

She wasn't sure if Strider's paranoia was rubbing off on her, but that feeling that something wasn't right nagged at her. It was the same feeling she'd had around the messenger who led her and Tevin into an ambush. Addy took another step back. Her instincts had been right before. She wouldn't doubt them now. Despite the part of her screaming to escape, she wouldn't run. Addy faced Renard, her resolve growing.

"You ran to intercept me. You knew I would go to see Strider, or you were at least concerned enough to try to stop me from coming this way. Why?"

"Because he is dangerous!" he spat. "Because he has some sort of spell or hold over you; I had to make sure you were safe. Protected from him."

His words were full of venom as he spoke. There was a hostility Addy had never heard come from the man's lips, as he spoke of Strider.

"He has no hold over me. He's my friend," she told him.

"He does! There is no way you would allow such a vile creature to be in your presence otherwise. He has somehow tricked you into thinking you need him, into wanting him! That is an unforgivable crime."

Addy looked at Renard in shock. "That is crazy!"

"Crazy or not, you're not going back to that man. He is unworthy to be in your presence. He should have had the decency to die in that room."

"That's enough!" Addy roared, raising her sword. "I will not have you speaking of Strider in such a way! Renard, you're no longer my steward. I want you to leave this castle immediately!"

The fury in the man's eyes was frightening, made more so by the glint of madness flickering within them.

"You cannot dismiss me!" he shouted. "I am your most loyal servant, your most devoted! That yulie has done something to you. He's warped your mind. When he dies, you'll be free and realize just how much you truly need me, how much you care about me!"

Renard advanced on her as he ranted, forcing Addy to back up. He had her pinned in the corner of the room. If she tried to dart for a door, he'd be able to catch her. He paced, his movements erratic.

"Renard, what has gotten into you? You're mad!"

"I am watching my lady be manipulated by a fiend! Of course, I'm mad! There should've been more men sent to kill that man! You must be freed, and I must have you back!"

All she could do was stare at him in shock. This made no sense! Her mind reflected back on the years she'd known him. At the time, she'd brushed off his possessive tendencies as overprotection of his charge. He'd always made her feel like a grown woman, telling her how smart and mature she was one minute, and making her doubt herself the next. With distance, she now realized how manipulative and controlling he was when her family wasn't around.

Creeping hands of horror clawed around her ribcage toward her heart. No, she had to be wrong. There was no way Renard could've been involved. He was misguided, yes, but he'd always been her friend, her protector. He'd never do anything to hurt her or her family. Fingers of fear curled around her heart. *Please, gods, tell me I'm wrong*, she begged silently. Her stomach twisted into more knots and bile burned the back of her throat; she didn't want to believe it.

"You were a part of my kidnapping, weren't you?" she said, her voice soft. She hadn't realized she'd spoken them aloud, until she heard them come from her lips.

Renard stopped pacing and looked at her.

"Of course, I was!" he exclaimed. "I had to protect you! They would've killed you otherwise!"

Chapter 69

Something's Afoot

Tevin tossed and turned in bed. He didn't know how long he lay there before deciding to get up. He wasn't sure if his inability to sleep was because the bed was uncomfortable, or if he'd become too used to sleeping on the ground. Either way, his losing battle with sleep left him feeling restless.

Figuring the rest of the men would probably appreciate not dealing with his noisy tossing, he quietly strapped on his sword, pulled on his boots, and left. As he walked down the small hall, he noticed the barracks seemed emptier than before. Far more beds were unoccupied than filled, which struck him as odd. Slipping out one of the side doors, Tevin stepped out into the crisp night air. He took a deep breath and let out a long, slow sigh.

Sir Tamous had found him a bed in the barracks while he returned to his own position at Sir Fenforde's side. It was the first time since being saved by Strider that he'd slept with a roof over his head and couldn't sleep. Leaning back against the wall, he looked up at the star-filled sky. He wondered how Strider and Addy were faring. They were both likely asleep. Like he should be. Hoping a walk would help, he pushed off the wall.

Something caught his eye while he walked past the stables. Figures moving atop the castle wall above him. Standing in the shadow of the stables, Tevin watched two figures approach the men standing guard. The men hailed them, which meant they knew each other. A changing of the watch, most likely. He couldn't hear what was said, but as he watched, one held up what looked like a waterskin. The watchmen laughed and accepted the drink. Each took a large draught from the skin.

The conversation continued for a moment until the watchmen grew unsteady. The other two moved in, catching them before they fell. Tevin stared in shock at what he'd witnessed. He looked along the wall for anyone to hail but saw several more guards drop. Others standing watch didn't react to seeing their comrades collapse. An icy chill ran up Tevin's spine. He heard footsteps and stepped back into the darkness of the stable doorway.

Men moved past him; more soldiers. They carried boards and hammers as they shuffled toward the barracks. The group split and set to work. Ramming great beams into the ground, they wedged them against the doors to the barracks before they began nailing other boards across the door. It took a moment before cries sounded within of the barracks as the soldiers awoke to being nailed inside the building.

So much for letting the other soldiers know what was happening. Likely, no one beyond the wall knew. Even if they did, they had no hope of getting inside. The walls of each ring were lower than the next, the inner being the highest. None of them had passages connecting them, ensuring that if one wall fell, the enemy couldn't use it to enter the next. The height advantage of the next wall also meant it was still defensible against attack.

None of the soldiers beyond the inner wall would even suspect there was a problem. When they looked back, all would appear well. Even if Tevin could tell them the gate was closed, with the drawbridge drawn, they were cut off from the outside.

"That should do it," the leader said. "You men come with me. We're to ensure no one escapes the keep."

Most of the soldiers who helped bar the doors hurried off toward the keep. The rest remained on guard to ensure no one escaped. Clutching his sword, Tevin looked to the keep, then back to the barracks. He had no hope of stopping the men that'd rushed off. He knew Sir Tamous and his men were still inside.

Hopefully, they'd be able to hold them off with the help of Strider and Kyre. If they could retake the walls and sound the alarm, they could bring in reinforcements. There was no way these people could've taken the entire castle. There had to be good men beyond the inner wall still. He just needed to find them.

Tevin wished he'd thought to put on some armor before leaving. Tulie let out a nicker when she spotted him entering the stable and a soldier glanced over. Tevin hid quickly behind the doorframe. He didn't dare breathe as the man stared. The traitor looked long and hard before turning back to watch the barracks. Tevin let out a breath. Backing further into the stables, he began devising a plan to release the trapped soldiers.

The men laughed and bantered with one another as they waited around the barracks. There were at least fifteen of them loosely surrounding the building. They could easily spot anyone trying to break out and call for help.

"We should burn it," one of them said. "Roast all the pigs inside."

"That'll draw too much attention, you idiot!" another snapped, slapping the would be pyromaniac on the back of the head. "Fancy trying to hold the keep against the rest of the armed forces outside?"

"It's not like they can get to us."

"And it's not like we can get out, if they trap us in. They'll starve us out and enlist more of the king's men to help ensure none of us escape. Just wait and trust the plan."

The other man was cowed into silence. A clattering sound erupted from the stable, followed by a startled whinny.

"What was that?" the same soldier asked.

"How should I know?" the man left in charge snapped. "Go check it out."

"Why do I have to?"

"You can either go, or you can lose your tongue. Your choice."

The man grumbled, as he unsheathed his sword and stomped toward the dark stable. He was still grumbling when he entered. Moving down the main aisle, he peered into each stall. Some of the horses looked at him quizzically, others ignored him, and a few glared at him for waking them up. His apprehension left him when he reached the last stall and found nothing. Turning back, he was about to call out that there was nothing there when something struck him in the back of the head.

The man fell with a quiet thud at Tevin's feet. Tevin clutched his sword in his hand, having used the metal pommel to clobber the man.

Grabbing the soldier's feet, he dragged him into the last stall. The horse gave a disgruntled snort before settling as it eyed the intruders. Relieving the man of his weapons, Tevin considered trying to pry off his chain mail, but discarded the idea. It would take too much time. Instead, he set about working.

"Braxton?" the leader barked. When no reply came from the direction of the stable, the man cursed and signaled for two more men to investigate. They vanished into the barn. A sharp cry soon followed. Then silence. All eyes were now on the stable, waiting for their allies to return. But they never did. The dark gaping maw of the barn loomed like the mouth of a silent monster that had swallowed three of their companions.

"With me!" the commander barked, as he stalked toward the stable door. Pieces of the broken door hung limply from the hinges, the remnants of the battle between Strider and Kyre. The remaining men gathered before the door with swords drawn. A rustle came from inside, then the sound of clattering hooves.

The men in front didn't have time to shout out a warning before over twenty horses charged out of the darkness. They plowed into the soldiers, who cried out, as they went down under the hooves of the panicked horses. Several leaped out of the way, using their companions as shields, as they dove aside.

Tevin leaped from the horse he'd been clinging to and ducked into the shadows on the other side of the barracks. The disoriented soldiers never noticed him. Their leader shouted for them to get back in line and take the stable. Only eight remained, though the commotion in the courtyard would no doubt attract more. Hurrying toward the nearest barrack door, Tevin used his shoulder to shove the beam that wedged the door closed aside before moving to the door.

Drawing his knife, he slipped it under the boards nailed to the door, prying them free as best he could.

"Get your swords and armor," he urged quietly; he was unsure if the men inside could hear him, but he didn't dare speak any louder. "We've got a fight on our hands."

Shouts from the other side of the barracks told him that the enemy soldiers had discovered the barn empty, save for the bodies of their allies. Working harder, he pried the last board free before yanking the door open. Thirty armed and angry soldiers poured out of the door. Tevin signaled for them to be quiet and stay out of sight of the walls.

"They've taken the walls and the gate is closed," Tevin said hurriedly. "We need to signal the outside that the keep has been captured, and we need to get that gate open."

The men looked at him with grim determination and barely suppressed fury at knowing that their castle had been taken out from under them. It was then that the howls started, muffled by the stone walls. The sound was haunting and sent chills up Tevin's spine.

"We'll take the west wall," an older soldier said, motioning to half their group. "Looks like half the barracks betrayed us. They can't have them all up on the wall."

Tevin nodded. "I'll take the rest and take the eastern wall."

That was as much as they could plan, since the enemy was searching for Tevin. Taking a deep breath, he led the charge from the shadows. Fifteen men followed him as they jumped the eight remaining men in the courtyard. The other fifteen stuck close to the buildings, trying not to draw attention to themselves, as they moved toward the stairs leading up the wall nearest them. The sound of battle soon filled the courtyard, and the men on the walls, already watching the strange sight of their horses prancing around the courtyard, took notice.

They shouted in alarm, drawing their bows. They aimed to rain arrows down on the fighting party, hesitating momentarily, seeing their own fighters in the mix. Their hesitation allowed the freed archers an opening. Being on the inside of the wall, there were no merlons for the men above to hide behind. A couple of men fell as arrows found chinks in their armor. The others had to duck for cover or get struck, as they began answering with return fire. They no longer cared if they hit their allies.

The bowmen in the courtyard tucked behind the buildings as best they could. One fell, struck by several arrows. The men fighting in the courtyard moved out of view of the west wall, leaving the bodies of the dead behind, as Tevin led them toward the eastern stairs.

The wall guards readied their bows, but a shout on the wall caught their attention, as more angry soldiers flooded the western walkway. Battle cries filled the air, ringing with the clash of steel as the west wall defended against an onslaught of men. The other sections of the wall that could see what was happening attempted to fire into the crowd, hitting friend and foe alike. More arrows flew up from the ground as the bowmen tried their best to disrupt the enemy, taking out several. Men screamed as they fell from the walls.

Horses ran about in a panic, creating more chaos. One went down, struck by several arrows as it ran in front of Tevin, who'd been leading the party. He leaped over the horse and continued his charge, keeping his head and shoulders covered by a shield he'd taken from a fallen enemy.

Arrows thudded into the wooden shield as he ran. He could see the stairs; his gut twisted at the thought of mounting them and the wall, but he pressed on. Soldiers rushed to block him. Keeping his shield up, he raised his sword to meet them as his men ran behind him. Blocking an overhead strike, he slashed at the attacker's stomach before blocking another strike from the same man.

Unbalanced, he fell off the stairs with a cry. Keeping as far from the edge as he could, Tevin pushed onward; two of his men bounded past him to attack the other wall guards trying to hold the stairs, making quick work of them with their spears before leading the charge up onto the walkway. The sound of battle on the walls drew the attention from the guards on the lower walls. Tevin could hear them shouting. Soon, a bell sounded, as an alarm was raised throughout the castle Timara.

"Get to the gate!" Tevin yelled, as he fought. "Open the gate!"

Chapter 70
Unease

Howls rang through the halls of the keep, like the wailing of a banshee. The sound woke Tymott. He bolted upright in bed, his skin crawling, as his heart gave a startled spike. Something deep inside him told him danger was close. That he should flee from the sound.

The howl came again, muffled by the wood and stone but still audible. How the call seeped through the thick stone walls and entered his soul, he didn't know. None of the hunting dogs sounded like it. None of the calls of normal wolves in the wild compared to the howls he heard now. That had to be Greer.

Tymott groped in the dark for a light. Finding the candle holder, he fumbled with the matches, finally striking one. His room was soon lit by candlelight, allowing him to see the lavish surroundings. Pulling on a pair of pants, he stuffed his nightshirt in them before buckling on his sword. In stocking feet, he walked to the door.

That sense of unease never left him, even after the howls quieted. He looked about, as if expecting something to jump out at him. Accompanying the sense of dread and unease, was an overwhelming worry for those he cared about. Opening his door, he peered out before leaving the safety of his room for the hall.

Candles, kept lit by servants who patrolled the castle, illuminated the hall with warm light. The door guards were gone, though the watch shouldn't have changed yet. No one was in the halls. Every ghost story flooded Tymott's mind, increasing his jumpiness, as he hurried toward Curthis' room. He felt exposed alone in the hall, and he practically flew through the door to his brother's room. Light from Tymott's candle spilled into the room as the door slammed against the wall.

Curthis fell out of bed, scrambling for his sword as he became tangled in his bedding. Cursing and fighting, he tried to break free with one hand while the other still searched the general vicinity he knew his sword was in. The sound of his door slamming shut didn't even cause him to look up, as he struggled to get free of the blankets wrapped around him like a warm prison. He only stopped for a moment to peek out from his cocoon when he heard laughter. Tymott was standing over him, a candle in hand, laughing at his plight.

"Shut up and help me!" Curthis snapped.

Tymott placed the candle on the nightstand beside the bed and helped him free, though he didn't stop laughing.

Glaring at him, Curthis asked, "Care to tell me why you came barging into my room at such an ungodly hour?"

The laughter died in Tymott's throat as a bleak, haunted look flashed across his face. He glanced back to the door, a hand rubbing the back of his neck nervously.

"The wolf howled," he said.

"The wolf what?"

"Howled."

"Wolves howl all the time." Something dawned on Curthis, and he smiled. "Did the sound of the big bad wolf scare you?"

"It wasn't a normal howl!" Tymott defended himself. "Something is wrong."

Curthis gave him a doubtful look. Tymott had always been the more emotional of the brothers. He was easy to scare, and Curthis and Elayis loved to freak him out with ghost stories. Curthis was not nearly as sensitive to the aura in the air as Tymott was.

"What's wrong is that you're acting like a mouse," Curthis said, not happy with being woken up. He picked up his blankets and threw them haphazardly onto his bed.

Tymott grabbed his arm before he could crawl back underneath them and go to sleep. "Come with me to check on Elayis first," he insisted.

Curthis groaned. "Go check on him yourself. You know how cranky he gets when he's woken up."

"Please, Curthis. I can't shake this feeling."

Curthis let out a heavy sigh. Sometimes he wondered if Tymott was actually the youngest son, not him.

"Fine. But you owe me."

"Deal."

Grabbing his sword, Curthis followed Tymott out into the hall toward Elayis' room.

"He isn't going to like this," Curthis muttered under his breath.

"We don't have to wake him."

"Oh, so you don't plan to come bursting into his room like Chaos is on your tail, like you did with me?"

Tymott's ears turned red as he led the way. "I didn't burst into your room."

"So, you threw my door open hard enough to make it slam against the wall, then slammed it shut, for fun?"

"Shut up," Tymott grumbled.

Curthis grinned. "Did you see a ghost in the halls? Maybe the late baroness, who died mysteriously a hundred years ago?"

"Shut up, Curthis!"

Curthis grinned like a pleased cat.

Tymott stopped abruptly, forcing Curthis to step aside quickly, to avoid running into him. When he did, he saw what had caused him to stop. Elayis' door was slightly ajar. Both brothers quietly drew their swords, before moving toward the door. Tymott pushed the door open further so the light of his candle and those of the hall spilled into the room. They fell upon the form of someone standing beside Elayis' bed. Metal flashed in his hand, and both brothers yelled out.

"Elayis, blade!"

Their elder brother's eyes flew open, startled, as was the attacker. Both locked eyes for a second before Elayis rolled aside. He cried out, as the blade sliced into his side. He kept rolling, falling off the other end of the bed, clutching his side. The attacker cursed before drawing his sword. Tymott and Curthis rushed him. He raised his sword.

Curthis was the first to reach the man, his sword connecting with the would-be assassin. Tymott's blade darted in around him, taking the man in the ribs. Curthis broke the man's guard and stabbed him in the stomach before backing away out of reach. The man stumbled back, clutching his abdomen. He tripped over the corner of the nightstand and fell with a thud. Tymott knocked the sword from his hand as he lay on the ground.

"Who sent you to attack Elayis?" Tymott demanded.

The man smiled up at him, blood bubbling from his lips, before his eyes glazed over.

Curthis ran around the bed to Elayis, who was getting to his feet, his hand still clutching the wound in his side. Curthis yanked a blanket off the bed and began tearing it into strips.

"Are you okay?" he asked, as he began binding the wound.

"I'll live," Elayis grunted. "Who was that?"

"He's dressed like one of our guards," Tymott said.

"Did he tell you who sent him here?"

"No."

"I guess I owe you guys one."

Curthis shook his head. "We both owe Tymott. He's the one who came and got me, saying something was wrong."

Elayis eyed his brother with a moment of suspicion. "How did you know?"

"The Hunter's wolf howled. Something felt wrong about it."

"He came storming into my room like he was running from a ghost. White as a sheet, and shivering like a scared child."

Tymott's ears grew even redder. "I was not!"

Elayis raised a bloody hand to silence them. "We need to alert the guard. This man might be a part of the group who stole Addy. She could be in danger."

Both brothers grew sober, as they clutched their swords tighter, their faces flushing with anger.

"Don't trust anyone. Get Addy and bring her to our parents' room," Elayis ordered, as he grabbed his sword and led them out of the room, not bothering with the body.

As the three brothers entered the hall, they encountered two men, each leaving Curthis and Tymott's room, each dressed as soldiers of the castle. When they spotted the three men, who were clearly alive and armed, they shouted. Three more men came around the corner, swords drawn. The castle alarm suddenly rang through the night.

"I think they're happy to see us," Tymott said, raising his own blade, no longer afraid, now that he faced a physical enemy.

Curthis and Elayis grunted and fell into a fighting stance, as the men charged them.

Lord Fenforde felled another man, before raising his sword to block another attacker's blade. Kyre battled another man to his left, while Sir Tamous fought to his right. The enemy had ambushed them while leaving the lord's study, having stayed up late discussing matters.

"Your plan worked great!" Kyre said, as he ducked out of the way of a blade, before slicing the fighter's sword hand off. He tried to call to his magic but felt it shrivel and die, blocked. Someone had prepared an artifact to counter his magic.

"As I recall, the plan was to use the Hunter as bait, not us!" Lord Fenforde shot back, as he shoved the body of a dying enemy aside before facing another.

"A minor detail," Kyre puffed, as he slashed a man across the back, slicing through gambeson, severing his spine. "The real plan was to draw out the traitors, and here they are!"

"Less talking, more fighting!" Sir Tamous snarled, as he nearly beheaded a soldier with a single strike.

More men kept coming as the three fought. Several soldiers, hearing the conflict, came running to aid their lord as the battle grew in intensity. Confusion increased, as the new soldiers tried to figure out who was friend and who was foe. The ringing of blades echoed off stone walls. Shadows of fighting men danced up and down the corridor. Cries of pain, anger, and fear became a familiar din in the warriors' ears as they battled. Sir Tamous' men, knights dressed in armor bearing the king's crest, fought their way to their commander's side. Sir Tamous pressed in front of Lord Fenforde, shielding him from any attacker, as the soldiers formed a wall of swords and shields. Slowly, the group began pushing back against the invading men.

Kyre appeared from behind them, like a whirlwind of blades. His sword was a blur of silver as he carved a bloody path through the men, with Sir Tamous bringing up the rear. The head knight was a terrifying force, as he and his most highly trained fighters smashed through the rest of the attackers, like multi-headed monsters made of steel. Slowly, the tide of battle turned, as the enemy began to retreat. Fear rippled through the group like a silent tidal wave. The foot soldiers scattered and fled before the terrifying onslaught.

"We need to find Adelin and Felice!" Lord Fenforde shouted, pushing past the knights. He ran down the hall toward his bedroom, where he knew his wife waited.

Chapter 71

Books Make Great Tripping blocks

Lady Fenforde was waiting up for her husband, having decided not to return to the discussion with Kyre. She never slept well when he wasn't in bed beside her. She'd decided to read, rather than toss and turn in a futile attempt to sleep, and was awake when the faint sound of the howls drifted through the walls. It caused her to pause mid-paragraph in her book. Lifting her head, she cocked it to one side and listened.

The dreadful howl came again, and she felt a shiver run up her spine. It had to be that man's wolf. Howling at an ungodly hour and likely waking up the entire keep! Strider and Greer apparently have no manners. Snapping her book shut, she called for the servant who always waited outside, in case the lord and his wife needed something. A young girl entered the room.

"Yes, my lady?" she said, bowing. She kept her eyes on the floor, as was customary.

"Go down to the room where the Dark Ranger is being kept and tell him to keep that wolf quiet," she ordered.

"Y-yes my lady," she stammered, a look of fear crossing her face as she hurried out of the room.

Opening her book, Lady Fenforde resumed reading. Her husband was staying up terribly late tonight. No doubt still in a meeting with Kyre regarding the ruffian now locked away downstairs. She frowned at the thought of the man. Strider, he called himself. What kind of name was that? Did he fancy himself a horse? Or did his parents name him after one? Likely the latter. Rangers were a strange lot.

No doubt his parents named him after a favorite steed. Or as a joke. It was truly distasteful. His name aside, she'd seen how her daughter had interacted with him. She had been far too familiar with him and he with her. She believed her daughter that he hadn't kidnapped her. But she still didn't care for the filthy half-yulie, and his influence on her daughter.

A new sound invaded her thoughts. At first, it sounded like

clinking silverware, but when she stopped to listen, she realized it was a heavier clashing as shouts drifted down the hall, followed by screams of agony. The castle alarm rang. Standing, she clutched her book to her chest with one hand as she carefully walked toward the door. She cracked it open to see her usual guard standing out in the middle of the hall, sword drawn.

"What is it, Yolin?" she asked, as the sound of fighting grew louder.

"Battle, my lady," he said. "Please get back inside and lock your door!"

Several men came around the hall, all dressed in the armor of her soldiers. They hailed Yolin, who returned the greeting.

"What is happening?" he asked, as the men came closer.

"The Dark Ranger got loose and is waging war against the entire keep," one said. "The man is Chaos Touched. Lord Fenforde sent us to guard Lady Fenforde."

They came closer. Yolin nodded, lowering his blade. The moment he did, two of the men lunged forward, driving their blades up under his guard. He fell to the earth with a grunt.

Lady Fenforde suppressed a scream, as she slammed her door shut. Using the key she always kept with her, she locked it. Keeping the key turned in the lock so they couldn't put in another one without forcing hers out, she backed away as someone tried the handle.

"Open the door!" the man ordered, who'd first spoken to Yolin. "It'll be very bad for you if you don't, my lady." The last two words dripped off his tongue in a sarcastic drawl.

Lady Fenforde ignored him, as she dropped her book and moved toward the writing desk on the wall next to the door. Putting her shoulder against it, she pushed. The desk groaned as it slid across the door. The soldiers pounded against the door, but the heavy wood wouldn't budge.

"Use the ax!" the soldier ordered.

The door shuddered as someone began attacking the door. Aiming their ax at the section around the handle. They didn't need to pulverize the door completely; simply separating it from the lock barring it in place would be enough. The handle was knocked off and wood splintered under the heavy blows.

Lady Fenforde ran to her nightstand and pulled out a dagger. Tucking it in her skirts, she blew out her candle before looking for a place to hide. Unlike other castles, her room didn't have an adjoining room, leaving her nowhere to run. So, she busied herself with moving every object she could in front of and around the door. Chairs, a table, drawers from her wardrobe, even books and perfume bottles were strewn all over the floor. Anything that would create an obstacle for the men trying to break in. Then she hid between the wardrobe and the wall, out of view of the doorway.

She wasn't completely helpless, nor was she clueless. She kept herself protected from any bolts or arrows that the enemy soldiers might shoot at her as they tried to clear away the ridiculous amount of mess she stacked before them. Finally, with a mighty crack, the door broke free of the handle, and the men combined their strength to push aside the writing desk and table. Two men rushed in, instantly stumbling over the debris and falling to the floor. They cursed as they got up and were forced to tread more slowly away from the door as several more men entered.

They looked around the room, not yet spotting her hiding in the shadows behind the wardrobe.

"Come out already!" the one giving the orders shouted. "Don't make me any madder!"

The men fanned out, easily casing the room.

"Got ya!" one shouted triumphantly, as he grabbed her arm. She shrieked and slashed at his face with her dagger. The man fell back with a scream, blood streaming from his face. The others drew their swords.

"I told you, you wouldn't like what happened if you made me mad!" the leader snarled, as he advanced on her.

"You won't like what will happen to you either, once my husband is done with you," she snapped back.

The man snickered. "He's likely dead by now, as are your sons. You will be too, eventually."

Lady Fenfordes eyes narrowed, and she brandished her knife. "You'd do well not to underestimate my family."

The man chuckled. "Feisty, I like it." With a flick of his sword, he knocked the blade from her hand. "But like all Rachian women, you're beautiful, yet terrible with a blade."

He advanced on her, and she flattened herself against the wall to get away from him. He grabbed her arm to jerk her out of her hiding place, as the others made catcalls and howling noises.

The man jerked but didn't pull her out as he grew incredibly stiff. His eyes went wide, and he let out a squeaking groan, before crumpling to the floor. A black shafted arrow protruded out of the back of his armor, its rigid form dissolving into smoke. The soldiers turned in time for two more to catch arrows through their necks. Strider stood in the doorway, his face hidden in the shadows of his hood. He killed another man with an arrow before casting his bow aside and drawing his sword as the men rushed him.

Lady Fenforde watched as the darkly clad figure glided like a phantom, his bluish blade flashing as he danced through the men. All fell to the ground, their blades never touching the Hunter. He stepped over their lifeless bodies, as he pulled his hood away from his face. Greer came in behind him, his nose twitching as he surveyed the carnage. Lady Fenforde sagged against the wall with relief, before stiffening as she met the gaze of her rescuer.

She offered a curt nod. "Thank you."

Strider returned the nod. "Where is your daughter?"

"Her room is down the hall. Not far."

"Greer, stay with the lady. Get her somewhere safe."

Greer let out a whine, as the man turned and walked toward the door. Strider stumbled into the door frame with a grunt.

"Are you okay?" Lady Fenforde asked.

"I'm fine," he grunted. Using the doorframe for support, he leaned down and retrieved his bow.

"Stay in the shadows and follow Greer. He'll keep you safe," he told her, before pushing off the frame and stumbling into the hall.

Greer let out another whine, before walking over to Lady Fenforde. She eyed the large animal warily; her gaze never left him as she stooped to pick up her knife. He looked at it, snorted and shook his head, before trotting to the door. He paused in the doorway and looked back at her with an expression that said he expected her to follow.

She didn't understand why, but his presence had a calming effect, as she inched out into the hall, blade raised and ready to strike out at anyone who came too close. But no one was there. Not even the Hunter. The sound of battle was also more distant. Greer moved off, and she followed him.

Strider moved unsteadily down the halls, slashing his way through anyone who dared get in his way as he searched for Addy. A trail of bodies marked his passing as he searched. He came to what had to be her room and found it empty. Swearing, he turned around and continued searching, taking a set of stairs leading down to the main floor as he kept searching with growing intensity. He had to squash the overwhelming desire to call out her name. He couldn't attract more people to his location.

Another man appeared, dressed in armor. He didn't even have time to shout in alarm before he was dead. The blue yulie blade glistened red as Strider moved as fast as his body would allow him. He cursed again. Swearing as he urged his body to move quicker. But it wouldn't, it couldn't. His soul barely held onto his connection with his body, like a puppeteer trying to control a puppet on the end of a fraying string.

Everything felt so distant and starkly real at the same time, making him feel disoriented. He stumbled into a set of armor on display, knocking it to the ground with a loud clatter. He swore again and was forced to lean back against the wall or fall. His breath came in ragged gasps as his body fought to live, while his soul fought to leave. His chest throbbed, and for a moment, his vision darkened.

It returned in time to see someone rushing toward him, weapon drawn.

It took every ounce of willpower he had to make his body move as he parried the strike and thrust his blade, through gambeson, under the man's ribcage. The man fell to the ground. Strider struggled not to join him. One thing kept him going as he returned to wandering the halls. A desperate desire to protect someone who had become precious to him. Addy had been nothing but an annoyance the first time they met, and he'd been content to let her die. She was trouble from the start; a spoiled girl determined to make his life difficult. He'd resented her for that.

But his defenses had softened and despite never wanting to, he found himself taking her under his wing and caring for her. He'd been content to die the day they met, since he'd achieved his only purpose. Greer had known he wasn't done. Addy needed him. He fought against it. It frightened him. Everyone he cared for ended up dead. He couldn't lose someone else. He had to get to her. Had to find her. He had to make sure she was safe. Only then could he let himself die. The Hunter kept going, no longer aware of anything but his need to get to Addy.

Chapter 72
Obsession

Addy stared blankly at Renard as her stomach knotted itself. "What do you mean I would've been killed?"

"That doesn't matter. What matters is getting you to safety."

"I am not going anywhere with you until you tell me what you mean!" she shouted, keeping her sword raised. "Who is trying to kill me?"

"The men who sent me here!" Renard stated, exasperated. "I was to infiltrate your family, gain your trust, then see to your deaths! But I could never kill you. Never."

Addy's throat grew tight, as she took a subconscious step back. The tip of her blade wavered as her breathing grew shallow. She couldn't believe what she was hearing. "You were supposed to kill me?"

"I would never harm you! And they allowed it. They said I could keep you, as long as the rest of your family was taken care of. So, I suggested a plan. We take you and use you as a hostage. Your father would be forced to do as they wanted. When we had the fort in the Bayvar Pass and Timara castle, we would dispose of them then."

Addy gazed at him in horror as he explained his entire plan. Renard looked like a man possessed as he spoke. She tried stepping to the side, steering closer to an exit, but Renard shifted to cut her off, forcing her further into the corner.

"They were furious with me at first. But they accepted. I did this for you, Adelin. I did this all for us. Can't you see I am trying to protect you? And now that yulie has come and tainted you. But he will be gone soon; all of them will. And then I'll take you. We'll live somewhere peaceful and raise a family."

"You really are insane," she whispered. This wasn't Renard, this couldn't be. The faithful, kind man that'd grown up beside her.

His face stiffened. "You're unwell now, but you'll get better. You'll see how blessed you are to have someone who cares for you so much. You'll realize you love me."

The horror of who Renard truly was finally hit her, and she flinched back. He walked closer. She stepped back again, holding her blade up. Her heart was a torrent of emotions. Fear, betrayal, sorrow, and anger whirled within her. How could they have been so blind? How did none of them see it? He was the one who'd taken her, and now he was planning to kill her family and take her again. He was insane, manic! He'd murder her family if he wasn't stopped!

A cold resolve settled in her chest like someone had thrust a stone through her ribs, calming the storm raging within her. She forced her muscles to loosen, as she fell back into a stance Strider had drilled into her a thousand times. She raised her defense once more. Her gaze was as hard and sharp as her blade. She wouldn't bow to Renard, and she wouldn't let him hurt those she loved.

"I will never love you," she spat. "You're a filthy, delusional pig."

He frowned. "That is the magic talking. You'll see it soon enough. Now put down that sword."

Addy struck out with her sword, and he jumped back, drawing his own weapon with a resigned sigh.

"Adelin, please. This is ridiculous," he reasoned.

She didn't lower her blade as she glared at him. "Drop your sword, and surrender."

He shook his head in a hopeless gesture before bringing his longsword up sharply in a move intended to disarm her. But Addy's sword wasn't there. Not expecting the lady to predict his attack, his blade overshot, providing enough space for her own to slip in with a powerful thrust.

The blade bit deep into his stomach, and he stepped back, a look of shock on his face. Addy mirrored his look, as her resolve faltered for a moment, upon dealing the man a mortal blow. She watched as his face changed from shock to betrayal to pure fury.

He came at her with all his strength, as he rained a series of blows upon her.

Grim faced, Addy did her best to counter or dodge the attacks, but they came with increased strength and reckless abandon. Her strength ebbed, as her arms cried out from fending off powerful attacks that forced her back against the wall. But she wouldn't give up. Her resolve to defend her family returned. She called upon her magic, as Strider had taught her. Strength returned to her arms, and she began forcing Renard back. But he kept coming, no longer caring to guard. Addy went to attack him and dealt several more blows. But he didn't fall, spurred on by his anger.

They tangled in a furious duel, as Addy tried to steer the fight so she could reach a door to escape. But Renard blocked her with reckless abandon, keeping her from reaching an exit. With a furious slash, he knocked her blade aside. She could only watch as the weapon cut upward, slicing her from her abdomen and up across her ribcage. She stumbled back, gasping. Her mind was dulled to most of the pain, but she still reeled back. She looked up at him in disbelief. Their eyes met and the man's anger turned to abject horror as he realized what he'd done.

"No," he said. "Oh no, no, no!"

He kept repeating himself as blood soaked her nightgown. Addy wrapped her left arm over the wound in a vain attempt to slow the bleeding. But she refused to fall, as she stared Renard down.

"No, Adelin!" he sobbed. "I'm so sorry. I didn't mean to."

She raised her sword and said through gritted teeth. "Drop. Your. Sword."

Renard let his sword fall from his hands as he fell to his knees, still begging her to forgive him. Addy didn't reply, using her fading strength to kick the sword away. He tried to grab the hem of her skirt as he cried, tears streaming down his red face.

She brushed him off, not sparing him a glance or a word. He was dead to her. Still holding her sword and clutching at her wound, Addy maneuvered around Renard. Determined to leave the man behind. That same feeling within her that had warned her before sprang to life as she felt intense anger and hatred behind her. Without thinking, she turned, raising her sword as she deflected a knife aimed at her back.

With a sidestep, she moved with the block, circling around Renard where she brought her blade down upon his own back in a fluid slicing motion. He screamed, as her sword bit deep into his spine. He flailed about, trying to twist, to reengage her with his weapon. But his legs wouldn't respond. Addy stared at him, her gaze emotionless, her face blank. A numbness spread within her, dulling her emotions toward this creature who lay before her, screaming and cursing her name. Had he really once been her friend? He looked nothing like the person she'd loved.

A shudder ran through her, and she took a wider path around Renard, staying out of his reach as she left the man to die in a pool of his own blood. She didn't revel in her victory; the numbness was spreading. Her vision was becoming splotchy. Addy knew her body had only so much left. She'd spent all her magic, and she was bleeding out. She had to find Strider or Kyre.

"Kyre!" she called weakly. "Strider!"

Chapter 73
Sacrifice

Tevin led his men forward. Blood streamed from a wound in his thigh. His shirt was torn in several places where swords had cut, though only one area showed any sign of having drawn blood. His men roared, as they attacked the guards with a vengeance. They pressed on, determined to get to the wheelhouse. They had to lower the bridge and open the gate. Tevin bashed a soldier in the face with his shield, sending him tumbling from the wall as he killed another.

Keeping to the center to avoid seeing how high he was, he stepped over the bodies and moved on. The soldiers who'd been fighting them watched the man armed with a wooden shield, and a blade cut through their fighters like a scythe slicing through wheat. A group of snarling warriors stood behind him, their swords and spears drenched in blood. As more and more of their men fell, they gave ground. On the other side, soldiers loyal to their lord were making quick work of the traitors.

The soldiers gathered on the lower castle wall outside the inner keep, helpless to save their lord from the attack within. Both fighting parties above wore the armor of their castle. They didn't know who to shoot at with their bows as they watched the slaughter. Until a man with a wooden shield raised his sword and shouted.

"Protect your lord, open the gate!"

Deciding that the warrior shouting about letting them inside was their ally, the archers began firing upon those standing between that brave swordsman and the gatehouse, doing their best to strike the soldiers that weren't sheltered by the merlons. The traitors fighting above were not expecting an attack from below. Their will broke the moment a storm of arrows hit. They'd had enough. First, one man abandoned the fight, then another.

The remaining survivors ran over each other, trying to flee to the nearest staircase. Tevin and his men rushed forward, closing in on the structure that housed the great wheel that lowered the drawbridge and raised the gate. Several soldiers grabbed the wooden wheel as

Tevin threw himself against the release lever. The chains clanked and rattled as the bridge lowered. Its counterweights rose, pulling open the gate as the bridge fell.

Soldiers from outside began streaming into the courtyard, surrounding the surviving enemy, who dropped their weapons in surrender. Tevin collapsed against the lever, breathing hard. The surrounding foot soldiers cheered in victory, and several clapped him on the shoulder in congratulations. But they couldn't stay to revel in their victory.

"It's not done yet," he breathed, straightening as he hurried to the door. "To the keep!"

"To the keep!" the men chorused, as they followed him toward another battle.

Strider heard Addy's call as he moved back down the hall that led to his rooms. He'd searched everywhere else. Or maybe he hadn't. Everything was a dim haze around him. He was only moving because of his drive to help Addy. That alone kept his feet walking, his hand gripping his saber, and his heart pumping. He stubbornly clung to this body through will alone, as his soul attempted to break the only remaining tethers he had to this world. Her cries drew him onward, and as he rounded the corner, the dim world came into stark relief as he saw Addy limping toward him, her dress slick with her own blood.

A relieved smile brushed her lips before she fell. Her sword clattered to the floor next to her, her pooling blood mixing with the crimson on the blade. Strider moved with new urgency as he stumbled forward. The Hunter fell to his knees on the other side of Addy.

"No," he said, a hand brushing her cheek.

Addy took a deep breath, opening her eyes, though they barely showed any light of recognition. She gave a soft smile.

"I didn't hold myself back," she breathed, before coughing. "But it still wasn't enough."

"Shh," he told her. "It was enough. Just don't leave."

He pressed his hands to the wound and began channeling every ounce of magic into healing her. Addy's eyes closed, and Strider poured more. Everything he had.

"Addy, stay awake," he said through gritted teeth. "Don't let go!"

The throbbing in his chest turned to a roaring fire of pain that closed off his throat. He felt his soul screaming, breaking, tearing, and burning, as the magic devoured it. But he kept pushing, sending his own soul, his own life, into her.

"Don't leave!" he choked out, when he felt her own soul drift from her body. "Please, Addy, don't leave me!"

He wasn't aware of the tears that stained his cheeks as he reached out with the last remaining parts of his soul toward her. All he knew was that he couldn't lose her, he couldn't fail her like he'd failed Kinri and his parents. He pulled her back as his magic mended organs, tissue, and bone.

The Hunter held her close in his arms with the desperation of a father holding onto his child. He wasn't aware of himself as he hugged her, head bowed, as he gave her everything. At that moment, he knew nothing but his desire to save her. Even the pain was no more as he felt her soul return to her body and the injury seal.

He let out a gasping sob as he pulled away, laying her on the ground with shaking arms. He felt for a pulse, and was rewarded with a strong, steady beat. She let out a deep breath as she lay there, eyes closed. He tenderly brushed her hair out of her face.

The sound of clambering feet filled the hall as people shouted Addy's name.

Addy's father and brother rushed toward them, Sir Tamous and Kyre close behind. As they ran to Addy, Strider stood and stepped away, allowing her father and brothers to fall to their knees around her. Saying her name as they tried to get her to wake. She didn't stir. Strider stepped further back and turned away.

He walked down the hall several paces before stumbling, clutching at his chest as a sharp stabbing pain shot through it. He fell, throwing out an arm, trying to catch himself on a side table in the hall. Instead, he knocked over a vase displayed there as he and the glass decoration hit the floor.

"Strider!" he heard someone yell. "Curse it all. What did you do? You idiot!"

Was that Kyre? He thought it might be.

"What happened?" Sir Tamous' voice drifted from somewhere far away. "Is he injured?"

He didn't hear Kyre's response. The threads holding him to the world snapped, as he slipped away into the embrace of eternal cold.

Chapter 74
New ties

Addy woke to her father and brothers kneeling around her with tears in their eyes. She was confused as they hugged her fiercely. Nothing hurt, though she knew she was wounded. Maybe this was what dying felt like? She had been hugging her father when she heard the crash. Like everyone, she looked. When her mind registered the form of Strider laying on the ground, Kyre and Sir Tamous standing over him, she screamed.

"Strider!" She pushed her father away and stumbled toward him, her body weak and shaking. It didn't respond right. It felt strange, as if she were in a different body. But she fought her way to him, nonetheless. Sir Tamous tried to step in her way, but she dove around him as she fell to her knees beside the Hunter. She sobbed as she shook his shoulder.

"Strider!"

She snatched at his cloak, trying to turn him over, but his body was too heavy, hers too weak; she cried harder.

She clutched her stomach as she bent over Strider's still form. A terrible, soul-shattering wail filled the hall as a gray form lunged toward the fallen body. Addy grabbed Greer, as he continued to let out a series of strangled cries that sounded far too human as he screamed out his agony. Behind him, Lady Fenforde stood, white as a ghost.

"Fetch the healer!" her father ordered.

"Medicine won't help," Kyre stated somberly, before swearing. "The idiot overused his magic. He gave everything to save her."

"How do I give it back?" Addy sobbed, as she hugged Greer.

"You can't," Kyre said.

"Watch me!" the words caused her breath to catch in her throat. She reached out and took Strider's hand. She called to her own magic, begged it to come, to give Strider his life again.

Kyre cursed and jerked her away. "You idiot! He died to save you!"

"Then you do it!" she pleaded, jerking on his cloak violently. "Help him!"

Kyre cursed again, and Addy turned back to heal him. He pulled her away; she kicked and shouted.

"Someone, hold her before she kills herself!" he ordered.

Elayis and Tymott took hold of her, and she swore and screamed, fighting them with everything she had.

"Help him!" she demanded, before slumping into Elayis' arms.

Greer joined in her pleas, as he looked up at Kyre. The Ranger cursed as he knelt before Strider and turned him over. He hesitated a moment as he stared into the man's lifeless face.

"This will make us even," he muttered, as he placed a hand on Strider's shoulder before calling to his magic. He didn't know if he could retrieve the Strider's soul before it slipped too far, or if the Hunter would be willing to return. But he wasn't inclined to give up without a fight. He focused entirely on channeling his magic and didn't notice Greer, who'd collapsed onto Strider's chest, whining pitifully.

Strider drifted in the darkness. Down, down, down. He didn't fight it this time as the chains of ice wrapped around his body, tightening into a bone-crushing grip. He gasped for air as they squeezed, but he otherwise made no sound, or attempted to relieve the pain. He was vaguely aware of where these chains were dragging him, and he wished they'd take him to his parents and Kinri.

The Hunter longed to see them again. Longed to tell them goodbye. To tell them he was sorry. But where they rested, a soul as tainted as his couldn't travel. Even spending his own life to save Addy wouldn't have been enough to wash away the blood that stained him. But that was okay. He knew that. And he knew he would do it again. For her.

He watched with disinterest, as the light above him faded, and he was dragged down to the lower depths of Tarn. The realms of darkness. He vaguely wondered if he would recognize any of the faces. The Hunter had killed plenty of men and women worthy of the pain-filled prisons said to fill the different depths of Tarn.

He wondered if they'd recognize him and decided that it really didn't matter. He chuckled briefly at the random thought of meeting one of them. Of them, asking who'd finally killed him, and telling them with a sly smile.

"No one."

No one had the satisfaction of claiming his head, and he felt a satisfied pride in that thought. His thoughts turned to Greer. His brother would be heartbroken. He'd never known life without him. For the first time in his life, he would be alone.

Would Addy's parents let her keep him? She had sworn to care for him and would make sure he had a happy life. A life far safer and better than anything he could ever provide. All he ever brought to those who loved him was death. It was only a matter of time before misfortune stole Greer from him. Now he would be spared.

Strider found himself uttering a small prayer to Layura and Takari, the goddess of monsters and the god of people. The sibling gods of life. He wasn't sure they'd care; he'd never cared for them. He still didn't. But maybe they'd honor it, considering what he'd done for Addy. He asked them to watch over Greer and Addy in his place.

Closing his eyes, he found breathing even harder, as his insides began to freeze. He was still drifting down, down, down. The crushing pressure surrounding him, pressed into him from all sides, adding a new sensation of pain that he ignored. He'd gladly bear far more. He likely would, if half the stories of the dark realms were true. Strider didn't care, knowing that she was still alive.

A weight pressed into his chest, pulling at his heart and taking the last of his breath away. He opened his eyes. The light above him shimmered and shifted. The weight increased, and slowly, a warmth trickled into him. His eyebrows knit together in puzzlement.

The chains yanked him deeper, as if trying to pull him away from something. The ice inside him hissed as the heat touched it. It crept into every recess of his body, and he cocked his head. He couldn't muster the energy to care or take more than a mild interest. The chains jerked again. The light above him shifted. Was it growing closer?

"Please stay," a voice whispered from somewhere. "We still need you."

It echoed softly around him. He blinked lazily, watching the light change. It twisted and swirled together, forming a braid of silver and orange. It drifted toward him.

"Come back," the voice whispered. The warmth continued to fill him as it waged a war within him against the ice, like the touch of summer trying to drive away winter's chill.

"Strider!" the voice shouted, as the thread drew closer, casting off silver and gold sparks of light.

Sluggishly, he reached a hand toward the thread. It wrapped around his arm and tightened. He gasped in agony as he was jerked to a sudden stop.

Memories flooded through him. Greer as a puppy sitting with him near the fire. The little creature looking up at him with large brown eyes that seemed to know more than they should.

"I'll let you stay," he heard his voice say. "But you have to promise me that you won't die before I do."

The little Greer seemed to smile and let out a happy yip. His vision blurred, as memories washed over him. He found himself watching Addy sitting by the campfire, laughing as she combed her fingers through her hair before jumping to a memory of him riding with her and Tevin as Greer ran around them like an excited puppy.

"Come back to us," Addy's voice whispered once more, as he dangled limply between two fighting forces.

He could hear her crying. He could hear the whines and howls of Greer as he called for him. They were begging him to stay. They were hurting because of him. But would they be safe if he returned? They'd be better off without him. Their wails filled the surrounding void. It brought more pain to him than anything he'd ever known as he listened to their heartbroken pleas. He looked up at the threads wrapped around his wrist. He was unsure how long he stared at them, before finding the strength to grab hold.

The chains shattered, and he was yanked back toward the surface. The world slammed into him like a wall of bricks, each one exploding into a tumultuous cacophony of sights, sounds, and sensations as soul collided with body. He gasped for breath, as his body demanded air and his chest flooded with fresh pain.

"He's alive!"

Strider recognized the voice of Kyre. He opened his eyes and saw the tired face of the Ranger. Strider uttered a particularly potent tahrvin curse, before all thought ceased and the warm darkness of living unconsciousness claimed him.

Strider slowly opened his eyes. His eyelids felt as if they had been sewn shut and lined with stone. The sight of a wooden ceiling greeted him as light filtered in from a window somewhere. His brow knit in confusion for a moment when he realized he was lying on a bed. He didn't remember how he'd gotten there. The Hunter tried to sit up, but a great weight on his chest held him down. He looked down, and saw the sleeping form of Greer, snoring softly. It was probably for the better. He didn't have the strength to move, anyway.

Something brown to his right caught the attention of his sluggish brain. He tilted his head and saw Addy. She too was asleep, as she used his bed as a pillow. She held his hand, clutched tightly, even in sleep. As if she were afraid he'd disappear while she wasn't watching. The idea was amusing, considering the hulking body of Greer trapping him.

Chaos, he was hot! Trapped beneath the self-heating Greer and blankets, he felt like he was being smothered. But he couldn't find it in him to wake either of them. The room was quiet. For a moment, things seemed peaceful. As he lay there, his muddled mind began reassembling what had happened.

He closed his eyes and let out an annoyed sigh. He'd probably made the stupidest decision in his life in choosing to come back. But at the moment, he didn't mind. Laying here in the quiet with Addy and Greer made it worth it. He'd likely rethink his actions when the brown-haired girl woke up, but things were nice for now.

"You lived," a voice said softly, sounding one part pleased, one part disappointed.

Strider opened his eyes to see Kyre. The Ranger was frowning at him.

"If you didn't want me alive, then why'd you help?" Strider asked. "Addy never would've been able to keep me here."

"I didn't honestly think I'd be able to bring you back. I probably wouldn't have been able to if not for Greer," Kyre said, eyeing the sleeping animal suspiciously. "He shared his magic with me. I didn't know di'horviths could do that."

"Neither did I," Strider grunted, as he looked at his brother.

"He is your wolf, and you never knew?"

"He never brought it up," Strider said.

"He's an animal. He can't talk."

"Try telling him that."

The silence stretched between them for a moment before Strider spoke up.

"If you'd let me die, it'd have made things easier for you and the Rangers. Why did you save me?"

"Addy asked me to, and who am I to refuse the request of a fair maiden?"

Strider snorted derisively.

"I don't plan to let you live for long," Kyre went on. "I will best you, Ruther Longstride, son of Ruther. When I do, I will take your feather back. Under my own strength."

It had been decades since Strider had last heard his name. It sounded foreign. That name belonged to a young boy, who had a far too positive outlook on the world. It was a name he was no longer worthy of. It belonged to happier times.

"Strider," he corrected, then smiled. "You should kill me now. It'll be the only chance you have. If you can even manage it."

"Don't tempt me."

Strider rested his head back on the pillow and sighed. "How long have I been out?"

"You've been coming in and out for about three weeks now," Kyre told him. "Addy has barely left your side the entire time."

Both Kyre and Strider rested their gaze on the sleeping young woman.

"You risked everything to bring her home safely. You were prepared to give your own life for her," Kyre said softly. "You acted in a way that honored the title of Ranger. Aside from leaving The Wilds, as far as anyone else is concerned, you never broke your other oaths. I'll make sure our leaders hear of that. They'll decide what to do after that. Until then, I won't attack you."

Strider offered a slow nod. "Until then, I won't beat you."

"You really make it hard not to punch you!"

"It is one of my many talents."

Kyre sighed and shook his head, his lips curling into a smile. He turned and walked out, muttering under his breath as he disappeared, "You really are a Chaos touched idiot."

The conversation left Strider feeling drained, and he was about to fall back asleep when Addy stirred.

She let go of his hand and stretched her arms high over her head as she yawned.

"Sleep well?" Strider asked.

Addy jumped in her chair, and Strider couldn't help but offer a small smile, as her face filled with relief and joy. She fell onto him, wrapping her arms around him in a tight hug.

"Strider!" she cried, her voice tight with barely suppressed tears. "I thought I lost you."

"I'm annoyingly hard to kill, or so I'm told."

She drew back and scowled at him. "You did exactly what you told me not to, you idiot! Stop laughing. This isn't funny!"

She punched his shoulder, which resulted in him chuckling harder at her display. The commotion woke Greer, who, upon seeing Strider awake, attacked him with wet kisses as he whined and chattered as if he too were lecturing him. Strider tried to fend him off with little success.

"I'll go tell Tevin and the others you are awake."

"Don't," Strider said, his tone serious and tired, as he grabbed her hand to stop her from rising. "Don't."

Greer, sensing Strider's weariness, stopped licking him. He rolled off him and lay beside the Hunter, his head still resting on his chest. They all sat in silence for a long moment. He wasn't aware of when he fell asleep, surrounded by the two most important people in his life. The only important people in his life. But, for the first time in a long time, he was at peace.

Chapter 75
Aftermath

It took another moon for Strider to regain his strength. At first, Addy came every day, fretting and fussing over him. But her visits grew less frequent. Her mood began to darken as his health improved. Strider noticed the normal fire within her had faded.

He tried to ask her about it, but she retreated within herself, insisting she was fine. He didn't have the strength to pursue the matter, so he stopped and observed. Being there for her in silence. One day, she didn't come at all. He waited a couple of days before finally inquiring about her.

Tymott was the first person to appear at his doorway who could answer his question. He'd popped in to visit, likely to see Greer more than Strider. The middle son of the Fenforde family had grown quite attached to the large mutt. He stopped by every day to see him and take him out to play.

All three brothers, including Curthis, now that his opinion of Strider seemed to have improved, would occasionally ask Strider if he was up to sparring yet. They'd wanted to test their mettle against the Hunter, especially after they'd seen the carnage he'd left in the halls in his search for their sister. He declined every time, allowing his body to rest.

"Where is Addy?" Strider asked Tymott.

Tymott stopped playing with Greer's ears to look at him, a worried expression wiping the smile from his face.

"She's sequestered herself in her room. No one knows why. She won't come out, or let anyone in. It's why I came here, actually. I was hoping maybe you could try talking some sense into her."

"I doubt she'd listen." Strider shrugged. Addy wasn't easily swayed when she'd set her mind to something.

"I think you're wrong," Tymott argued, softly but confidently. "She respects you and listens to you. Addy told me about your travels and all you did for her. She's changed, for the better, and I believe it is because of you."

Strider was about to scoff but caught the look Greer gave him. He shook his head instead.

"I'll see what I can do," he said. He had little confidence that he'd be able to change anything. While he preferred being alone, Addy was inherently social. Worry settled in the back of his mind as he suspected what might've caused her to shut everyone out.

Tymott smiled and nodded his head. "Thank you."

He left the Hunter and di'horvith alone. Both looked at each other, and Strider sighed as he rubbed the back of his neck.

"It isn't too late to cut and run," he said to Greer, who snorted his disapproval. "I figured you'd say that."

"Addy, could you open the door please?" Tevin said, as he knocked.

Addy ignored his muffled voice coming through the door as she stood before it.

"Please talk to me," Tevin begged softly.

She clutched her hands to her chest, fighting off another wave of tears. She didn't know why she'd left her bed to walk to the door. She couldn't face him. She couldn't face anyone. She was a wretched monster, and each time someone tried to get her to come out or speak words of useless comfort, she felt even worse. Why couldn't they go away? She wanted to be alone, forgotten.

Was it too much to ask that they leave her be to fade away? Tevin seemed to give up, and she heard his footsteps walking away. A part of her wanted to open the door and apologize. That part made her heart stab with pain. She stood still, hands clutching tighter against her chest as she bowed her head and bit back tears.

She'd thought she'd cried herself dry. But her body kept making more tears for her to spend. She took a deep, shuddering breath, and turned around to return to bed. She stopped dead, her back growing straight with alarm as she stared at the person sitting on her bed.

"How did you get in here?" she asked, as she gazed at Strider.

Strider sat on the unrumpled side of the bed. His back resting against the many pillows piled there. His shoes were still on, and they only barely extended over the side of the bed as he lounged like a content cat.

"I have a few useful tricks," Strider answered, head tilting to one side as he looked at her unkempt hair, red puffy eyes, and wrinkled nightgown. "You look terrible."

She glared at him. "And you're a jerk."

He gave a shrug, not arguing the point.

"Now that you've kindly pointed out my physical appearance, get out," she ordered, gesturing toward the door.

He made no move to leave as he crossed his hands on his stomach and settled in.

"We need to talk," he growled.

"If you won't leave, I'll have someone remove you," she stated hotly. "Father will have you flogged for breaking into my room."

He didn't look bothered as he casually gestured for her to proceed.

Addy turned back to the door, intending to call Tevin back to have him drag Strider out. A thought caused her to pause as she shot him a suspicious look.

"You want me to open the door," Addy began, her tone slow. "If I do, Tevin or someone else will come in and talk to me or drag me out of here."

Strider's lips curled into a wicked smile. "You're learning."

She frowned and stepped away from the door, glaring at the man on her bed.

"I'm still not going to talk to you about it," she stated. "You won't convince me otherwise."

"I don't expect you to," Strider answered, pulling his hood down over his eyes as he leaned back against the preposterous amount of pillows that occupied the bed.

"You said we needed to talk," she pointed out.

"We do. But I'd have an easier time forcing a dragon through a keyhole than forcing you to talk."

Addy continued eyeing him, like one might eye a tiger, as she skirted around her bed. He didn't move or seem to notice as he lay there. She moved about the room for a short time before deciding to sit on the other side of the bed. She pulled the blanket she'd been huddling under most of the day over her head and sat there in silence, ever conscious of Strider's quiet presence beside her.

She sat there, trying to ignore him. But she was aware of him. Her irritation flared to anger.

"Get off my bed!" she snapped.

He said nothing as he lay there. The silence stretched between them until she poked her head out from under the blanket.

"I said move!" she tried pushing him off, he didn't budge. "Get out already!"

Her anger and inability to move Strider was the final straw, and she burst out crying as she began hitting his arm and trying to shove him.

Strider watched her, as she took her anger out on him. He moved his arm. She began hitting his chest instead, unaware of him stretching out his hand to comfort her before stopping. He hesitated as she cried, still hitting him. It didn't hurt, but he didn't like seeing her so distraught. What exactly should he do? Patting her head like before didn't seem like a good idea. Annoyed by his own hesitation, he made a decision. If it was the wrong one, he'd find out quickly.

Addy was still beating her fists against Strider's chest when she felt arms wrap around her. She continued to try to hit him, each blow growing weaker until finally, she stopped and cried into his shirt.

"Why did you save me?" she sobbed. "I thought you weren't coming back this time."

"I always come back," he answered softly, in his simple, straightforward manner.

"You shouldn't have," she hiccuped. "I don't deserve it. I-I killed him!"

Her tears resumed as she cried, curling in on herself, as Strider hugged her. He held her, letting her cry for several moments, considering his words before he asked her a quiet question.

"Your brothers and father have killed as well. Do they deserve to die?"

"No," she sniffled.

"Why are you any different?"

"Because..." she began, but her argument died in her throat. She hated the man's logic, hated how he always asked questions that made her stop and think. But this time, she would beat him. "They're trained for it."

"You can never truly train to kill. Everyone, trained or not, who takes a life, has to come to terms with it. They're no different from you."

"They're men; they have a different mentality than I do. Plus, they were protecting themselves, us, it's their job."

"Women protect as well," Strider said. "Your mother was prepared to kill to defend herself. Does that mean she needs to die?"

"No!" she shouted at him and hit his chest again. Well aware that she was losing the fight, but not caring, she wasn't in the state of mind to think clearly. "Shut up!"

She pulled away from him, turning her back on him as she wrapped her blanket tighter around herself. Her shoulders hunched as she hugged herself.

"Why did you kill him?" Strider asked, after a long pause.

Addy ignored him, her shoulders hunching further, her head bowed under her blanket as if making herself smaller would help her hide from the question.

He asked her again. "Addy, why did you kill him?"

She didn't answer; she refused to.

"Did you want to kill him? Was this finally your chance to take his life without anyone growing suspicious?"

"No!" she shouted, whirling on him. "I never wanted to kill him!"

"Then why?"

"Because," she whispered. "He was going to kill my family, and he- he..." Her voice caught in her throat, as she remembered that night. "He was going to- to take me and force me- he..." she couldn't say it as she began crying once more.

"He gave you no alternative," he said softly, gently touching her shoulder. "You had to protect yourself and your family. That is why the price was so high."

Addy shook her head. "If I'd talked to him, maybe I could've stopped him. I could've done something, I-"

"Stop," Strider said, his voice firm. "You can spend your entire life looking back at the could haves. All it will do is destroy you. You made the decision you felt you had to make at the time. No amount of wishing for a different outcome will change that."

"How do you do it?" she pleaded. "How do you get rid of the guilt and pain?"

He looked away, unable to meet her gaze as he looked at his free hand, calloused from decades of fighting.

"The day you completely rid yourself of that feeling is the day you become a monster." His voice was hollow as he looked at his hand. It often surprised him how it hadn't been stained a permanent red. To the world, his hand looked clean. How easy it was to wash blood away, and yet it never truly left. The memory of it, preserved by the killer. Even if he couldn't remember who he'd killed, their blood was still there.

"Then how do you live with it?"

Strider blinked, Addy's voice drawing him from his reverie. He let out a heavy, weary sigh. The sigh of a man, burdened by too many years, too much darkness.

He wanted to tell her that she was asking a monster. He'd long since grown numb to taking another's life and accepted that he'd lost the part of himself that made him ummanie. Instead, he told her, "You should ask Tevin, your brothers, or your father, men better than me." He finally met her gaze again. "What you can't do is lock yourself away and starve. What you can't do is give up. You took a life, but never forget the reason. Honor that, stick to it. Or else you killed for no reason, no purpose."

She didn't look consoled by his words. He didn't expect her too. But she looked to be considering them, as her shoulders relaxed slightly. She still cried as she came closer, curling up beside him.

"I don't think I can," she whispered. "I am not that strong."

Strider put an arm around her shoulder. "You are," he told her softly. "You have to remind yourself every day until you remember."

She snorted derisively. "So, I'm not only holding myself back, I'm lying to myself?"

"People do it all the time," Strider breathed. "It's stupid, really. But we can't seem to break the habit."

She gave another snort as she continued to cry. She felt the bed jostle as something large jumped onto it and a furry head pressed itself between her arms.

"Greer?" she exclaimed. "How did you get in here?"

"I brought him," Strider said. "I wouldn't have heard the end of it if I'd left him behind."

The di'horvith gave a soft whine, licking the tears from Addy's cheeks as he snuggled close. She hugged him as she rested her head on Strider's chest. She hadn't stopped crying, and the sight of Greer brought on more tears as she hugged him tightly. It took a quarter watch before she finally cried herself to sleep. Neither wolf nor Hunter moved, remaining with her until they, too, drifted off.

Chapter 76
The Debt

Addy didn't miraculously feel better the next morning. Her guilt wasn't gone, and her heart still hurt. She hadn't slept well, the nightmares still came; they still left her sobbing and fighting for air. The only difference was, Strider and Greer were there for her when they happened.

He didn't hold her as he consoled her during her night terrors. If he had, it would've caused more panic. He seemed to sense that as he helped her separate her dreams from reality. Only then did he hold her, patting her on the head as she cried. The dreams always left her sobbing.

She didn't have the strength to get out of bed, and she curled against Greer, snuggling into his soft fur for warmth. No one had come into her room to keep the fire going. She'd locked her door and ordered the servants to keep out. No one had come since Tevin's last visit. They likely knew Strider was with her.

She looked over at the Hunter to find that he was awake and watching her. He didn't say anything when their eyes met. He studied her, as if searching for something. She was too tired to notice any details about him other than those golden eyes. She wasn't sure if he found what he was looking for, as he patted her softly on the head before looking away. Addy frowned. She wasn't a dog. Neither one exchanged a word as he got up and left. He didn't ask Greer to come, leaving the wolf to remain with her.

He returned later in the day. She woke up to him sitting in her reading chair by a crackling fire, drawing in his sketchbook. Greer lay at his feet eating a ham Strider must have stolen from the kitchen. She noticed a tray of food sitting on the end of her bed. Her stomach rumbled, but she didn't feel like eating.

She took a deep breath, grabbed a small piece of cheese, and forced herself to nibble on it. It wasn't much, but she told herself that it was a start. When the nightmares came again that night, she held onto Greer while Strider stroked her head. She ended up falling asleep between them.

She wasn't sure how many days went by. She ignored everyone who came to her door. But she slowly found the strength to get up and move around her room. Strider came and went. Confirming her assumption that her family knew he was there when he left out of her door. He'd return with food, or a book, or something for her to do should she want to keep her mind off of things. Most of the time, she ignored the items he brought. He didn't seem to mind, bringing something else the next time, until there was a sizable pile on her desk.

He remained a quiet presence, listening when she needed to talk. He let her yell at him, let her scream her frustrations without batting an eye, then held her as she cried. He was always there for her at night, when things were the hardest—a quiet presence, keeping guard against the monsters that plagued her.

One morning, when she woke, he seemed quieter than usual as they sat on her bed, Greer snoring between them.

"I am leaving today," he told her.

She let the words sink in as she held onto Greer, her chin resting on his head.

"Do you have to?"

"I either leave today or fight my way out when that Ranger returns with his partner."

"So, Kyre isn't here right now?"

"No, he left to give his report to the Sanctuary while his partner reports to your king."

"Did you hear that King Elias has been cleared of any charges?" she inquired, only half paying attention to the conversation.

"I did. They blamed one of his lords who spoke out quite often against their alliance with Myvara. I've not heard the entire story, but he had to have spun quite the tale. Whoever planted the evidence was quite skilled as well, to have thwarted the Rangers. Though I suspect if given the time, they'd find the truth."

"So, you believe the king was behind everything?"

Strider shrugged. "That's something I'd have to confirm for myself, but I don't believe this lord was the mastermind."

He grunted, as he stood up and began stretching the stiffness out of his neck and shoulders. He turned and looked at Addy, cuddling Greer.

"He can stay if you need him," he told her.

She looked at him, surprised. Addy had seen firsthand how much Greer meant to Strider. They were more than simply wolf and master. They were brothers. Strider had shown that he would trade his life for Greer's. Here he was, willing to continue on alone if it meant she could heal. She felt her eyes watering and closed them, shaking her head.

"No, you need him more than I do," she insisted. "I'll be fine."

His eyes narrowed.

"I will be!" she told him, heat entering her voice. "I am strong, remember?"

"So long as you remember," he said, in a low voice.

Walking over to the bed, he tapped the snoring di'horvith on the head. Greer snorted as he woke, looking up at the Hunter, confused.

"Time to go."

Greer let out a whine when he looked at Addy. He fixed her with a worried, questioning gaze, and she repeated what she had told Strider.

"I'll be fine." Her voice cracked, and she had to take a breath before forcing a smile.

Greer looked unconvinced. Despite that, he gave her a kiss before hopping off the bed.

Strider gave her a meaningful look. "If I hear you've remained sequestered in your room, I will come back and drag you out of it, even if it means being hauled off to whatever prison the Rangers have waiting for me."

Addy felt her lips twitch in a ghost of a smile. She wasn't completely better, and for a moment she felt herself curling back in on herself as she realized she would be alone tonight. She felt a hand on her shoulder and looked up to see Strider crouched before her.

"You have many people here who want to be there for you," he told her. "You're not alone. Don't tell yourself you are."

She bit back tears, as she embraced him in a fierce hug. Not for the first time, she found herself wondering what had made Strider who he was. What pain had he gone through that helped him to understand? He, too, had taken his first life, she reflected, as his words came back to her. She hugged him tighter.

"No matter what you or anyone says," she said. "You will never be a monster to me. Thank you, Strider."

She felt his arms wrap around her as he returned the embrace with a tight hug of his own before pulling away.

"Don't forget what I taught you," he told her, his voice tight. "And stop hol-"

"Holding myself back," she finished for him.

He smiled. "You're learning."

He moved quietly to the door. Letting Greer out first, he turned to look back at her. He gave her a final half-smile before silently closing the door.

Strider rode Copper, leaving castle Timara behind.

"I don't see why we had to take the horse," he growled down at Greer.

The di'horvith smiled up at him, as he trotted alongside Copper. The mutt had stopped outside the stables, crying and howling, while they were trying to leave. He only stopped when Strider went in and saddled the scruffy, faded roan. No one stopped him. A letter from Lady Fenforde, giving him permission to leave, fended off anyone who asked too many questions. The word of the Dark Ranger and what he'd done for their lady had spread like wildfire until he'd become something akin to a folk hero.

The loyal soldiers had watched as he and Greer helped weed out the remaining traitors in the castle guard and staff. Many had tried to hide among the loyal, using the chaos of the fight to blend back into the ranks of the soldiers they'd fought against. Greer had quickly and mercilessly sniffed them out. The castle dungeon was full of conspirators awaiting execution.

Everyone who saw him smiled and nodded as he rode Copper down the street toward the final castle gate. People hailed him, praised him, thanked, and cheered for him. He hated it, and was glad when he finally left the castle behind him.

"You know he's going to die," Strider continued to argue with his brother. "You've seen my luck with horses. It'd have been best to leave him."

Greer sneezed, shaking his head vigorously.

Strider scowled at him. "Don't blame me when he dies."

They rode on in silence, as Strider took the first of many roads that would take them back to Fair Fork and Toris's tunnels. He'd considered returning to his cabin. It had been fifty years since he'd left it to hunt the assassin that'd killed Kinri and his father. He'd only thought about returning there when Tevin had asked him what he would do after helping Addy. It was the only skeleton of a plan he had at the time. He honestly didn't think he would be alive to consider other possibilities.

Strider wasn't sure how long he had left to live, having given so much of his life force to save both Greer and then Addy. The idea of living out the rest of whatever life he had left at the cabin sounded nice. But he couldn't return yet.

There were people left out there that had plans to harm Addy and her family. He intended to find them. It'd be easy enough to have a Ranger stumble upon the information he found, assuming he didn't kill the person, or persons, first. Then he'd return home.

It was mid-afternoon when Strider spotted two figures sitting on small horses on either side of the road. His eyes narrowed in suspicion, but he kept Copper moving at a slow trot. They were both tahrvin; neither one wore a recurve bow, or felaris feather marking them as Rangers. They seemed out-of-place wearing the traditional colorful clothes of their people. The two hailed him when they saw him. He stopped Copper as they rode up to meet him.

"Are you the one known as Strider?" the younger of the two tahrvin men asked.

"Who is asking?" Strider responded, eyeing them both.

"Lady Tourmaline, High Priestess of Zircion, has sent us to bring back the Hunter known as Strider," the tahrvin said, eyeing Greer, as he and his companion's horses dipped their heads to greet the di'horvith. "She told us to wait here for a man riding a faded red roan, accompanied by a large, light grey, dire wolf."

Strider gave them a stern look. "What does she want?"

"She is calling in her debt."

Thank you for reading

If you enjoyed the first book in the Hunter of Fareldin series, please consider leaving a review.

The Hunter of Fareldin series will continue in book 2, The Debt. For news of its release please consider signing up for my newsletter at kaagard.com.

Pronunciation Guide

Names
- Su'lris (Sue-L-ris)
- Sephyra: (Seph-fie-ra)

Organizations
- Syliceon (Sigh-lis-eon)
- Ry'arie (Rye-Ar-E)
- Userith Femiera ([u]-sir-eth Feh-mere-ah)
- Tolvers (Toll-ver)

Races
- Yulie (You-lee)
- Ummanie ([u]-mah-nee)
- Tahrvin (Tar-vin)
- Ravack (Ra-vawk)
- Anumie (ah-new-me)

Misc Words

- Liely'pine- To walk unseen paths. Magical paths throughout the world that can be traversed quickly. (Lie-lee-pine)
  - Difit- Tahrvin Swear or exclamation (Dif-it)
  - Shyter- Tahrvin word for Soothsayer, charlatan (Shy-tur)
  - Chwite- Tahrvin equivalent of bastard. (Sh-white)
  - Tarn- Hell/Heaven consist of 13 levels
  - Chaos Ridden- Strong Insult
  - Chaos Touched- Mad/Crazy/Insane
  - Child/son of Chaos- Son of a B*
  - Chaos Blessed- Devil's Luck
  - Golden Stag- big reward, striking it rich, etc
  - Unmiera = Brother (Un-mere-rah)
  - Femiera = Family/Family relations (Feh-mere-rah)
  - Lumiera = Sister (Lue-mere-rah)
  - Daya = Mother (Day-ah)
  - Lonia = Father (Low-nee-ah)
  - Do'lonia = Grandfather (Doe-low-nee-ah)
  - Do'daya = Grandmother (Doe-day-ah)
  - Usereth Femiera= Family beyond blood ([u]-sir-eth Feh-mere-ah)
  - Usereth = Strong ties, loyalties, or bonds/ Bonded beyond blood. ([u]-sir-eth) Example, Usereth Unmiera = Someone not of your blood that you consider a brother ([u]-sir-eth Un-mere-ah)

Monsters
  - Di'Horvith (Die-hor-vith)

Additional Maps

Beyond this point are additional maps of the areas Strider, and Co. traveled on their journey. Visit kaagard.com for a map listing the path taken to return Addy home.

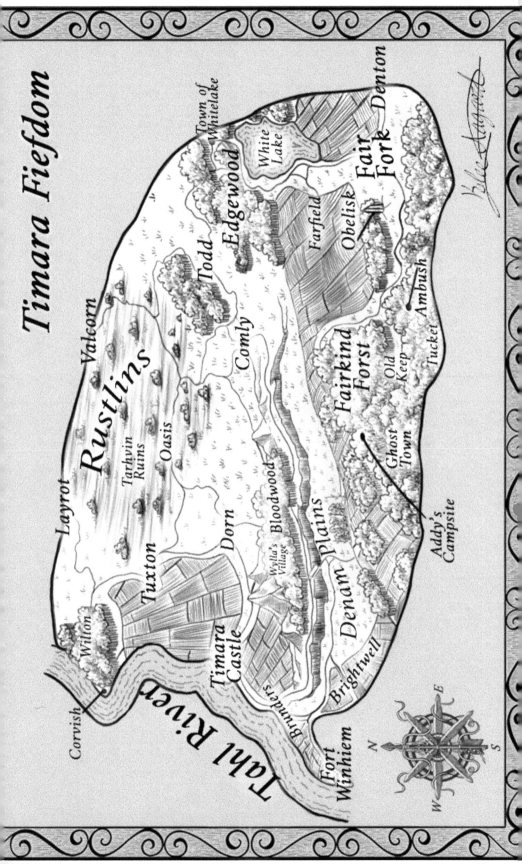

Myvara Territories

Kylee August

Legos — Venmar, Hoons
Haldon — Daxbi
Kernie — Tomkin
Ruden — Halloway
Godrey
Timara — Timara Castle
Cettlin — Alvenir
Darkmont — Wolx
Kenly — Corles
Wolphy — Bentla

About the Author

Kylee Aagard has been in love with making stories ever since she was a young child. She was writing tales before she understood proper grammar, the use of periods, or that everything doesn't need to be written in caps.

Drawing, writing, and games of imagination occupied most of her childhood. Saving her from boring car rides while she traveled with her family to deliver her dad's artwork.

She fell in love with the fantasy genre at age 8 and spent much of her time drawing dragons and imagining tales of adventure. She expresses her love for the fantasy genre in her writing as she creates her own imaginative worlds.

When she isn't writing, she spends her time with family; reading, drawing, making jewelry and other crafts, playing video games, crafting D&D campaigns, or just getting lost in her own head.

Milton Keynes UK
Ingram Content Group UK Ltd.
UKHW022334051024
449185UK00017B/139/J